SAVE
A SONG
FOR ME

SAVE A SONG FOR ME

DELON NICOLE STARKEY

COPYRIGHT

This is a work of fiction. Names, characters, places, and incidents are either the product of the author's imagination or are used fictitiously, and any resemblance to actual persons, living or dead, business establishments, events, or locales is entirely coincidental.

ALSO BY DELON NICOLE STARKEY:

It Crescendos: A Poetry Collection:
The Oklahoma Years

The House on Monarch Street

Genesis

ACKNOWLEDGMENTS

First, I must thank my Heavenly Father for getting me this far. I wouldn't have accomplished any of this without His endless love, mercy, and grace poured over my life. Thank you, forever.

Secondly, my family. For all your encouragement, kind words, and continued support throughout this entire thing. Thank you for pushing me to never give up. Third, thank you to all my friends, all my readers, my ARC team, as well as my Hype team. Thank you for taking yet another chance on me. I am forever grateful for your enthusiasm, encouragement, and support behind the scenes. I see you and appreciate you more than I can say. You guys are awesome.

Finally, a big, big thanks to Stacy, my editor. You guys, she is not just an editor. She is magic. She makes the words come to life and is amazing at what she does. My story would not look like this without you. I owe you big time. Thank you.

And a big thanks to YOU if this is your first time reading anything of mine. Thank you for taking the time to dive into this story that I poured my heart and soul into. It's spoken to me in a thousand different ways, I hope it speaks to your heart in a thousand more.

All my love,

On my wedding day, I believed love was the final chapter —the one thing you never recover from losing. I never imagined there might be something after. Ben Jennings was the love of my life. *Benny.* My soulmate, if you believe in that sort of thing. *I did.* He was my first real love, and the one I thought would be my last. I didn't know how to open my eyes and heart to another. It was unthinkable.

The day I lost Ben was the worst day of my life. I couldn't function, and mundane things such as eating and breathing took too much effort. Yet, I did them because I had to. Not only for myself, but for our two young children. Time certainly doesn't heal all wounds, but it does make each new day a little more bearable than the last.

I had to learn that I was fractured, not broken. I could heal, it would just take some time. Little did I know, life—and even love— could go on, even after the kind of tragedy that shatters everything.

The day I married the man of my dreams, was also the day I met the man I'd end up spending forever loving. It would take a sea of tears, and the most unlikely person on the planet, to realize that love was waiting for me again.

I know what you're thinking right now. But it's a long story, and one worth listening to, so stay with me.

My husband is dead, and now I am in love with someone else. It didn't happen overnight. I tried to deny, deny, deny. All of it was so sudden and absurd, and I put up a big fight. But he was relentless, and eventually won my heart over.

I thought that when my husband died, all the music in my life was silenced. Our song had ended. In the end, I could only hope that maybe, just maybe, he'd save a song for me.

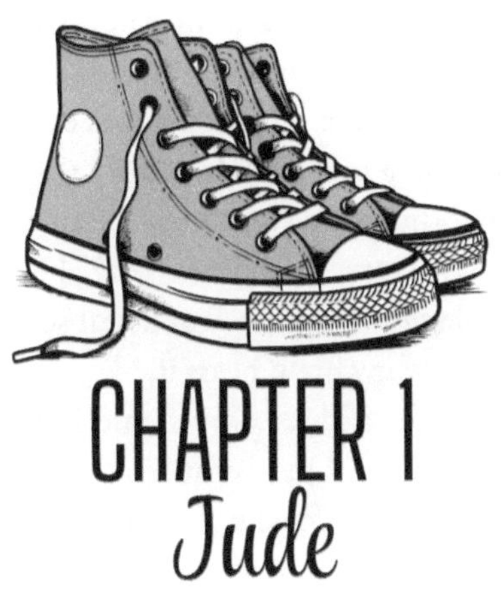

CHAPTER 1
Jude

Will you please stop fighting with your brother, Nova? For crying out loud," I snap at my daughter, who is relentlessly pestering her younger brother.

It's an everyday battle. Always the same thing, and she's usually the instigator.

I'm on the phone with my husband, trying to figure out if I should start dinner now or wait until he's on his way home. Did he already tell me when he was coming? If he did, I wasn't listening, or I didn't hear him through all of the commotion.

Six-year-old Novelle (Nova) is a diva. She's my firecracker who knows-it-all. She's basically a tiny version of me. On the flipside, my three-year-old son, Riley, is my sweet little relief, most days. When he's not busy fighting with his older sister, he plays quietly, putting together puzzles, drawing, or building Legos. But when Sissy is in the picture, all of that is thrown out the window. Along with my sanity. Needless to say, today is one of those days. Some days, I want to throw myself out of one of our windows.

"When will you be home, Ben?" I ask again, exhausted. It's

only Monday, but it feels like the longest day. Nova started first grade this year and is gone all day, but Riley is still home with me. All day, every day. My precious little "mama's boy." Except when Sissy's home. Then they are mini-tornadoes destroying everything and everyone (including me) in their paths.

"I'm wrapping things up right now. Brian said he could close for me tonight. Have you started dinner yet?" he asks.

I don't think he *means* for it to come out sounding accusatory, but that is exactly how my brain hears it.

Riley's now in tears and screaming, and Nova's yelling back at him. I can't think straight. I just want him home. Somehow, when he's here, the chaos stills. There's something about his very presence that calms the storm. A storm that I can't weather on my own.

"No, was I supposed to?" I ask impatiently. He's not reading my mind the way he's supposed to right now. I need him to get here. I should probably hang up. The kids need to be separated *right* now, and I need to figure out dinner. There's a pause on the line, and for a second, I think he's hung up on me. I can almost picture him running his hand through his wild, unruly hair—he does this whenever he is stressed. His hair is so dark it's almost black, and his eyes are a close match. We met while I was still in college. He was working at a bar close to campus at the time, and even though he graduated four years before I did, we hit it off pretty quickly. We dated my senior year and married six months later.

"You know what? There should be plenty of leftovers here. I'll grab some food and bring it home for you guys. How's that sound?" he offers. I breathe a sigh of relief. I love this man. He's a miracle worker.

"Yes, please. Oh, that would be great! Thanks, babe." I bend down to scoop Riley into my arms. He's got a head full of curls like his father. The moment I pick him up, he lays his head on my shoulder, and I gently stroke his tear-stained cheek.

"Okay, give me about thirty minutes and I'll be on my way. Tell the kids if they can't be nice, they don't get dessert tonight."

Ooh, he's good. Sometimes *too* good.

He doesn't bring home dessert every night, but on the nights he does, they become angels. It may be a form of bribery, but it works most of the time.

Tonight, I'm willing to throw in anything to get them to behave—even if that means decadent Oreo pudding pie, made fresh from the tavern. *Our tavern.*

Second Verse Tavern has been in Ben's family for years, and now he owns and runs it. It's in an old historic building downtown that used to be a bank—or maybe a grocery store—back in the early 1800s. It's since been restored, but when Ben's mom and stepdad bought the property, they kept as much of the original structure as possible. The fireplace is original, and many of the walls still contain bricks from when it was built.

I always enjoy taking the kids to the tavern on Friday nights. Not just because they love seeing their daddy at work, but also to listen to the live entertainment at Friday's Open Mic Nights.

If only tonight were Friday…

"Okay, I love you, Benny." I end every call the same way—with my favorite nickname for him.

He sings into the phone, his voice soft and familiar—the same Beatles tune he always serenades me with. The song that has my name in it. My real name is Judith, which only my parents are allowed to use. Well, them… and apparently my mother-in-law, who insists on calling me that despite my repeated requests otherwise.

Growing up, I was always Judy with close friends and family. Then I started dating Ben, and he rebranded me as Jude. It stuck.

He's also the *only* one allowed to sing the song with my name. It's cheesy and cute. I secretly like it, but I always play it off like it bothers me.

"Stop it. You know I can't stand it when you do that," I tell him, laughter bubbling in my voice. He knows I like it just as much as he does, but I'm too stubborn to be the first to back down. It's our little game we always play. I never want him to stop singing it to me.

He laughs. Both kids are currently quiet, and I don't want to break the peace. I feel like we are on the phone for the first time, and I don't want to be the first to hang up. *No, you first. I'm not hanging up this phone until you do.*

"Okay, I'll see you soon, Jude," he says.

I smile, even though he can't see me. "I love you," I tell him.

"Love you too."

He hangs up the phone first.

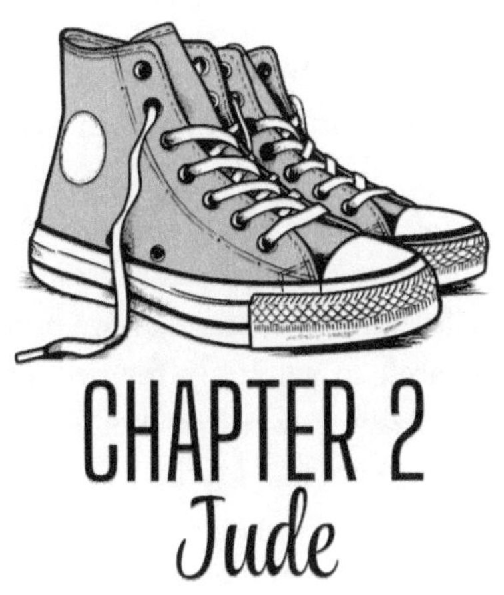

CHAPTER 2
Jude

I t might be strange—or even borderline creepy—but sometimes I track my husband's whereabouts on my phone. It comes in handy during moments like this, when I'm hungry and need to know how close he is to home.

The kids also think it's fun to watch the little dot move across the map. Tonight the dot is moving, but not towards home. Instead, the dot is going in the opposite direction, and I'm very confused.

Kids are dangerously good at sensing things about their parents. Nova is eyeing me suspiciously, and she never hesitates to speak her mind.

"Mom? Where's Dad going? He's supposed to be coming home, right?" she asks, looking from my phone screen back up to me as if I have all the answers.

I nod because I'm not sure what to say. That's what he told me. He said he'd be heading home in about thirty minutes. The problem with young children is that they take everything literally.

If you tell them thirty minutes, it has to be thirty minutes. It's now been forty-five.

It's not like him to run late, but something might have come up. Running a tavern has its perks, but it can sometimes be unpredictable.

"Yes, sweetie, that's what he said. Maybe he forgot he has to run an errand," I say, even though doubt threatens to creep in. I'm not even sure I believe that. It's later than we normally eat dinner, and the kids will need to get ready for bed soon. It is a little concerning that he's heading away from home.

This time, Riley chimes in, "Maybe he needed to stop for gas, Mommy."

My sweet boy. I look over at him and ruffle his curls a little. He shies away from me, smiling.

"You might be right. We can watch for a little longer, but if he's not heading home in five minutes, I'll try calling him again."

Nova nods, not arguing with me for once, and Riley intently watches the tiny dot moving across my screen. I called a little bit ago, and don't want to seem like I'm worried. It's probably nothing, and he wouldn't want me to worry the kids.

We all watch it for a moment longer, our eyes transfixed on the screen. The dot seems to stop moving altogether, somewhere far from home.

There are no streets around the dot, and it looks like he's in a field. And then the realization hits me. He's not at the restaurant, and he's not heading home. He's gotten a fire call.

A call that suddenly feels more important than mine, urging him to hurry home before I strangle our kids. I don't mean that. I'm just tired. *So tired.*

He's out somewhere saving lives, and I'm here complaining about mine. What kind of monster am I? But still, he should have called me, right? He should have, but he didn't.

I sigh in frustration and switch off my phone screen. Both kids look up at me with the saddest eyes in the world. I'm about to become the worst Mom, but I have to tell them.

"Hey, guys, listen. Daddy's on a fire call, and I don't think he's going to be able to bring us dinner tonight. It's getting late, so let's make something quick, like cereal or toast, before bed. I'm so sorry," I say to them and mean it.

I know how much they want him here with us, but this isn't anything new. While this doesn't happen often, it has happened on more than one occasion.

My son's lip starts to quiver, and just as quickly, he calms it. "That's okay, Mommy," he says.

I want to reach over and hug him for being so understanding at his age, but I hold back, waiting for the outburst that I know will come. But not from him. Three, two, one…

"Waaaaaaah!"

There it is. The wailing cries from my six-year-old diva. Bless her little heart.

I try to console her. "It's okay, baby. He'll be here in the morning when you wake up, and you can give him all the hugs and kisses you want."

It doesn't work. When she gets like this, nothing helps. She dramatically flops on the floor like a dying fish, flinging her arms in the air, and wails even louder, "I want my daddy!"

I lean down to stroke her forehead—something that used to calm her when she was younger—but she's not having it this time. She immediately swats my hand away. Riley, unsure what to do, tries to hug her, but she shoves him a little too hard. He falls backward and hits the ground. Now he's crying too. Wonderful.

"I'm sorry Daddy couldn't make it tonight. But if you're hungry and want to eat, now's the time."

Neither kid responds. They're both too busy writhing on the floor in tears to hear a word I'm saying. I can't deal with this right now. I excuse myself to the kitchen and pour a bowl of cereal. I'm not even hungry anymore, but I know that if I don't eat, I'll get cranky. And I'm *already* cranky.

If they're hungry, they'll find me. They know where I am and what I've asked of them. If they don't come in the next few minutes, they will have to go to bed hungry. I hate that, but I can't make them eat.

Why tonight, of all nights, did Ben have to get a fire call and go do something courageous? He's braver than I am in a lot of ways. I couldn't do half the things he does, and I'm thankful that I don't have to. I honestly don't know what I'd do without him.

As I quickly scarf my bowl of cereal so I can get the kids in bed, I decide to try calling Ben. It immediately goes to his voicemail. I try again. And again, and again.

The fifth time, I leave a voicemail. "Hey babe, it's me. I was wondering when you'll be home. The kids are really upset that you aren't here tonight. Just know that you're missed. Okay, bye. Oh, I love you, and can't wait to see you. Be safe."

As soon as I end the call, a text comes through. I open it immediately.

Hubby: Hey hun, sorry I won't make it home tonight in time for dinner. Brian and I got an emergency call. Please don't wait up for me. I'll see you soon. Extra hugs and kisses for the munchkins. Love you, babe!

I can't help but smile as I type out a response. He's impossible to stay mad at. He's a good man. The *best*.

Me: Love you even more! You know I can't sleep well until you're here.

My message shows delivered, but it hasn't been read yet. He's probably busy or already lost signal.

The kids still refuse to eat anything for dinner, so I put them to bed. I kiss them each on their heads and tuck them in. Nova tugs me close to her as I give her a kiss. "I *need you*, Mommy," she says to me.

I can't tell her no, and I don't want to. I know eventually she'll stop asking. I climb into her twin-sized bed, barely big enough for two, and I hold her close. We both cuddle until we fall asleep.

I don't wake up until two a.m. There's a loud thumping sound somewhere in the house. Did Riley fall out of bed again?

There it is again.

No, that sounds a lot like someone knocking.

Knocking at our front door.

But who in the world would be banging on our door in the middle of the night?

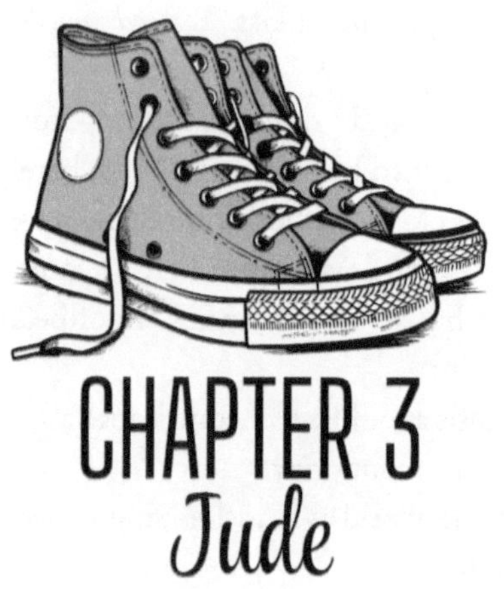

CHAPTER 3
Jude

t takes a moment for my eyes to adjust to the person standing at the door. He's in a uniform I'd recognize almost anywhere, black with reflective yellow stripes. My eyes quickly flash across the name patch, which reads STARK in big, bold letters. He's one of my husband's good friends. What's he doing here at my house at two in the morning?

He avoids my gaze and looks down. He keeps wringing his hands and shifting from foot to foot. Why is he here now? Shouldn't he have called Ben instead? He's in bed asleep, right? I didn't hear him come in, but that doesn't mean he never did.

"Brian? What are you doing here? Is everything okay?" I force down the lump in my throat.

Stay calm, everything is fine. Don't panic.

He clears his throat, slowly raising his gaze to meet mine. "Uhh, excuse me. I'm sorry to have disturbed you like this," he starts, but stops abruptly and looks past me, a devastated expression on his face.

I feel small hands wrap around my fingers. I look down and see my son standing next to me in his footie pajamas. I don't know what's going on, but he should go back to bed. We both should.

I ruffle his curls like I always do, and tell him to go lie back down. I promise to come in a minute to give him hugs and kisses.

"Why is Daddy's friend here, Mommy? Is Daddy home?" Riley asks, not making any movement towards his room.

He's still holding my hand, and I give it a gentle squeeze. *Did Ben come home last night?* I never thought to check our room on the way to answer the door.

I scoop Riley up into my arms and look back at Brian. This time, my gaze is stern; I need answers.

"Please tell me what's going on, Brian. What is this all about?" I demand, trying hard not to raise my voice because I'm pretty sure Nova is still sound asleep in her room.

His eyes suddenly look glassy. He continues to fidget and clears his throat again. I've never seen him like this. Something must be wrong. What is it?

Could it have something to do with Ben? Please, anything but *that.* I can't allow myself to go to the darkest place imaginable. Stay positive. It's most likely nothing. But showing up at two a.m. is definitely *something.*

"Jude, I hate being the one to tell you this... but Ben was with us, fighting a fire. He never made it out. He saved the family, but the whole thing collapsed before he could escape."

I can't believe what I'm hearing. That's impossible. When I'd looked earlier with the kids, he'd been somewhere in a field. Not in a neighborhood where a building could collapse on him. Riley is tugging on my chin, trying to get my attention. I know he has questions, but so do I.

"No, that's not possible. My phone showed his location in a field. He was in a *field,* Brian. You're mistaken." I want to shake him until he understands, because the expression on his face makes it apparent that he doesn't.

He shakes his head. "The house was surrounded by fields. It

belonged to an old farmer and his wife. Grass fires have been brutal this year. The fire was really bad, Jude. He helped get the elderly couple out safely, but as soon as they were clear, they panicked because their grandson was still inside. Ben wasn't about to leave that little boy behind.

"He found the boy in a room on the upper level, but they got trapped by the fire. We used a ladder to rescue them. Ben handed the boy to me through the window. It wasn't until I got to the ground and passed him off that I looked back up—and the whole house had already started to collapse.

"I'm so sorry, Jude. There was nothing we could do to save him."

Nothing we could do. While we sat here, hungry and worried about getting our food, he was busy saving another family. He saved strangers in a burning field and left his family in our newly built home, alone.

How did this happen?

I can't think straight. I still don't believe what he's just told me. He keeps talking, but I don't catch the words over the loud ringing in my ears. Instead, I slam the door in his face. I can't listen anymore.

I almost forget I'm still holding my youngest in my arms, and I numbly set him down at my side as I sink against the closed door. The door my husband was supposed to walk through earlier, like he always does after a long day at the tavern.

The door my husband will never walk through again. Because he's—I can't even say it. Can't even *think* it. Someone's crying, asking what happened to Daddy, but I'm too numb to answer. I can't form the words, even if I tried. I don't have any left to give. Oh, *no.* I'm all these kids have left. It's all on *me.*

I can't do this. Why would he do this to me? This isn't real. None of this is real. I'm going to wake up in Nova's room and realize this is all some terrible dream. That's it. It has to be. I cannot accept this as my new reality. I won't.

I won't... Ben, please hurry home. This isn't funny. I *need* you. I need you here with me.

We need you... please, come home. *Please, be okay.* Because I can't even think about what it means if you aren't.

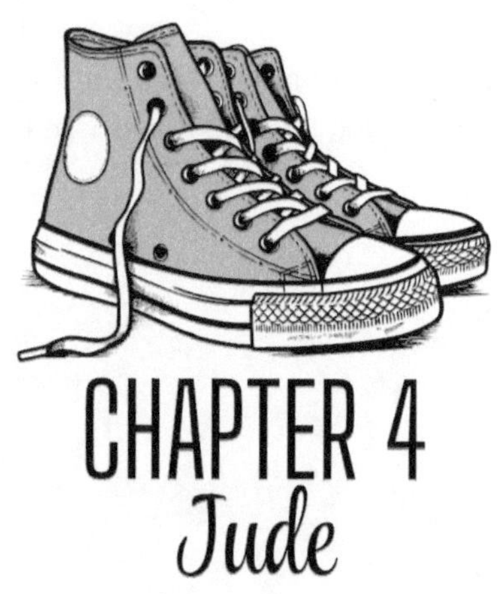

CHAPTER 4
Jude

wake up in my bed. I'm not sure how I got here, or when I managed to fall back to sleep. I guess my exhaustion from the day finally caught up with me. I don't hear the kids, so they must not be awake yet. I tap the screen on my phone to see that it's 6:55 a.m. They will start stirring any moment. I don't have long.

I roll over and reach out to wake up Ben. Only he's not there. I jolt upright. His side of the bed is pristine. The covers are drawn up, and his pillows are still in place. Ben was never here. He didn't come home last night. Suddenly, I remember the unexpected guest at our door this morning, and hot tears instantly spring to my eyes.

No, no. This is not happening. Ben can't just be... *gone.* I pick up my phone to check for any missed calls. I only have two from an unknown number. I bring the phone to my ear and listen to the voicemail. It's Brian Stark, telling me he's on his way to our house. He must have tried calling me before he arrived. I don't remember hearing my phone ring. Suddenly, I remember the last text I received from Ben.

Hey hun, sorry I won't make it home tonight in time for dinner.

Brian and I got an emergency call. Please don't wait up for me. I'll see you soon. Extra hugs and kisses for the munchkins. Love you, babe!

I know I'm not thinking rationally, but I can't help but feel like I'm missing something. Something important. He tells me everything. We don't keep secrets from each other.

About four or five years ago, his buddy, Brian, decided he wanted to become a reserve firefighter. Not long after, he convinced Ben to join too. Ben rarely says no. Yes is his default.

Was.

Was his default.

I don't think I'll ever get used to that—thinking and breathing in the past tense.

He'd come home from work one day and told me he wanted to become a volunteer firefighter. I nearly fell over. My jaw was on the floor. At first, I told him no. Absolutely not. Nova was a toddler, and we weren't sure if we wanted more kids.

I just couldn't say, *"Oh yes, honey, that sounds wonderful. Please, go risk your life. I'll only be worried sick anytime your phone rings or you're inside a burning building. No biggie, sweetie."*

I know the world needs brave first responders saving people. I get it. I really do. I just didn't want that person to be my husband. *My* Benny.

I don't hear the kids yet, so I open the phone app, go to my favorites list, and select his name. It immediately goes to voicemail. I'm not sure what that means, but I try again. And then again, and again. Eventually, I don't hang up, but I listen to the message I know so well. "Hey, this is Ben—bar owner, firefighter, and currently unavailable human. I'm either pouring pints or putting out fires."

The message cuts out as I hear my voice in the background. "Ben, come on. Just record the message, I think it's about to time out on you!" I hear myself snort laugh. It's one of my most unattractive traits, but Ben loved it.

And then there it is, rich and full, the sound of my husband's deep laugh. How I would give anything to hear his laugh right now.

"Oh, okay. Sorry! Leave a message, and I'll get back to you after the last round... or the last flame. Whichever comes first... Ben!" Followed by a loud beep on the other end of the line.

I don't leave a message because what's the point? Instead, I call his number again so I can listen to it one more time.

The moment doesn't hit me until I look up from my phone to be greeted by two small children who are curiously watching me listen to a recorded version of their Daddy over and over. Again, I have no words.

"Mom? Is that Daddy? Is he coming home?" Nova asks, holding her little pink teddy bear as she walks over to my side of the bed. My side of the bed. There will only ever be one side to this bed now. Because their daddy won't be coming back home.

The lump from the night before finds its way back into my throat. I can't swallow it down this time. Suddenly, my eyes blur with tears. I hold my arms out to my babies, ushering them to me. I can't get the words out that I need to say. I can't even mother them right now. All I can do is hold on tightly to them, praying they won't let go.

Nova comes around to my right side, while Riley climbs onto the bed and wraps his whole body around my waist. I love these two so much. I can't imagine a world without them. I never thought I'd have to imagine a world without Ben, but here I am.

I squeeze them tight because they're all that I have left of him. And now, *I* am all that they have.

How will we ever survive this?

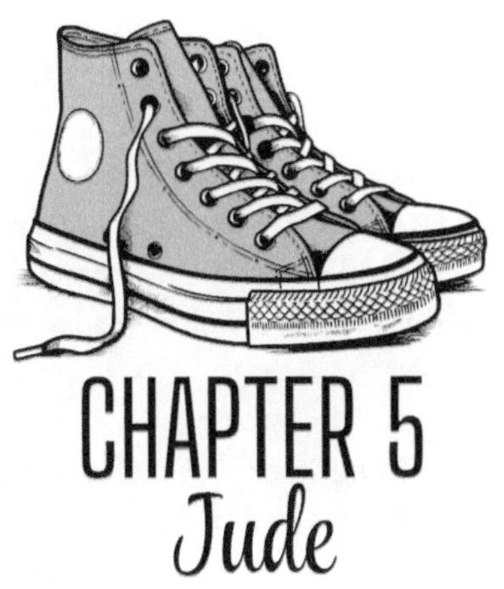

CHAPTER 5
Jude

This has been both the slowest and fastest week of my life. I wouldn't even know what day it is, if not for my husband's funeral tomorrow. Ben's mother had shown up shortly after I told the kids—I don't ever want to relive that moment. Telling my two children that their daddy will never come home again broke me. I break every time I think about it.

Nova and Riley both understand what it means for someone to die, but neither of them have been a part of it like *this*. Never seen death up close. Truthfully, neither have I.

Not like this.

His mother showed up unexpectedly, not long after my talk with the kids—just like Brian had a few hours earlier. I wonder if he called her too. It's almost comical how many people decide to show up at a time like this. When I'm barely functioning for my kids, let alone myself. I can't possibly be expected to cater to anyone else's needs... even if they're hurting too.

Rita, Ben's mom, took charge of the arrangements. Which is a good thing, because I'm not sure that I'd have been able to handle it. When I told my mom the devastating news, she scheduled a flight from Indiana to Oklahoma immediately and arrived Tuesday afternoon to help.

"What do the kids eat these days? I was thinking about grabbing a few items from the store," my mom asked me one morning.

I drew a blank. I feed my kids three times a day, along with snacks, but I honestly can't remember the last time I ran to the store.

"What?" I asked her, half listening.

She made me a steaming cup of coffee, yet I couldn't make myself drink it. Ben always had a cup with me every morning before he said goodbye to me and the kids. It doesn't feel right to drink coffee without him. Nothing feels right.

"Grocery store, dear," she reminded me. "I can take the kids with me, let them pick out some things they like. Whatever you need, I've got you."

I'm grateful she came, honestly. I'm not sure how I'd handle things if she weren't here. Everything is too much to think about right now. All I can manage is one minute at a time. Because that's all I know anymore.

Life is so unpredictable and unbelievably unfair.

Nova is quieter than usual and clingy. Riley senses that something is wrong, but keeps asking me when Daddy's coming home. It breaks my heart every time. We've had many talks about life after death with our kids. I think they know better than I do that Daddy's in Heaven, but nobody says it. I leave all the hard questions alone for now. And when that isn't possible, my mom answers for me.

Rita had originally wanted his funeral to be today instead of tomorrow. But Fridays are my favorite. Well... they used to be. I don't think I have a favorite *anything* anymore. And I'm not sure I can ever go to another Friday night Open Mic again. But I'd rather not share the day that means so much to our family with the day I have to say goodbye. I need one more day.

No, scratch that. I need a lifetime. I doubt I can ever say goodbye to the love of my life. I thought I had forever with him. I realize I had more time than a lot of people ever get, so I shouldn't complain. Yet, it isn't enough. It'll never be enough.

So, instead of having the funeral today, tonight they are dedicating Open Mic Night to Ben Jennings. All of our family and friends are invited.

I wasn't sure if I wanted to come. Part of me wants to stay home. But right now, I need to be away from home and everything that screams his name. *Benny! Benny! Benny!*

Please, make it stop.

Somehow, I don't think this will be much better. After all, this is a night dedicated to him. He chose *them* over us, and now, as a consequence, we all lost him. *I* lost him. The love of my life. I know it's a selfish way to look at it. I know, I know, I know. I can't help it.

I'm not sure what to expect at the Open Mic Night. Mom drove me and the kids here. My phone has been going off nonstop from friends and family trying to get in touch so they can tell me how truly sorry they are. They have no idea, though. No idea at all.

I wasn't exactly sure what I was supposed to wear to Ben's... special night. It's too close to a celebration, and there's nothing to celebrate. We're essentially throwing a party in his name, without him. It's only a small consolation to me that I know that this is exactly what he would have wanted.

Ben once made me promise that if he died first, I wouldn't have a traditional funeral. No sad songs, no black clothes—just a party. He wanted me to dance in my favorite dress while he celebrated in Heaven. I hadn't taken him seriously, but I promised anyway.

I never dreamed I'd have to keep that promise.

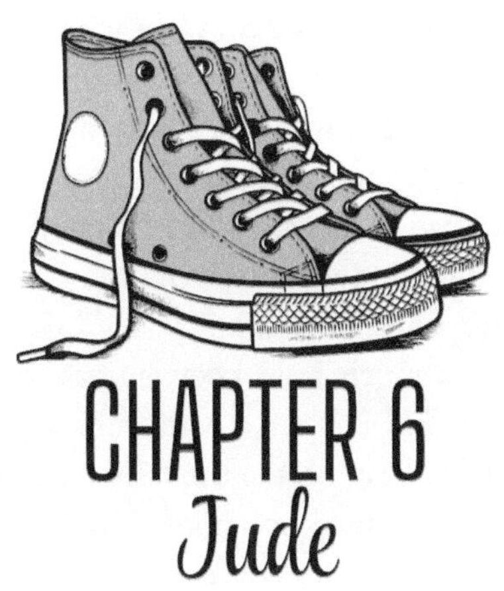

CHAPTER 6
Jude

All eyes land on me as soon as I walk through the doors of the tavern for Open Mic Night. His tavern. It's technically ours since we were married, but it's always been more his than mine.

Second Verse Tavern has been in Ben's family for over twenty years. His mom and stepdad first ran it, and then Scott's health started to decline. His stepdad had undergone a minor surgery for a heart condition during Ben's first semester in college. The surgery went well, and Ben was able to finish his degree.

He fell in love with the area and stayed close to campus after graduation. He landed a job at a local bar that he fell in love with. He hoped to one day own it and run it himself, but when we met, something in him changed. He had been away from his family long enough. It was time to return home. His mom and Scott were getting up there in age, and he wanted to be close to help them.

We moved back to Oklahoma, and Ben took over managing Second Verse Tavern so Scott could focus on his health. Barely three years into our marriage, his stepdad suffered a heart attack and passed away. Running the family business hadn't been a dream of his when we first met, but it didn't take long for it to become his *everything*.

The old building stands in the center of the town's historic Main Street. Many of the original shops are still open over a century later. Ben had always cherished his family's restaurant. He loved the home-cooked food, the live music, and the community. And naturally, the people loved him.

Ben never said as much, but I know he was hoping his brother, Jay, would come home and run it with him. Jay left home right after high school and hasn't come back. I remember Ben trying to reach out to him on several occasions. But after a while, it just began to feel pointless. Jay wouldn't answer most of his calls. And if they did talk, the calls never went anywhere—they were always cut short.

How can two men, born of the same mother, be so different from each other? Even with twelve years separating them, Ben still tried on countless occasions to connect with his brother. But Jay was always so closed off. Like he didn't want or care to make the effort in return.

I do believe they could have made a great team running the tavern together, but they will never get that chance. Jay blew it. Now it's my turn to try and make something of it. But one thing I don't ever want is to make it completely mine. Second Verse Tavern will *always* belong to Ben.

Except everyone in the room sees me now. They are all staring. The one time I wish I could become invisible, I can't.

If I were to take a guess, it's probably due to the hot pink dress I'm wearing. I never wear high heels, even though I'm barely over five feet tall. Ben always towered over me, and I used to tease, calling him my giant. He was six feet tall. I secretly loved it though. He wasn't scary, he was quite the opposite. His eyes were dark, but rich like chocolate. His features had a softened, roundedness to them that made him approachable. It's what drew me to him in the first place.

Ben said if he died first, I wasn't allowed to wear black. So I'm wearing only bright colors to honor his wishes. I just can't do anything about my dark tresses. When Ben and I met at the local bar near campus, I had my hair loosely pinned up in a messy bun on top of my head. He told me he wanted to see what my hair looked like down.

My hair is often long, wavy, and an untamable mess. I warned him it would probably resemble a lion's mane, but I did what he asked. He did two things as soon as I released the bun, letting it tumble down my back in waves—he whistled at me and asked me for my number.

Tonight, I'm wearing my hair up. I don't have the energy to style it and leave it down, and frankly, I have a feeling it might draw some unwanted attention. I don't feel like my lion's mane will help the cause.

Nova holds my hand on the left, Riley on my right, and my Mom stands beside him. We all walk in together, and we seem to move in slow motion as we make our way over to the booth reserved for us and sit down. I let loose a sigh the second my bottom hits the cushy seat.

Nobody comes up to us right away, but it's only a matter of time. I don't know if it will be out of obligation or because they are concerned about how I'm doing. I'm not sure how I'm doing, so I'd rather they not ask. I'd give anything to avoid the upcoming conversations, but I take a deep breath and steel my nerves for the night ahead. I'm doing it for Ben.

I take the opportunity to look around. Everything looks mostly the same. Ben decorated the place in warm, rich shades of mahogany, chestnut, and cherry. The large stone fireplace in the middle of the room is the focal point. It always has a fire merrily crackling, and plenty of seating around it, along with tables featuring board games and card games.

To the right of the front entrance is a small stage with tables nearby. It had originally been set up in the back of the restaurant so it wouldn't disturb anyone who just wanted to talk or enjoy the fireplace. But Ben was adamant that the stage be one of the first things people would notice.

This tavern has hosted a lot of talented people on that stage, and I'm not sure if it would've been so popular tucked away in the back. The customers love it. There is such a variety of talent, and you never hear the same thing twice. It's why I started to fall in love with it myself.

A large part of me lives for coming here on Friday nights. After the kids were born, we started bringing them with us. It's a tavern, but I never had to wonder if it was okay to bring my kids with me.

Tonight, there is a large banner hung across the ceiling in front of the stage that reads: KEEP ON KEEPING ON, BEN!! RIP.

I hate the term RIP. The only thing that has *ripped* is me.

I notice every table has a photo card of Ben, front and center. A reminder of who's missing here. This might be a party in his honor, but it doesn't feel the same without him. I hope he's right about celebrating in Heaven, because it sure doesn't feel like a celebration here.

Nova is sitting quietly at the table, reading Ben's card with my mom, aka Nana, while Riley keeps asking me why Daddy's picture is on every table and why we're the only ones not wearing black. Nova is sparkling in a pretty blue dress—her favorite color—while Riley wears a light pink shirt because he wanted to match his mommy.

My mom is wearing a top that's a coral color with flowers on it, like she's about to go on a beach vacation. She also has on black pants. Close enough, I won't complain.

"It's just a card talking about Daddy and all the wonderful things he's done," I say, absently. I'm not here. I can't be here without him. I don't know *how* to.

"Kind of like a birthday card, right? But there aren't any

balloons here. I think they forgot. Daddy would have liked balloons at his party," Riley tells me, looking up at me with eyes that mirror his daddy's. Eyes that I will never look into again.

I force a smile and give him a light squeeze, glancing away while blinking rapidly to hold back the tears before I start crying in public. This is the first time I've set foot outside my house all week. Every part of me wants to run away, but I know I can't. That wouldn't be fair to the kids or everyone else. What's fair anymore, though? There's nothing fair about any of this.

Rita is the first to approach our table. She carries herself with confidence, even after the loss of her son, and I can't fathom how she's doing it. Her eyes look sad, but her body language doesn't. She is wearing a long, black dress and elegant black beads to complement the dress. She looks gorgeous.

Her nose scrunches slightly as soon as she notices what I'm wearing, but then it disappears just as quickly. I'm sure she has more important things to discuss. She always has an agenda.

"Judith, hello," she greets me, using my full name, even though I've told her countless times to please call me Judy, or even Jude. Yet, she insists. Same with Ben. It was always Benjamin. If it bothered him, he never admitted it. Either she doesn't care, or... I'm not sure of her reasoning, but I guess it doesn't matter. I'll let it go like I always do.

"Um, hi," I respond. I don't have much to say these days. I'm empty. A bottomless pit. Is that what I'm becoming?

My mom smiles beside me and cuts in. "Hello, Rita. I can't tell you how sorry I am for your loss. We all love... loved Ben very much." She wipes her eyes, and gives my hand a gentle squeeze.

Rita's eyes look glassy, but not a single tear falls from them. I don't know how she does it. Sometimes I wonder if she's human. I know everyone grieves in their own way, and I shouldn't have those thoughts about her.

"Thank you, Mina. I'm glad you're here. I'm sure the kids are too." She nods in their direction. For a moment they look up, before going back to whatever they were doing, uninterested.

Ben has always been close with his parents. But with me, Rita has always been, well... she's hard to crack sometimes. I think she likes me okay, but I've always gotten the vibe that she thinks Ben could have done better than me.

"Are you planning to speak tonight, Judith?" she asks me.

I wish I had something to drink. A glass of water, wine, *something*. My throat is dry, and words have left me once again.

"Oh. I—I haven't... I mean... I..." My words fail, and I can feel them all staring at me, waiting for me to get something out. But I can't. My eyes instantly well up with tears.

Nova, my little diva—the one who makes me find gray hairs at almost thirty-three—decides to finally speak up. Always speaking her mind, she, on the other hand, never runs out of things to say.

"I can say something for you, Mommy. I have lots to say about my daddy. I'll do it."

I can hardly see her through the tears blurring my vision. She's so much braver than I am, stronger too. Here she is, six years old, offering to do something I can't. Simply because I can't seem to get any words out. I feel pathetic, yet grateful for her willingness to jump right in.

"Excuse me for a moment," I say, and scoot out of the booth.

I hear my son start to call for me, but my mom steps in and takes over for me. I can feel eyes on me once again, but I don't make eye contact with any of them. I don't want to make this night about me. I'm not trying to cause a scene, I just can't be here right now. It's too much, and I can't handle it. Maybe we should have gotten everything over with today. If I can't celebrate with some family and close friends, then how will I make it through the burial tomorrow?

I push my way through the double doors at the front of the building and welcome the warm May air. Summer is around the corner, and everything is starting to heat up. I've always enjoyed the warmth spring and summer bring, while Ben's always preferred the colder months. I can't think about the future right now, though. I can't even think about the next *minute*. Nothing is certain anymore.

I need to feel him here with me. I need to know that I'm not alone. My feet carry me over to the metal railing out front, and I grasp it. Expecting the metal to feel cold beneath my fingers, I am disappointed to find it warm to the touch. And *that's* when it hits me. I *am* alone. Forever. *This* is my future. I am a widow. A *widow*. A word that might be more condemning than "death" and "burial." The word that now defines me.

Here I am, in my pink party dress as promised, and I couldn't feel more alone than I do right now.

It's not until moments later that I finally realize I'm *not* alone. There's somebody else out here with me. Somebody else who has escaped from the party and has come out here to seek something. Something that isn't found inside. Because it simply isn't there.

CHAPTER 7
Jay

am not alone anymore. I came outside for a smoke, but I finished my cigarette a while ago. I recognized a few people inside, but most of them were strangers to me. This town doesn't know me, and I don't plan on sticking around long enough to change that. I plan on putting this town in my rearview as soon as I can.

I haven't set foot in this town in ten years. I left this place for good as soon as I graduated from high school. I had an apartment and a new job waiting for me in LA, and I couldn't get there fast enough.

Ben and I are half-brothers. We have the same mom, but different dads. I don't know the full story, but Mom had been married to Ben's dad until he was about ten. I heard it had been a nasty divorce, and she'd been fairly quick to remarry.

I was born two years later. Ben was twelve when I came along. We weren't close—we were like two opposing magnets. Maybe it was the age gap, or maybe it was because we were half-brothers instead of full—even though that shouldn't have made a difference. But for some reason, it always seemed to matter to Ben. He was a senior in high school by the time I started kindergarten.

We didn't even have the same interests. Sure, we lived in the same house and essentially grew up together, but Ben had a life before me. I was always vying for his attention, but he wanted nothing to do with me. Can't say I wouldn't have acted the same way if I'd been in his shoes, but still. It stung.

While he was busy with late night baseball games and hanging out with his buddies, I was home watching Blue's Clues and sneaking an extra fruit snack packet from the pantry. But when my brother was home, I wanted to be with him. Wherever he was, I wanted to be too. Unfortunately for me, he wasn't interested in having a little kid tagging along after him.

That was probably the biggest problem he had with me. He didn't need me like I needed him. When someone makes it clear they don't need you, it gets easier not to need them back.

So, why am I here, in a town where I don't belong, around people I haven't seen in a decade, celebrating a brother who I barely knew? I've been asking myself that question since the moment my plane landed at the dinky little landing strip they call an "airport." But he was family. He was my brother. Even if he's only ever been half of one to me.

Mom asked me to come, and I couldn't bear to tell her no. Not again. She already lost me the minute I graduated. I jetted out of here and haven't laid eyes on this place since. I didn't even fly out when my dad passed away from a heart attack seven years ago. I was a coward and didn't think I could handle it.

I'm not sure Mom's ever forgiven me for missing Dad's funeral. Can't say that I blame her. Would I have come now if she hadn't asked me to? Maybe. Probably. I don't know. But I'm here anyway. And apparently, I'm not alone anymore.

It's a woman, and she rushed out here like she couldn't get away fast enough. Guess it was all a bit too much for her, too. Well, join the club, princess.

"Hey," I offer in her direction.

She's out of breath, and her dark, wavy hair looks like it started out in a neat bun, but is now spiraling out in every direction. It's hard to tell exactly how long it is, but if I had to guess, I'd say it lands close to the curve of her hips. It takes me a moment to drag my eyes away from her lower back, picturing the wind tugging her hair in gentle waves with the rhythm of the breeze.

The outside patio lights illuminate her just enough to make out her bright pink dress, the color of tulips, and matching pink Converse. Hmm, interesting. She's not wearing the typical high heels girls like to wear to make themselves appear taller. Her dress is snug enough to hug her curves, but she's petite and probably no more than five foot two.

Her hands grip the railing, and we're no more than a few feet apart. Her hold is so tight, it's like we're on a sinking ship, and she's holding on for dear life. Maybe to her, that's exactly what she's doing. She hasn't responded to me. Perhaps she didn't hear me, or maybe she'd rather be alone right now. I try again. "Some party in there, huh?" I say, as if this were really a party, and we aren't here celebrating and mourning my brother's loss.

This time, I have her attention. She turns and looks at me. Her skin is darker than I thought; it's a gorgeous olive color, and her eyes glimmer in the outdoor lighting. It's both satisfying and terrifying at the same time. I dare to lean in a little closer.

Up close, I can see that her eyes are a hazel, greenish gray mixed with gold. This woman is fire. But I'm suddenly struck with recognition so strong, it jolts me back to my senses. Fully aware of my near mistake, allowing my gaze to linger a second too long, I take a small step back, away from her—the woman who is not a stranger.

"Excuse me?" she finally responds, her eyebrows pinched up in a scowl. Yep, definitely who I think it is. Who I *know* it is. She hasn't aged a bit. I wonder if she remembers me like I remember her.

I know that wasn't the right thing to say. Had she come out

here crying? Were there tears in her eyes? I didn't even notice. I feel like a complete jerk. Per usual, I've been too stuck inside my head.

I clear my throat. "Sorry, I shouldn't have said that. Um, are you okay?" I try instead. I'm not sure why she came out here, so I may as well ask her if she's okay at least. Not that I care that much. But still, I'm trying. Especially now that I know exactly who she is.

I get drawn into her eyes again. They remind me of the color of honey or flecks of gold. I don't know what it is about her eyes that keeps pulling me in, but they are mesmerizing.

She's the first to break eye contact. Instead, she stares down at her hands, letting her hands fall to her sides as though she remembered something or is lost in her thoughts.

I've been out here long enough that I'm starting to crave another smoke. Just one more.

"No," she whispers in the air. I barely hear her response, and I'm close to her. But I'm getting her to talk, and that's something.

"Yeah, me neither," I admit honestly. I fumble in my back pocket for my lighter.

"Why are you out here?" she asks, glancing back in my direction while she subtly wipes at her eyes.

So she had been crying. Great, now I really am the biggest jerk. But this doesn't feel like the right time or place to comfort her. Especially if it were to come from me. I can feel her golden eyes lingering on me, assessing who I am and what I'm doing here.

Has she finally come to her senses? Figured me out like I did with her a moment ago? Tension hangs between us like a weighted blanket.

Why did I come out here? Other than to literally blow some smoke?

I pull out another cigarette and light it, bringing it to my lips and inhaling the familiar smoke into my lungs.

I can feel her watching me, studying me. Is she judging me? I don't look in her direction right away. I only see her out of my peripheral.

"I don't like large crowds," I settle on. It's not the full truth, but it's not a lie either.

"Oh," she says.

There's a slight hesitation in her voice, like she wants to say more. She's figured out who I am too, I'm almost sure of it. I'm ten years older, but I'm still the same broken shell of a man I was the day I walked away.

I blow out a big cloud of smoke on my next exhale. My lungs burn from the sensation, yet I ache for more. Every time I think about quitting, my body screams *more, more, more.* One of these days I'll quit for good, but today isn't going to be that day.

Probably not anytime soon.

"What about you?" I ask, scooting a little closer. A whiff of her perfume wafts over me. It's something floral... maybe rose or jasmine. It smells a thousand times better than the cigarette pressed to my lips. I throw it to the ground and stomp it out.

Her familiar golden eyes blink a few times at me. She's staring, watching me closely. I can't tell what she's thinking. She's not easy to read, and it frustrates me because most women are an open book to me.

But she isn't like most women. My brother married her after all. I watched them exchange vows: "Till death do us part." Well, death has parted them, so now what? What does this mean for Jude's future?

Jude.

"Is it really you?" she finally asks, avoiding my question altogether.

Wow. Okay, so she does recognize me. That's a good thing. Isn't it? I'm not sure of anything right now. Sure, she's a sight for any man, but I've never been that guy... and never will be. She's been off limits the moment I met her, and that hasn't changed. I'm not proud of this, but I don't have the best record when it comes to relationships. One-night stands? I'm excellent at those. But love and romance? I'll pass, thank you.

Her perfectly shaped eyebrows are pulled together in the form of a question. I haven't set foot in this tiny Oklahoma town in ten years. Bethel. Sounds like the name of someone's grandmother. Or an old church, which I wouldn't know anything about.

Her eyes are locked on me. She's waiting for me to confirm what we both already know. I don't say anything, though. It's been ten years. What is there left to say? I'm sorry? It's not enough and never will be.

"You're... Jay," she says, confident enough to speak my name with only a slight hesitation in her voice.

I give her a small nod of acknowledgment.

"...Ben's younger brother," she continues confidently. "And you're here. Like, really *here*. Hmm." Her expression is dark and dancing with more questions simmering beneath the surface.

Ah, there it is. After all this time, somebody finally remembers the forgotten brother. The "younger" one. That's all I am, and all I'll ever be. Don't worry about me, I'll just be here living in my brother's shadow.

This is exactly why I never came back. I didn't want to be just Ben's brother. I wanted something different, something more. Here I am, back where it all started. And this woman—correction: Jude—thinks she's got me all figured out. Well, she's wrong. She doesn't know me at all. And it's better that way.

I know I should respond to her revelation about my identity, but I've suddenly lost the nerve. I turn my back and start walking towards my rental car. I can't stay here any longer.

I feel a light tug on my arm. I glance down and see bright pink polished nails digging lightly into my bicep. My gray eyes flash back up to hers.

"You're leaving?" She spits angrily.

Yeah, I guess I am, princess. I've had enough. I shouldn't have come in the first place. I should've known it'd be no different than when I left ten years ago.

"Yeah, you're right. It *is* me, the 'younger brother,' as you so kindly put it. I'm sorry for your loss, okay? Bye, Jude," I say, my words empty and bitter.

I want her far away from me. I never thought I'd say that about anyone, but especially about my dead brother's wife.

"Eff you, Jay," she says firmly.

Little Spitfire.

This time, she says my name with full confidence—no wavering or hesitation in her voice. Funny how she can't even be bothered to say the full word. I can help her out with that. I'm not sure what's gotten into me tonight, but I'm done. Tonight is a joke. I gently peel her fingers from my arm and step out of her reach.

"Don't you mean to say fu—" I start to say before she shoves her hand over my mouth.

Is she serious right now? Unsure what she wants me to do now, I do something she probably isn't expecting. I nibble gently on her fingers. Her skin is warm and soft, a sharp contrast to my rough, calloused hands from years of hard work.

"Don't." Her eyes flash angrily. "My children are inside, and I don't cuss. You, of all people, should know that my husband just died, and that I'm out here because I can't handle one more second inside that place. *His place.*"

Let it all out, girl. Let it out.

She continues, "I have to go back in there because I need to give a speech, but I can barely speak. I've only said a handful of words this entire week, and yet here I am, spilling my guts to a man who dared to show up at his brother's funeral. I can't believe you're here. How noble of you."

By the time she finishes, she's panting and out of breath. Realizing she still has her hand over my mouth, she draws it back, her eyes suddenly apologetic.

"You're right, you know," I say, nodding.

"Right about what?" she squeaks, her eyes suddenly filling with tears.

Great, now she's crying, and this time it's my fault.

"I knew coming back was a mistake. I shouldn't be here. I'm sorry I came. I'll stop ruining your night..." I say, defeated and a little embarrassed.

This is low, even for me. I'm being a jerk. She doesn't deserve to be treated this way. I need to go before I continue making things worse... for both of us.

She stops me again. "No. You didn't ruin my night. How selfish of you to think that. Ben ruined everything when he died. This isn't your fault, but it'd be a lot easier if you were the one to blame."

She has the saddest look in her eyes. The last time I saw her plays in my mind like a movie. She had tears in her eyes then, too, but they were happy ones. She was overjoyed to be spending the rest of her life with Ben. My older brother. She would spend the next decade getting to know him better than I ever could.

I was at the wedding, but she probably doesn't remember me. I was in the background. I hadn't even been chosen as my brother's best man.

I want to take her in my arms, comfort her, and tell her that everything is going to be okay. But I can't promise her that. I can't promise anyone that. Because I don't even believe it myself.

I'm the last person on the planet to try to offer her solace. She's gone this long without it. She doesn't need me.

Everything is *not* okay, and I've just made it all worse.

CHAPTER 8
Jude

When I make it back inside, it's as if I never walked out at all. I'm still fuming about my encounter with Ben's half-brother, Jay. The nerve of that guy! I'm shocked he came at all. He moved to LA the day after we got married and hasn't been back at all.

It's not like we haven't tried to reach out to him over the years—we have. I've even invited him to visit a few times. But it's always the same excuses, and he never comes. My kids have no idea who he is because they've never had the chance to meet him. And now that he's finally here? Well, that chance is gone.

I'm heading back to the booth with my mom and kids when someone steers me aside. It's Brian's wife, Kelly, who is as bright and bouncy as my Zumba instructor. She always wears her white-blonde hair in a high ponytail that swishes as she walks.

Even her steps have a peppy bounce to them that I envy. She has a map of freckles across her face and the bluest eyes I've ever seen. She's taller than me, as most people are, and has four girls: Juniper, Pippy, Lanie, and Alona. I have no idea how she manages, but somehow she does. She is what I often refer to as Miracle Mom, and I strive to be like her.

Kelly wraps me in the biggest hug, squeezing the life out of me —what's left anyway. Again, I'm speechless. How is it that running into Jay—the last person I expected to show up here, smoking and cursing in my face—suddenly brings my vocabulary back? She must sense my body tense underneath her grasp, because she pulls away.

"How are you, love?" she asks me. I don't know if Brian is also "her love," but she's called me this for as long as I have known her. Ever since Brian was hired as one of our head chefs at the tavern. She also works here as both a waitress and a hostess. Kelly is the type of person who will fill in wherever needed, no questions asked.

I shake my head, tears clinging to my lashes. I can't stand crying in front of people. I don't know why, but I always try to avoid it. I wouldn't say Kelly and I are best friends, but we're pretty darn close.

She wraps her arm around my shoulder and starts leading me across the room. I don't realize where she's taking me until her feet stop suddenly, and I nearly crash into her. My gaze flicks up to hers. She's brought me to the stage.

The stage that feels as familiar to me as my own children. There's no way I can get up there and give a speech tonight. Talking about my Benny? I'm not ready—not in front of all these people. I won't let them see me fall apart, because that's exactly what'll happen if I try.

"I know you don't feel ready, but you *can* do this. It doesn't have to be anything long or fancy, they just want to hear from you. Everybody knows how much he meant to you, love. I'll be right here, okay?" she offers gently, squeezing my hand in hers. Tears gather in her crystal blue eyes, but somehow, they still don't look sad. I don't even want to know what mine look like right now.

I shake my head as tears begin to fall. I hear people around us shuffling in their seats, waiting for me to get up on stage and say something in Ben's honor. But I can't make myself get up there. I can't do it.

That's when I feel something warm and small grasp my other hand. I look down and see my son Riley gazing up at me with big brown eyes and a head full of hair. Oh, my sweet boy. Just when I needed you.

"It's okay, Mommy, I'll go with you," he tells me. I choke back a sob.

"Me too, Mommy," says my six-year-old from behind her brother. As much as they fight and bicker, they're a team when it counts. A team for me, and a team for their daddy, who can't be here. But I like to believe that there is a part of him here with us tonight.

Hand-in-hand, we walk onto the stage together. I don't have anything prepared, I'll have to just speak from the heart. "Hi there, um... Thank you all for coming out tonight. Friday nights were always our favorite. Music has always been a big part of Ben's life," I pause, close my eyes for a moment, and collect my thoughts.

Breathe.

"He saw a need in our community and wanted to fill it. He recognized talent and dreamed of creating a safe place where it could shine. That's what he was aiming for when he started Open Mic on Friday nights. Whether it was reading poetry, sharing a scene from a story, or singing a well-known song. He wanted people to be bold enough to do it all. I've never been as bold as my husband..."

I stop as soon as the word 'husband' escapes my lips. He stopped being my husband the day he died. The day he left and never came back home. What does this mean for us? What does this mean for our marriage and our future? There is no 'our' anymore, it's just me. A *widow*.

"Excuse me," I apologize into the mic, my eyes blurring and my voice croaky. This is now the second time in one night that I have to make an escape. It's all too much. I should have known it would be. But staying home hadn't felt like an option.

I turn and start making my way off stage. But before I can make my exit, I hear the softest, most precious voice start singing into the microphone. Bold and unafraid. Not at all a coward like I am.

Nova stands there with the mic to her lips, softly singing *Hey Jude*, the song I know by heart. I didn't even know she'd been paying attention when Ben would sing it to me, but kids' minds are like sponges. Hers apparently absorbs everything.

She doesn't skip a single beat. There's no band playing tonight, but someone pulls up the instrumental version of the song on their phone and plays it to accompany Nova.

I can't believe she would do this. This isn't for me, though; this is for her daddy. She was Ben's little princess, through and through. I can't think about what that means for her now. We all have a long road of healing ahead of us, and this is only the beginning.

But tonight, for the first time since I found out he died four days ago, I feel him here with me. Everyone in the crowd starts to sing along to the familiar tune. Riley has returned to my side, and I pick him up in my arms. With tears raining down my face, I sway with him to the music.

Ben would have loved to see his daughter on stage. We tried many times, but she was never ready. She always chickened out as soon as her song choice started and refused to sing a single note. Now look at her. She's a natural up there. And I can't help but think of who she reminds me of—someone who hasn't had the guts to get up there in a long time. Not for any dramatic reason, just time... and life as a stay-at-home mom with two kids.

I'd do anything to get back on that stage and perform, just like the old days. But those days are gone. The past can't be changed, but it sure changed everything for me.

CHAPTER 9
Jay

didn't end up leaving. Shortly after she made her way back inside, I did the same. For being in a place where I spent a good chunk of time, the only people who would even recognize me would be my mom and the woman with gold and fire in her eyes.

I could probably handle Jude if our paths cross again, but my mother—she's a different story. Growing up, I was always close to my mom. She was stern with us, but I think she may have grown a bit softer after I was added to the picture.

Sometimes I wonder if I was an accident. Ben was almost a teenager by the time I was born. Most people don't plan their families that way on purpose.

I wouldn't say she babied me more than Ben, but she was certainly less strict with me. Probably because she was older and more laid back by the time I came around. As a result, I got into more trouble than my brother.

Ben moved out of the house the summer after he turned eighteen. He left for college in Indiana, only returning for holidays and occasional birthdays. I really only got six years with him.

After that, I was on my own. I wasn't an only child, but it often felt that way. I could be friends with whoever I wanted, date whoever I wanted... There was no competition between us, ever. Because of our age gap, we never fought about girls, sports, or what we should be doing on the weekends. It wasn't like that and never would be. He lived his life, and I lived mine. Basically, I could do whatever I wanted with little to no consequences.

I did, however, get my license suspended at least twice by the time I graduated. I've lost count of how many speeding tickets I've racked up over the years. Luckily, I'm mostly past all of that now.

But no matter how hard I tried at anything, Ben always seemed to do it better than I could. I knew this because, whether they realized it or not, both Mom and Dad often spoke highly of their oldest son. Even though he was only Mom's biological child, they both doted on him. Ben could do no wrong.

I think a part of me has always resented my brother. I don't hate him; my distaste for him isn't that strong. But if someone told me tonight they were sorry for my loss, I'm not entirely sure what it is I've lost.

My thoughts are quickly interrupted by the sound of Jude's voice. She's standing on stage with a little boy in her arms and a girl who must be her daughter, because they look almost identical.

"Whether it was reading poetry, sharing a scene from a story, or singing a well-known song. He wanted people to be bold enough to do it all. I've never been as bold as my husband..."

Her voice trails off at the word husband, and I can hear a low murmur of voices surrounding me. Whispering, wondering, waiting. Her eyes find mine across the room, and she quickly moves to exit the stage, placing the microphone on an empty chair. I move unconsciously towards her. I need to know if she's okay. And that's when I hear the sound of singing. It stops me short.

The voice is small, childlike, and pure. This kid is pretty good.

She's hitting all the notes with a precision I'm not sure I could match. I'm in awe of this little voice.

I take a closer look at the girl. Her hair is long, dark brown, and wavy. Her eyes are a greenish gold. I wasn't paying attention before, but now I recognize the song she's singing. It's a song everyone would recognize. It's the famous Beatles song *Hey Jude*. I find myself closing my eyes and quietly singing along, even though I'm sure my voice is out of tune. I'm a bit rusty. I don't sing much anymore, and if I do, it's not songs as sweet as this.

I open my eyes and refocus on the girl—until I notice Jude. She's off to the side, holding a little boy with curly hair, hugging him close as she watches her daughter with tears in her eyes. And that's when it hits me.

The harsh reminder that I don't belong here—the flare in her eyes, the words that slipped from her lips: it'd be easier if someone were to blame. And that someone... is me.

Maybe that's fair.

Maybe she *should* blame me.

Maybe if I hadn't been so stuck-up, so self-absorbed, I wouldn't have left.

And maybe if I stayed... he'd still be here.

Maybe my one and only brother wouldn't have died.

I mean, we all go eventually, but maybe it wouldn't have been so tragic.

Maybe I should've been the one who burned in that building instead of him.

The thought alone guts me... but maybe it's not so far off.

Maybe it should've been *me* in that fire.

Across the room, I lock eyes with Jude, the woman my brother loved. A woman I have no business locking eyes with, let alone exchanging small talk. We weren't friends then, and we certainly aren't anything now. If I was smart, I'd stay away from her. She's grieving, and so am I. I'll just make a mess of things if I get involved. I don't have a clue what it means to fall in love with someone, and I've never committed myself to anyone.

I'm not my brother, and I've come to realize that maybe I never will be. I was happy for them when they got married, but I also knew that I would never be lucky enough to find a love like theirs. Love emanated from them in waves.

He was lucky enough to find someone in this lifetime. And now she's here mourning my brother. For her, she did lose something. She's experiencing a terrible loss. I may have lost my brother, yet I feel little pain. This woman staring at me from across the room feels everything. Because the man she's in love with broke her heart into a million pieces.

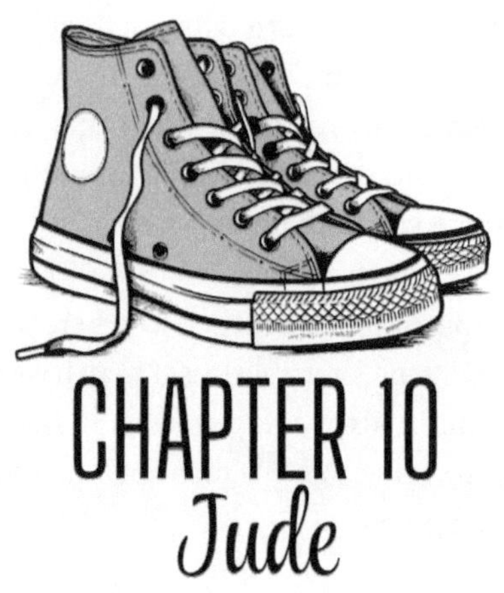

CHAPTER 10
Jude

t's after ten by the time we make it back home and tuck the kids into bed. Mom retires to the guest room in the basement shortly after. I'm not sure how long she plans to stay, but she did mention that Dad would be here tomorrow for the burial. Saying the word out loud feels wrong. It leaves a bitter taste in my mouth, and the moment it slips out, I wish I could take it back.

Burial.

It sounds so... final. Because it is. That's exactly what it means.

Both kids go to sleep without a fight. Not that bedtime is usually a struggle, but there's always someone who needs another drink of water or one last potty break. It's always something with these two. But not tonight. Tonight, they are out as soon as their heads touch their pillows. I wish it were that easy for me. But I can't sleep. The other side of the bed remains cold, the sheets still smooth and untouched. His side.

There's still a small part of my brain that believes if I leave his side untouched, he will magically appear. I know it's impossible... but what if? What if they're wrong? What if, by some crazy miracle, he didn't die in a horrible fire and is out there somewhere trying to make his way back home? It's a ridiculous thought, yet I can't shake it.

Nova's song had been a huge hit, and I couldn't be prouder of her. Afterward, the tears kept coming, followed by a few bouts of laughter too. One by one, people found the courage to get up on stage and share a story or two about Ben.

I was too choked up to finish the rest of my speech, and even though no one commented, I'm sure they all understood why I couldn't.

At some point, Jay made his way back inside, but he didn't seem to want to be noticed by anyone. *So why did I notice?* I barely know the guy. I met him once at our wedding. But even then, he'd barely said a word to me and disappeared from our lives until now.

He couldn't bother being around while Ben was alive, but decides to show up now that he's gone.

Maybe I shouldn't be too hard on the guy. I don't know his story, only the little bit I've heard from Ben. And Ben never had much to say about his brother. They were twelve years apart. Ben was forty when he died, and so that would make Jay... twenty-eight. That's a pretty big age difference for siblings. So maybe it isn't anyone's fault they aren't close, but just the way of the world. Their world. I'll be five years older than Jay when I turn thirty-three at the end of this month.

I'm not ready to spend the rest of my life without the love of my life. I don't want to think about that. Not yet. Someday, I'll have to. But not tonight. Now, I'm just taking it one day at a time. I close my eyes and pray sleep comes quickly. Surprisingly, it does.

I dream of Ben.

I jolt awake to the smell of smoke. Where is it coming from? Jay smoked a cigarette right in front of me, not a care in the world. Is he here? Surely, not. Maybe I'm still at the tavern, and I couldn't drive myself home after a few drinks. But people aren't allowed to smoke here. What's going on?

It only takes a moment for my eyes to adjust to the darkness surrounding me. I'm in bed, and Ben is asleep next to me. I nudge him. At first, he doesn't budge, but when I nudge him again, he rolls over and groggily looks up at me. He must have been deeply asleep. But something isn't right. My eyes are stinging from the smoke, and it's starting to become hazy.

"Ben! Get up! There's smoke in here." I tell him sternly.

This time, he sits up straight in bed, runs a hand over his jaw, and scans the room. That's when he notices it too, and he flies out of bed.

"What's going on? What should we do? Is something wrong?" I'm trying to be calm, but panic is setting in.

He steps into a pair of slippers and throws on a jacket. I have no idea where the jacket came from. My heart is racing, and my hand rubs my chest to try to slow the beating.

"You're right, there's smoke in here. I'm going to get the kids and come back for you, okay? Stay here," he commands.

I don't want to be left behind. I start to argue with him, but he's already racing out the door and across the hallway to get our kids. I can't stand here and do nothing!

I'm a mess. I jump out of bed. Where are my shoes? Do I need my phone so we can call 9-1-1? That's what you're supposed to do in emergencies, right? My thoughts are racing, and my heart is fluttering. I don't know what to do. Ben, please hurry up. Don't leave me here.

I start rushing around the room. I think my shoes are in the closet. The smoke is getting heavier. Shouldn't our fire alarms be going off? Why aren't they working? All I hear is the thumping sound of my heart. Everything else is silent. Where are my husband and kids? Why are they not coming for me?

Quickly, I find a pair of shoes. I'm pretty sure I put them on the wrong feet, but I don't have time. I need to be ready to bolt the moment he returns. I yank one of my favorite cardigan sweaters off its hanger, sending the hanger flying in the air, and quickly put it on.

I rush back into our bedroom only to find the entire room covered in flames. It's engulfing the ceiling and crawling across the floor towards me. I'm trapped. There's no way out. Flames lick and dance around the room. Suddenly, the large window that overlooks our front yard shatters. I scream.

"Ben, where ARE you? Ben... Ben... Ben." I keep screaming over and over and over until I open my eyes again.

I wake up in a cold sweat. My sheets and clothes are both soaked. My heart is thumping so loudly that my ears are humming.

Soon after, Mom rushes into the room. I must've been screaming for her to hear me from the guest room. She sees me and knows exactly what to do. She wraps me in a dry towel and pulls me into her lap, just like she used to when I was a child. It's at this moment that I break.

I sit there, wet and sobbing, in my mother's arms as I recover from my nightmare. Except this isn't a nightmare, because I'm living it. It was Ben's life that had been lost in that fire, not mine.

But maybe it should've been.

Maybe it should've been me.

CHAPTER 11
Jude

Today is the day I have been dreading all week. No, that's not true. Today is the day I have dreaded all my life. From the moment I said I do, I never imagined I'd go from exchanging vows at the altar, to saying goodbye forever at my husband's gravesite. We only had ten years together. He promised me a lifetime.

Well, not forever, according to my son. Riley reminded me that someday we will get to see Daddy again. He's in Heaven, we just can't go there until it's our time. I used to believe this, but as we draw closer to the place where his stone will go, I'm not sure what I believe in anymore.

I've always considered myself a person of faith. I grew up going to church every Sunday. Ben and I had been more consistent in our early years of marriage, but somewhere along the line, we drifted. I want to believe there's a God and Ben's in a better place, but I'm just so hurt and angry.

Angry that Ben could leave me and the kids like this. Angrier at God for letting it happen. Maybe there are just some things I'll never understand. My human brain won't let me. But I have to hold onto the tiny sliver of hope I still have that this isn't a permanent goodbye.

Today, I'm wearing black. Ben isn't here to make fun of me for looking so depressing, and honestly, I want to blend in with everyone else. Wearing dark sunglasses to hide my puffy eyes feels a little too cliché, so I don't bother. Isn't it what people expect anyway? If I don't look like I haven't slept all week, or spent the whole time crying, something would be seriously wrong with me. People would talk. They'd start rumors that I didn't love my husband. The grieving widow.

I don't know why widow is such a taboo word. It's almost as bad as saying the F word. I don't care if other people cuss, I just choose not to. It's never been a part of my vocabulary. But who knows what will slip out of my mouth after today, after becoming a widow.

My mom has been a true blessing this past week. I haven't had to lift a finger, thanks to her. She's not babying me necessarily, but she's been through her share of grief with the loss of her sister and her mother recently. I think she's genuinely happy to be here helping me with the kids and everyday things I can't remember to keep up with. It's given her something to do, something else to focus on, and she can relate to my grief.

Rita requested this intimate graveside ceremony—even though we'd all been together just last night in a much more pleasant setting, instead of here, where everything seems to echo the word *death*.

Last night turned out to be a good night. I wasn't sure when we first arrived, but seeing Nova on stage singing her little heart out made everything else melt away... for just that moment. She heard her daddy sing it to me many times, it traveled with us wherever we went, and now my daughter carries it with her.

Mom drove us to the cemetery, and I'm back to barely saying anything. I try extra hard when I'm talking with my kids, but everything I say sounds empty and scratchy to me, like a broken record on repeat.

The kids don't seem to notice, thankfully, they are still themselves, running around and playing. It's at bedtime when the realization settles in again, and extra bedtime stories are required, as well as one more lullaby, and two more hugs and kisses—one from me, and one from Daddy in Heaven.

We make it up the hill to the site they've picked out for Ben. I haven't spoken a word the entire way here, and I don't plan to say anything to the small group that is starting to gather around the grave. Heads are bowed as though they are saying a prayer, but I think that's just the mood we are all in. There's a soft murmur of whispers, but not much else.

Kelly and Brian are already here, and when she sees me, she gives me a soft smile and reaches out so she can squeeze my hand lightly. "It's going to be okay, love. I know it doesn't feel like it right now, but someday it will be."

I nod, because that's all I know how to do. I'm not sure what kind of response she expects from me. I scoot off to the side and stand next to my mother, who wraps an arm around my shoulder and tugs me close for comfort. I lean my head against her shoulder. After a moment, I feel someone else wrap their arm around my waist. I glance up and see that it's my dad.

He made it here. I know he said he would, but for some reason, I didn't believe he meant it. I can't stop the tears. They slide down my cheeks before I even realize it. I don't say anything, because if I do, I will surely lose whatever composure I have left. It's not much.

By the time everyone settles in around the gravesite, I'd estimate there are about twenty people here. On my side, it's just my parents and kids. On Ben's, there's his mother, along with a few aunts and uncles I haven't seen since the holidays.

His brother Jay, on the other hand, is nowhere to be found. My eyes scan the small crowd, but I don't see him anywhere.

Figures. Maybe he was right when he said that he shouldn't have come. Why *did* he come last night?

The remaining few all work at the tavern. There's Brian, Kelly, Lexi, Mitchell, Zach, and Tanner. Not everyone was able to make it, some had to stay and run the tavern. But they'd all been there last night, and if I had been given the choice between everyone showing up to an Open Mic Night in honor of Ben or coming to this... the answer is obvious.

CHAPTER 12
Jay

I didn't arrive at the cemetery late on purpose. I overslept this morning. After seeing Jude last night, I couldn't sleep. I lay in bed for hours, going over our encounter and thinking about Ben. My nights are often like this, where my body and mind are restless. Only this time, my thoughts are invaded by the one person I can't help thinking about.

Unlike last night in a room full of people, I can't blend in here. So, once I make it up the small hill where everyone's gathered, I find a discreet place in the back. From here, I can see the pastor at the front of the half circle that's formed, as well as a straight shot view of the woman I ran into last night.

Someone I need to forget about as soon as this is over. I don't belong here. I'm going back home, because this isn't where I'm meant to be.

The ceremony is going well. Er, about as well as these types of things can go. Even though Ben and I haven't spoken in years, I still can't wrap my head around the fact that he's gone. The moment I got the call from our mother, I was filled with regret.

I should've called ya, man. I should've made an effort to come visit you and your family.

After a while, Ben quit trying. He stopped calling me, probably because he was tired of hearing me tell him no. I can't say I blame him. That was all on me. I'm the one to blame. But I couldn't fathom why, after spending most of our lives apart, he wanted me in his life. It made no sense to me at the time, and so I did what I do best—shove everyone I love away, because it hurts less than having to face it head-on.

I know that makes me a coward. But I didn't have the courage to face someone who was both my brother and a stranger. I didn't know his life, and he didn't know mine. And I planned to keep it that way. It was the only way I knew how to protect my heart.

In hindsight, though, I was wrong. I don't know what I would've done differently—only that maybe I wouldn't be standing here, hating myself for all the things I should've done but never did. All because my pride had gotten the better of me.

The pastor closes with a prayer, and even though I haven't set foot in a church since I was still living with my parents, I don't shut it out like I normally would; I listen. After the prayer, the pastor opens it up so people can say something in honor or remembrance of Benjamin Jennings.

I glance over at Jude, who has kept her eyes glued to the ground this entire time. I can't see the fire glowing in her eyes. I wonder if her eyes glow at all today, or if the flames have been completely snuffed out. I'm not sure why I'm so curious, but I am. I expect she will want to say something, especially since she never finished last night, but she doesn't make any effort to speak. I can't say I blame her. She's lost something far worse than I have.

Mom speaks first. "This day is so hard. A mother should not have to bury her son. It just isn't fair," she says, dabbing at her eyes with a tissue.

I've never seen my mother cry in public. She can't stand crying in front of anyone, but I'm glad she's letting it out. I want her to be real. I want her to allow herself to feel, rather than try to keep it all inside like I still do.

"Anyone who knew Benjamin knows how well he loved. He didn't do anything half-heartedly. When we first mentioned him partnering with us in the family business, he said: Wherever you need me, that's where I'll be. He was devoted to our restaurant, but love and family always came first for him. When he married Judith, my late husband was still struggling through some health issues at the time, but truly, she was a Godsend. She stepped right in alongside him and helped out wherever and whenever needed, especially after the passing of his stepfather.

"Benjamin gave his whole heart to this life and the people in it. And though we'll miss him more than words can say, we'll carry that love with us, in everything we do. We'll see you again soon, son." She ends her eulogy and dabs at her eyes again, joining my aunt and uncle off to the side of the pastor.

I'm not much of a crier, but I find myself wiping away a stray tear after that speech. I move a little closer to get a better look at Jude. It strikes me that today she's wearing mostly black. Her hair is tamed in a bun high on her head. She's wearing a long, black dress with a nice jacket, even though it's really warm.

I can't help but wonder what shoes she's paired with such a somber dress, and I lean over to take a peek. Sure enough, she's wearing another pair of Converse sneakers. Only this time, they're black. I wonder how many pairs she owns. I'll probably never get the chance to ask her, because I'm leaving after the ceremony. I'm booking a flight back to Los Angeles when I make it back to the hotel.

When Jude still doesn't make any effort to say anything, suddenly all eyes turn to me. Wait, what? Why is everyone looking at me? How did anyone notice me? I'd slowly started to inch forward without even realizing it.

I've been found out. I suppose it was only a matter of time.

All eyes are on me, and my mother starts motioning me to the front. I shake my head at her. I wasn't planning to say anything. I don't even have anything prepared. What would I say? Surely, Mom understands exactly why I don't want to do this. I didn't bother to show up at my dad's funeral, and here I am at my brother's, years later, representing a man I barely knew.

I didn't know Ben. Not in the way a brother should. Not like everyone else here does. They're all better equipped to make a speech than I am.

Mom motions for me to join her again, and I make my way slowly towards the front. The sea of people part down the middle like I'm Moses with the Red Sea. Only I can't perform any miracles or do anything remotely amazing. All I seem to do is make things worse. Like when I said the wrong thing to Jude and she ran off. I didn't mean to, but I hurt her.

Before I realize it, I'm standing front and center. Someone grabs me by the shoulders and spins me around to face the crowd. Everyone is staring. It's so quiet you could hear a pin drop. I hear nothing but the stampede of my heart inside my chest.

Jude is standing closest to me. I want to glance over and see what color her eyes are, but I don't move. I take a deep breath and release the words I should've said a long time ago.

CHAPTER 13
Jude

So, he decided to make an appearance after all. I didn't notice him here earlier. Maybe he had been trying to blend in. But his mom saw him and is gesturing to him to come forward.

Sure enough, here he is. Not only is he walking through the parted sea of people, but if I'm not mistaken, he's looking in my direction... at me. No, that's silly. Don't be ridiculous, Jude. But I see him more clearly now—without the dim glow of the city lights last night.

I take a good look at him for the first time. At a glance, I can't tell he's related to Ben. While Ben's hair was so dark it was almost black, Jay's is much lighter, like the color of fallen leaves in autumn. His hair is neatly combed to one side, but he doesn't appear to use any gel in it. His hair is short, slightly longer on top, yet even in this Oklahoma wind, he doesn't have a single hair out of place. How is that even possible?

I couldn't tell what color his eyes were in the dark, but now, when he's only a couple of feet away from me, I can clearly see them. They aren't one solid color but rather a kaleidoscope of colors. They're a light green mixed with a touch of blue and a dash of gray. I've never seen anything like them.

I immediately force my gaze back to the ground. What am I doing studying another man's eyes? And not just any man's eyes, but my brother-in-law's. That's technically what he is to me, right? Or does that disappear when your husband passes? I don't know. There's a lot I don't know anymore.

I did come prepared with something to say, but I haven't mustered up the courage to say any of the things I have scribbled on the back of a grocery receipt yet.

I'd take Kelly's kind offer to have her read it for me, but I doubt she could make it past the first line. It's smudged, with words crossed out and rewritten, like I couldn't quite make up my mind.

I couldn't.

Still can't.

A voice breaks through my thoughts. And it isn't Pastor John from my church. It's coming from a voice I heard last night. Jay.

"Um, hello. You might already know who I am. Then again, maybe not. I'm Jay Whitley, Ben's brother. By the look on some of your faces, you're just now finding out that he even had a brother. Well, no surprise there. That one is on me." He laughs nervously to himself.

My eyes snap in his direction. He's standing right next to me. So close, if I extended my arm, I'd bump right into him. I'm not going to do that, of course. I can't move away, though, there's nowhere else for me to go.

Crickets. Nobody laughs. I have second-hand embarrassment for him. What is he doing? He better have something good to say, or I'll be forced to rip the hypothetical mic out of his hands and start reading my grocery receipt eulogy.

"Look, Ben and I had always been at odds. I think from the moment I was born—fate, if you believe in that sort of thing—just wasn't on our side. Ben was twelve when I came into the world. By the time I was starting school, he was already leaving.

"I had six years with my brother. But those earliest years? They're the hardest to remember. And now, looking back, it wasn't enough. Not nearly enough. Not enough time to know him and bond the way most brothers do. We were at a disadvantage from the start."

When he speaks, his hands stay tucked inside his jean pockets, and during the pauses, he pulls them out. In, out, in, out... A nervous habit, I suppose. I catch myself wondering which pocket holds his cigarettes. Maybe he'd rather be anywhere else smoking, rather than standing here, giving this speech.

But he continues, and I listen.

"I know that doesn't excuse my behavior. I wasn't exactly the 'poster child' for my parents. Sorry, Mom. Anyway, I could've made a better effort at being a part of Ben's life as we got older. By the time I graduated, I was more than ready to leave this place. Not that there's anything wrong with Bethel. But it never felt like home to me, and I didn't know who I was. It was something I had to do to figure myself out, without worrying about following in my brother's footsteps.

"There were a few times Ben reached out to ask if I could help run his restaurant with him. We weren't on good terms, and I think it was his way of trying. Trying to extend an olive branch and mend the broken pieces of our relationship. But I turned him down. Told him no. Over and over. And it's been almost five years to the day that I last spoke to him. My own brother."

His voice breaks on the word *brother*. I can't see his eyes from my position, but a tear escapes down his cheek. And then another, and another. Part of me wants to hate him for how he treated Ben, but I don't have it in me. I think he's genuinely sorry for the pain he caused his family and his brother... Only now, it's too late. And it's something he'll have to live with.

"Ben, if you're listening, I'm sorry. I'm so sorry I failed you. If I had another chance, I would tell you yes and try to be the little brother you need me to be. But I'll never get that chance. I hope, wherever you are, you'll forgive me. I—I mean it, brother."

And with the crowd still parted, he walks back out the way he came. Out of sight like a ghost. I surprise myself, and probably everyone else, by what I do next. But I don't care.

I run after him.

CHAPTER 14
Jude

His stride is a lot longer than mine. I'm practically at a jog before I finally reach him. He must know I'm here, but he doesn't stop until he reaches a small gazebo in the middle of the cemetery. He finally turns around to face me, folding his arms across his strong, solid chest. He seems to be in good shape.

Not that I'm looking at his chest. That would be absurd. Inappropriate. We're standing beneath a gazebo in the middle of a cemetery at my husband's funeral—I'm not too quick to forget the real reason we're both here.

The air is getting more and more humid by the minute. I'm starting to sweat underneath my jacket, but my dress is a spaghetti strap, and I don't have a bra on underneath. I don't want that to be obvious, especially to *him*, so I keep the jacket on.

I'm the first to break the silence. "Hey, I just wanted to say that I'm sorry," the words quickly tumble out of my mouth.

His hair still looks perfect, but I never realized how tall he is.

Ben was an even six feet, but Jay appears to have him beat by at least a couple of inches. But now, I'm not so sure. I can't remember. I chew my bottom lip, thinking about it.

"Sorry? What for?" he asks, as confused as I am.

"Oh, uh, for cussing at you last night. I wasn't myself, and I wasn't being very friendly. I'm sorry for that."

He wasn't very nice either. He was petty enough to call his own brother's celebration a "party." But it doesn't excuse my actions, and I need to apologize.

He waves off my apology. "Nah, don't be. And you didn't cuss at me. You didn't even do it properly, remember?"

Seriously? Is he seriously baiting me right now? Here? Believe me, I remember. All too well. Maybe I should retract my apology.

"Don't be a smart-alec," I retort. I feel like I'm talking to my children. I've said this exact phrase to them numerous times.

"You mean a smart-a—"

"Don't." I quickly stop him. "That's not what I meant, and you know it." I huff, folding my arms across my chest just in case he happens to be staring. I don't even care if he is. Let him stare for all I care. This man is infuriating, to say the least.

"Do I, though? I don't think we know each other at all," he tells me.

He's right, and we both know it, but I'm not giving him that satisfaction. Why can't he accept my apology and move on?

"Look, I just came to say that I was sorry, that's all. Oh, and I never knew all of that stuff you said about you and Ben. He never told me any of that. So, I didn't know. Is it true? Everything you said?" I ask, genuinely wanting to know, the anger in my voice slowly fading.

Ben hardly talked about his brother. He said they weren't close and probably never would be. When he first took over the family business, it was me who encouraged him to reach out to his brother. He reluctantly agreed, and I had so much hope back then.

I wasn't sure what went wrong between them, but I thought maybe this could be the start of mending whatever had been broken. But I was wrong. Jay turned him down every time Ben called, and he finally gave up. They never spoke again after that.

Both of them quit trying to repair their relationship. Just like that. I didn't have any siblings growing up, but if I had, I can't imagine not talking to them for years.

He reaches a hand into his back pocket, pulling out a dark green lighter and a pack of Marlboros. He lights the cigarette and brings it to his lips, taking his time on the inhale and blowing out smoke on the exhale. I'm close enough to get a whiff of his smoke. It smells almost the same as my dad's used to when he smoked. It's an oddly comforting sensation.

"Yeah, it is," he finally says. "I'm not sure why I admitted all of that, but it felt good to get it off my chest, I guess. For what it's worth." He takes another drag from his cigarette. He can feel me watching him and offers it to me.

"Do you smoke?" he asks me.

I shake my head, suddenly feeling shy around him. I should be getting back to my family—to my kids. They're probably wondering why I ran off in such a hurry. Especially if they saw who I ran after.

I'm not sure how to explain my quick departure, but maybe it's not a big deal. We're just talking, and I'm a grown woman. That's allowed, right? Just maybe not with *him,* per se. Even his own family doesn't talk about him, as though he died a long time ago.

Part of me feels a little sorry for him, but it's probably silly of me to feel that way. Sure, he just confessed his remorse, and I think he meant it, but what he did wasn't exactly fair to Ben. Or his family.

"No thanks. I don't," I say, finding my voice again. "But it doesn't bother me if you do," I offer. Truthfully, it doesn't make me uncomfortable. He can make his own choices about what he puts into his body.

"Hmm, okay," he chuckles, blowing out a slow stream of smoke.

I really need to get going, but for some reason, I'm still standing here. I've barely been able to talk to anyone, yet here I am, talking to someone who is mostly a stranger.

"I think it would have meant a lot to Ben that you came today. I do believe he's watching over us, and I don't think your words were empty or meaningless," I say. "For what it's worth," I add, repeating his words back to him.

I can hear people approaching in the distance. They're probably heading this way. That means it's over. I have to get going before everyone sees us standing here, sharing whatever this is that's happening between us. Nothing is happening, though. This is probably the last time I'll ever see him, but for Ben's sake, I'm glad he came.

He stomps out his cigarette and looks up at me with his grayish-green eyes. "Thank you, Jude. For saying that."

Only those close to me call me Jude. It sounds strange coming from somebody else. Coming from *him*. I don't like it. But I also don't hate it.

"Yeah, no problem. Uh, I gotta get back," I say, turning to head back towards the crowd of people descending the hill in our direction. From here, I can spot Nova's pigtails swinging as she walks, and Riley's soft curls bouncing around him as he chases after his sister.

"Me too. Hey, see you around," he says.

I chance a look back in his direction and offer him a soft smile. *Will I?* It's highly unlikely, given that he doesn't live here anymore. Last I heard, he was still living in LA. He has no business being here in a small, rural, dusty town. It's probably for the best that he doesn't stick around. It's the kind of place where everybody knows everybody, and they will eat him alive. He wouldn't survive here.

There's a look in his eyes that I've seen in my own reflection lately. A mixture of sadness, fear, and regret. But there's something else I notice, too. He looks just as lost as I have felt since losing Ben.

And I'm not sure what to do about it.

CHAPTER 15
Jay

don't wait around after my conversation with Jude. I take off in the direction of my dented navy Prius rental car. Normally, I wouldn't be seen driving something like this, but I didn't have a choice. I had to accept what they'd given me at the airport. It drives okay, but I'm really missing my sleek, black Range Rover.

I'm not sure why I spoke up at the gravesite. I hadn't planned to speak at all, much less in front of everyone. I'm not used to all eyes being on me. Before I came here, I was working for the new contracting company my best friend's dad started. Praying this time, things would work out for us.

When I graduated from high school, I thought I had it all figured out. One of my buddies, Kyle, was moving to LA with his girlfriend and asked me to tag along with them. His dad lived out there and promised us jobs when we arrived. I had no reason to say no, and every reason to stay. Yet I went.

His dad owned a bar, and for the first few years, Kyle and I were bartenders and partied it up. Kyle and his girlfriend had partied a lot in high school, and that didn't stop when we were on our own. We were either high or drunk most nights after work.

After two years, the bar went bankrupt, and we had to start over. I remember feeling panicked and wondering if this meant I needed to suck up my pride and go back home. I should have listened to that gut feeling, rather than sticking around.

It wasn't even a year later that his dad decided to start up a landscaping business. Kyle's dad was full of talk, but very little walk. But we were young and dumb, and trusted him when he said that this time things were going to work out. And they did, for a little while... until they didn't.

I don't know all the details of what went wrong that time, but eventually, the landscaping company also failed. Kyle remained faithful to his father, and I stuck with Kyle because he was my best friend. I also didn't want to use my alternative option. The option I kept on the back burner, just in case I ever needed it, which I hoped I never would. Life isn't perfect, I know that, and neither are people. I truly wanted to believe that his dad was a good man who was down on his luck and had been burned too many times.

So, after seven years of jumping from job to job, I should have taken the folding landscaping business as my final sign to return home. But instead, I chose to give his dad the benefit of the doubt when he presented us with yet another opportunity that sounded too good to pass up.

Finally, this was it. The moment we both waited so long for. How could I go back now?

It was a construction company. His dad was responsible for designing floor plans and bringing them to life. I wasn't used to the early mornings, the high physical demand of the job itself, and the long hours. I'd come home after nine or ten hours of solid labor and pass out. I was exhausted. The main thing it was good for was my physique. I grew lean and muscular with the manual labor.

By the time the weekend rolled around, I did everything I could to escape from it all. Smoking pot and drinking eventually led to bringing girls home with me. I couldn't tell you how many women I've slept with over the years. Eventually, I stopped counting, because what was the point? There was always going to be another.

I should have known better by now. This time would be no different from the time before that. And before that. And before that. I guess there had been some shady stuff going down behind the scenes that neither Kyle or I knew about, and it resulted in yet another one of his dad's businesses to crash and burn.

This time I got the message loud and clear. I was trying to figure out what I should do for a living—stay in construction, find a gig bartending, start my own company, or something else—and then I got the call about my brother. It suddenly felt like the universe was working against me. I had no choice now but to come back to the very place I'd run away from. At least for a few days.

A loud rapping against the window startles me. I was too lost in my thoughts to see anyone approach the side of the Prius.

My gaze shifts to the woman looking at me through the glass. Mom. I quickly turn the key in the ignition, and the little car roars to life. I roll down the window and look back up at her.

Her hair is dark, like Ben's. I don't remember what Ben's dad looked like. There weren't any pictures of him around the house growing up—just of our family since I came into the picture.

To be honest, I don't look like our mom at all. My hair is light brown, almost the color of sand, and it's softer and straight. Recently, I've kept it short. From what I remember, Ben always let his grow longer than you think he should have. As though he was due for a haircut but couldn't find the time to have it cut regularly, like I did mine.

"Hey, son," she greets me.

I can't remember the last time she called me her *son*. She called me for every holiday, every birthday, and if there was a death in the family. It wasn't until recently that I called her back. She left me a voicemail because I was too drunk to answer when she called. I never expected to hear her broken voice on the message, telling me about my brother dying in a fire.

I may be her son, but I'm a terrible one. I've said and done some horrible things over the years, and I wish I could have come home a changed man. But I'd be lying if I said I've changed. Sure, I've matured a bit from my partying days, but I'm still rough around the edges. I'll always be in Ben's shadow. I can never live up to him. Especially now that he's gone.

"Hi, Mom," I say weakly, because I don't know what else to say. I'm not a man of many words, and right now, I don't have any. I need to leave. I knew coming here would be a mistake.

She scans the outside of the car, as if she's assessing the type of car I'm driving, but then her eyes find mine again.

"Can I talk to you for a minute?" she asks.

A lump settles in my throat. It's about my speech, isn't it? I shouldn't have opened my mouth. I never should've said anything at all. People were here to mourn the loss of Ben, not listen to me go on and on about what *I've* lost. Somehow, I made it all about me.

I don't argue. "Sure," I say, patting the seat next to me. She nods, and I unlock the car as she makes her way around to the passenger side. She's taller than I remember, and I've noticed how she walks when she's around others, like she's someone important. But now, her shoulders are slumped, and I can see dark circles underneath her eyes. It's all for show.

Once she's seated, she closes the door and angles the air vent towards her. The cool air gently blows her dark hair around, and her body relaxes a little.

"I have a lot to say, but I won't say it now. I'll keep it short. I'm glad you're here. Whatever force brought you home, I'm glad it worked. What you said at the ceremony was both stupid and brave. Stupid because you've missed out on so much over the last ten years, but also brave for admitting it. I'm proud of you."

I can't see her face because she's staring out her window with her body angled away from me. I can't tell if she's crying, but I hear her sniffle as though she's trying to hold back tears. She's always holding something back.

"Mom... I—" I start, but she doesn't give me a chance to finish.

"No, don't. I'm sorry if I sound angry. I'm not," she pauses. "Okay, that's not entirely true. I am angry. But not with you, I don't think." Her words are rushed and all over the place.

It's like she's forgotten how to have a normal conversation with me, and maybe she has. Maybe we both have.

I try again. "Mom, listen. I am so—"

"No, don't. Listen, it's okay... we can talk about that later. There's something else I need to talk to you about. I was hoping we'd be able to discuss things over lunch."

Wait, discuss what? She wants to have lunch with me? As if this isn't awkward enough. I wasn't planning on staying that long. I suppose I owe her that much. I'll have lunch with her, and then I'm booking the next available flight back to LA. I don't want to spend another minute in this place. There's nothing here for me, maybe there never was.

"How about right now?" I ask, suddenly craving another cigarette.

I've really got to slow down.

"Starving, too, I take it? I skipped breakfast, too anxious about today, but now it's caught up with me," she says, her warm brown eyes finding mine. Her eyes are glassy, and something twists hard in my gut.

I don't have time to process the sudden change in my plans, so I just nod. "Okay, Mom. Where do you want to go?"

A small tear escapes the corner of her eye and trails down her cheek. She ignores it and lets it fall. She doesn't care if I see her weakness. Maybe I'm the only one who's allowed to see her like this. Maybe.

"I want to go to Second Verse," she says.

Ben's tavern is the last place I want to go. I was there last night, and it'd been enough. But now all I can think about is Jude. A woman I have only one thing in common with. We both lost the same person. And now Mom is asking me to go back to the very space he breathed in. Lived in. A place we were supposed to thrive in, together, and I had told him no. *No.*

Ben's tavern. It could have been *our* tavern, but I'd been too selfish. Too caught up in myself to ever give that a chance. To give us, as brothers, a chance. And now, I'm too late.

"Okay," I say, resigned. She agrees to meet me there since she drove herself. I put on my seat belt and reverse the car out of the cemetery. I leave my brother's grave without looking back.

CHAPTER 16
Jude

I make my way back to Ben's grave while my kids are off somewhere close by with my parents. I'm not ready to leave him yet. The kids each placed a homemade picture on their daddy's grave as soon as the service ended. Nova colored a picture of a bright rainbow so Ben would have something pretty to look at in Heaven whenever he misses her. Riley's is an array of colors all swirled together. When I asked him about it earlier, he shrugged and said Daddy would know what it means. I left it at that.

Nova's busy reading the names off the other graves, while her brother follows closely behind. They are close enough to keep an eye on, but I know I won't have long when it comes to the two of them. I still haven't taken off my sweater even though it's extremely humid and sticky out. I reach inside the large pocket on the right side and pull out the grocery receipt I tucked in there, waiting for the right moment. Well, I guess this is it. As good as it'll ever be. Nobody can prepare you for this level of hurt.

My hands begin to shake as I unfold the letter that took me

forever to write. I use the few moments of alone time I have to read it out loud.

> *Dear Benny,*
>
> *I didn't have the words yesterday, and I don't really have them now. But I'll try my best. If you could hear my last words to you, what do you think they would be?*
>
> *Probably something like: How dare you? How could you do this to me? Why did it have to be you?*
>
> *Every selfish thought has crossed my mind. I'm constantly living in rewind mode, trying to forget the present, and do everything I can to relive our past. I know that's silly, and I'm sure you're rolling your eyes right now. But you've always taught me to be honest, and this is the truth. I don't know how I'm expected to move on with my life without you in it. It sounds impossible. It sounds like a mistake.*
>
> *Another honest truth: I don't want to. I don't want to know what it's like to wake up another day without you beside me. I don't want to know what it's like to watch our kids grow up and grow older than you ever had the chance to. Because there's a good chance that they'll outlive you someday. I'll outlive you, Ben. And I hate that. I absolutely can't stand it. But there's nothing I can do about it.*
>
> *I have no choice but to wake up tomorrow, get out of bed, feed myself and the kids, and move on with our*

lives. Life without you... is a life I never dreamed of living. And now, I have to face this.

I know I can't stay angry at you. It's really not your fault. You were doing an amazing thing. Something I never would've done. Something I can't do. You gave up your life to save somebody else's. It's not fair, but it's the way it worked out.

I'm trying to be strong. I'm trying to hold on. It's hard, though. You have no idea. I don't know how we're going to make it through life without you, Ben. But we have to try. Sometimes that's all you can do.

I truly hope that this isn't goodbye... but just "see you later." So, I won't end this letter with a farewell... because I do believe someday, we will see each other again. I have to hold onto that hope.

I love you always, Benny. I'll never stop.

Your songs for me will forever be my lullaby. Save a song for me when I make it back to you someday.

See you, Benny

Love,

Your Jude

It might be due to the chaos in my head, but the house has seemed quieter, stiller, since Ben left us. The kids haven't wrestled each other or yelled as much, and neither have I. I worry that my mom being there has a lot to do with it... maybe everything. The moment she heads back home to Indiana, and it's just me and them... I have a feeling the floodgates will open. On all fronts.

I'm not ready to think about that yet. She still hasn't told me when she's leaving, and I haven't dared to ask her. Dad, however, is very clear about his plans. He says he'll stay today and tomorrow and leave early Monday morning. Whether or not Mom is joining him is either undecided, or I'm not supposed to know yet. Either way, I'm not going to ask. Not yet anyway.

"Are you up for lunch, dear?" Dad asks me as we head back to our vehicles.

I glance at him. He isn't a tall man, standing at around five foot six. His hair is white now, and is starting to thin a little in places. I have my mother's skin tone, but my father's eyes. His eyes are still warm and inviting, even though I don't get to see him much. And when I do, our conversations don't last long. Not because we aren't close. He's just a man of few words. He doesn't need to say much to enjoy someone's company. I, on the other hand, enjoy conversation. Well, I used to.

I bring myself back to my dad's question. The real answer? No, I don't think I can eat. Not after today. Maybe not even tomorrow. Maybe I can be like Jesus and fast for forty days. But I don't think that's a likely scenario here. I should say yes and be agreeable. I'm a sucker for giving in to Mom and Dad. Especially now, given the circumstances.

"Sure, that sounds great. There's a new diner that opened up not too long ago, and I've heard it's pretty good," I say.

He smiles and shakes his head at me. "And pass up your place? Are you kidding me?"

Suddenly, I know exactly where he's referring to, and instantly, my stomach pitches. "Dad, I—"

"I didn't come all this way to let you turn me away from eating at your tavern," he says with a glimmer in his eyes that I don't return.

I shake my head, adamant. "It's not *my* tavern... not anymore..." I trail off.

He gently grabs my shoulder, forcing me to look at him.

I do.

Mom's trailing close behind with Nova and Riley, who keep stopping every few seconds to try and read all the names on the headstones. Nova's proud that she's learning to read this year, but I don't want to be here any longer than I have to be. I'm ready to go.

"Oh, don't be silly! Of course it's yours. Just because Ben di—"

This time, my mother stops him. She's caught up with us enough to know where this conversation is going. I'm thankful for the sudden pause.

A part of me has never truly felt like the tavern belongs to me. We'd moved here and gotten married so that he could help run it. His stepdad's health had ups and downs, and we were newlyweds —how could I have said no? He knew he might need to run the tavern someday, and it didn't take him long at all to fall in love with it, the same way his family had.

There are things I love about it, too. I love the people—Brian and Kelly are amazing and are some of my closest friends. There's an entire kitchen staff, including a guy named Tanner, who is super reliable and valuable to the restaurant. A girl fresh out of college, named Lexi, just recently got hired full-time.

Mitchell and Zach are the main bartenders. When I first met them, I thought they were brothers—they look so much alike—but they're not related at all. They're friendly and always have a good story to tell. Like the time someone got tired of waiting for their drink, attempted to hop the counter, missed, and caused a big scene.

These people have become like a second family to me. Since mine lives states away, this is the closest thing I have to family. Honestly, they have been there for me the entire time I've been with Ben. It's silly to think that they would leave me high and dry the moment he's no longer a part of the picture. But I can't help but worry about it. What if they don't need me anymore? What if they only put up with me because of Ben? The thought alone is enough to make my head start to spin.

"I think that's enough. If Judy doesn't want to eat there today, we won't eat there today," Mom says as she gently pats Dad on his shoulder.

I sigh. I don't want to cause a scene. We are nearing the parking lot, and I don't want anyone to hear that I'm avoiding the tavern.

"Won't eat where?" Nova pipes up from beside me, handing me a flower.

I look down. "Where did you get this? Did you take this off somebody's grave?"

She smiles and shrugs. She's a stinker sometimes. I should probably use this as a good teaching moment, but instead, I bring it up to my nose and take a big whiff. It's a pink tulip, my favorite.

"Next time, ask me first if it's okay. But thank you. It's beautiful."

"You're welcome," she says.

"She picked it because pink is your favorite color," Riley chimes in.

He's right, it is my favorite. Ben always told me I looked best when I wore pink. The brighter the shade, the better.

"That's not why I got it," Nova argues.

We all stop walking and look at her.

"Then why did you get it, sweetheart?" my mom asks.

"Because Daddy told me that was the kind of flower he always used to get for her."

My eyes instantly well up with tears. I lose it. I break down right there, in front of my family. She isn't wrong. It's because she's right that I can't handle it.

It's something only Ben would have known. I don't think I ever told our kids which flowers are my favorite. But Ben knew because every year on my birthday, he'd get them for me. A vase full of vibrant, pink tulips. Or maybe like the song he always used to sing me, she miraculously remembered this little piece of us, too.

My knees hit the soft grass, and I fall apart. I'm crying so hard I can't see anything in front of me. That's when I feel their warmth. One arm, two arms, suddenly my entire body is encased in a sea of arms. I'm surrounded by the people who still love me. The people who are still here. Here for me and with me. Here because not only are they my family, but also because of their love for me.

This is what love looks like.

This is what love feels like.

This is something I don't ever want to forget.

CHAPTER 17
Jay

By the time we walk through the doors at the tavern, it's after one o'clock. I haven't booked my return flight yet, and I'm sure Mom has brought me here to try and talk me out of it. She may have a shot... I don't have a job anymore, and the lease on my apartment is up at the end of this month. There's not much holding me to LA currently.

I'm immediately hit with déjà vu the moment we step inside. Despite the tavern being part bar, it doesn't smell like a typical bar. The air isn't stale with beer or the usual cocktail of spilled alcohol. It smells like fried onions, burgers, and freshly baked bread— exactly the way I remember it.

While I don't carry the same memories here that my brother does, I have plenty of my own. As soon as I was capable of entertaining myself, Mom started bringing me here. I remember the specific booth, too. She'd set me up in a booth, which faced the stage, with coloring books, crayons, Play-Doh, and whatever else she could bring me to entertain me while she worked. But it was the live music I enjoyed the most. I remember being mesmerized by the people that had the guts to get up there and sing their hearts out to a crowd of strangers. It baffled me that people could do that. I never imagined that someone being me. Mom tried to get me on the stage as soon as Dad gifted me his guitar, and I started playing. But I never had the courage like these people did.

When I was in high school and Ben was long out of the house, I started earning a paycheck at the tavern. Mom put me to work doing all sorts of odd jobs. Washing dishes, taking orders, filing papers in her office, and running errands all over town the minute I was handed my license. There was a part of me that loved it here, and the other part of me that couldn't wait to get away from it all.

Dad had an underlying heart condition, and when I was about six years old, he needed heart surgery. It was minor at the time and he healed well. It wasn't until a few years after Ben married Jude that my dad passed from a sudden heart attack. When Ben had first moved back, I had thought he'd come back for me. Silly, thinking that way now. Dad was okay then, and finally, I was at an age where I felt like maybe Ben and I could at least be friends. Work together. Become business partners. Something. Anything. He came back to be close to Dad again, but he also had planned to take over the tavern if things got bad again with his health. And they did.

Things had taken a turn for the worse, and the most frustrating part was that I had already left by then. As soon as Ben wanted no part of me, once again, I couldn't handle any more rejections from him, and I left. I had to. I felt like I had no choice. Nobody really wanted me there, until suddenly they did. It wasn't until Dad died that they reached back out to me. Needed me. By then, it was too late.

I was gutted.

If they didn't need me, I didn't need them. That was the final push I needed to leave everything behind, including this place. The tavern belonged to my brother.

Mom's already made her way over to a booth tucked into one of the corners. I've had friends tell me that my mom intimidates them. I think it has to do with the way she always carries herself around others. She always walks with confidence. Her shoulders are rarely ever slumped, and she keeps her head held high, no matter the circumstances. I've never seen her with her chin down until today.

She's actually soft beneath all the steel armor she wears. She's tenderhearted and one of the most caring people I've ever known. She doesn't often let that side of her show. I'm not sure why, but she's always been that way.

I slide into the booth across from her, right as a waitress walks over to our table with a bright smile and menus. She's smiling at me as though she can tell I'm not from around here. In a town this size, a stranger doesn't go unnoticed. Not that I'm a stranger, but I may as well be.

"Hello there! My name is Lexi, and I'll be serving you guys today. Can I grab you a couple of beers or anything to drink to start you off with?" she asks, her hair is a light brown with blue highlights, and she has a silver hoop through her nose. Her eyes are a soft green, but I find myself thinking about honey-colored eyes. I'm not really in the mood for her chipperness, but it's a little contagious, and I offer her a crescent of a smile back.

"A beer sounds great," I tell her.

"Okay, sure. What would you like?"

I shrug. I honestly don't care. Anything will do right now. "You pick. It doesn't matter to me."

She flashes me another one of her infectious smiles. "You got it. And for you, Mrs. Whitley?" she asks, turning to my mother.

Mom hasn't been paying any attention to us. She's looking down at her nails, chipping away at the red polish. A habit I didn't know she had. I'm not used to seeing her like this. But I know her, and she's not usually someone who is anxious or fidgets. She glances up at the sound of her name. I wonder if she's been like that recently, distracted ever since she lost her firstborn son.

Losing someone changes you.

"Oh, I'm sorry, Lexi. I'll just have an iced tea with lemon. Thank you." Her eyes trail back down towards her nails. Pick, pick, pick.

Lexi walks away, and I use this opportunity to reach across the table for her. I grab hold of her hand gently, and she lets me. Her dark brown eyes find mine again. There's an ocean of sadness in them that I hadn't noticed before. It's heartbreaking to see her like this.

I know nobody is to blame for this, but I suddenly feel angry. Angry that Ben died and left my mother in pieces. She's lost both husbands and now her oldest son. I'm the only man she has left in her life, and I'm not even really a part of it. I haven't been for a long time.

"Mom, are you okay?" I ask, even though I know the answer. Neither of us is *okay*, but I want her to know I genuinely care.

Her eyes gloss over, but she doesn't look away. She faces me head-on, her eyes searing into me. Tearing my heart into tiny little pieces.

It was a stupid thing to ask. Of course, she's not okay.

She gives my hand a light squeeze and shakes her head. "Yeah, I'm fine," she says, even though we both know it's a lie.

"It's going to take some time, ya know?" She dabs her eyes with the corner of her napkin and places it back into her lap.

She waves the hand she was picking at around in the air. "Getting used to coming here and not seeing..." She trails off without saying his name, but she doesn't have to. We both know who she's referring to.

I nod. Because what else can I do? I don't know what it's like to come in here and *not* see Ben at work. I haven't spoken to my brother in five years. He might as well be a stranger to me. I didn't know him. Not like a brother should. He's everywhere I go. Every place reminds me of him. Yet time and distance haven't replaced him.

"I know, Mom," I say.

She sniffles and sits up straighter. "But that's not what I want to talk about right now. There's something I wanted to discuss with you."

My stomach pitches at the thought of "discussing" something with her. I have a feeling I know what it involves, but I'm not sure. We haven't discussed anything in years. Again, that's all my fault. Not hers.

"Okay," I say nervously.

"I want you to come back home, Jay." Her voice wavers slightly.

Hearing it breaks me a little more inside. Please don't start crying, Mom. I can't handle her crying right now. *Please.*

"Mom..." I start, but she puts her hand up to stop me, she isn't finished. She's just warming up. Here it comes.

"No, please let me finish before you say anything," she says, her voice strained, but gentle.

I nod, letting her continue.

Lexi returns to our table quietly, understanding that we are in the middle of a conversation, and places our drinks on the table. She looks over at me and whispers, "I'll come back whenever you are ready to order. Take your time." Then she walks off.

"I want you to move back to Bethel. You've been gone for too long, and I'd like you to come back. Time, distance, and circumstances, whatever you want to call it, has pulled us apart—and I want to put an end to that. I want you here, Jay. I *need* you here." Her voice cracks on the last part, and she quickly grabs her glass of iced tea and takes a long sip. Her lipstick leaves a burgundy stain against the glass when she's done.

I had a feeling she was going to do this the moment I came back. But I can't do this. I don't want to break her heart all over again when it's already been broken, but I have to. I can't stay here.

"Mom, I don't—" I try a second time, and again she stops me.

"No, Jay. I don't want to hear your excuses this time. I need you to come home. Even if it's for a little while, I need you here.

Just give me six weeks to figure things out. This place is yours too you know..." Her voice drops an octave as she says this, and for a moment I can't catch my breath. I reach for my cold glass of beer and take a long sip from it.

My mother doesn't ask for anything, so it's a big deal that she's asking this of me now. I know that. But I also can't promise her anything. I can't give her that.

She must see the answer on my face, because she quickly continues, "I don't have your dad around anymore, and Benjamin was quick to step up and take responsibility for the tavern." She holds up her hands to stop my rebuttal before it comes. "I'm *not* asking or expecting that of you. I *know* you aren't your brother. Benjamin ran the show ever since the passing of your dad, and he's done wonders with the place. But it's still missing a big piece. It's missing *you*, Jay.

"This tavern doesn't just belong to Benjamin and Judith... it belongs to you, too. We won't dig into the past right now, but it's something I want you to consider. I still manage all the finances, and I've never minded helping your brother with that part. But running this place? Think about Judith... She'll need help. All I'm asking for is six weeks to allow me time to find somebody else who can run it if you absolutely don't want to. But I need some time to figure everything out. Please give me that."

Think about Judith. Jude.

How can I tell her no? How can I shut her down at a time like this? But what does it mean if I say yes? She's right, I'm not my brother, and I don't want to take his place. *Think about Jude.* Where does she fall into all of this? Surely she would have more say in the matter of running this place than me or even my mom?

This isn't where I belong. I've never belonged here. Not then and not now. I need some air. The room is closing in, and I really need a cigarette. I've lost track of how long it's been since I had my last smoke, but I don't think I can take it any longer.

I know this isn't fair to her. She didn't ask for any of this, but neither did I.

"I need some air, Mom. Give me a minute," I say, pushing up from the table and scooting out of the booth. Her eyes look even sadder than before, if that's even possible, and she nods. I'm the one doing this to her, not Ben.

I hate myself for any pain I've caused her, but I can't wrap my head around this. I had come here to pay my brother respect. To honor him in his death, since I'd been too much of a coward to face him while he was still alive. I guess this was my effort at trying to turn over a new leaf, but it's a wasted effort. I see that now.

She doesn't say anything else as I walk away from our table. She doesn't try to stop me as I push through the double glass doors. The same doors I escaped through last night.

This feels too familiar. Mindlessly, I walk over to the railing out front, and I grip it hard. I want to scream. I want to curse every obscenity into the universe. But I don't. I growl and run my hands through my hair, closing my eyes. I can't do this. I don't want to do this. But what choice do I really have here? I don't have a home waiting for me in LA, and I don't have a job anymore. I have some in savings, sure, but eventually that's going to run out too. I have nothing to return to.

But what is there for me here?

When I open my eyes, I notice that my vision is blurred. I'm crying. I'm standing outside my brother's tavern—and apparently mine too if I just say the word—cursing him and the universe for allowing him to die, and I'm crying.

I'm *crying*.

I suddenly don't care who sees me. I can hear people whispering around me as they quietly pass by to make their way inside. I don't care who hears the sob escape my throat as my hands grip the warm metal. I do care though, when my vision suddenly clears, and I see a flash of gold standing before me. I wouldn't miss her eyes anywhere. There she is again, standing in the exact spot I'd met her less than twenty-four hours ago.

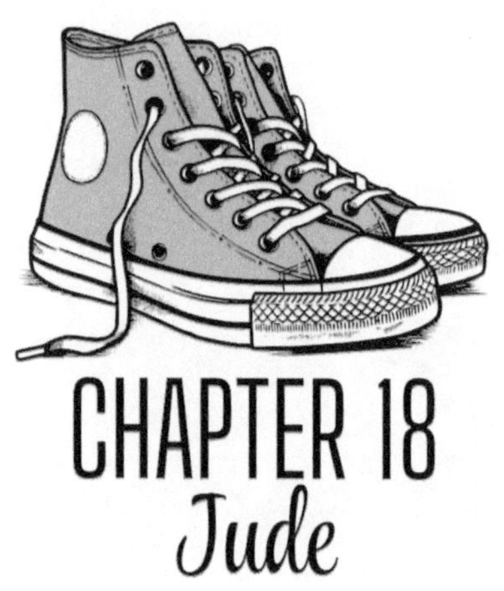

CHAPTER 18
Jude

He's the last person I expected to see. Jay Whitley, here again at the tavern. My tavern, apparently. Because it's mine too—always has been—it has never really felt like it was something I could claim. Not with Ben's family always at the forefront of it all.

Of course, I supported Ben from the start, but it never felt like mine. This place was always his thing, and I was simply a part of it because I was Ben's wife. And that was enough for me. I loved being a part of this tavern with him. I can't even begin to fathom what will become of this place now that he is gone. Now that it's in *my* name alone. It could've been both brothers running it side by side, but Jay didn't choose that path. He'd made that very clear.

So what is he really doing here? Did he really come here to pay respects to a brother he never knew? Or is he planning to rip this place out from under me and claim it all for himself? The tavern was in Ben's name, and now it's mine. If he suddenly decides he wants it now after all this time, I don't know what I'll do. He doesn't know the tavern, its people, or the vision Ben had for it. I can't trust him or his motives.

My plan is to quickly skirt past him and hope he doesn't notice me. Don't make eye contact or stand out.

Only... I can't.

Everything in me screams to run from him, but I simply can't. Because what I'm seeing is someone deeply broken. A man who doesn't even realize exactly what he's lost, yet feels the weight of it in his soul. He didn't just lose his brother, he's lost himself, too.

He is no longer standing at the railing, he's down on his knees, sobbing into his hands. I can't see his face, but I can hear the gut-wrenching sobs. People are staring at him, but they don't stop to help him. Instead, they step around him, whispering or shaking their heads like they feel sorry for him. I'm beginning to feel sorry for him as well. Should I? Not even a moment ago, I wanted nothing to do with the guy.

This guilt—if that's what this is—or grief that he's feeling out of regret and remorse for his brother is all on him. They *both* had many chances to figure their stuff out, yet neither of them did. And now, a decade later, after the passing of my husband, Jay's heart finally splits wide open.

I'm stunned and don't know what to do. A moment later, I feel someone's warm breath tickling my ear. I turn my head in their direction, away from the man breaking apart in front of me. I know I should look away instead of staring like everyone else, but his grief speaks to mine. We're both broken over the same loss.

"We're gonna go inside and find a table, okay? Want me to order you anything?" Mom asks me, her voice soft.

I nod and whisper back, "Sure, that sounds good."

I'm not sure why I'm whispering, but it feels like the right thing to do.

"What would you like?"

I could go for a cold beer right about now, but I don't say that.

Now doesn't feel like the best time to be enjoying a beer. Despite where we're at.

"A water is fine. I'll only be a minute," I say, my eyes already turning back towards Jay. I've never seen somebody so broken before. Except for myself... It's a little unnerving how much he looks like I did when I was crumpled on the floor after finding out the news.

She squeezes my shoulder, and her and Dad walk inside with the kids. I'm not sure why I'm still standing out here. It doesn't feel right to leave him like this. Did he come here alone? Why?

I slowly approach him and crouch down to his level. His shoulders are tense, heaving up and down every time he cries.

I don't know what to do or say to comfort him. I gently rest my palm on his back and let it sit there for a minute. I don't know if he knows I'm here. I don't know if he's aware of anything outside the world he's in right now. I don't want to startle him.

I slowly start to rub small circles along his back. Gentle strokes back and forth like my mom used to do when I came to her as a kid with a scraped knee or bad dream. She was always the person I ran to when I needed someone to comfort me. I wonder if Jay has anyone like that in his life to comfort him. A girl back home in LA, maybe? I wonder if this is the first time he's needed someone to be there for him, and why he's struggling alone. The thought saddens me, and I push it aside because I hardly know Jay. I don't know him at all.

He cries harder. His entire body shakes like an earthquake beneath me. Images flash in my mind of a time similar to this, when Ben heard the devastating news about his stepdad. They may not have been as close as they could have been, but I'd never seen my husband so broken before. It looked a lot like this. A lot like the man crumpled in front of me.

What am I doing? I should be inside enjoying a meal with my family, not out here comforting the man my husband hasn't spoken to in years.

Five years, to be exact.

But I can't bring myself to walk away either.

"Hey, are you okay?" I ask gently, not expecting him to answer. He doesn't seem okay, but I don't know what else to do. How to help him.

I feel his body tense beneath me at my words, and he shifts. I remove my hand and freeze. I don't move as his gaze sweeps up to meet mine. His grayish blue eyes are glassy, tears and snot running down his face. I should offer him a tissue. I think I have some left in my purse. I fumble around for a tissue in my bag, but I can only find a napkin. It's the best I can manage, and I offer it to him. He takes it and wipes his eyes and nose with it.

"Thank you," he says, his voice coming out raspy and gruff.

"Are you okay?" I ask again.

He wipes himself off and stands. I do the same. I almost forgot how tall he is, but I'm reminded once again as he towers over me now. He's so unbelievably tall.

"I'm fine," he says unconvincingly.

He doesn't sound fine. He doesn't look fine. He looks anything but. I'm sure I don't look much different though.

"Okay, if you're sure," I say, hesitating. I know my family is inside waiting for me, but I can't leave him here like this, knowing as well as he does that he is *not* fine. But I'm not sure there's anything I can do... or if he would even want comfort from me.

"I'm sure. Go be with your family. They need you," he says, his voice more even this time.

I nod. He's correct, yet something isn't sitting right with me. He's not okay, but maybe he will be.

And technically speaking, he *is* my family, too.

"Are you here alone?" I ask him. I'm not sure why that spilled out. I shouldn't have asked him that.

A slow smile creeps across his face. There it is.

"No, Mom's inside," he says, the smile quickly vanishing.

Okay, good, so he's not alone. He has family waiting for him inside as well. I wonder what he's still doing here. He seemed ready to leave town when I spoke to him in the cemetery. I honestly didn't think I'd see him again. I don't blame him for wanting to leave, but this is one of the last places I expected to see him.

Especially not here.

"I should go," we both speak at the same time.

I want to hate him, but there's something about him that makes hating him hard. When he's not being irritating, he might even be the tiniest bit likable.

"Okay, well, best of luck to you, Jay. I mean it," I say. And it's the truth. I do mean it. I wish him well.

He nods, stuffing his hands into his pockets. "You too, Jude."

There it is again. He had to go and use my nickname. Not Judith, like his mom calls me, or Judy, like my parents. Jude, as though I'm still Ben's girl. Right now, hearing my nickname coming from his lips is too much. It's too much.

I start to walk past him when he darts in front of me. What now?

I'm shocked to see that he's holding the door open for me. He's not pushing me away or running, he's staying. I offer him a small smile as I glide past him. I get a whiff of him as I walk by. It's an intoxicating smell. It's a mixture of leather and maybe cinnamon? Not sharp, like chewing gum, but subtle and lingering, like a soap or body wash. I don't know exactly what it is, but it's pleasant.

I find my parents quickly and sit down at their table. I busy myself with a menu even though I don't need one. I know everything that's on it already. I've ordered everything at least a hundred times, and it's all delicious.

I can't stop picturing Jay crying in front of the tavern, on public display. Not everyone can do that. Break in public. I'm not even sure I've allowed myself to do such a thing. But it does something to me. And I can't help but think that maybe I've been wrong about Ben's brother. Maybe Ben had been wrong about him, too.

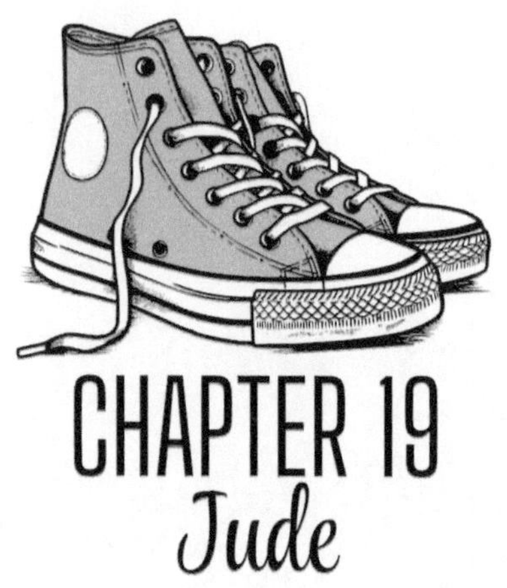

CHAPTER 19
Jude

can't help but notice Jay and his mom from where we're sitting. I saw him walk past our table and around the corner not that long ago. I wonder if he's having one last meal with his mom before taking off.

What caused him to leave Bethel in the first place? What could have been so bad about this place that you would leave everything behind, including your own family? It made no sense to me. As far as I knew, Ben and his brother had a great childhood.

Mom and Dad are in the middle of telling me something, when I notice I'm zoned out. I'm not paying any attention to the conversation. I steer my gaze back to my parents and try my best to stay engaged, but I'm lost.

"Are you with us, dear?" Dad asks.

I am now.

"No, sorry. I'm listening."

Mom smiles and shakes her head at me, offering me one of her hands across the table. She knows my thoughts are elsewhere, yet always finds a way to pull me back. I reach across and give her hand a gentle squeeze in return. The warmth brings me back to the present.

"Sorry, Mom. What did you say?" I ask.

Riley and Nova are busy coloring on a kids' menu, a new addition to the tavern since they came into the picture.

There hadn't been a kids' menu when Ben took over the tavern, but after we started bringing Nova here as an infant, I wanted to make it more of a family establishment. I wanted families to know that they, too, are welcome here.

Ben and I sat down one night and designed a kid-friendly menu, with the help of Brian, of course. After all, they have four little mouths to feed, so they know better than anyone. It's been a hit ever since. And that was almost six years ago now. Six years.

I had Ben for ten. I don't think any amount of time would ever feel like long enough, because the amount of life I have left to live without him could very well surpass that.

"Your dad and I were just asking what you thought about having the kids come stay with us for a little while, after Nova finishes school for the year, of course. She only has a week left. I can stay here and then have the kids fly back with me once school's out," Mom offers.

I hadn't even considered that as an option, to be honest. I can barely think about tomorrow. Let alone the weeks ahead of me. It's already too much to focus on the next few minutes and seconds of each day. I can only live in the now. Nothing beyond that is promised. And even then, I feel as though my entire body is stuck in slow motion, half steps at a time.

"Are you sure? I mean, Nova's flown before, but Riley was so little. He won't remember it," I start, and she shakes her head as if it's no big deal.

"It's fine. They'll be fine. I would love for the grandkids to spend some time with us. I can get the pool set up and everything," she says, and I know without a doubt that she means every word.

Dad doesn't say anything as he sips his beer, but that isn't unusual for him. His silence doesn't mean he disagrees, it means he's leaving this one up to Mom.

"What about me? What am I supposed to do?" I sound like a whiny child asking my mom for help. Right now, I don't feel like an adult. I need someone to take me by the hand and tell me what to do with my life. I don't feel capable of making those kinds of decisions on my own.

"What do you mean? You keep doing what you've always been doing," Dad says matter-of-factly, like the answer has been right in front of me this entire time. Maybe it has, but it's not as simple as he's making it out to be.

"How? You mean help out at the tavern? Fill in as needed and sing every Friday night like I did before?" I ask, a slight irritation creeping into my tone.

Dad takes another sip from his beer and nods his head. "Yeah, exactly."

He says it like this is easy. And maybe it is. But he's not the one who lost the love of his life. He's sitting right next to her, and pretty soon they'll be back home doing life together.

I don't get to have that. Not anymore.

He doesn't understand the depths of my pain. And part of me hopes he never has to survive this pain. How can he expect me to carry on as if nothing happened? As if this is normal. Normal doesn't exist anymore.

When I leave this place, I have to face the cold reality that I'm alone. I don't have anyone waiting for me at home. I no longer have someone to warm the other side of the bed. I don't have someone to laugh with and share stories with after the kids are asleep. All of that was ripped away from me the moment Ben died. How dare him for leaving me here like this. *'Til death do us part.* It's a load of crap. I didn't sign up for *this*.

Not this.

I know our food will probably come out soon, but I suddenly don't have an appetite. I don't want to be here anymore. In *his* place. I can't take his place. I can't walk in here and act like everything is fine and pick up my life where he left off. It doesn't work like that. I can't live as though nothing has changed because *everything* has changed. Dad's wrong.

I stand up to leave, throwing my purse hastily over my shoulder. At this, Nova and Riley look up at me. Their eyes glistening with questions I probably can't answer.

"Judy... please sit down. I know this has all been hard on you. We just want to help you out. Give you and the kids a bit of a break," Mom says, her voice smooth and soft like a lullaby.

I know she means well, they both do. They don't deserve my frustration, yet I don't have anyone else to unload it on. If I'm going to be angry at anyone, it should be at God for taking my husband too soon. I wasn't ready. None of us were.

But right now, my parents are standing in my line of fire. I reluctantly lower myself back into my seat and take a breath.

"Been hard on me? Excuse me? It's been a week. *One* week. I have to live the rest of my life like this. You get to go back to your lives like nothing even changed. *You* had a hard week, I'm stuck with a hard life," I spit out. It's petty and hurtful of me to say this to them. I know my mom isn't immune to grief.

She went through all of this a year ago when she lost both her sister and mother, within months of each other. She knows *exactly* what I'm feeling, yet there's a part of me that wants to separate her grief from mine.

The stubborn part of me knows I should be softer with her, with them both, but I can't. I'm tired of being soft with everyone. Neither of them has dealt with the pain of losing their *spouse*. Therefore, it's not the same. It's not the same at all.

Mom's lips part as though she wants to say something, but then she closes them, choosing her next words carefully.

"Please think about it, okay? Nova only has one week left of school, and I'll stay as long as you need. Unless you want me to leave sooner, then I will. But if you'd like some time to grieve on your own and process all of this, we'd like to give you that," Mom says.

Dad butts in. "What your mom is trying to say is that we are here for you and want to help in any way we can. Think about it. You don't have to decide anything right now. We love you."

Tears form in my eyes, and I choke back a sob. It takes everything in me not to break down in front of them again.

"I want to go to Nana's house." Riley chimes in.

Of course he does. He loves it there, and we haven't been in a while. They should go. But they've never gone anywhere without me. Without *us*. What kind of parent does it make me to send my children away? They wouldn't be alone, though; they would be with my parents, who are so good with them. They're probably better off in their care right now than mine.

"Me too," Nova adds. She looks up at me from her coloring page with wide eyes.

How can I tell them no? As much as I need them here with me, maybe it'll be good for all of us. We could all use a reset, or a "break" as Mom calls it. I'm not too sure I can figure it out with them all here. I need some time to clear my head, figure out how to live without him. Without Ben.

But on the flipside, I can't fathom the thought of being alone for the first time since Ben came into my life.

It's not something I have to decide now, though. I feel more tears bubbling up underneath the surface, threatening to break through. To gush out of me like a raging river.

Like Jay.

I stand back up. "I'm gonna go. Just get my food to go, please, I'll eat it later."

"Are you sure?" Mom asks, her last effort to try and keep me here.

But I can't. It's too much. Everything is. "Yes. I'm sorry. Can you bring the kids home in a little while?"

Mom nods, knowing full well what I'm asking without saying it.

"Alright. Are you sure you're okay? Do you want me to come with you?" she asks.

At this, Dad places his hand gently over Mom's arm.

I shake my head. I can't say anything else. I'm moments away from breaking down completely.

"Don't worry about us, we're fine. We'll find a ride home when we're done. I was pleased with my Uber driver from the airport. I'm sure he'd be happy to give us another ride. Go home and get some rest."

Mom and I have been sharing my vehicle since she arrived. I'd rather be the one to find a ride home.

"No, you take the car. It has the kids' car seats. Don't worry about me. I'll meet you at home."

This time, nobody argues or stops me, and I'm grateful. Because the moment I push through the doors, the dam bursts wide open, and the tears start coming.

And they keep on coming.

CHAPTER 20
Jay

ordered a platter of chili cheese fries, smothered in all the fixings, along with another beer. I had at least two, or maybe I'm already on my third. I should probably slow down with the drinks. I'm with my mom, I'm not out for drinks with my buddies. A fourth one will probably do me in, and I'm already starting to feel a little buzz.

When I first sat back down at the table, Mom's eyes were wide and full of concern. I'd been quick to dismiss her and ordered my meal and drink. I needed something to distract me.

Maybe it isn't the healthiest way to take my mind off everything, but I can feel the effects of the alcohol smoothing out the sharpness of everything. Not enough to feel drunk, but just the right amount to take the edge off.

I can't believe I broke down like that, and Jude witnessed the whole thing.

Mom's eyes darken. She reaches for her purse and digs around for her wallet. She's ready to get out of here, I can tell by her body language. Her shoulders are stiff and her movements aren't as loose. I think my presence has somehow made her uncomfortable. I hope it's because we haven't been around each other in so long. We have to re-learn what it's like to be in each other's company.

But now that I'm finally here, I don't know if I can walk away from her. I left once before. I could do it again. Only this time, I'm not sure how well she would recover from it. She's already lost more in her lifetime than a mother should have.

Mom breaks into my thoughts. "Jay, are you alright? If this is all too much for you to talk about right now, it can wait a little while."

My eyes are red and puffy from crying, and I'm sure I look as much of a mess as I feel. "I'm not ordering any more drinks. I'm done."

"Oh. I wasn't referring to that, but I'm glad you know your limit. You look awful, dear. Like you're running on empty... It's been a hard day, and I think I should drive you home, my car is fine here for the night. It might be nice to have some peace for a little while. Everywhere else just feels too loud. If you know what I mean."

I do know what she means. My tank is running exceptionally low right now. I barely have the energy to finish my plate, which never happens. There's so many things we need to talk about that I've missed over the years. But right now, I don't have any energy for conversation. It's been a very emotional morning. It's not smart for me to commit to anything right now. Especially committing the rest of my life to our family's tavern—a place that's meant so much to everyone except me.

Guilt stabs me in the chest.

"Mom, I'm really sorry," I say, not knowing what else to add. I am sorry. Sorry and ashamed for getting buzzed when I probably should've just dealt with the pain, like she is. She's not using drinks to cope. But I'm also sorry for a lot of other things.

Missing her calls over the years. Never returning home for a visit, even though she asked me to more than once. Pretending my father didn't pass away. I thought if I acted like it never happened, maybe it never really did. That's how I handled pain in the past. Staying far enough away to avoid the grief and hurt. Only instead, I ended up hurting everyone.

Especially Mom.

Mom starts to say something else, but I don't hear her. Something catches my eye out the window. A flash of golden skin, wild hair whipping around in the wind, and a puddle behind her eyes as tears streak down her face.

Jude. Jude is outside.

And this time it isn't me crying my eyes out, it's her.

Maybe we're both lost and broken.

I quickly excuse myself, tossing enough cash on the table to cover the bill. Before I can explain, I'm heading out the door.

Straight for *her*.

I don't know what it is about her that draws me in. Everything in me screams to run away from her, but I do the opposite. I move towards her until she whips her head around in my direction, and then it's just the two of us. She turns her face to mine, and for a moment, we stay like that, frozen in place.

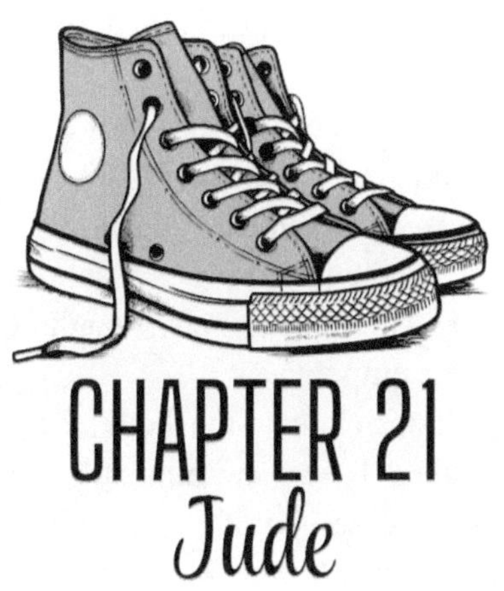

CHAPTER 21
Jude

My fingers tremble as I try to call an Uber, but I keep hitting all the wrong keys. I can't keep my fingers steady, and the numbers blur behind the stream of tears pouring from my eyes like a leaky faucet.

I wipe my face with the back of my sleeve before glancing up. Whether I consciously heard the door open, I'm not sure, but it only takes a second to realize who I'm suddenly with... *again.*

How does this keep happening? Maybe I should've had that drink. I shake my head. That would've been a mistake. But wasn't he just in the tavern with his mom? What's he doing out here?

It doesn't matter. I'm calling an Uber, and I'm getting out of here. I'm not sure home is where I want to be right now, but anywhere away from here will do.

I peel my eyes away from him and glance down at my phone, willing my fingers to work. I've got the app in here somewhere, I'm pretty sure. I just have to find it...

Tap, tap.

Someone is tapping my shoulder. Not someone, Jay is tapping

my shoulder. I feel more annoyed than anything else right now. It's worse than the persistent little taps I endure from my kids daily.

I force my gaze up to meet his, and I get a whiff of his leather-and-cinnamon scent again. It's the perfect combination. Why does he have to smell like *that?* But, then again, it's better than if he came out reeking of alcohol like a lot of people do. Maybe he's not like everybody else. There's definitely something different about him that I can't quite pinpoint.

He takes a small step closer to me. I can see that his eyes are still red from earlier when I first saw him out here. Whatever he's battling right now, I can see that it's wearing him down. He looks as though he's lost a battle. Maybe we all have.

"Jude," he says my name like a statement.

He's not asking me a question, just stating my name. I'm not sure what to say. I just want to get home. I feel a little bad for leaving if he purposely sought me out to talk, but I don't feel like chatting right now. I'm not even sure I'd know what to say if he tried.

I take a small step back, almost bumping into a small table behind me. I stop. I have nowhere else to go. I need to find that app. It's my ticket home, unless I want to go back in and join my family until they're ready to leave. I don't want to go back in though, I really don't.

I can't help but wonder what there is to talk about with Jay. We said everything last night and today at the cemetery. I thought for sure he'd be on his way back to LA by now.

"You should go back inside, Jay," I try to say it in a way that doesn't sound like I'm barking orders at him, but judging by the look on his face, I'm not sure I succeeded. I don't know why I suddenly feel angry and defensive, but I do.

I want to be alone. Or at least I think I do. *Maybe.*

"I just wanted to see if you're okay," he says.

Wait, he saw that? He saw *me* falling apart? Is that the real reason he came out here? It doesn't matter. I'm not in the mood to talk. Maybe if I quit responding he'll get the hint and leave.

I don't say anything. I wait a beat, trying to gauge his next move.

Leave me be.

"Is it because of Ben?" he asks.

His question stuns me. I stop and stare at him.

"If you really must know, yes. Of course, it's about Ben. Why else would I be out here crying on the day of the funeral? At his tavern for heaven's sake?" I retort as though it's the most obvious thing in the world. And to me it is. Why else would I feel this way? He's to blame for all of this. *Right?*

As soon as the words fly out of my mouth, I instantly regret them. I may not feel like having this conversation right now, but he doesn't deserve that kind of response. Yes, I may be angry with him, and I have every right to be after how he's treated Ben and his family all these years. Maybe he has changed, I don't know. But it doesn't matter or excuse my behavior.

I look away so I can't see if there's hurt in his eyes. I didn't mean it. Not like that. Maybe it's best we both just move on so we don't hurt each other.

I think for a moment that's the end of this. Hopefully, Jay goes back inside. I turn my attention back down to my phone. Aha, there it is! Finally found the app, buried inside a folder titled Useful Resources. Obviously.

I open the app and click on the next available driver. It says he'll be here in ten minutes. Perfect. Ten minutes can't come soon enough.

Tap, tap.

He's tapping my shoulder again to get my attention, instead of just saying something like a normal person. What's with all the tapping anyway?

I look up, and the moment my eyes meet his gray-blue ones, every trace of anger and hurt drains from my body. He's not looking at me like he hates me. He's looking at me as though he understands some unspoken truth—as if to say, *It's okay. I'm hurting too. You're not the only one.*

"What is it, Jay?" I ask.

He shrugs. "I... I'm not sure. I just... wanted to make sure you're okay."

I shrug back at him. Because I honestly don't know if I'll ever be okay again. But of course, I don't tell him that. I don't say anything.

He seems to accept the silence for now. He turns to leave, but pauses mid-step.

"I'm truly sorry for your loss, Jude. I meant every word I said at his grave today. I know I haven't been around... But I do care. I'm not as callous as I may seem, and I'd like to help if I can. Can I call you an Uber or something?" he offers, and I think he genuinely means it.

He must not have heard me mention waiting for a ride earlier. A sigh escapes me. I don't want to be angry. It has very little to do with him, and I'm not being fair. In fact, now I owe him an apology.

"It's already on its way, but thanks," I say with a small smile. "And I'm sorry for being a jerk. It wasn't really meant towards you, I'm just struggling."

He nods, stuffing his hands into his pockets. For the first time, I see the bags underneath his eyes. He looks as tired as I've felt all week. Maybe he isn't getting much sleep either.

"Can I ask you something?" he asks.

A lump forms in my throat, but I nod my head.

"Okay," I say, unsure what he's about to ask.

"Do you believe in life after love?" he asks me, and the absurdity of it almost makes me laugh out loud.

What? Did he just say what I think he did? Maybe he had a couple of drinks after all. He's not drunk though, he's talking fine and still steady on his feet. But did he really ask me that?

I stifle a laugh. "Are you really quoting Cher right now?"

A smile tugs at the corners of his mouth. "Yeah, maybe. So, do you?" he asks again.

Okay, wow. He's serious about this.

I can almost hear the all-too-familiar tune playing in my mind, like I heard it a thousand times over the radio as a teen. But what does it mean? And what do I believe? I'm not sure what I believe in anymore.

"Uhh, I'm not sure. I don't know," I answer honestly. I shrug again.

"Do you?" I ask him, truly curious now.

He doesn't even hesitate. "Yeah, I do."

"But what does it mean?" I ask. I glance at my phone. Five minutes until my driver is scheduled to arrive.

This time, he really thinks about his answer before he speaks again. "For me, it's learning to love again after something tragic. Believing in love even after it's ended. I believe just because love dies, doesn't mean it won't ever live again."

Tears instantly form in my eyes again. Okay, maybe he is of sound mind, but surely I'm not hearing him correctly. Besides, what does he know about falling in love? Or, even worse, losing the one you were supposed to love forever?

That's right, he doesn't. Hopefully, he never will.

I snap back to reality and check my app once more. The Uber driver's right around the corner.

"My ride will be here soon," I say. Coldness sweeps back over my heart.

For a second, I see it in his eyes. Hurt. But then it's gone, and this time he takes a step back from me, giving me the space I need.

"There's one more thing I want to ask you about," he starts, but I hold up a hand to stop him.

I don't have time right now. Whatever it is is going to have to wait. The car is pulling up.

The driver rolls their window down and waves at me. I wave back and start walking towards him.

I glance back over my shoulder at Jay before I go. "It's going to have to wait," I say.

Jay holds up a hand, giving me a gentle wave as a peace offering. One I don't deserve.

"I'll be here," he promises.

I climb into the passenger seat of the car, my eyes fixed on Jay.

I'll be here.

Before I have the chance to ask him what he means by that, we drive away, leaving him standing there alone outside my tavern.

I'll be here. And apparently, I will be too.

CHAPTER 22
Jude

I can't seem to shake Jay's words. *I'll be here.* What did he mean by that? Did he overhear the conversation between me and my family about the kids visiting their grandparents while I stay here? Unlikely.

He also wanted to ask me about something when I was leaving. What could it be? Now, he'll likely never get the chance since he's leaving soon. For good.

I didn't say much to the driver from the time we left Second Verse until we rounded the corner of my street. What was there to say? Normally, I'd make small talk, even if it was the typical commentary about the weather and if this was his full-time job or just a side gig. But not today. I can't find it in me to handle any small talk. I try not to dwell on it too much.

He weaves down my long, gravel driveway that's surrounded by forest and fields of wildflowers. He comes to a stop just shy of our wide, farmhouse-style garage. I sit there for a moment, staring at the house. The house we built from scratch less than a year ago. A house that will now be in my name only, and that I'd never be able to afford on my own. I can't think about that right now. There are a lot of things I can't bring myself to think about.

My mind is frozen, my body along with it.

I jerk back in place when I hear someone talking to me. Oh, that's right.

"This is your house, yes?" the Uber driver asks me. His skin is darker than mine, and he has soft, kind eyes. Guilt eats at me, even though I don't think it should. Maybe he assumes I'm shy, or maybe every stranger I pass somehow sees it written across my face... this horrible word that now defines me and follows me around like a shadow... *widow.*

I nod my head. I can't seem to form words. I still haven't made any effort to remove myself from his car. Jay's words echo again through my thoughts: *I'll be here.* Where will he be? And do I even want him anywhere near me? He's just as broken as I am. What does he want from me? He said he had something else to ask me. But what? What could he possibly have to say to me? There is nothing left. Nothing.

I feel like a ghost. I nod my head again, not paying attention to the driver. I grab a wad of cash from my purse, without bothering to count it, and I place it on the console within his reach. I know it's more than enough.

My hand finds its way to the door handle, and I push it open, forcing my feet to finally get out of the vehicle. I exit his car in slow motion and stand there staring up at my house—at the bright blue front door and the flowers out front that I planted with Ben a few weeks ago. How crazy life can change in a flash. In a single moment.

I don't look back as the car slowly backs out of the driveway, and I hear the gravel crunch underneath his tires. I dig my key out of my purse and slowly turn it into the lock, waiting for the familiar *click.* I push my way inside, not bothering to turn on any of the lights.

I make my way slowly to our bedroom and head straight for

the closet. I yank one of Ben's sweatshirts off a hanger and throw it over my head. I'm instantly wrapped up in the smell of it. The smell of *him*. Tears burst forth like a flood, and I let them. I let them fall. I let my vision blur as I breathe him in like he's still here with me, even though I know that he's not.

I pull back the covers on his side and bury my face deep into his pillow. There's the faintest hint of him there, too. But I know it will soon be gone. Eventually, I'll have to force myself to wash it or give it all away so I don't have to see it every day as a big fat reminder of what I've lost. Of the man I've lost forever.

I cry for what feels like eternity, even though I know that's not possible. But I've cried so much, so hard, my entire body is trembling, and my ribs ache. The weight of losing him is crushing me. I can feel the heaviness lingering in the air like the smoke when you blow out a candle.

Will it always feel like this? Like I'm drowning. And when I'm not drowning in sorrow, I'm suffocating. Suffocating from lack of oxygen, as if I've forgotten how to breathe. That's how it feels. This constant stabbing, drowning, suffocating tightness in my chest that doesn't go away.

I cry until there are no tears left—at least for the moment. I know they'll return the second I open my eyes and face the painful truth of my new reality.

How do people survive this?

How do they find the strength to wake up each morning and carry on, as if something terrible hasn't robbed them of everything they once knew?

How do they keep pouring love into their children when they're barely pouring enough into themselves to survive?

How?

I'll be here.

I close my eyes and succumb to the darkness.

CHAPTER 23
Jay

'll be here.

The words I said to Jude earlier still echo through my head at Mom's house, long after she's gone to bed. She'd met me outside the restaurant and drove my rental car to her house. She said I could give her a ride back to the tavern tomorrow. There was hardly a word spoken between us during the ride.

She offered to drive since I had a few beers, and I didn't argue with that. It's much better to be safe than sorry. It's not worth the potential risks, I've taken plenty of those to know. Silence fell like a cold autumn wind, but neither of us knew how to break it. There was a heaviness in the air that hung between us.

Void. Empty. Hollow.

I expected her to climb out with the same silence that cloaked us during the trip, but instead, she invited me to come in and stay the night. She said I could sleep in my old bedroom, and that it was pretty much the same as I left it. After everything we've been through, how could I turn down her offer?

From the moment I cross over the familiar threshold, I'm immediately hit with déjà vu. It was like I never left.

There were a few differences I noticed immediately, like the carpet had been updated since I was here last, and there weren't any toys or video games lying around. But other than the small things that typically change over time, everything was the same as I left it a decade ago. As though I had never set foot out of this house, and I was simply coming home.

Home.

It was strange being back here now. In a way, it was comforting that not much had changed. It was welcoming and warm like it had always been. Only, I'm not sure it can ever go back to that for me. My home may not have changed much, but I have. I'm not the same boy who grew up here.

I'm not the same boy I was when Ben left for college and quickly forgot all about his little brother. I'm not the same man I was the day he tied the knot and got married to his beautiful bride, Jude. In a way, I guess you could say I'm jealous of my older brother.

He got to experience everything first, and it all came to him so quickly and effortlessly. I always had to work harder to get the things I wanted in life. While he made straight A's and hardly had to study, I pulled all-nighters, trying to memorize information I knew would be forgotten by the time the test was handed out. By default, I always came in second place.

He got the grades, the scholarships, and the girls. Not to mention *the* family business that had been handed off to him, simply because he had gotten there first. Did all the time and work I put into Second Verse during my high school years amount to nothing? I was the afterthought.

The only reason it is within reach now is because Ben was removed from the picture completely. With Dad gone and Mom keeping up the finances for the business, I'm all she has left. Besides Jude, of course, but she has her kids to take care of and a new life to navigate. Second by default. And I can't even fault my parents for that. It's just the way the world works. Unfair as it may be at times.

Speaking of fair, Ben had offered me a partnership with him, and I not-so-politely declined. I turned him down rather than swallowing my pride and saying yes to my brother.

We could have been business partners. What then? Would everything else have fallen into place as it was meant to be? Yeah, maybe. But I didn't choose that path. I chose my own. Now here we are, five years later, Ben's gone, and Mom's asking me to finally say yes. *Yes.* Such a simple word, yet so hard to say.

In a way, it feels like I'm being offered a second chance to stand up and accept my ownership in the bar. A second shot at saying yes this time. And I know that I should. I can't say no again. I won't let pride get in the way. Not now, not after this crazy turn of events that none of us saw coming. How could we?

Jude.

Somehow, my thoughts keep veering back to her. Why? I don't know. I have no idea. I can't imagine what she's going through. Losing the one person who she was supposed to be promised to forever. What a joke. Does anything last forever? I once believed in an afterlife, with streets of gold and no pain or sorrow. But now, I'm not so sure. I certainly don't believe in forever. After losing my brother, I was very quickly reminded of how short life really is. And how much time I've wasted. Years and years.

I'll be here.

What did I mean by that? I haven't exactly given Mom a solid answer yet, but I know what my gut is leaning towards. Six weeks. That's the time frame she offered me. It doesn't sound like much, and maybe it isn't, but maybe it'd be just enough time to figure out where to go from here. Figure out what I should be doing with my life, because who knows how many days I have left here? But I can't go there. It's too much.

I want to ask Jude what her plans are for the tavern, but when I tried, the Uber had shown up. And from the looks of it, she was done with our conversation. It sure seemed that way, anyhow. I'm willing to help her to the best of my ability.

After all, I know how things are run at Second Verse tavern. At least, how they used to be run, back when I worked there. Now, I'm sure I'll be a little rusty starting out, but I'm a quick learner. It didn't look much different from the last time I was there. That is, a big fat *if* she even wants me around.

I need a cigarette. But I think I used my last one. It's late, and I don't feel like going back out now. And just in case the alcohol hasn't fully worn off, I'm probably better off staying here for the night. One night, and then I'll figure out how long I'll be in town for. Maybe things will make more sense in the morning. I need sleep. I can't even remember the last time I got a full night's rest.

The house feels eerily quiet without Dad here. Mom immediately showers, and then we fall into the familiar pattern of watching reruns of Criminal Minds together, like we did ages ago.

After a few hours of mindless watching, she heads off to get cleaned up and ready for bed. I can see the exhaustion written across her face. She tells me I can order myself a pizza later if I want to, but truthfully, I don't have much of an appetite. I wander through the house after she retreats to her room, eyeing all the pictures still hanging on the walls from our childhood.

From the pictures, you'd have thought Ben and I were best buds. Ben's senior year, Dad got us all tickets to an Oklahoma City Thunder basketball game. Mom bought my brother and me matching jerseys, which I'm pretty sure Ben only wore because of how good the seats were.

I don't have a lot of memories with my brother, but I remember this one clearly. The Thunder won that night, and we both lost our voices from cheering so loud. Mom captured our excitement on camera. We both have huge grins on our faces, and his arm is draped across my shoulders in a warm embrace.

Another is a family portrait: we're standing on the front porch, surrounded by fall leaves and decorative pumpkins, with Ben holding me up on his shoulders.

If it's fake or real, I couldn't tell you. But we both had smiles painted on our faces. If I didn't know better, I'd say we look happy. Was it possible it hadn't been all bad between us? Maybe there were more of these little blips of happiness, but I just can't remember them. I wish I could remember the day this was taken.

From the outside looking in, we look like an average, happy family. Nobody would ever guess that Ben and I hardly spoke to each other. We didn't wrestle like most brothers, and we hardly argued because we weren't around each other long enough to have anything to fight about.

I feel a slow burn forming in my chest, and I rub it in gentle, slow circles, easing the ache. Tears well up in my eyes, and I flash back to earlier when I was on my knees, sobbing in front of the tavern. Ben's tavern, which would now be mine for the next six weeks. It isn't lost on me that Second Verse could have been ours, *together*. But I was too selfish at the time and robbed us both of that chance.

Another thought catches me off guard. It isn't that I have no clue how to run a business or follow in my brother's footsteps. No, my first thought is something else entirely. What will Jude think about me stepping up and taking Ben's place? How will she feel about that?

And more importantly... Why do I care?

CHAPTER 24
Jay

t's been a week since we buried my brother. Some days, time seems to move in slow motion. Other times, I feel like I'm living in a sped-up version of my life. Now it's the latter.

The day after Ben's funeral, Mom and I had a deep conversation about the tavern. I agreed to give her the six weeks, as a favor, but I was clear that I was planning on going back to LA at the end of our agreement. I feel like I owe my mom, but I'm not prepared to be stuck here forever. I don't know if I want that.

She agreed with a soft smile and immediately put me to work. First, I was a host—greeting people at the door, passing out menus, and showing people to their tables. Next, she put me behind the bar, pouring drinks. I enjoyed bartending from my years doing it in LA.

Every minute that I spend at Second Verse is a rush of adrenaline. I don't have time to feel, or even think, because my feet are in constant motion. When my body is busy, so is my mind. I don't have time to ponder or question if I'm doing the right thing. If this is meant for *me*. If I'm truly cut out for *this*. And the work came back to me easier than I hoped.

"Hey, Jay! Do you mind helping out in the kitchen for a bit?" Tanner hollers at me from behind the swinging double doors that lead into the kitchen.

Mom has me working up front today, and despite the May rain showers, there has been a steady flow of traffic since we opened the doors at eleven.

"Sure, man. Just a sec." I look around for Kelly, who's been showing me the ropes around here. She's a ray of sunshine. Maybe a little too much for my taste. Besides, she is married to the head chef, Brian. Which, I quickly came to find out, had been best buds with Ben. And Kelly spoke fondly of Jude.

Jude.

As much as I want to escape any thoughts of her, she keeps bubbling back up to the surface. One way or another. Always present. Always there.

I'll be here.

That was the last thing I said to her. I'm here, but she's not. I have not seen her since the day of the funeral. Maybe that's normal for her. Maybe she needs some time and space. I don't blame her.

Kelly finishes taking orders at her table and wanders back over to our host/hostess podium. She punches the order into the computer, which sends it back to the kitchen staff. I eye her carefully and clear my throat.

"Hey, I'm needed for something back in the kitchen for a little while. Are you okay out here?" I ask.

She takes a moment before glancing up at me. Her sky-blue eyes dance with something I can't quite pin down. How is she always so happy? It's as though she doesn't have an off switch. Despite the gloom that seems to hang over me in waves, nothing seems to stop her or get in her way. How does she do that?

She smiles at me and waves me off in the direction of the kitchen. "Yes, yes. Go. I'm totally fine out here. Lexi should be getting off break soon. I should be asking *you* that question, though."

Her eyes dance with curiosity. It looks like she has something more to say. I pause for a moment, allowing her the space to speak.

"So..." she pauses, waiting for me to respond.

I don't. I'm not sure what she wants me to say, so I stuff my hands into my pockets and stare out the front entrance, willing somebody to walk in and steer this conversation away from me.

The silence is beginning to drain me.

I sigh and look back in her direction. Her eyes bore into mine, patiently waiting.

"So, what?" I retort back at her.

"So, are you doing okay?" she stifles a laugh. Is she making fun of me, or is she being serious? Does she even care about how I'm doing? Even though I've been here a full week, I'm still practically a stranger here. I haven't decided to stay, and Jude hasn't asked me to co-run this place, I'm just here. *I'll be here.* Whatever the heck that means anymore.

I don't know how to truthfully answer her. What does she expect me to say? *Yeah, I'm fine. I love it here.* Should I stay and take my brother's place? Would Jude even want me here? What if she doesn't want me here at all? This place has never *really* belonged to me. I'm part owner, but I've never had anything to do with it. Maybe it'll never be something in my grasp. Ben offered me that chance, and I didn't want it. Kelly wants me to be honest with her? How's this for honesty?

The moment I returned to Bethel, I wanted to run. Bolt. Leave. Never return. Just because Jude has a pretty face, doesn't mean she can convince me to stay.

This feels a little like dying. Dying inside. Dying to myself. And everything I thought I knew. Because now, I'm just as lost as I was before I left this place. Like I've said before, I don't belong here... I don't fit in.

I have a split second to decide how to respond to Kelly. Do I give her a small piece of the truth, or feed her a simple white lie? Would she be able to tell the difference? After all, she doesn't know me. Nobody here does. And after six weeks, I'll be completely forgotten. Replaced. As though I was never here. As though I never returned.

I choose to ignore her question and walk away. It's a jerk move, but something in me doesn't care. I don't want to be here, not really. Even though nobody would be bold enough to say it to my face, I'm pretty sure the feelings are reciprocated.

I spend the rest of the morning helping out in the kitchen. Their daily delivery truck arrives, and they need help getting everything unloaded. It's amazing how much food people eat in a day.

After stocking the fridge and the freezer, I'm put to work washing dishes. I don't mind anything that keeps my hands and mind busy. The kitchen is where most of the excitement takes place anyway. Wait staff are constantly entering and exiting through the double doors. Taking orders out, bringing empty plates in return. Constant movement.

The people in the kitchen are fun to watch as well. Brian is a different man when he's in his element. He's quick, efficient, and works hard to perfect every entrée before it's served to his customers. Classic rock music blares from the kitchen speakers overhead. Some cooks dance and sing while they prepare the dishes, others remain steady and focused, not letting a single thing distract them from the task at hand. And the most incredible part of the whole thing is that they all seem to work well together.

They have a steady rhythm that I can't quite figure out or emulate, yet they all have it down to a science. They are confident in what they're doing, while I'm over here terrified of screwing something up. Even if I'm just floating around wherever they need me. I don't have a place here. I don't jive with their beat. I'm the odd one out, and it's obvious.

They've all been kind to me since I showed up here. They knew of me by default, but that's about it. After their initial greeting, they turned their attention back to their work, as though I wasn't even there.

I'll be here.

My own words now haunt me like a lingering ghost. Maybe that's it. Maybe nobody else feels it, but I do. The ghost of the man my brother left behind. Who am I kidding? I can't run this place. *His place.* Who am I to show up here, unannounced and unwelcome after all this time, and tell all of these people that I'm going to take over? No. I can't do that to myself or them. They belong here. I don't. Jude. I can't do that to her.

What was I thinking? Who was I kidding?

I was a fool to come in the first place. I'm only doing it as a favor to my mom.

As soon as the clock hits one o'clock, my designated time to take a break, I bolt out the back doors into the alley. The rain has stopped, but the sun is nowhere in sight. Dark clouds coat the sky in a heavy blanket. I reach into my back pocket and pull out a pack of cigarettes. I can't light the thing fast enough.

I close my eyes as soon as the smoke hits my lungs. The familiar burning sensation brings me back to life, just for a moment. It's enough, and yet it isn't. It's not enough to drown out this pain that lingers deep inside my chest. I don't understand what it means.

When my eyes flutter open again, I know what I need to do. And that's to get out of here and never look back.

CHAPTER 25
Jude

The sunlight streaming through the blinds wakes me up. I glance at my phone: Tuesday 10:05 a.m. Ugh.

It's a weekday, so I shouldn't be lying around in bed still. Yet, here I am. Wearing the same clothes I wore all day yesterday and quite possibly the day before. It's been over a week since Ben's funeral. Mom left three days ago with the kids. Which also means my birthday is in four days. May thirty-first. But I can't bear to think about growing a year older without Ben.

I was hesitant to send the kids with my mom and stay here on my own, but in the end decided it was probably the best thing for all of us. Who even knew what was "best" anymore?

Eyes closed, I allow my body to sink further into the bed. The bed I never want to leave. Because getting out of bed requires me to actually do things. Make myself something to eat. Force myself to do laundry. Every day, mundane things. Things that should be easy and simple. Yet nothing is anymore. Everything is complicated and everything is hard.

Lying in bed, wasting the morning away probably isn't ideal, but without Mom and the kids here, who's stopping me? Absolutely no one.

I sigh. Well, no one except for whoever is on the other end of that call. My phone is vibrating loudly on the nightstand, moving closer and closer to the edge.

I roll over onto my side, and without even glancing at the screen, I swipe to accept the call and press it gently to my ear. "Hello?" I answer groggily, wishing I could fall back to sleep. At least when I'm asleep, the spiraling thoughts cease. Just for a moment. But it's a moment I would take in a heartbeat. Anything to help me escape from my heart breaking in real time.

"Thank God, you're alive," Kelly sighs on the other end.

Kelly has always had a flair for dramatics. I try not to cringe too much at her choice of words. *Alive.* Technically speaking, yes, I am. But it doesn't feel like it. This doesn't feel like living to me. I might be breathing, but I'm not living. Not in the same way as she and everybody else around me is.

This feels pretty close to dying.

"Yup," I retort, because that's all I've got. Nothing more, nothing less. I'm simply existing.

"Good. How are you doing today, love? I mean, really," she asks.

I can hear other people in the background, and based on the time, I'd say she's already at the tavern, preparing to open for the day. She's always been so much more organized than me. I don't know how she does it, day in and day out. She always shows up early for her shift, no matter what.

How am I? Well, that's a loaded question. I roll onto my back and force my eyes open, staring at the ceiling. Does she really want to know the truth, or is she just being polite?

In all seriousness, I know she cares. Ever since Mom left with the kids, Kelly has been checking on me daily, sometimes multiple times. My answer is always the same. Short answer: No, I'm not okay. I'm not sure I ever will be. Long answer: I don't want to get into that right now. I'll go into a mental spiral, which will send my body into a spin, and then it's downhill from there. I can't go there right now. I don't want to. Which is why I can't leave this bed.

"I want to stay in this bed forever," I admit, twirling the charging cord around my finger as I wait for her to respond to my absurd remark.

She doesn't hesitate. "I know, sweetie. But you can't, unfortunately. What can I do? Can I bring you something? Does anything sound good from the tavern?" she offers.

While I appreciate the offer, tears spring to my eyes before I can stop them. Spontaneous combustion. I'm a ticking time bomb. Literally. I can't help it. One moment I'm fine, the next I'm falling apart.

Ben was supposed to bring us home food that night. *I can't believe it's been two weeks; it feels like it happened yesterday.* I delayed dinner plans because the kids were fighting, and I couldn't come up with anything to make for dinner. Ben was off saving lives, and I was worried about myself and my own needs. I'd never been so selfish. Sometimes I hate myself for it. I blame myself until it makes me sick. The thought of food now makes my stomach churn in the worst way possible.

Silence. A pause. Kelly clears her throat before speaking again. "Love, are you there? Do you need me to stop by? Jay will be here in a few, and I'm sure he won't mind if I step out for a bit," she offers.

At this, I bolt upright in bed. Wait, what?

Just to be sure I heard her correctly, I demand, "Whoa, hold up. Did you say *Jay*?"

I can't hide the shock in my tone. It's been a week. Why is he still here? *I'll be here.* Is this what he meant? No. No freaking way. He has no business being in *my* business. Second Verse could've been his business years ago, but he made it clear how he felt about that.

I can hear the slight hesitation in her voice, "Uhh, yes. I

thought you knew this... Jay is still here, and he's been helping out a bit. It's not that big a deal."

Not a big deal. Is she kidding me? Of course it is! It's a *huge* deal.

I yank the charging cord out of my phone and swing my legs out over the side of the bed, forcing my body to move as soon as my feet hit the floor. I waste no time making my way over to my closet to quickly throw on something.

"Not a big deal? Do you even hear yourself?" I say a little too harshly. What's gotten into me? Something in me has snapped. I know it. I feel it, yet I can't stop it. I'm a force to be reckoned with.

"Love, please calm down. Seriously, he's not that bad. He's pretty quiet, honestly. Mostly keeps to himself. He's just helping out," Kelly says, trying to convince me.

Convince me of what? I'm not sure.

"I bet he is," I mutter under my breath. I wedge the phone between my chin and shoulder so I can pull on a pair of socks.

"I'm not sure why you're so upset over this, but really, it's fine. I promise. Look, I'm serious. Let me take the day off. We can hang out. Go somewhere. Or sit and do nothing. I don't care. Let me come to you," she offers again.

While I appreciate the offer, I have something else in mind. "Thanks, Kelly, but no need. I'm coming in. I'll be there in about fifteen minutes."

This stops her. More silence. This time, the pause is longer.

"Wait, what? What do you mean you're—"

I hang up the phone without letting her finish. I honestly don't know what's gotten into me, but not even I have the power to stop whatever is about to go down. All I know is that I have to get to the tavern.

Now.

CHAPTER 26
Jay

Jude is the last person I expect to come bursting through the front entrance of Second Verse Tavern. The fire in her eyes catches me by surprise as she barrels towards me with startling speed. This girl is on fire... in more ways than one right now. This is a look I recognize. Just not from her. There's a flash of anger on the surface, simmering with a flicker of hate. I don't know what has Jude riled up, but this woman is here to destroy me.

And she might succeed.

"You." She points at me, seething.

Yep, she's not here to make peace. She's ready to pounce.

"Hey, is everything oka—" I start, but she jerks her finger back behind her.

"Outside. Now." She pivots back towards the entrance and storms back out, expecting me to follow. I guess I don't really have a choice. I don't want to make anything worse.

Kelly witnesses this whole unfortunate debacle, and frankly, I still have no idea what's going on. She quirks her eyebrows at me and shrugs her shoulders.

"Good luck. I just got off the phone with her, and she didn't sound like herself," Kelly cautions me.

I nod and reluctantly start heading in the direction Jude stomped off. The fire awaits.

My hand is on the handle of the door when someone stops me. I glance over, and I'm met with Kelly's crystal blue eyes.

She clears her throat once before speaking.

"Look, Jay, I know that this has been tough on all of us. Just go easy on her, okay?"

Is she messing with me? Did she not witness the same storm that thundered in here not even a minute ago? Go easy on *her*? I've seen that look in a woman's eyes before. And it doesn't mean anything good. Nothing good could possibly come from this. If anything, I'm praying Jude will lighten up a little and go easy on *me*.

I gently shrug Kelly off. I've already kept Jude waiting a beat too long. Let's get this over with.

"Thanks, but I don't think we'll have to worry about that," I say as I give the door a strong push.

I prepare my heart the best I can as I head for a fuming Jude standing there waiting for me. What's one more battle wound going to hurt?

CHAPTER 27
Jude

’m sure I look every bit of the hot mess I feel right now. I’m a loaded cannon, ready to fire. Moments ago, I’d been lying in bed wallowing in my despair, and with one phone call, something ignited within me. I’d leapt out of bed, a lit fuse moments from detonation. I was ready to burn something or someone down.

I’ll be here. His words ring in my ears like an anthem. Only one I’d rather forget. Like right now.

It’s the last week of May, and the air already feels like it’s pushing ninety degrees as I wait for Jay.

Hot. Muggy. Sticky. But that’s an Oklahoma summer for you.

Jay finally makes his way over to me. His eyes hold mine for a split second before darting away, and he pushes his hands into his pockets.

Are his cigarettes in one of them? Ugh, I remind myself that I don’t care where he keeps them. He’s not smoking one right now. I’m a little embarrassed I’ve approached him in this manner, but I’ve already taken it too far to back down now.

"Let's talk. My car's over there." I nod my head in the direction of the side parking lot. I turn and start walking at a quick pace. I don't have to look to know he's following me. It doesn't take long for him to catch up and his shadow to swoop in beside me. For a moment, my breath catches. I almost forgot how tall he is when we are standing this close.

I glance over at him once we reach my car.

"How tall are you, by the way?" The question slips out before I can help myself. Why did I just ask him that? I don't want to know how tall he is. I know what I came here to say, and I need to get it over with.

He takes one hand out of his pocket and runs it through his smooth, sandy hair. I can't help but notice how long and slender his fingers are. Quit that. Quit staring at this man... At Jay.

I shake my head. I'm being ridiculous.

"Six-foot-three," he says so matter-of-factly that at first, I think he's lying. I glance up at him again. He's over a foot taller than me. Nope, he's not lying.

I nod my head because this isn't what's important right now, and I motion towards the passenger side of my car. If he will fit. Yikes. He might need to do some minor seat adjusting when he gets in.

I unlock the car and climb into my seat. Once he's seated, he turns to me, waiting. Anticipating. I can't quite read his expression. Am I making him nervous right now? A part of me feels bad if I am, but then I remember why I dragged him out here in the first place and hide any hint of amusement from my face.

"Why are you still here, Jay?" I ask him point-blank. I want him to answer me honestly. Why did he come home? Does it really have to do with losing his brother? He didn't come to his dad's funeral. I know, because I was there with Ben. So, why is he here now? I can't seem to wrap my mind around it.

A sinking feeling hits my stomach... What if he didn't come here to pay respects to his brother at all? What if he came back because he decided that now that Ben is gone, he can run the business? Maybe it never was about partnership, maybe he wanted it all to himself this whole time.

My hands are suddenly sweating and nervous, and my car is warm from the late spring heat.

I gently ease my foot on the brake and hit the start button, bringing my Honda Odyssey to life. Ahh, air conditioning. I almost close my eyes at the sudden sweet movement of cool air on my skin, but fight to ignore the sensation.

"Why am I here in your car? I honestly have no idea. You tell me," he bites back.

I was right, he barely fits in here. He's already reaching under his seat for the lever to adjust it. Fortunately, for his sake, there's room right now without the kids' car seats in the back. Mom took those with her on the plane.

"You said you weren't staying here, Jay. So, what are you doing? It's been two weeks." Not that I'm counting or anything.

I have no clue what he's still doing here. But I can't trust his intentions. He never wanted to come back in the first place. His own brother couldn't convince him. Somehow, after his brother's death, he suddenly had a guilty conscience and decided to come here... to what? Make peace of sorts? That's BS, and we both know it.

I want the truth. The real reason.

"Am I not allowed to change my mind?" He leans slightly forward in his seat, fumbling with the air vents, trying to direct the cool air at himself. That's when I catch a whiff of him.

A faint musk of cigarettes, a subtle hint of cinnamon, and leather. Leather.

Why won't he give me a straight answer? He's toying with me. But why?

"Well, have you?" I fire right back, crossing my arms across my chest, goosebumps coating my upper arms even though I'm not cold. I feel as though my skin is on fire. Like my entire body is burning up.

Fire... Ben.

Isn't Jay supposed to ask me something? I can't think straight. My head feels funny.

I can't breathe. My chest tightens, and suddenly I can't get any air out of my lungs. Trapped. Suffocating. Just like he did. My husband. *Benny.*

It's happening again. I'm having a panic attack. Not here. Not now. Not in front of *him.*

"No," he responds, so quietly I almost miss it. His eyes are fixed on me, frozen on my frame. Can he tell what I'm feeling right now?

"Are you... What's wrong, Jude?" he asks gently, his hand moving closer to mine on the steering wheel. "Hey, Jude. Talk to me. What's going on?"

Hey, Jude.

"Get out of the car," I say, my eyes glassy, my vision starting to blur with tears.

My body starts to tremble and shake. It's a slow rumble at first, but it doesn't take long for the avalanche.

"Jude... I'm here. You can tell me what's wrong," he offers again.

"I said, get out of the car, *Jay,*" I spit out his name like it leaves a sour taste in my mouth. Maybe it does. His name shouldn't be on my lips at all.

The only way I'm going to be okay is if he leaves. But he just sits there.

"Please, don't do this. I can help you if you let me..."

"Get out!" I slam my hand against the top of the steering wheel. The impact causes my palm to sting with a pulsing pinch. At this, he doesn't utter another word as he throws open his door and slams it shut.

I got what I wanted. He's finally leaving me alone. Alone to try and work through this stupid panic attack. I never even got to say what I wanted to say. I'd been too angry and let it get the best of me. Gripping me like a vice. I couldn't let go.

And now, I've let go completely. Because I'm back to where I started my day.

Alone.

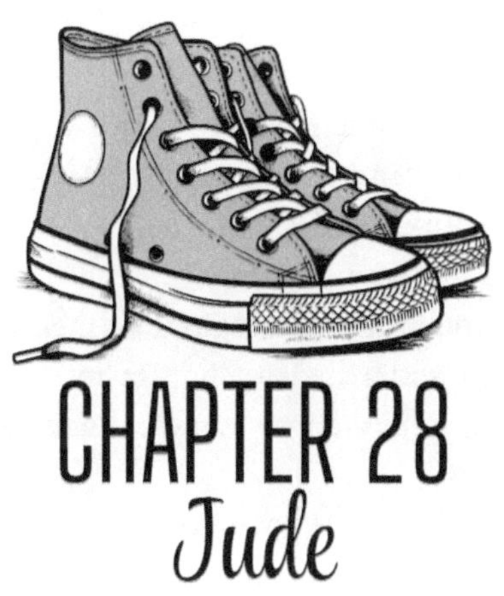

CHAPTER 28
Jude

After leaving the tavern, I head to the Y to blow off some steam. I don't normally get that fired up, but Jay struck a chord with me this morning. After finishing up with my much-needed Zumba session, I spend the rest of the afternoon cleaning up the house. I do anything I can think of to keep me busy, to drown out the quiet, and to silence the noise inside my head. It's inevitable, of course, because nighttime always comes around too soon these days. There are never enough hours in a day to escape the burden that comes with the night.

Without Mom and the kids here, I have no distractions. I turn my phone on silent and get to work. I clean the main level and downstairs, all the bedrooms and bathrooms—until my legs and back ache and I need to rest.

I try to sit down and start reading a book, but my thoughts keep wandering off. By now, the sun is starting to set, and I haven't even thought about dinner. Without Mom here to cook, clean, and remind me to take care of myself, it's all up to me now. Which isn't all that comforting.

The fridge is mostly bare. Half a carton of milk that's almost expired, and a couple of slices of cheese that smell questionable. Ugh.

The freezer isn't much better. I find a package of ramen noodles in the pantry and tear open a bag. My daughter loves this stuff and would eat it every day if I let her.

At least once a week, we had what we called Kid Choice Night. Nova and Riley took turns picking one of their favorite meals for dinner. Both Ben and I had to indulge in whatever meal they picked. The kids often chose ramen, knowing it wasn't my favorite.

But this is what it's come down to.

This is my life now... ramen noodles, and it isn't even Kid Choice Night. It feels weird eating it without them here.

I heat the noodles in the microwave because I don't feel like dirtying up a pan. I cleaned the entire house from top to bottom, I think this can slide.

I pour it into a bowl and head to my bedroom and turn on the TV. I proceed to watch four episodes of Gilmore Girls, because why not? I'm the only adult here right now, there are no rules.

I'm getting ready to start a fifth episode when several things happen at once. First, the lights flicker. Then, I jump at the sharp clap of thunder as the sky suddenly opens up with the heaviest downpour I've heard in a long time. It doesn't rain much in Bethel, or the entire state of Oklahoma, but the folks that live here know all too well: *when it rains, it pours.*

I mistake the loud knock at my front door for another clap of thunder, and in my surprise, my arms flail out, sending my empty bowl of ramen and the TV remote crashing to the floor. At least I finished every last drop, so nothing spills out, but the remote batteries are now scattered.

I glance outside. The sky is pitch black, save for the occasional streaks of lightning that light it up like fireworks. The motion light on the side of the house by the garage has kicked on. It could easily be the winds—it's picked up fast—but there's also a chance someone's really out there.

The thought sends chills up and down my spine. I'm watching the coziest show on the planet, and yet here I am, almost thirty-three years old, shivering and cowering underneath my blanket in fear.

I'm pathetic. But I'm also home alone. Alexa's playing soft acoustic music from the kitchen to help drown out the terrifying sounds of the house creaking and settling. It wasn't so bad when Ben was here. His very presence calmed my nerves completely. Without him here, it's like every nerve in my body has gone on high alert. I'm hyper-aware of every creak, every groan, every single sound the house makes.

There it is again. *Knock knock.* Who could be out there? It's pretty late for anyone to be standing at my door. I reach over and tap the screen on my phone to reveal the time: 9:13 p.m.

Yeah, nobody should be here this late. There's a chance it could be Kelly. She seemed worried after our phone call this morning, and I haven't exactly explained my rash behavior. But she doesn't typically just show up without calling or texting me first. So, who is it?

I hope I remembered to lock the front door when I came in. Did I? I can't remember...

There's a long pause. I can't hear anything over the rain slapping against the windows and the wild thrumming of my heartbeat. I close my eyes and take a deep breath.

It's okay. It's going to be okay. I'm okay. I'm safe here.
Right?

Who in their right mind would be out in a storm? And who could have decided to visit me this late? What if I'd been asleep? What then? I've gone through enough already... Leave me alone.

And then I hear something else.

A voice.

Someone familiar. Someone I told to leave earlier today. Someone I never imagined I'd find at my doorstep.

Ever.

CHAPTER 29
Jay

"Hey, Jude. It's me, Jay. Can you open the door, please?" I shout over the sound of the storm.

My shoes and jacket are soaked, but somehow it hasn't hit my pride... *yet*. I know she's home because I can see the soft glow of lights inside. I also think I hear music playing from somewhere inside, but I could be mistaken. I know she's here, though, because where else would she be at this hour?

Far away from me, that's where.

I have my left hand raised to her midnight-blue door, ready to try one last time, while balancing a large, hot pizza box that's starting to burn my other hand.

Suddenly, the door cracks open a sliver. I can sense her standing there before I open my mouth to say anything else. I lower my left hand and use it to stabilize the pizza box. I search for her eyes in the darkness, but I can barely make out her shape. She seems to be trying to put as much distance between us as possible. I still don't know what set her off earlier in her car, but I can sense that she's still angry with me. I sort of get it. I didn't exactly treat my brother the way I should've. I know it, she knows it, this entire town knows it. But that was between Ben and me. So, why is she angry with me *now?* Did I do or say something wrong?

If only I could get a glimpse of her eyes to see if the fire's still burning.

The rain's still coming down hard, but at least for now, I'm able to stay dry under the safety of her porch covering. She shuts down any chance I have to smooth things over. She doesn't open the door any wider, but her words break the silence between us.

"What do you want, Jay? Why are you here?" she snaps, barely above a whisper.

I'm not the best at reading people, especially if I can't see their face to make a judgment call, but I think I detect a slight tremble in her voice. Like she's scared.

I knew coming here was a bad idea. I just thought... I'm not sure what I thought, but it wasn't this. I mean, I'm not expecting her to jump with joy at the sight of me—I'm pretty sure she hates me. But I didn't expect this kind of greeting. Not after seeing her so broken and vulnerable earlier.

"Hello to you, too," I retort, unable to help myself. She needs to take this box out of my hands before I burn myself. It's surprisingly still hot.

"Can I come in?" I ask with a sigh after she doesn't say anything.

"No. You can't. What do you want?" she barks in return.

I sigh again. This isn't going anywhere. This is what I get for trying to be nice. Bit back in return. Ouch. She doesn't even realize why I'm here yet. I'm starting to wonder how long it's going to take her.

The door creaks open a fraction wider, and our eyes meet. Her pink, soft lips part into an O as realization sinks in.

"You have a pizza from the tavern. Why didn't you say so?" she says softly, eyeing me carefully.

"Well, if you'd open the door like a normal person instead of growling at me, you would've noticed sooner," I say, smirking.

I can't help myself.

"Hmph! I didn't *growl* at you. That's absurd." She folds her arms across her chest.

She's wearing a bright pink T-shirt that says, "Mom Life is the Best Life," paired with a black cardigan and leggings. For the first time, her hair is down—flowing well past her shoulders and arms, settling in gorgeous waves just above her hips. Wow.

Get a grip, man. You've seen a lady with her hair down before.

Yes, but not her. Not like this.

There's nothing tame about the curls and waves cascading all around her. I can just make out the faintest glow from her golden eyes in the porch light.

"Okay, you didn't growl. Got it. So, can I come in now?" I nod towards the box I'm still holding, and her eyes break free from mine as she glances down.

She uncrosses her arms from her chest and reaches for the box. Finally. I don't let my eyes linger, but as soon as she takes the box from me, I notice... Yep, definitely not wearing a bra. She might've been sleeping for all I know. Or maybe she's a bit of a night owl like me, just getting the night started. Before I can ponder Jude's night routine any further—especially now that she doesn't have someone else to go to bed with—the door starts closing. Right in my face.

She mutters a soft, "Thank you, really," as I hear the door click shut in front of me, followed by the second click of the lock sliding into place.

Wow. I brought her a large pizza from the tavern after work, and she can't even thank me to my face?

Yeah, that sounds right. I've had my share of rejections, and it's not like we even know each other. She's probably wondering how I even knew where she lives.

Kelly seems to be close friends with Jude. She was a little hesitant at first to give out Jude's address, but when I explained that I was just trying to make a peace offering, she quickly changed her mind. She even suggested food that Jude would enjoy.

For the past ten years, I've been the hardest one to track down. Besides Kyle, I wasn't close with anyone. It wasn't that my life has been terrible, I think I was just tired of living in my brother's shadow. I wanted to experience life for myself. I didn't know what that was like, not really. In order to do that, I had to start over somewhere new. And that's exactly what I did, even though it came with a price.

And now I'm back, where it all began. But I can't stay here. There are far too many ghosts.

With the door still shut and no signs of Jude wanting to pick up our conversation, I glance towards the large front window. She's drawn the curtains, of course, and a soft glow spills out from within.

Well, I hope she enjoys the pizza. It's the least I can do. Kelly mentioned that Brian made an extra pizza, and that it's Jude's favorite thing on the menu. I knew I wanted to do something small for her, especially after seeing her panic in the car earlier, so I asked if I could have it.

If I didn't know any better, I'd swear it was a full-blown panic attack that Jude experienced. I've had my fair share over the years. So I know all too well what one looks like.

I run back to the Prius I rented and wait for a moment before putting the key in the ignition. I take one last look at her house before shifting into reverse, and that's when it happens.

Like a match struck, the entire sky lights up like it's on fire. The biggest streak of lightning I've ever seen dances across the horizon.

A threatening clap of thunder shakes the windows and rattles the car, swaying it slightly from side to side.

Glancing back at her house one last time before reversing out of the long driveway, I notice all the lights in her house are out. It doesn't take a heartbeat to realize what has happened.

She lost power.

Jude is alone in the dark.

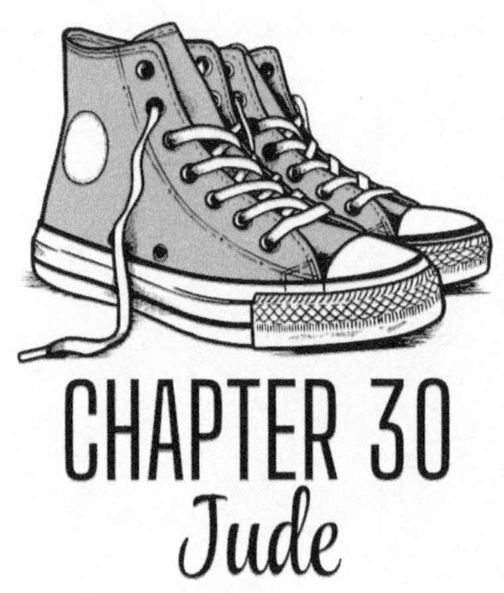

CHAPTER 30
Jude

D on't get any ideas." I warn Jay as I light another candle in the kitchen. Only moments before, I'd been bathed in utter darkness when all the lights flickered off. After nearly dropping the steaming pizza box in shock, I quickly feel my way over to the cupboard and pull out a candle and lighter.

The second the candle ignites with a tiny shimmer of flame, Jay is knocking at the door again.

He's one of the last people I expected to see standing on my doorstep. How he found my house is beyond me. Whatever, none of that matters right now. He's still here. But why?

First, he surprised me by still being in town and working at the tavern. I hadn't set foot back there since I walked out during the meal with my parents. Until earlier today, when I stormed in, ready to throw some punches. Then, he brought me a pizza after his shift. After the way I treated him and yelled at him to get out of my car so I wouldn't break down in front of him? And this wasn't just any pizza. Oh, no. He brought me Ben's special pizza that he put on the menu just for me.

"*Pickles on pizza, are you kidding me? That's so disgusting, Jude!*" Ben said as we sat in bed flipping through the movie options on Netflix.

"*No way! It's so good. You have to trust me. Have you ever tried it?*" I pleaded with him, my mouth watering at the thought of pickle pizza.

"*I'll take your word for it, because I'm never trying it. Eww!*" he said.

But I didn't back down. "*What's so gross about it? Don't knock it until you've tried it!*" I poked him in the ribs, and he squirmed while his eyes tried to remain glued to the TV.

"*I don't like pickles. That's reason enough.*"

At this, I gasped in mock shock. "*Seriously?*"

"*Seriously,*" he retorted.

"*Challenge accepted,*" I said.

"*What does that mean?*"

"*Oh, I think you know. I'll go make you one now.*" I started scooting off the bed.

"*Stop it. I'll make it for you tomorrow at the tavern,*" he said it so casually that I just blinked at him, stunned. Wait, what?

"*Hold up. You're going to make me disgusting pickle pizza at your tavern tomorrow?*" I asked in disbelief.

He clicked on an action movie and hit the pause button before turning to me. His expression was serious as he said, without flinching, "*Yeah, sure. And I'll name it "What's the Big Dill?*"

I smirked, my eyebrows quirking up at him. "*You can't be serious.*"

He winks. "*Guess you'll have to wait and find out if I am or not.*"

And with that, he hit the play button.

I hadn't paid much attention when I spoke to Jay on my front step, but now that he's in my house, I can see that he's soaked from head to toe and dripping water all over my floor. I light a third candle and set the lighter down.

I bite my lip, daring to meet his eyes once again. Eyes that reflect the tiny candle flames, casting shadows along the walls from the kitchen into the living room.

"Quite the storm out there, huh?" I laugh nervously, attempting to make small talk and failing. I don't know how to do this—make small talk and pretend like everything is normal.

My eyes catch on the water dripping off Jay in tiny rivulets. It takes me a moment to pull my gaze away.

"Sorry," I shake my head to clear it. "Let me go grab you something. I'll be right back. Uh, make yourself at home."

Ugh, why did I say that? That isn't what I mean. I don't want him making himself at home here. He doesn't belong *here*. I'm pretty sure I'm still mad at him for coming back to Bethel in the first place. The damage he caused Ben was already done and can't be repaired. Doesn't he see that he's too late? It doesn't matter anymore.

Now, he's just wasting both his time and mine.

"I'll be fine..." he starts to say, but I walk away. Using the torch flashlight on my phone, I light the way to my closet so I can find him something dry to wear. A lump forms unexpectedly in my throat at the thought of giving him something of Ben's to wear. But I don't have much of a choice. The sooner I get him some dry clothes to wear, the sooner he'll be on his way back home. Or wherever it is that he's staying. Doesn't matter, I just need to pick something.

But there's a small part of me that isn't ready for him to leave. Without the kids here, the house is eerily quiet at night, especially now with the power out. I'm not sure I can handle being alone right now. The very thought sends a shiver up my spine, and hot tears force their way into my eyes. Don't. I am so sick of crying. Is it too much to ask for one moment where I'm not falling apart?

Just one.

I pull a folded T-shirt from the bottom of one of Ben's piles. It's a shirt I hadn't seen him wear in a while—one I won't miss easily and can do without, at least for now. I hesitate when I get to the pants. I'm not sure if Jay is a jeans guy or what size he wears. I'm pretty sure nothing of Ben's will fit Jay's six-foot-three frame, but a pair of sweats will have to do for now. Surely he doesn't need a clean pair of underwear and socks too, right? I'm overthinking this. What I have is fine; he can make do. He's not staying.

I rush out of the closet and yank my towel off the rack as I head back into the kitchen. Jay hasn't moved from his spot. He looks up at me with a piercing gaze as I make my way over to him.

"Here you go, sorry about that. I didn't notice how wet you were and—" I'm talking so fast my voice starts to shake, and I cut myself off. I suddenly realize how nervous I am with him here. I know I'm not doing anything wrong. After all, he came to me, but there's something about it that reminds me a lot of when I was a teenager getting ready to lean in for my first kiss.

It had been both terrifying and exhilarating being that close to someone else. My nerve endings are shooting electricity through my body, standing this close to him. Too close.

"Thank you, Jude. Really. You didn't have to do this," he says, his voice coming out a little husky, but he also sounds sincere.

He doesn't strike me as the caring type. Maybe this is how he is with every woman. Gentle at first, but nothing about him screams, "I want a lifelong partner I can go through life with."

I shrug my shoulders. "No problem. You're the one who brought me food. I should be thanking you, not the other way around. I know it might be weird wearing his clothes, but maybe not, since he was your brother. Okay, I'm going to shut up now." I bite my lip, heat rushing to my cheeks. What has gotten into me?

He surprises me with a soft laugh. It's warm and deep and rich.

It also sounds very similar to Ben's laugh. My stomach clenches, and I fight back the urge to cry. *Not now, not here.*

"Where's your...?" he trails off, grabbing the clothing I set on the island counter for him and looking around for a place to change. Of course.

I blush again and direct him to the nearest bathroom. As soon as he leaves, I wander over to the large box of pizza and pop open the lid to sneak a piece. It's after ten now, and my tummy is grumbling. It's embarrassing. The aroma of roasted garlic, salted dill crust, alfredo sauce, freshly sliced dill pickles, and mozzarella cheese tickles my nose and sends me into the sweetest heaven on earth. Ahhhh. My senses are overwhelmed and fueled with the purest of fragrances.

This pizza concoction was created before Nova was born, but I was pregnant with her when the idea struck me. I've always loved pickles, but the thought of pickles on top of a pizza sends my senses into overdrive. I'm obsessed, and once an idea strikes me, I have the hardest time letting it go. Ben knew this about me, but I was so shocked when he kept his word and created this amazing delight for me. And not only that, he tried it himself and loved it so much he officially convinced Brian to add it to the menu permanently.

To our surprise, it was a huge hit. It's been one of my favorites ever since.

I nearly jump out of my skin when Jay leans over my shoulder and says, "So, they weren't kidding. They really did put pickles all over this pizza."

Yep. We absolutely did, and it was one of the sweetest things Ben ever did for me. It's something I'll never forget.

CHAPTER 31
Jay

I didn't expect her to ask me to stay, but she did. And I couldn't say no. Not now. Even though she made it very clear from the moment I walked through her door that this was in no way a date. If I were a stranger looking in, I'd call BS, though.

I mean, here I am with a woman, alone in her home. The power conveniently went out, so she lit about a dozen scented candles. It smells like a flower shop in here.

Between the two of us, we devour an entire box of pickle pizza. I didn't know what was inside until she opened it. Hot, white, melty cheese, a mix of Italian spices and seasonings, and yes, the whole thing is covered in sliced dill pickles. Pickles! That's new to me.

I don't despise pickles, but I wouldn't say that I love them either. I usually pick them off my burger or don't order them at all. But hey, this is obviously something she loves, and for that reason alone, I'm willing to try it.

Let's just say she won't have any leftovers tomorrow.

After we demolish the pizza, I'm surprised when she offers me a beer. Jude doesn't strike me as a beer gal. I wonder if they're hers or Ben's leftovers. Like the borrowed clothes I'm wearing now—a baggy gray T-shirt with a pocket on the right and sweatpants that fit more like man-capris on me.

I appreciate that she offered me dry clothes, but I should have headed home rather than take her up on the offer. I'm the one who showed up here uninvited. It was clear when she saw me that she didn't want me here. At all.

Now? I'm not so sure.

I've only allowed myself one beer. I decided that the moment I cracked open the first bottle and took a sip. Especially after I got buzzed with Mom the other day at the tavern. Embarrassing to say the least, and not something I'm eager to repeat with Jude.

After stuffing ourselves with the ridiculously good pizza—I can see now why it's her favorite—she asks me if I'd rather play a board game or do a puzzle. I manage to hide my surprise that she's not kicking me out. I'm not strong enough to leave on my own, so I'll follow her lead.

I can't remember the last time I did a board game or a puzzle, so I let her choose. She opts for a puzzle, which is a thousand tiny pieces that she spreads out over her living room coffee table. The room is pretty dim, even with the flickering light of the candles all around, but luckily, she finds one of Ben's camping lanterns in the garage. And because we're inside, we don't have to worry about the bright light attracting bugs.

I'm not paying much attention to the puzzle itself, I find myself more fascinated by her—by little movements like the way her eyebrows scrunch up and her nose twitches when she's focused and concentrating hard. It's cute.

She also prefers sitting on her knees. Even though the table is low enough to reach from the couch, she'd rather be on the floor, propped up on her knees.

I can tell that this is something she does often. Maybe she does this with her kids. Or maybe this was something she reserved for date nights with Ben after the kids were asleep. A sudden pang of guilt stabs at my chest, because I'm here now, participating in something so personal, so intimate, as putting a puzzle together, and Ben isn't.

I have a million questions I want to ask her.

Is it hard living without him? Are the bigger things, the more vibrant memories, the most painful part, or is it things like this? The small, simple things, such as putting together a puzzle. Solving something together. Partnering to accomplish a bigger picture. A piece of art to cherish and remember.

Do you regret inviting me in?

I spent the last decade living on my own. Alone is all I've ever known. It haunted me daily. After what she's gone through with losing her husband... I can only imagine how alone she's feeling right now. Even though the difference between us is that she's surrounded by a sea of people who love and care about her. In just the few weeks I've been here, I've witnessed firsthand the people in her corner. And it's a pretty big corner.

I don't have that. I can count on one hand the people who would notice if I died today. It's a sad truth I've come to terms with over the years, but it doesn't make it any easier.

I'm not my brother and never will be. I know Mom said there's no pressure if I don't want to stay after my six weeks are up. I'm already on my second week, four and a half more to go. Right now, I don't plan on staying past the promised timeframe. I don't want a life here. *Been there, done that.* But I'm here now, so I might as well make the most of it.

I'll be here. I don't know why I said that. Or what I meant by it. I could blame the alcohol, sure, but it goes deeper than that.

Funny how words can slip out before we are ready to give them life. Like right now.

"So, it's just you here?" I ask, glancing over at her. I've finished my beer and set it on the corner of the coffee table. We've spent at least an hour poring over the puzzle. She set the box up at the end of the table so we can easily reference it, but it's not helping me much. The puzzle is a picture of a couple sitting together at a bar, drinking beers and smiling. It looks a lot like the Second Verse Tavern. But maybe it just looks similar.

"Yeah," she responds, golden eyes focused on finding the perfect pieces to fit together.

I love watching how quickly her mind works. I want to ask how many times she's completed this exact puzzle, or if she's just good at it. But I don't want to ruin the moment. "How long are your kids gone?" I ask, genuinely interested.

I know I'm distracting her, but every time I'm around her, I find myself wanting to know more about her. More about the person my brother spent the last ten years of his life loving and caring for. I don't know what that kind of love looks like.

I never stuck around long enough to give anyone I've met a chance. I don't believe in a love that lasts forever. And I certainly don't believe it's a possibility for my future. I don't deserve that kind of goodness in my life. I'm sure to ruin it before it ever has the chance to begin.

I can sense that she's still a little nervous to be around me. I don't know why, but I want to fix that. I want to see a complete one-hundred-eighty-degree turn from how she approached me in the tavern earlier today. She's interesting, and she has my attention. Which is saying a lot from a man who chases one thing after another. Women included. Not that I'm chasing her... because I'm not. She's just different from anyone I've ever met before, and it's making it hard to walk away right now.

She raises the bottle to her lips, takes a slow drink, and sets it down again. Maybe she's a beer girl after all. I like that she's taking her time with it, not in a rush to get every last drop.

She gives me a small, rueful smile. "They're staying with my parents in Indiana for most of the summer. I'll head up there at the end of June to spend the last month with them before we all come back here when school starts again."

The end of June. Our timelines match up. She'll be leaving to go spend time with her family, and I'll be leaving behind the family I left. *Again.*

She speaks softly, carefully, like she's unsure what information she can trust me with. I don't blame her. She hasn't seen me since her wedding day. I could've been working at the tavern with my brother for the last five years, but obviously, that ship has sailed.

"Are you glad to have some alone time, or has it been hard?" I ask gently, watching her closely.

Her body is stiff, and the candles create a soft glow around her. I should try and pretend to be interested in the puzzle, but it's impossible. Something is drawing me to her. I can't look away.

She glances over at me, her golden-brown eyes blinking rapidly, as though my question caught her off guard and she wasn't expecting me to ask that.

Slowly, she nods her head. "Yeah, it has been. Hard, that is."

I nod and sit up straight on the couch, carefully studying her. Her movements have slowed a bit, and she now has her back pressed against the couch.

"Can I ask you a question?" she says.

I swivel my body slightly in her direction. "Sure. What's up?"

She peers up at me over her shoulder.

"Why did you come back?" she asks, curiosity flickering in her eyes.

Now it's my turn to be caught off guard. She could've asked me anything. I'm usually closed off most of the time, but for some reason, when I'm near her, there's a part of me that wants to let my guard down. Like she's someone who can hold my darkest secrets and never tell a soul. I see it every time I look at her. That she's someone I can trust with anything.

Why did I come back?

The easy answer: because of my brother's death.

The harder truth? Because I'd been away for too long, and it was time to come back home. *Home.* Even though I don't belong here, and this place holds nothing for me. Right?

"It's complicated," I settle on. It's not the full truth, but it's not a lie either.

I close my eyes. I can feel her eyes lingering on me, but I don't move to open them.

For a moment, neither of us says anything. Then she speaks up first, breaking the silence and slicing through my dark thoughts.

"Well, I hope it wasn't for nothing. I hope that when you decide to leave, it'll have been worth something," she says, her voice catching a little.

My eyes find hers in the soft light, and for a fraction of a moment, I almost forget where we are, who she is, and why I'm here in the first place.

I find myself wanting to be closer. I gently lift myself off the couch and sit on the carpet next to her. There's just enough space between the table to bend my legs, and I rest my hands on my knees.

We're close enough now that I can feel her warmth against me. Without thinking, I lean in, expecting a kiss—only to realize too late she's pulling me into a hug instead. I catch a whiff of her lavender-scented shampoo and quickly pull myself back together, settling into the hug.

Of course, she's not ready for that. What was I thinking? Good thing she can't see me right now with my face buried in her hair, still hugging.

Suddenly, we're blinded by the lights coming back on, and we quickly pull away. I realize just how close I'm sitting to a woman that'll never be a part of my life. Not like that.

I bolt off the floor as though I've been struck by lightning, letting her words hang heavy in the air.

"I've gotta go. Thanks for letting me stay for a while and for the dry clothes. I'm sorry for intruding on your night," I awkwardly say.

Suddenly, my skin feels hot and prickly. I've got to get out of here before I say or do something I'll regret.

I should've dropped off the pizza and left. But I'd feel a lot worse if I drove away, leaving her alone in the dark.

"Um, yeah. No problem. Thanks for the pizza," she responds flatly, confusion written across her face.

I flee before she can say anything else. The real question is, how am I going to survive these next four weeks with her nearby?

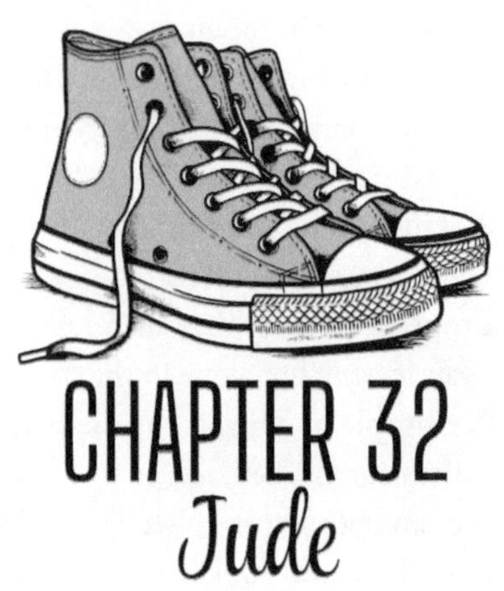

CHAPTER 32
Jude

t's the next day, and Mom and the kids are FaceTiming me in a few minutes to catch up. I set my alarm for seven a.m. for the call, something I haven't done since getting Nova ready for school in the mornings.

After Jay left last night, I decided I'd go into the tavern the next morning. Not to yell at anyone or cause a scene... but because I need to start trying to figure out how to run this business, my business, without Ben. It's been a little over two weeks since his death, and it still feels like it happened yesterday.

Time moves in slow motion, and I feel stuck in some sort of weird time warp. I can't rely on intuition right now because I have none. All logic and reasoning have left my brain. Last night was proof of that.

What was I thinking, inviting Jay to stay and share an entire pizza last night? Was it because he did me a favor, and that was my subtle way of saying thanks? Or did something in me want to know the man who knew a part of Ben I'd never get to know?

I know their relationship was estranged, but they were still brothers. I don't have any siblings, so I didn't get the same experience that they had growing up. I find myself wanting to know more about them. The brothers together, and the brothers apart. I want to know every little thing that I'm missing. Is that healthy? Probably not. I have no idea. But I have a million questions swimming through my head that I want to ask Jay, but can't.

I wouldn't call myself one hundred percent introverted, but whenever Ben and I were in a room full of people, he was always the center of attention. I prefer chatting one-on-one. Something about it feels more intimate, a private, shared space where true thoughts and feelings can be released without the pressure of a crowd. I've always been this way. It's probably one of the reasons Ben balanced me out so well.

Now? Now, I'm a mess. I'm all over the place. One moment I'm hot, and the next I'm ice cold.

It was almost eleven p.m. when the lights came back on. A part of me couldn't help but feel disappointed, because Jay bolted out of here quickly. I can't say I blame him, though. He already sat with me for almost two hours. *Two hours.* That's the most time we've ever spent together, not to mention he hugged me. As in, he wrapped his warm, strong arms around me. I can't remember the last time I was held like that. It's not something I can shake from my thoughts, and even if I could, I'm not sure I'd want to.

If he really is helping out around the tavern, that means we'll be seeing a lot more of each other.

I'm not entirely sure how I feel about that.

My thoughts are interrupted when I see two adorable faces appear on my phone screen. Nova has her hair up in two, bouncing pig-tails, and Riley's curls bounce right alongside his sister's. I haven't seen them smile like this since they last saw their daddy. I've missed this. Tears immediately well up in my eyes, and I do my best to quickly swipe them away.

Riley notices. Of course he does. I swear that kid notices everything. "It's okay, Mommy, don't cry. We are having fun at Nana and Papa's." I bet they're having the time of their lives. Nova butts in and takes over the screen.

"Guess where Nana is taking us today, Mommy?" She's still bouncing up and down with excitement.

I grab a coffee mug and place it under the Keurig machine, shaking a pod with my other hand and placing it inside. I select the size I want, and I move the phone away as the coffee starts to brew.

"I have no idea, Nov, where are you going today?" I ask, setting the phone against the napkin holder as I sit down at the kitchen table.

Riley comes back into focus, and at the same time, they both shout, "The water park!"

My mom has always been good at keeping these two entertained. Whether it's building blanket forts, movie nights, or scavenger hunts around her house, she loves doing it all. And they love her all the more for it.

"That sounds like so much fun, you guys. Make sure she takes lots of pictures to send me, okay?" I say, smiling for the first time in what feels like ages. The muscles around my mouth pinch, as though it isn't simple muscle memory, and they, too, have forgotten what it's like to be happy.

"What are you doing today, Mommy?" my son asks me.

I turn around, grab my coffee, and add in a splash of creamer before sitting back down.

"Well, I woke up early this morning and got ready so I can go into Daddy's restaurant today," I say, taking a slow sip from my coffee to fight the quiver in my lip so I don't start crying on camera.

The word Daddy is a trigger.

Everything these days is a trigger.

"I miss Daddy," Riley says quietly. His dark brown eyes suddenly grow sad and glossy. I wish that he were closer to me so that I could hug him.

"Me too, buddy," I say, offering him a small smile.

Nova is quiet as she tugs gently at one of her pig-tails, twirling her hair around and around.

"What will you be doing at Daddy's work?" he asks me, curious.

For only being three, he's always been in tune with people. He doesn't just ask things, he truly cares what you have to say.

"Oh, um. Well, I'm not entirely sure, bud. Daddy's office is probably a mess, so I'll need to clean it up."

Nova chimes in, "You know how Daddy is. He left messes everywhere." She gives a big eye roll for extra dramatics.

Always full of theatrics, this one.

"I mean was..." she adds, biting her lip. Suddenly, sadness sweeps across her face, and she wipes at her eyes. It pains me to see them struggling. I see my pain every day, but watching my kids fight back tears does something inside me. It's like little pieces of my heart are slowly chipping away. Does this pain ever fully go away, or is this how it's always going to be? I don't want this for them. I can barely handle it myself, but my kids? It's not fair. It's just not.

"I know what you mean, sweetie. Hey, you guys have fun splashing and playing at the water park, okay? Call me later and tell me all about it? I love you both so so much," I say quickly.

I need to end this before I'm not able to fight off the water works that are sure to come.

"Love you too, Mommy," Riley says, his smile returning.

As soon as I get to Indiana, I'm going to squeeze both of them and never let go. These next four weeks are going to feel like a lifetime. But I think Mom is right, I need this. It's not enough time to heal, and I don't think you can just "get over" something this big, but this time to myself is either going to make or break me. I'm hoping for the former.

"Nova?" I say gently, willing her to look at me again.

Her green-gold eyes meet mine, and a slow smile creeps across her face. "Yeah, yeah, I love you too," she giggles into the phone.

She's a goober, but she's mine.

The kids get distracted, done with the conversation, and take off chasing each other through the house. My mom has her hands full with these two, but I'm also grateful she and Dad offered to spend this time with them. I hope it's as meaningful to her as it is to me.

"Hey, Judy. How are you holding up today?" Mom says into the phone, talking louder than normal to be heard over the kids playfully yelling in the background.

"Today? Right now? I'm doing okay. That might change later, maybe even as soon as I hang up. But for the moment, I'm doing okay," I say honestly and distract myself with another long sip from my mug.

"That's great, dear. Life is full of little moments—some good, some bad, some easy, and some hard. Just take it one moment at a time, okay? Right now is a good moment, and that's great. There will be some not-so-good moments too, and that's okay. One moment at a time is all you can do. I love you, and I'm proud of you," she says, her eyes crinkling into a soft smile.

I love my mom so much. She might be miles away, but I have never doubted her love and faith in me. She's always been able to see the best in me, no matter what. I know she doesn't expect me to be a perfect version of myself right now, but I also don't want to let her or my kids down by constantly falling apart. I can do this. One moment at a time.

As soon as we say our goodbyes and hang up, the tears come like a flood. But somehow, I'm okay with it. I decide to let them. Because as soon as they're done, I've already moved on to another moment. The moment I walk out the door and head to the tavern. *My* tavern.

CHAPTER 33
Jay

don't take my lunch break until two o'clock today. For a Wednesday, this place is the busiest I've seen. Since the doors opened at eleven, it's been a constant flow of people. As soon as one group leaves, another enters.

There's a small break room off the side of the kitchen, but I'd rather spend my break in private. One of my first days here, I escaped to the office to eat in peace. Ever since, I always have my lunch at Ben's old desk in the office. I've never seen anyone come in here, so I figured I'm not bothering anyone by using it.

His office is a mess. I don't know how Jude can stand it. But maybe Ben was the only one who used it. Jude's house was spotless when I showed up there last night. Last night... I can't believe I spent almost two hours with her, at her house, putting together a puzzle. I'm curious to know if she stayed up after I left to work on it some more. At the rate she was going, she's likely finished it by now. And I can't forget that moment that we shared... It's been playing nonstop in my mind ever since. I almost kissed her. I can't believe I almost kissed her. It's a good thing she hugged me instead. I might've ruined everything with that kiss.

I'm halfway through my sandwich when the door opens. I nearly choke the bite down and glance up, wiping my chin in haste. Even though I'm not doing anything wrong, I can't help feeling guilty, like I've been caught.

She doesn't see me right away. Her eyes are on the ground, and she's holding a brown paper bag and a large drink in her hands. As she scans the room, her eyes land on mine, and she startles, not expecting to find me here. I gulp and scoot back the chair to leave. I thought this would have been okay, but from the surprised look in her eyes, I'm starting to second-guess if I should've just used the break room. But the idea of eating in a room full of people who I'm still not sure like me being here, twists my stomach into knots the size of a pretzel.

"Oh," is all she says.

I'm standing now, gathering up my trash and brushing crumbs off the desk onto the floor. I probably shouldn't do that either. I'm only making this worse. What is it about her that tangles up my insides? Something on the corner of the desk suddenly catches my eye, and before she has a chance to look up at me, I quickly stuff the piece of paper into my jacket pocket.

"I'm sorry. I'm leaving. I just thought... never mind." I push in the chair, and at the sound of someone clearing their throat, I glance back over at her.

Her wild hair is tamed and pulled up into a ponytail, she's wearing a maroon T-shirt with matching lipstick, and tight, black jeans with rips in the knees. I can't help but glance at her feet, and a smile creeps along my face when I see black high-top Converse to match her outfit. I should have known.

My eyes find hers again, and a sigh escapes her.

She motions back to the desk before speaking. "No, no, please. You don't need to leave. I wasn't expecting to find anyone here. That's all." She shuffles to one side, nervously pulling her lip between her teeth. My gaze trails towards her mouth, and I have to force myself to look away. Quit staring at her mouth. Quit thinking about her lips and what they might feel like on mine.

"It's okay, I'm finishing up anyway," I say, wadding my trash into a ball and looking underneath the desk for the trash can. There is one, but it's buried beneath a pile of trash that's already spilling over the sides. I can't believe my brother was such a slob.

"Oh, okay," she says, disappointment laces her tone. At least I think that's what I detected in her voice.

She hasn't moved from her spot, and she's blocking the door. I'm not in a hurry to leave, but I also don't want to burden her with my presence if she'd rather be alone. After all, that's why I came here in the first place. To get away from all the noise.

"No, wait." Her eyes flutter closed for a moment, and I'm mesmerized by her long lashes. How did I not notice them before? They are long and dark, matching her hair. She slowly opens them again, finding me in the soft, warm light of the office.

"I could use the company. But you don't have to if you don't want to," she adds quickly, unsure of herself.

Maybe she's even a little unsure of me. But she wants me to stay. Otherwise, she wouldn't have said it, right? This is the second time in less than twenty-four hours she's asked me to stay.

"You sure?" I ask gently, not wanting to push her too hard. It was only yesterday when she stormed into the tavern mad at me, and today her features are softened with something I can't quite pin down. But I like seeing this side of her. She was a force to be reckoned with when she was all fired up. She's a flame I'm drawn to.

"Yes, of course. Please," she mutters so quietly I almost miss it.

Almost. I gesture to the chair for her to sit down in my place, but she shakes her head as she makes her way over to the couch and plops herself down onto it.

I hesitate, half considering sitting down on the couch next to her, but quickly change my mind. We're just getting to know each other, and I don't want to push anything. But I don't know exactly what we're doing or what this is; maybe she needs someone to talk to. Maybe she's just lonely, and I'm somebody who doesn't already know all of her secrets. Even if it's only temporary, I can be that for her.

I sit back down and rest my hands on top of the desk. A slow smile tugs at her lips, and she looks down at her bag, pulling out one item at a time and setting each beside her on the couch.

"What'd you bring for lunch today?" I ask, urging her to talk to me. To break the silence between us. I'd never admit this out loud, but I like hearing her talk. There's something about the layers in her voice that I find fascinating.

When she talks fast, or slow, or soft, like listening to the steady rhythm of a drum. I can only imagine what her voice sounds like singing through a microphone on Friday nights. Speaking of... maybe I can get her to come to Open Mic this Friday. She doesn't even have to sing. It would just be nice if she came. Otherwise, she'll be sitting at home alone like she was last night and possibly every night.

She responds to me with a mouthful, "Don't laugh, but it's an Uncrustable." Only it doesn't come out sounding like Uncrustable, more like Uncrumbable.

I can't help but laugh.

She laughs in return, and it immediately sucks me in. I can't get enough.

Again, again.

"Like the circle sandwich without crust?" I ask, grinning at her from behind the desk.

She nods as she wipes her mouth with a napkin. "Yeah, exactly like that. My kids love these things, and it's all we have. Another reminder that I need to start doing adult things again. I haven't been out of the house much since..." she stops mid-sentence, suddenly frozen mid-chew.

She collects herself a moment later and takes a long sip of her drink before finding me again.

"Sorry about that," she apologizes.

"Nothing to be sorry for," I respond, offering her a sliver of a smile. I want her to know it's okay. Whatever she's experiencing, I want her to know it's okay to experience it. While seeing somebody cry is never an enjoyable experience, I want her to feel comfortable enough to do so.

"It just feels weird being here without him, you know?" she finally says, her eyes searching mine for answers.

Answers I don't have.

I nod and move my hands onto my lap. It's been a couple of hours since my last smoke break, and I can feel the itch creeping back up. I force it down because I don't want to leave and ruin whatever this is. Even though it's probably nothing. Not to her anyway.

The truth is, I do know. I do know what it's like without Ben, because most of my life has been spent without him. Living without him is all I've ever known. I'd give anything to have a different outcome, but I can't go down that rabbit hole. It'll send me into a spiral I'm not sure I'd be able to escape.

"Yeah, I can only imagine," I say instead. Hoping she feels my sentiment and that it's enough. Because I do care. Maybe a little too much, more than I should.

"I guess I'll start in here after I finish up my pathetic lunch." She laughs again, looking down at her lap. Her cheeks turn pink, and I memorize the color of them. The pretty way it paints her golden skin.

"That sounds like a good plan. Do you need any help?" I offer. I'm not sure how much I'd be able to help her sort through this mess, but I don't mind.

She shakes her head. "Thanks, but that's okay. I think this is something I need to tackle myself. But I appreciate it, really. And uh, thanks again for last night. I'm almost done with the puzzle, by the way."

Again, her cheeks bloom like tulips.

"Really? That's impressive! I'm guessing you do a lot of puzzles? And sure, no problem. I was happy to do it." And I was. I'd do it again if she gave me a chance. Why is she suddenly being so nice to me? Why am I thinking about her like that? What is wrong with me?

I need to get out of here before I embarrass myself. "Well, I'd better get back to work. Nobody but you knows where I disappear to on my breaks. Good luck! Let me know if you change your mind."

She smiles again, and it tugs at my insides.

"I don't do puzzles often anymore... but I enjoy them. Okay, I will. Thanks," she says, our eyes lingering together for a moment.

It's only a moment, but I carry it with me for the rest of the shift and all the way back to my childhood home.

It's a moment that is burned inside my head.

A moment that I need to forget, or it's going to be the very thing that destroys me.

I'm only here for a short time. I'm leaving. I can't be spending hours with Jude. It's not that I don't want to, because I do. But I don't want to cause her any more pain than what she's already going through. Her heart already broke once, and I don't want to be the one to break it a second time. I care about her and want whatever's best for her and her kids.

I won't hurt her. Leaving is the best option. I won't be the one to break her heart. It's already been broken once by the man she loved. I don't want to be the cause of it shattering again.

I can't let that happen.

CHAPTER 34
Jay

The next two days, we end up sharing our lunch space in the privacy of the office. My brother's old office. I'm constantly reminded that I don't belong in this tavern. Nonetheless, I'm here for a reason. Whatever that may be.

It's Friday, the end of another week that has both flown by and spun in slow motion. In the moments it's had a chance to slow down a little, I've learned a few things about Jude.

Her favorite color is pink or anything bright. She's always sporting some pop of color. I did finally ask her about her collection of Converse. She has fourteen pairs—fuchsia, light pink, yellow, orange, neon green, aqua, navy, cream, black, white, red, violet, coral, and her special-occasion tie-dye pair.

Her favorite food is pickle pizza. It's quite possibly a new favorite of mine as well. Although admitting that isn't going to happen. At least not anytime soon.

Her favorite types of music are jazz, indie-pop, and acoustic anything. When I asked her when was the last time she sang, her eyes got all teary, and she excused herself from the room.

She returned a moment later, changing subjects, but she didn't force me to leave like I expected. She hasn't been completely transparent around me yet, but I don't expect her to. Yet somehow, it was different from how my mother handled stress, or any feelings she didn't consider normal.

I never get the impression that she's trying to put on a show for me. While her guard isn't completely down, she isn't fully guarded either. Sometimes her emotions will spill over, and she allows herself to feel them for a moment, before pulling herself together and carrying on. She's strong. Stronger than she even realizes.

I don't know how she does it. She doesn't act as though everything is fine, but she also isn't walking around with her shoulders slumped either. She's trying her best to be okay, whether or not she really is. But there's just something about her that's real to me. Genuine.

It's Friday, and we've just finished our bagged lunches, and so far neither of us has made the first move to leave and get back to work. The office still has a long way to go, but I can already see improvement. There isn't a slew of papers cluttering the desk space anymore, and she's started reorganizing the walls filled with Post-it notes, old calendars, and fliers that should've been taken down ages ago. I know it won't take her long to turn this place around. I don't know how I can help her, but I'd like to try if she'll let me.

Starting with what I'm getting ready to ask her.

"Jude?" I ask from the couch. This time, she's at the desk that's mostly cleared off with everything in neat little stacks on top of the faded oak.

She throws her bag into the trash can underneath the desk, and her bright eyes find mine.

"Yeah, what's up?" she asks, folding her hands on the desk as though she's the teacher and I'm the student asking for extra credit.

I feel my throat tighten, and I'm not sure what to do with my hands, so I tuck them under my legs to keep from fidgeting.

Okay, I can do this. I finally have the chance to ask her what I've been meaning to ask her since Mom first approached me with her proposition. Where do I stand in all of this? Would Jude even want me to be a part of this business with her? I don't even know if it's an option yet.

I decide to just go for it.

"Have you thought about what you might want to do with the tavern?" I ask, feeling my face flush hot with embarrassment. Did that come out right?

From the startled look on her face, I'm guessing not.

I hurry and try again. "What I mean to say is, now that you're running things around here and Second Verse Tavern is yours... how do you feel about it? Of course, it's always been yours and Ben's, but are you doing okay with it all?"

She folds her hands in her lap and stares down at them. She doesn't say anything for several minutes, and I worry that I've asked the wrong thing. She just lost her husband. She was handed his business whether she wanted it or not. I can't begin to imagine how it feels to be in her shoes. All fourteen pairs of them.

She doesn't look up when she answers, not right away at least.

"I, uh... I haven't thought about it much, honestly. My brain has two modes currently. Silence, where I'm not thinking about anything at all. Or it's so loud and overstimulating that the only thing that seems to bring it back to a quiet space is sleep. Which is a funny thing too, because sometimes I sleep for hours and hours, and other days I can barely sleep at all. So, to try to answer your question: I have no idea what I'm doing. But I'm here, and I guess that's gotta count for something, right?"

She cracks a laugh that doesn't ring quite the same as the ones I've heard before.

I offer her a small smile and nod my head.

"I think it does. It definitely counts. I'm sure it's all a lot."

At this, she snorts. Not a half-laugh, but a full-on snort. She's beautiful and quirky.

I want more.

Speaking of more... there's something else I'd been meaning to talk to her about.

"I'm hoping I'll see you tonight at Open Mic." As soon as I speak it into existence, I feel a gnawing of regret. I shouldn't have said that. It's too soon.

This is the longest I've been in town since I left it, but two weeks is nothing compared to what she must be feeling right now. I wish I could take it back.

"Oh," she says, startled.

"I'm sorry. I shouldn't have asked you that. Sometimes I have no filter," I admit honestly. If I said every thought that came to mind, we'd both be in trouble. Sometimes the wrong thing slips through the cracks.

"No, it's okay. Really, Jay. I want you to be able to ask me things. I'm just processing. Give me a minute," she says, massaging her temples, as though my question is causing her a great amount of stress.

I'm the cause of this. I did this. This isn't okay.

"I didn't mean it..." I blurt out. Apparently, I'm on a roll today.

She opens her eyes and flashes her gold irises at me. "So you don't want me to come?"

I know I'm not making any sense. I'm even starting to confuse myself. Anxiety's getting the best of me. I'm not so good at saying exactly what I mean sometimes. My words come out all scrambled. It's why I tend to keep quiet most of the time, afraid of what might spill out if I don't. Like now.

"No, I do. It's just... I don't want to pressure you to come if you'd rather stay home. Which is fine too." I avert my gaze and stare at my legs, now bouncing up and down like the nervous wreck I am. What is wrong with me?

I feel the couch move as Jude sits down next to me. It's impossible to keep our legs from touching on this tiny couch. Why did Ben put such a small couch in his office? When I'm not acting like such a spaz, I'll offer to buy her a bigger couch.

"Jay, look at me, please," she pleads gently.

I don't want to look at her. I don't want to know what she's thinking. I can't handle whatever look of disappointment or doubt she's holding in her eyes.

Small, slender fingers gently wrap around my thigh, squeezing gently. For a moment, I forget how to breathe.

She has her hand on me.

She's touching me.

This time, I force myself to fully look at her. The look I find in her eyes isn't one of pity, but of sorrow or concern. She's beautiful even when she's sad.

"Why is it important to you that I come tonight?" she asks carefully. Her hand hasn't left my leg, and they stop shaking beneath the heat of her hand.

There it is again. Her warmth. Every time I look at her, really look at her, I feel this blanket of security wrap me up tight. I would trust this woman with my life. I'm out of my mind for even thinking something like that, but it's true. One look and I'm gone for her.

I'm not sure how she expects me to answer her with her hand on my leg, but I do my best to offer her the truth. She deserves that from me. And a lot more that I can't give.

"I'd love to hear you sing," I say, hedging on the little strand of hope I have left. I don't expect her to say yes. I've only heard her daughter's sweet voice the night before the funeral. I've heard people talk about Jude's voice, and can only imagine how sweet a sound it must be. I came to Open Mic for the first time last week, and while it was great and the energy felt alive, something was still missing. And I knew right away what that something had been. *Her.*

"Oh, that. I don't know, Jay... I don't know if I can." She draws her hand back into her lap, and I have the urge to grab it and hold it steady in mine. But I don't.

"I don't either. Let's make a deal," I say, offering my hand to her, and she just stares down at it like it might bite her.

"Say yes to coming tonight, and you won't have to sing if you don't want to. It'll be totally up to you," I offer.

Her eyes dance back and forth as she studies me. Watching me. Trying to figure out my next move.

"And if I don't?" she asks.

"If you don't, I can order us another pickle pizza, and we can watch one of your favorite movies. Your choice." I mean it. Either way, she wins. She gets to be the one in charge. I've been in charge for the last ten years of my life, and look where it's gotten me.

Back to where I started.

She tilts her head to the side, a knowing smile tugging at her lips. A small laugh bubbles out, and it's so pure I almost ask her to do it again. Every little thing about her fascinates me. Why didn't I get to know her sooner? But I know why. The realization hits me hard in the chest, and I hope she doesn't notice the shift in me.

"You'd do that? You'd skip the *best* talent in this town for a pizza with weird toppings and watch a chick flick that I'm pretty sure is not your jam?"

"Hey now, that pizza is surprisingly delicious. And the type of movie won't matter," I say. I don't feel like I can say no to her, and I don't want to.

"Why?" she asks, truly wanting to understand why I could possibly choose to spend my Friday night this way.

Isn't it obvious?

"I just want to be with you." From the look in her eyes, I can't tell if I've said the wrong thing again. I think I did. I should've taken more time to think about it before the words spilled out, but I can't undo it now.

My skin suddenly feels hot and itchy, and I can feel my entire body tense up. I'm really craving a cigarette. It'll help calm whatever is happening to me. I keep messing up because I don't know how to keep my mouth shut.

"You like hanging out with me?"

Her question startles me, but I'm too afraid to say anything else, so I don't. I try to calm my breathing and relax some of the tension in my shoulders.

"Jay, it's okay. I've enjoyed it so far, too." She gives me a sweet smile. "I'm glad we're becoming friends," she adds.

Friends. Yeah, that's what this is. That's what we are and all we'll be.

Because once again, Ben had her first. Ben had a lot of things first. Like going to college, finding the love of his life, and taking over the family business. Not to mention a gorgeous wife that he got to love for a decade, and two spunky kiddos... while I spent the last ten years lost and wasting time—partying, drinking, smoking to ease my anxiety, and sleeping around.

All to fill the void inside me and to help erase the pain of the choice I made when I left home.

We can never be more than friends.

Whatever I might think I'm feeling, I've got to push aside. I'm only here for a few more weeks. Soon we'll both be gone. When the smoke clears, it'll feel as though I was never here in the first place.

I'll be here.

For now, but not for long.

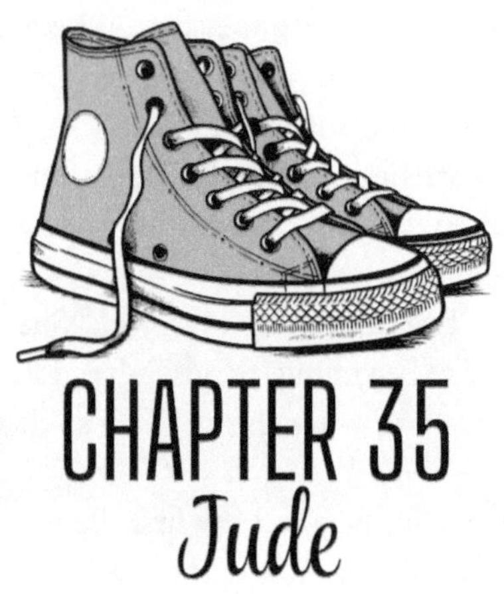

CHAPTER 35
Jude

haven't thought about singing since losing Ben. Music had been such a large part of our lives, and when he suddenly died, so did music. I didn't do it on purpose, it just happened. I stopped turning on the radio in the car.

I keep my phone on silent because even hearing my phone ring could be a trigger. Because every time it rang, it reminded me of the call that never came. I tried to call Ben and he didn't answer. I still replay his voicemail on nights when I can't sleep, which is often.

Jay seemed so nervous to ask me about performing again. I don't know why he was so hesitant. I'm not always open about the details of my life, but I try to answer honestly. Ask me and I'll be honest with you. No point in wasting time. Time that we aren't guaranteed. I know that a little too well.

I was starting to notice that about him more. He will say or ask me something, and then his entire demeanor will change in a flash, as though something strange has come over him.

I wonder if maybe he struggles with anxiety, too. Mine isn't usually that bad, but I do my best not to make him feel bad about it. We haven't exactly talked about it in detail, but the signs are there.

I still remember the first time I got up on stage nearly seven years ago, not too long after Ben's stepdad passed. The moment the lights hit my eyes and the music started playing, I almost lost my nerve. I missed the first few beats and asked the band playing with me to start again. I closed my eyes, said a quick, silent prayer, and was able to make it through the entire song without panicking. Afterward, I rushed into the restroom in tears from my near failure. I was so embarrassed. Fortunately, Kelly came to my rescue and gave me one of the best pep talks I've ever had.

She told me that if I didn't go back onstage the following week, she was going to kick my butt. We'd both laughed, but I knew that she meant it. She was scary when she needed to be, but also a good friend who supported us and the tavern.

I'd do just about anything to get back on that stage again. But I don't think it's going to happen tonight. It still feels strange being in this place without him. I can't get up there in front of everyone and pretend everything is fine when it's not. Especially with Jay here. He's not expecting anything from me, and I do think he means it. But even though the pressure isn't there, I can still feel it. Every time I walk in through the front doors, I can almost hear the words they're probably saying behind my back.

I'm surprised she's still able to come in here after what happened. How tragic, poor thing.

I can only imagine losing a spouse. If that were me, I'm not sure I could keep on living.

But she's got two kids to care for.

Yeah, but they aren't even here right now. She sent them away to stay with her parents... what if that's her way of getting rid of them, too?

Maybe she really would be better off if she just...

I shake the thoughts loose the best I can, because they won't do me any good. They'll send me into such a negative spiral that I won't do either of the things Jay suggested. I'd still be at home, lying in the dark, praying for Jesus to come and take my soul.

But I don't want to do that. I shouldn't even be thinking like that. Sometimes I can't help it, though. I could use the distraction, even if it's for a little while.

I don't want to be alone right now. I try not to think about the one person I don't want to be alone with.

Fridays always bring in a multitude of people to the tavern. Of course, there are the regulars who come in multiple times a week. Our small, Oklahoma town doesn't have much in terms of entertainment or recreation, and people from all walks of life find themselves here on Friday nights.

Every Saturday morning, we post a sign-up sheet on our socials and in the tavern for people to claim their time in the spotlight for the following week. Since Second Verse started doing this, I can't think of a single week with an empty spot.

It's been a bit since I signed up to sing at Open Mic. The week right before Ben passed, one of the kids had been sick, and I stayed home. The week before that, I was down with the flu. And in the two weeks he's been gone, I haven't been able to get back up there. Thankfully, nobody has pushed me. But I can almost sense the weight of it hanging over me.

Jay and I are sitting together at a small table in the far right corner, where we have a pretty good view. We're not right up against the stage, but we can still see who's up there.

We order a large plate of fully-loaded nachos to share, and a round of beers. I don't drink often. I much prefer white wines over the taste of beer. But it's Friday night, the start of the weekend, and everyone in the room has a drink in their hand. Nothing sweet or froufrou.

Open Mic starts promptly at nine. That's when Ben would typically get up on stage and give a toast. Glasses raised, laughter in the air, people were ready to have a good time. Then, he'd call the first person in line to come to the stage. A variety of talent was always in the line-up. Sometimes someone would read their poetry, sometimes it was a short stand-up set, and others would hook their phone into the speakers for karaoke.

On rare occasions, we'd get lucky and a full band would show up. We keep hoping someday someone famous will come waltzing through our doors, but so far that's yet to happen. But no matter who gets up on that stage, the crowd always supports them.

The applause is always loud, vibrant, and full of cheer. Nobody leaves feeling defeated or like they aren't good enough. It's never been like that, and that's my favorite part about Open Mic. That no matter who you are and what talent you bring to the stage, your passion will be supported. Ben made that happen, and that's never changed.

Tonight's no different. Jay and I haven't said much during the show. There are small pauses between each performance as they get set up. Every lull in the action, Jay turns to look at me like there's something on his mind. What comes out is usually something small and polite about the last performance. Not once has he asked me if I plan on getting up there. And it's a good thing, because I don't have any plans of getting up there tonight. The very thought makes my stomach twist and churn into knots.

Some nights, depending on how long the performances go, they wrap up shortly after ten; other nights, it can go all the way to eleven o'clock or later. We do have a cut-off time, though, just to allow those who came for their last call to get their drinks before they head out for the night.

It can be a bit tricky with the kids sometimes, because of the late nights. The first half of the sets are usually family-friendly and are okay for the kids to sit and watch. They may love Friday nights as much as I do. But I usually take them home by ten. It's now nearing eleven, and the performances are winding down. I'm grateful because I think I'm ready to call it a night.

That is, until Kelly skips over to our table, quite tipsy, with an idea up her sleeve.

"You," she points a finger at me, or at least tries to. It's somewhere in between me and Jay.

I glance behind us, but don't think she's motioning to anyone else. Yep, she's had a few too many drinks. I haven't seen her kids running around anywhere, so I'm assuming she got them a sitter for the evening so she could stay out. Good for her.

"What about me?" I ask, not liking where this is heading.

"You, love, need to get up on that stage. I've heard just about the entire town tonight, and I've had enough. It's your turn to shine, darling." Even drunk, her blue eyes glitter and sparkle in the soft light of the tavern. Her hair is still pulled up, swaying with every movement as her hips dance slowly to the music.

"I think that's a compliment. Thank you, Kelly, but not tonight. I'm tired and ready to go home." I say, a little buzzed from my beer, but not enough to be persuaded by her charm.

Maybe some night soon I'll be brave enough, but not tonight.

"Aww, come on. If you don't get up there, I'll have to take your place, and you know that won't be pretty," Kelly snorts, followed by a hiccup.

I quickly scan the room for any signs of Brian, but don't see him anywhere. He's probably cooking tonight.

She's right, though. As beautiful and self-confident as she is, I've heard her sing, and it wasn't pretty. She knows it's not her strong suit and is baiting me, throwing anything out there to get me on that stage. At least, she's trying to.

Why does it matter so much?

Suddenly, I feel more than just her eyes on me in the room. My head starts to spin as I grip the sides of my chair to keep my balance. I've got to get out of here.

This is the second panic attack within a week. My eyes flare in a silent SOS to the only person who can save me from a full-blown panic, and somehow, he catches on quickly. Within moments, I hear the scraping sound of his chair as he gets up, and then mine is pushed away, and he's helping me stand, draping my light sweater over my shoulders.

If Kelly tries to stop me from leaving, I don't hear her. I don't hear anything but the *thud thud* of my heart and the whoosh that escapes my lungs as soon as I sit in Jay's rental car. Jay's car. Oh, no. What am I doing here? I can't go home with him. What if someone sees us leave the tavern together? They already have enough to gossip about with Ben gone and my kids away. I can't bear to add rumors about Jay and me to the mix.

Ben's barely been gone a breath, and already, the ground under me feels like it's shifting again. I just need someone to support me tonight—not the whole town staring while they try to decide what that means.

This isn't what they think it is. Not yet. Maybe not ever.

CHAPTER 36
Jay

Jude doesn't say much the entire ride to her house. From her panicked expression inside the tavern, to the even more worried look when she realized I took her to my car rather than her own, I knew I needed to clear the air and fast. Of course, I didn't want her to get the wrong impression about my intentions. I'm not even sure what they are at the moment, but I'm doing my best to read Jude and give her whatever she needs.

We're friends now, she said as much the other day, but I don't want to give her any reason to feel uncomfortable around me. She's friends with Kelly, but I get the feeling Kelly is friends with everyone she comes into contact with. It's simply who she is.

But Jude? Jude is guarded like me. We aren't the same, not by a long shot. She's quiet when she chooses to be, but also doesn't let the conversation run dry. She's a good listener, doesn't interrupt me, and just might be the most patient person I've ever known. Which is nice because I'm not so patient with anyone, including myself.

When we pull up to her house after a silent drive, aside from the low hum of the radio, I'm not sure what to say as I shift the car into park. I glance over at her in the passenger seat. Her head rests against the window, both knees drawn to her chest as she hugs them tightly.

For a moment, I think she's asleep. If she's sleeping, I have no idea what I'm supposed to do. Wake her up? Dig through her purse until I find her keys? And then what? Carry her inside? No, I can't do that. Someone who's only a friend would never do that. That's way too... intimate. And we are definitely not that.

"Jude?" I say softly, unsure. I turn down the music, and my hand hovers over her for a moment, wondering how she'll respond if I nudge her. But she shuffles slightly against the window, still not looking in my direction, and I quickly lower my hand.

"Sorry. I'm fine, I just need another minute if that's okay," she says, her voice quiet and raspy.

"Yeah, of course. Take all the time you need." I lean back in my seat and close my eyes, listening to the echo of our breathing and the low hum of the engine.

I'll give her all the time she needs. I don't know what's bothering her tonight, but it could be a multitude of things. She's not an open book, but neither am I. I don't want to pry, but I also don't want her to think that I don't care.

Because I do. More than I should.

"Is it because Kelly asked you to sing tonight?" I tread gently, stealing a glance at her. Her hair is pulled back in a low ponytail, long dark curls trailing down her back.

Another beat of silence passes between us, but it isn't uncomfortable. I fidget in my seat, trying to locate my lighter in my pocket. I find it and grab my pack of cigarettes off the dashboard.

"Do you mind if I smoke one?"

"Nope. Go ahead," she says, still not looking my way.

I wish that I knew the right words to say. Words that could

help her, touch her in some way. But I'm not sure I know how. I'm not enough.

"And... yeah, I guess so. The Kelly thing, I mean. That's part of it," she finally offers, answering my question.

I roll down my window as I take a slow drag from my cigarette. I inhale and release, watching the smoke swirl out the window into the warm summer air.

"What's the rest of it?" I ask gently. "If you don't mind. You don't have to answer that if you don't want to." I don't want her to feel like I expect her to tell me everything. We might be friends, but I'm still closer to a stranger than anything else.

"It's okay." Her ponytail swishes against the leather seat as her body turns towards me.

There are tears in her eyes, threatening to spill over at any moment, and I witness firsthand just how fragile this woman is. I have to be careful. She can't afford for me to blurt out whatever comes to mind, it could destroy her unintentionally.

"I want to sing again. Really, I do. I miss it a lot. More than ever... I'm just not sure that I can do it anymore. I don't know how to find my voice again after losing the love of my life. And they just expect me to get up there and sing like I'm not... like I'm not broken." At this, her tears spill over, onto her cheeks, streaking the side of the leather seat where her cheek rests against it.

I'm tempted to reach out and brush her tears away, but I fight the urge. I don't know what she needs from me right now. It would be crossing a line that I'm not sure I'm allowed to cross. That's not something we've discussed. She doesn't feel the same way about me. My thoughts are not her own.

Instead, I tell her softly, honestly, "Jude, you are *not* broken. You're just grieving. As you should be. We all are, but *you* most of all."

She nods her head, tears continuing to soak the leather. There's got to be something I can give her to wipe her tears, if I can't do it myself. I snuff out my cigarette and drop the burnt-out stub into an old water bottle I keep in the driver's side door. I find a napkin in my center console and hand it to her.

She wipes her eyes and blows her nose before looking back at me.

"Why are you still here, Jay? I need the real reason why you stayed," she confronts me again.

My throat is dry. I'm in desperate need of a glass of water. But I know I can't put her off anymore. She needs the truth.

I don't understand all the reasons why I'm still here. Why didn't I walk away from all of this? Leave this place the same way I left it once before. It started because my mom asked me. But, honestly? The real reason I'm still here? She's sitting next to me.

It's stupid and crazy, and doesn't make any sense. She was my brother's true love. She isn't mine and never will be. I don't even deserve her friendship after the way I've treated her and her family since she married Ben ten years ago. Yet here she is.

Whether it's fate or the result of tragedy, I was brought back here for a reason. And I can't think of one that doesn't begin and end with her.

"You," I say in a single breath, shocking us both. I watch her body as it tenses, and her hand closest to the door starts to reach for the handle. Escape.

"You are the reason, Jude. I'm still here because of you."

It's true in more ways than one. I stayed since Mom asked, but honestly, it's because of Jude. She shouldn't have to figure all of this out on her own. Unless that's what she wants. I wish she'd tell me.

Before I can say anything else, she exits the car in a single motion. Her body is a blur of colors as she shuts the door without so much as a goodbye. There are a lot of things I regret in life, but this? No... I meant what I said.

I watch her enter her house without a single backward glance. I finally will myself to reverse out of her drive before regret has time to settle in.

I have no idea the extent of the damage my stupid mouth has caused this time. Only time will tell. And that outcome is going to happen a lot sooner than either of us is ready for. Because I'm ninety-nine percent sure I'll be seeing her soon.

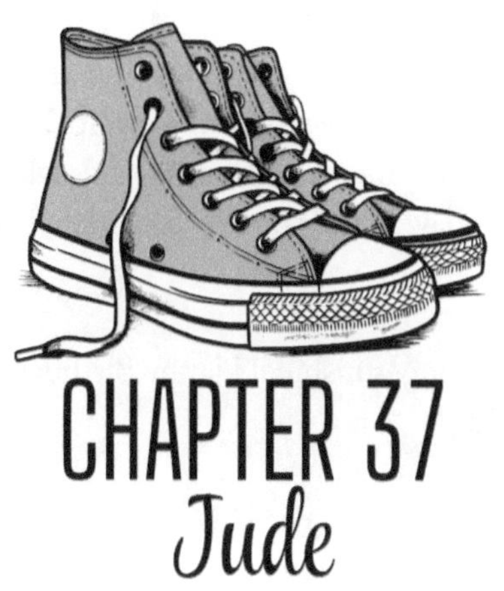

CHAPTER 37
Jude

Me? What does he mean—I'm the reason he's still here? I don't have a clue how to even begin processing that. All I know is that every time I think about it, my head starts to ache. So much so that I woke up this morning with a pounding headache. Maybe it's the alcohol I drank last night, but I doubt it. I didn't have that much. No more than usual.

Sunlight streams into my room. Time to rise and shine. What time is it? I reach over to unplug my phone from its charger and glance at the day and time: Saturday, May 31st, 10:08 a.m. Good thing today is my day off, or I'd be in trouble. As soon as I walked in the door last night, I shed my shoes by the door, my clothes were tossed as I made a beeline for my bed, my head hit the pillow, and I was gone.

It isn't unusual to have unread texts when I wake up, but I have more than normal today. It's to be expected, because I'm turning thirty-three today. Age is just a number anyway, right?

As I unlock my phone, I see that I have six unread text messages and two missed calls from my mom. Must be the kids calling to wish me a happy birthday. And here I am, mid-morning, still buried underneath my covers.

I could easily lie here all day. Sleep the entire day away, and escape it altogether. Because what's the point? I don't have anyone here to celebrate with me. And even if I did, what's there to celebrate anyway? Today is just another Saturday. I pull up my texts first.

Mom: Good morning, sunshine! Happy Birthday! Do you have any plans for today?

Mom: Hey, are you up yet? The kids want to call and wish you a happy birthday. Call when you see this.

Kelly: HEY HEY HEY! Today's your big day! I have a bad hangover today, whoops! But I have a surprise for you later. Text me, I might be napping.

Brian: Happy B-Day, Judy! Kelly is definitely napping today. We can bring your gift any time. Let me know.

Mom-in-Law (Rita): Happy Birthday, dear. I know if Benjamin were here, he'd have the whole day planned out for you. Just know that I'm here if you need anything. I don't have anything going on today. Please don't be afraid to ask. Love you.

Dad: My sweetest Jude. How I love you so. Hope you're doing well. Kids are doing great. Take care of yourself, okay?

By the time I'm done reading through all the messages, my eyes are blurry, and I can feel snot leaking out of my nose. Great. This is not how I want to start my morning. I'm wasting the morning away in bed, every bone in my body aching, because while I am blessed with people who truly love and care about me, I can't escape the pain that today is already bringing me.

Ben isn't here, and he should be.

This is only the first of many birthdays he's going to miss. I can only imagine what this will feel like during the kids' birthdays. Ben had always been the king of birthday celebrations. Heck, his whole life was a celebration. That's just who he was.

I don't want my phone to start exploding with people responding to me, but I quickly type out a message to each person, thanking them for their kind words, before setting my silenced phone back onto the nightstand.

I reach beneath the bed for my green fuzzy headphones. Ben bought these for me a couple of years ago as a silly gift for one of our anniversaries, but I love them so much I can't bear the thought of ever getting rid of them. I select a soft indie station on my phone before sliding the headphones on and closing my eyes.

I'm not tired, I got plenty of sleep. More than I usually get on a night when the kids are here and we have to get up early for school. But my entire body feels exhausted. Everything hurts. Everything aches. The past couple of mornings I've seemed okay... fine even. But today is a new first. I was wrong that today was an ordinary Saturday.

For the next couple of hours, I find myself distracted by my phone. I keep it on silent. I'm still not ready to hear the sound of it ringing. And even though I know it's ridiculous, I kind of hoped I might hear from Jay today.

I don't have his number, and I doubt he has mine. Why would he text or call me? He doesn't even know that today is my birthday. Yet, there's a small nagging feeling that keeps creeping back in. I've enjoyed talking with him, our little conversations in the office over lunch are nice. My opinion of him has changed as I've gotten to know him. He's not as bad as I thought he was. It wouldn't be so bad if I heard from him. Something. Anything. Even a simple, *"Hey, Jude"* would suffice.

But, that doesn't happen, and I can't wallow around forever. Not today of all days. I should get up and do something: play a tune on the old guitar, sit outside with a steaming cup of my favorite coffee, anything.

But I don't do any of those things. Instead, I pull the sheets back up to my chin and slowly drift away. Sleeping is better than feeling. Dreaming is the sweetest escape. Even when it's your birthday.

CHAPTER 38
Jay

didn't sleep much last night. I came home ready to crash, but my brain wouldn't shut down. I lay there in my bed, staring at the constellation of stars I put on the ceiling back in high school. It's so strange being here at twenty-eight, in a room with the ghost of who I used to be.

Some people look back on their lives and can list their defining moments, but what do I have to show for my life? What have I gained in all the years I've been away?

What would Ben say to me if he were still here? I can't help but wonder how things could've been different if I had been strong enough to accept Ben's olive branch. The thought hits hard, knocking the air from my lungs. I reach for my phone and notice Mom standing in my open doorway, eyeing me carefully. She's made it a point to check in on me at least once a day since I've been back home.

It doesn't feel smothering, it's actually nice to have someone care. She's teetering on the fine line of trying her hardest to keep me here, while also trying to give me space so I don't bolt. I don't blame her.

"Hey, Jay. You up?" she asks, one hand resting along the doorframe, the other holding a mug of steaming coffee. She holds it out, and I slowly sit up in bed, re-fluffing my pillows before reaching out to take it.

"Yeah, thanks." I offer her a small smile and take a slow sip. The maple pecan scent hits my nose before the drink reaches my lips. She doesn't forget a thing. It was my dad's favorite, and when I turned fourteen, she started letting me have a cup every morning with him. It quickly became mine as well.

She pulls the old office chair out from my desk and sits in it. Her eyes are shiny and bright, but she looks more tired than usual. Although I don't know if this is how she looks every day, since I haven't been here to notice.

"Do you have any plans today?" she asks me, crossing her right leg over her left.

I take another sip, letting the rich aroma wrap me around like a warm hug. I could use a real one. My eyes water slightly at the thought. Before the funeral, I can't remember the last time someone comforted me with a hug. I sniffle, hoping Mom won't draw attention to it. Thankfully, she doesn't.

I shake my head. "No, I don't. Am I supposed to?" I say, forcing a small smile over what little composure I have left.

"No, that's fine. I just wondered. I've heard you and Judith have been spending time together at the tavern. That's good. She doesn't have many close friends, and could use the company," she says, surprising me a little at this.

She's noticed? She's hardly been to the tavern. She pops in every now and then, but her visits are rare. What's more likely is that someone's noticed us spending more time together and it got back to my mom. And that's... that's a problem.

I don't want to be on anyone's radar. It's no secret how the people here feel about me. But if they see me hanging around someone as pure as Jude, it could damage her reputation. I ruin everything I touch, and the thought of hurting her in any way makes me sick to my stomach.

I'm not one to care what others think, but when someone else is involved and gets hurt at my expense—that's not okay. Especially when that someone is Jude.

While I like being around Jude, it's clear we're spending too much time together. Enough to draw attention, which is the opposite of what I want to do. She doesn't have feelings for me, and most likely never will. It's a "wrong place, wrong time" kind of thing. *I* am the wrong thing.

What Jude needs is space. Time. I am the last thing she needs in her life right now. If anything, I'm just a distraction keeping her from successfully running her tavern. I haven't mentioned to her yet that it's in my name too. But none of that matters if I make it harder for her in the end. I can't do that. I won't.

"Oh," is all I can think of to say. I almost forgot what we were talking about with my spiraling thoughts. Oh, right. Mom mentioned that Jude could use the company. Sure, she needs someone in her corner. Just not me. I can't be that person for her. Anyone but me.

I take another long sip, offering myself a sliver of a distraction. It's not enough.

"Jay... is there," she pauses, thinking about how to ask me whatever she's about to ask.

My stomach pitches. I don't like where this is heading, but there's not much I can do to stop it.

"Is there something going on between you two?"

At this, I set my mug down and focus my attention solely on my mom. Judith. Nobody else calls her that. Of course, my mother would be the only one to call her by her full name. I wonder if Jude has tried to tell my mother otherwise, and she was too proud to listen.

"She likes to be called Jude, and we're just friends, Mom," I defend myself like I'm still a child living under her roof. I feel like she's about to ground me if I don't say the right thing. It only reminds me of last night when I told Jude she's the sole reason I'm still here. I let the truth slip, more than I intended to. But it came out faster than I could stop it. This was my problem, and I needed to fix it as soon as possible.

"Friends," she repeats, staring at me. Trying to see beneath the cracks in the surface.

She won't... She might... She probably will. Moms have this scary intuition I'll never understand.

"Yes. Just friends," I repeat. "It's her tavern. I'm just helping her get back on her feet until she figures out her next steps."

"Next steps?"

"Yeah, if she wants to take over full-time and run everything, or if she wants to hire someone else to manage the tavern."

The question has been nagging me since I got here. I tried to ask her once, but she blew it off. Maybe she's not ready to decide. I know I should just come out and ask her point-blank about running the tavern, but I don't. Possibly because I know she will give me the truth—a truth I may not be ready for.

At this, her eyes go wide, and she quirks an eyebrow at me. I know what she's thinking.

"You haven't told her?" she asks, surprised.

"Told her what?" I play dumb.

"That you might be partners in running the tavern. That she doesn't have to figure this out on her own, because you're thinking of stepping up and running it with her. It's not just her business now, Jay, it's yours too. You know that."

"Key word: *might*. Of course, she doesn't know, and I don't plan on telling her. There's nothing to discuss. I don't know if I want to run the tavern, Mom. That's why I'm here, so I can figure that out. But you have to let me figure that out on my own." Maybe I'm more afraid of finding out that I'm not cut out for this. That maybe I won't ever be.

She looks at me, her eyes softening, and she nods her head, understanding.

"I know. You're right. Just please be careful with her heart, okay?" she pleads with me.

Her heart? What is that supposed to mean? We're just friends; whoever said anything about her heart? The moment our hearts get involved, we'll both be in real trouble.

"We're friends, Mom. Her heart is going to be fine," I say, even though I know that's a lie.

Her heart is anything but fine. The moment she received the news about my brother, her heart shattered into a thousand tiny pieces. A thousand pieces that I don't have the power to fix, and that thought breaks me.

"I trust you to make the right decision when it's time. And speaking of friends and Jude..." She pauses when she says her nickname. She quickly adds, "Have you wished her a happy birthday yet?"

Today is her birthday? She hadn't mentioned anything to me. Of course, she didn't. She's far too humble to boast about that, although I wouldn't have minded. Birthdays are worth celebrating. At least hers is.

I shake my head because I had no idea. "No, I didn't know it was today. Can I get her number from you?" I ask.

Friends. Am I still her friend? I was the half-brother to her husband, and now I'm nothing. We don't share any kind of connection other than the person who is no longer here. So what are we? Who are we to each other? I don't know, and maybe it doesn't matter anyway.

I don't know if she has anything planned for today, but my guess is that she's home alone. It's her first birthday without her husband, and her kids are away. I can only imagine how alone she must be feeling. I'm not sure my presence will help, but it doesn't hurt to try. That's what a friend would do.

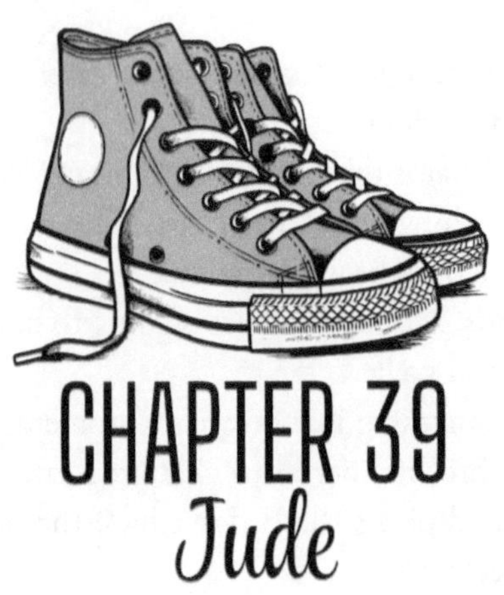

CHAPTER 39
Jude

When I finally open my eyes again, it's nearly one in the afternoon. I've spent my entire birthday morning in bed. But the moment my eyes first opened, I knew in my soul that I didn't want to celebrate today. Or any day for that matter.

I'm disappointed that it's *only* one o'clock. The sky is as bright as ever, mocking me in my pathetic state.

If Ben is looking down on me right now, he's shaking his head in disgust. This is not how he would've wanted me to spend my day.

Well, you know what, Benny? You're not here to have a say in the matter. So, there.

Yelling at my dead husband in my head doesn't make me feel any better. I know what he'd tell me to do.

Make yourself the largest cup of coffee you have. Then take two aspirin for your head and go outside. Go for a walk around the block, or just sit outside on the back deck and read a book! But don't lie there doing nothing. It's your birthday, Jude, wear something sparkly or pink. Celebrate already!

Nope, thinking about him is not helping me one bit.

Reluctantly, I roll out of bed and straighten the cover, like it's a normal day. Then I follow imaginary Ben's advice and pop two aspirins before taking a much-needed hot shower.

I feel a little better. Baby steps. At least I'm finally out of bed and moving. Doing something.

Then, I call my mom. I hope to avoid explaining what I've done with my day so far, which is absolutely nothing. Luckily, she doesn't ask. The kids are just happy to see me again, even if it's over a screen.

I miss them. More than I ever imagined I would. But they need this time away from the immediate pain of losing their daddy. I can't even think about it, or I'll be sucked back under again. Not now, not today.

They tell me all about their waterpark adventure and an art camp they are both going to next week. It sounds wonderful, and I'm thankful that they're doing so well, despite the tragedy that has taken over our lives.

Of course, by the end of the call, they are ready to take off, only stopping to ask me how many more days until I get to come see them. I give them the countdown—twenty-eight days—and they run away to play, happy that I'm coming soon. So far, they seem to be holding up better than I am.

After we end the call, I finish getting ready, grab my phone and a book, and sit outside on our back deck. As I'm scrolling through, looking for a song to play in the background, a new text pops up. I open the message, only to realize it's from a number I don't have saved.

Unknown number: Hey, Jude. Wanted to wish you a happy birthday. What are you up to?

Before I can type out a response, another message comes through.

Unknown number: Sorry, I forgot to say who this is. It's Jay.

My stomach swoops when I see who it's from. Jay. The text surprises me a little, although it shouldn't. I'm sure he got my number from his mom. All I've been able to think about since last night is the last thing he said to me. That *I'm* the reason he's still here. Why me? It doesn't make any sense, but I'm not going to discuss that with him over text message.

I type out a response.

Me: Hey, Jay. Thanks. I'm not doing much. Getting some vitamin D and attempting to read.

Jay: Attempting?

Me: Yeah.

Jay: How's that working out?

Me: Not so great. I thought a thriller sounded fun. No romances for me right now. But I'm having a hard time concentrating.

Jay: Why no romances?

Me: Isn't it obvious?

Jay: Not to me.

Me: Do you read?

Jay: Yeah, some. You skipped my question.

Of course, he would notice. Even in text, he holds nothing back. I like that about him... I think.

Me: Because they all hit too close to home. I can't read about falling in love right now, not when I don't even get my own happily ever after.

I watch the tiny bubbles appear on the screen to show he's typing, but then they disappear, and a few minutes tick by. For a moment, I'm worried I've scared him off. I give up waiting and start to swipe back through my song list when another message from him appears.

Jay: Who says your happily-ever-after has to end?

Me: What do you mean?

Jay: Remember when I asked if you believed in life after love?

Me: Of course. How could I forget something like that?

Jay: Just checking. I was a bit buzzed that day. Sorry about that. Anyway... I don't want to come across as insensitive, believe me, that's not my intention at all. But just because one love story ends, doesn't mean you won't get to experience another.

I ponder his words. I read them again and again, trying to make sense of it. I get what he's trying to say, but I don't see how it's possible. Not for me. It's way too soon to be thinking about falling in love again. The very thought makes me feel sick.

I can't do that. Not to Ben, the love of my life. My soul mate. There is nobody after him, and Jay can't see that because he's not in my shoes. I can't fault him for thinking that way and trying to cheer me up, but he's wrong. I need to make that clear to him so he knows.

After all, we're just friends. I thought we were both on the same page, but maybe I gave him the wrong idea about me.

Me: I disagree. Ben was my love story. Epilogue and all. Our love story was a standalone romance, nothing more. There will never be a sequel. It's not in the cards for me.

Jay: Why not?

Me: I don't know. Why are you asking? Why do you care?

I don't mean for my words to come out sounding insensitive, and I instantly regret hitting send. I start quickly typing out something to undo the harshness in my words, but his message comes through first.

Jay: Because I believe that you deserve to be happy. I'm not saying right now. But someday. Anyway... I'll let you get back to your reading. Unless you haven't had lunch yet... I can take you somewhere if you'd like.

Jay: Not a date, of course, because we're just friends.

I smile to myself when that last text comes through. I can't explain it, but his need to clarify brings a smile to my face. I guess we're on the same page after all.

I don't think I'm going to get anywhere in a book today, and honestly, getting out of the house sounds great. Even if I don't agree with Jay on the whole "finding love again" thing. We don't have to see eye-to-eye on everything for us to be friends. Because that's what we are, friends.

Me: Lunch sounds great. I haven't eaten yet.

Jay: Got anywhere in mind?

Me: Yes, I do. How do you feel about Mexican?

Jay: Great. I can be there in fifteen. Sound good?

Me: Perfect. I'll be ready.

Me: Looking forward to lunch. Not a date ;)

He doesn't respond, but he doesn't need to. I'm just glad to finally be celebrating. Even if I don't entirely feel like it. I'm going to do it anyway, simply because I can.

CHAPTER 40
Jay

The first thing I notice when I pick her up is that her hair is down. I'm instantly reminded of the night I brought her pizza in the pouring rain. Her hair had been down then too. It's still just as gorgeous. She greets me at her front door with a soft smile, wearing a light yellow shirt the color of dandelions, white shorts, and matching Converse, of course.

Whether or not she feels as bright as she looks on the outside, I'm glad she agreed to come.

I'm used to eating lunch at random times, but she strikes me as someone who abides by daily routines. Then again, I know better than to make assumptions.

We arrive at a local Mexican restaurant around three, and while it's busy, it's not even close to how busy the tavern gets. She orders a steaming plate of fajitas, and I order one of the lunch specials that will also be my dinner tonight.

There's a lot of food.

Jude came with an appetite. As petite as she is, that girl can slam down some chips and queso.

It's almost four in the afternoon by the time we head back to my car, and I can instantly feel sweat tingling along my neck from nerves. Why does she make me so nervous?

Sometimes it feels like that, though. Like we never met ten years ago at her wedding. It was so long ago, she probably doesn't even remember me being there. I hadn't really wanted to be seen. Ben didn't ask me to be his best man, and it nearly killed me. I didn't end up staying for their reception. I called up some buddies of mine from school and got wasted so I could forget the hurt I felt.

Now, all I'm left with is regret. Regret for the things that I can't undo.

For a moment, we sit in the silent car, neither of us wanting to be the first to speak. To break the spell. *Friends.* I'm not ready for my time with Jude to end. I like spending time with her. I feel different around her than I do anybody else. At least she's here trying to give me a second chance, the rest of the town pretends I don't exist.

Maybe to them, I don't. And I might have this whole thing wrong, it wouldn't be the first time. But when I'm around her, she makes me feel *seen*. And it means a lot to me.

"So, would you like me to take you back home? Or..." I trail off. I don't want to put ideas in her head. This is supposed to be *her* birthday celebration, it has nothing to do with me.

She runs a hand through her hair, shaking it out a little before glancing my way. My skin is still tingling. Nervous energy buzzing.

"Or what?" she asks me.

"I don't know. Whatever you want to do is fine by me. Really." I'm so bad at this. Why can't I hold a normal conversation with her?

She doesn't act like it fazes her one bit. She tilts her head to the side, thinking. Probably about how to politely tell me off. This friend thing is a bad idea, and it's better if we just stick to our separate roles when we're at work.

I'm in my head again.

She pulls me out of my spiraling thoughts. "Actually, I do have something else in mind... if you're up for it."

Of course, I am. I'm up for anything. It's not like I have anything else to do on a Saturday in a place that's long forgotten me. I don't blame them. If I were them, I'd have done the same.

"What is it?"

"I'll just have to show you," she says with a hint of challenge in her voice.

I can't help smirking. "Where to?"

"Back to my place. Unless there's somewhere you need to be right now."

I shake my head. Even if I did, I'd cancel. This is better. Something tells me I should say yes.

There's a smaller voice whispering, *Do you know what you're getting yourself into?*

No, I have no idea. And that's okay.

CHAPTER 41
Jude

The temperature outside has dropped a couple of degrees, and the sounds of Jay strumming my guitar go along perfectly with the soft hums of nature.

It's been too long since I've sang. I can't believe it's finally happening. It surprises me that not only can Jay play the guitar, but he's good at it. *Stupid good.* I had no idea.

When I first mentioned to him that I wanted to try out a few notes and see how they made me feel, I never would've guessed we'd be out here for two hours singing songs together like we did this every night.

It's the strangest thing, and I never saw it coming. Never in a thousand years did I imagine sitting here with Ben's brother on my back deck, on my birthday, playing with reckless abandon.

It's so absurd that a laugh suddenly escapes me. I instantly clamp a hand over my mouth, and Jay smiles over at me mid-strum. I don't have a clue what's gotten into me. I can only imagine what Ben would be thinking right now if he could see us.

"What's so funny? Did I sing something inappropriate just now? You're making fun of me." He laughs.

I've never heard him laugh so openly like this. It's a vibrant sound I wish I could play again.

It's crazy to think that he's only been here a few weeks. We could've had a whole decade to know each other as family, yet we never got that chance. *He* never gave us that chance.

I decide not to hold that over him, though. I shouldn't hold grudges or stay bitter about something that happened so long ago. I may never fully understand what went on between the two men, but it no longer matters. He's here now. He's here because of *me*. I just wish he were here for another reason... anything but that one.

Being here for me makes the least amount of sense. If it's true, it makes me question everything. It makes me question him and what his true intentions are. That's why I drew a clear friendship line. That's all we can ever be, and I hope he knows that.

My mood suddenly shifts, and I cross my ankles in front of me as I stare down at my bare feet. I can't look him in the eyes.

"No, that's not it," I say honestly.

"Then what is it?" He sets my guitar down in his lap and rests both hands on the top of it.

"I was just thinking that if Ben could see us right now, he'd think it's funny. Seeing us together, I mean," I say, hearing literal crickets in the summer breeze.

I sneak a glance over at Jay and notice that his entire body has gone rigid. In a flash, my words turned the tables. But maybe this is a good thing... We need to talk this out. Too many things get swept under the rug, and I feel like this is a safe enough space to say whatever it is we're feeling right now. We need to clear the air.

Because I can sense the tension. It's something electric and terrifying.

I'm positive we can both feel it.

"Hmm," he says after a minute. He sounds distant and suddenly checked out.

Moments ago, we were laughing and singing the most random songs we could think of—together. I hadn't felt an ounce of anxiety singing in front of him, because it hadn't felt like a performance. Neither of us had done it to put on a show. It was simply two friends making music. Now, the silence between us hangs heavy and as sharp as a knife.

"Yeah, you're probably right. Where do you think he is right now?" he asks, surprising me with his question.

I expected him to change the subject, rather than diving in deeper. But he didn't. He embraced it.

"Well, my kids believe he's in Heaven," I say, pulling a chunk of my hair over my shoulder and fidgeting with it.

"Do you?"

"Oh, um. Yeah, I guess I do." I don't know why I hesitate. I truly do believe that he's in Heaven. I have to. I have to hold onto the hope that I'll get to see him again someday, because if I don't...

"Well, that's good. I'm not sure what I believe in anymore," he admits. His light brown hair reflects the sunlight, giving it a golden hue.

I'd never admit this out loud, but he's rather good-looking. His hair isn't perfectly combed tonight like it usually is when he's working with me at the tavern, it's slightly messier. His grayish-blue eyes sparkle as the sun begins its descent in the sky.

I quickly pull my thoughts away from him and stare up into the vast expanse of the universe. It's been a while since I've admired it all.

"Yeah, me neither. Some days it's hard to believe that a good God would allow something like this to happen," I say, holding back tears.

"I know, I've wondered that too. And for what it's worth, I'm sorry about Ben. You don't deserve to go through something like this." He sets down the guitar and turns his chair to face me.

I can feel my heart pounding in my chest.

There's still a quiet buzz around us, and I don't think it's mosquitoes.

A tiny "Yeah" is all I manage to squeak out.

"What do you need right now, Jude? What can I do for you?" he asks me softly, gently.

He really, truly cares. I don't know why. I don't know why he suddenly showed up and decided to stay, but he cares.

About me.

About what happened to me and to his brother. He understands the gravity of it all.

Possibly better than anyone else. He came with his own burdens to bury.

I shake my head because the tears are on the verge of falling now.

Don't. Please not now.

"I don't know... I don't think there's anything," my voice shakes when I speak, there's no hiding the tremble in it now.

I watch Jay lift slowly out of his chair, making his way over to me. His movements are slow and cautious. He's waiting for my permission to close the space between us. I've noticed that about him. He often waits for a sign from me. Has he always been this way? Or is this something he only does with me?

Electricity crackles through the air.

"Anything. Anything you need. I don't care what it is."

A single tear escapes down my cheek, and before I have a chance to keep my plea locked inside where it belongs, my mouth opens against my will and says, "Can you hold me? Please. Just for a little while."

He doesn't bat an eye at my request, and swiftly scoops me up into his arms and carries me over to the porch steps. He places me gently in his lap, wrapping his arms securely around me. It's at that moment I break. All of me falls apart.

This is what it feels like to let go.

This is what it looks like to let my heart split open wide. Yet somehow, it doesn't feel the same as hiding under my covers, crying myself to sleep.

No, this is a different kind of pain.

The healing kind.

Because my blanket is in the form of human arms. Something I never thought I'd experience again.

CHAPTER 42
Jay

quickly find out that Jude is full of surprises. Like when she said she wanted to sing a few songs. I agreed immediately because I was hoping I'd get to hear her sing. I still have an old guitar I was gifted by my father back in high school, sitting in my room, untouched. As soon as I get home, I plan on tuning it up and messing around on it for a bit.

I'm a bit rusty tonight. It's been a while since I played anything, and it feels good. Refreshing. I haven't played a single chord since I moved out. Music is something I left behind. But tonight, seeing an old Martin acoustic with sunburst coloring collecting dust in the corner of her living room, something about it calls out to me.

When she mentioned it was one of the first gifts Ben ever gave her, I almost changed my mind about asking to play it. I didn't want to touch the sacred and precious gift from the person she loved the most. It didn't seem right.

But then she's crossing the room and placing the guitar in my hands. She said she's still learning to play, and asked me to play something. That was all the permission I needed.

The moment my fingers strum the first few chords of a song we both know, it becomes second nature. I don't have to think about the motions, they just come to me.

And Jude's voice, it's pure gold, like I knew it would be. She has this quiet confidence about her that's mesmerizing.

The moment she opens her mouth and the first few words pour out, I'm sucked right into her spell. She has a natural singing voice. She surprises me with her talent in the best way. I don't deserve to spend all this time with her, and there's a part of me that feels a little selfish accepting it all so easily.

But then my brother's name is brought up in our private space. I mean, how could it not? As if being here isn't already enough reminder of the person we both lost. If Ben were still alive, I wouldn't be here. Would I have ever come back if he hadn't left for good?

I honestly don't know.

That truth might turn June away from me. She wouldn't give me a single glance again. She'd be done with me for good.

I have to accept that Ben is still the love of her life. I get it, really, I do. It's stupid of me to think otherwise.

I'm snapped back into reality the moment she drops his name into the space between us. Bursting the bubble of my silly fantasies that clutter my brain as we sit together on her deck, making memories with our music.

Music that isn't really for me to share with her, yet here I am, doing it anyway. Again, I had the wool pulled over my eyes.

But then, she asks me to do something impossible. It's all my fault. I offered myself to her in the first place. I take her in my arms and try to hold her through her pain. What she probably doesn't realize is that she's holding me through mine as well.

At that moment, she begins changing something within me that I can't explain, even if I try to. So I won't. Not now.

It isn't long before we make our way back inside. Gathering up the shards of our pasts with us, as though we aren't both a little lost and broken. Because that's exactly what we are. Maybe me in more ways than she is. But her pain is far greater than mine.

We're sitting on opposite sides of her couch, getting ready to start a movie. She mentioned *The Princess Diaries* being one of her favorites, but didn't want to force her girly chick flicks on me. It honestly doesn't bother me at all. Anything to help settle my inner turmoil sounds great. The back and forth in my mind about all the reasons I should be here, and the reasons I shouldn't.

It's both strange and nice to be here. Lately, I feel like a life-size puzzle. There are many gaps between my brother and me, yet Jude seems to fill in those missing pieces.

Pieces of her I never knew, but also pieces of him, too. The fact that he didn't own a record player but collected vinyl records. They're showcased along one of the walls as an accent piece.

These are things I could've learned about him on my own. But every time I'm in her presence, I get a small glimpse of who my brother really was, and just how much he meant to the love of his life.

I let her steer the ship. I want her to have the first and final say. She allowed herself to be completely vulnerable in my arms for just a moment. That alone is both too much, and not enough. I can't seem to get enough of her lately, and it doesn't make any sense.

The first day she saw me, anger and hurt flashed in her eyes. Because of the damage I caused to her and Ben over the years. While that look has softened over the last couple of weeks with her, every now and then, I can almost feel it simmering at a low boil underneath the surface.

One wrong move, or word, and she might boil over. It's a difficult balance, because while I understand she's grieving, she's also strong and capable of more than she realizes.

I have to erase all the dangerous thoughts I keep having about Jude from my mind. But the more time I spend with her, the more vibrant they become. I know I should keep my distance, but she wouldn't have said yes to lunch if she didn't mean it, right? And this time, she's the one who invited me into her home. I didn't just show up unannounced like the other night in the pouring rain. She asked me to come.

But I'm getting too far into my head again.

Making something out of nothing.

We're friends, and she doesn't want to spend her birthday alone. Who would?

I'm embarrassed to admit that I've never watched this movie. But I don't hate it. It's pretty good.

As we're watching, Jude explains how she relates to the premise of the movie. That we often feel ugly and unqualified because the world's telling us we should. But we can do anything we set out to do. We don't have to live by the world's standards, we're created for so much more.

Before I have the chance to ask her to explain what she means by that last part, her eyes grow heavy and she drifts off. I leave the movie on and watch it until the end. I'm already in deep, and I have to know how it ends. I can easily see why this classic is one of her favorites.

When the movie first started, we were both on opposite ends of the couch. Sometime during the film, like magnets, we inched closer and closer together. By the time her long lashes flutter closed, and her chest rises and falls with the gentle rhythm of her breaths, her head has made its way onto my shoulder. The left side of her body is pressing into mine, and I don't mind that either.

Her long, wild hair spills around her. When the credits start to roll, I just watch her breathing. Her breaths are slow and steady, like the soft beating of a drum or the hum of a hummingbird's wings. With her head on my shoulder, I don't want to move. This is the closest we've ever been to one another, and I'm not ready for this moment to end. But I also know we can't stay like this all night, as much as I would love to.

I shift away from her as carefully as possible, trying not to wake her up. She's so calm and peaceful. I wonder when she last slept this deeply. Heaven knows I haven't been sleeping lately.

I grab one of the pillows that had fallen to the floor at some point. I use the pillow to gently prop her head up, tucking her in with a soft blanket.

I don't want to leave, but I force myself to turn away from her. If I don't walk away now, it'll make it that much harder to go. I hope when she wakes, she won't remember the pain that had knocked her down earlier. How often has she been trampled by the weight of grief on her own? The thought is crippling.

I hope she remembers how good it felt to sing. For a moment, I saw her come alive again. Something I never thought I'd get to be a part of. Not this soon. Not today.

She invited me into her space and let down some of her walls around her heart. I know that wasn't easy. It's something I'm working on doing in my own life.

But she taught me a couple of things tonight. Sometimes surprises come in the small things—moments worth remembering. Tiny sparks. A reason to keep going. To keep living. To fight for another tomorrow.

And to be here for her—to remind her on the days she forgets. On the days when grief clouds everything, and she can't see past her own two feet.

I know her grief isn't something that will ever disappear completely. I'm grieving too. Much more than I show. Jude isn't afraid to feel, even if she doesn't like it. Even if it means being uncomfortable for a moment. I like that about her. There are a lot of things I like about her. When she's with me, I feel that she's being real—no masks, no games.

I can only hope that she keeps on surprising me, because one of these days she might even surprise herself.

CHAPTER 43
Jude

So, love, tell me how you're really doing." Kelly asks from across the booth we're sharing during our lunch break. It's Monday, the second day of June. A new month, a new week, a new beginning. Only I wish it felt like that. Everything lately feels like the end of something.

I know that's just my bad thoughts taking over.

I take a long sip from my iced caramel latte before answering my friend. She hadn't given me her gift on my actual birthday, so as soon as I opened the tavern at eleven this morning, she'd been there to surprise me with a scrapbook she made herself.

She had tears in her eyes when handing it to me, and she told me to save it for a day when I needed a good cry. But not now. I tucked it away in the office. Maybe I'd glance at it later. The gesture was super kind and thoughtful of her.

Summer is just beginning, but already this Oklahoma heat is insane. People in Bethel like to joke that our weather is bipolar because of how up and down it can be. It might reach one hundred degrees today. Kelly has a pool, and she told me I'm welcome to use it anytime.

"Fine, I guess? Okay, not fine. It's weird, though," I say as I lean in a little closer, like what I'm about to share is a secret. It's not, but it's a small town and people talk. Anything you say can be used against you. There's a group on Facebook called Bethel Knows Best where people say whatever they want just to stir up drama.

I left the group ages ago, but I'm pretty sure Kelly is still in it to stay in the loop of the latest gossip around town.

"Some days it hits me like a freight train. I wake up and my body feels as though it's been run over, like a physical pain. I have trouble sleeping, too. I lie there tossing and turning, trying to shut off my brain."

Kelly's blue eyes pierce mine as she takes a large bite of her deli sandwich. There are surprisingly a decent number of coffee shops in Bethel, but this one has been our favorite for a while. It's quiet and cozy. Plus, they serve food during the lunch hour.

"And then other times I do feel fine. Like I can still go out and shop for groceries or make it to the Y for a Zumba class. It's like I can breathe. My schedule is more sporadic now, but sometimes it's like I almost forget that it ever happened. Then, as though someone flipped a light switch in my brain, I suddenly lose it. I'm so hot and cold right now, it's exhausting. This is my life, Kelly."

I ordered the chicken salad sandwich, but I haven't taken a bite yet. I'm too amped up. There's something I want to ask her, but I'm not sure it's a topic I can talk to her about. It's not that I don't trust her, because I do. If there's anyone I trust, it's her, but I'm not sure I want to know her opinion on the matter.

"Aww, sweetie. I'm so sorry. I don't even know what to say. This is all so hard and fresh for all of us. Brian is taking his death really hard. He's been so depressed, Jude. He might start seeing his therapist again." Her eyes go from light baby blues to an intense shade of ocean water.

I had no idea everyone was taking it so hard. But it makes sense. He was as big a part of their lives as he was in mine. Of course, losing your spouse is different than losing your boss... but he was also Brian's best friend. I'm not even sure I have a best friend. Kelly is the closest I have, but I'm not sure *best* describes our friendship. Maybe someday.

"I'm sorry to hear that, Kelly," I say, finally taking a big bite of my sandwich. I don't have much of an appetite, but I try to eat anyway.

She nods as she takes another bite.

"We're gonna be okay. It doesn't feel like it right now. Probably not for a long time. But I just have this feeling, you know? We're all gonna be alright. You, me, Brian, and the tavern. Speaking of which... Do you have any idea what Jay's plans are?"

I almost spit out my food. What?

"His plans?" I retort stupidly. I have no idea what she's talking about. I haven't spoken to him since Saturday, when he watched me fall apart in front of him, and then I fell asleep on the couch. I hadn't woken up until two the next morning, and when I checked my phone, he left me a message that said:

Jay: I had a great time with you tonight. Let's do it again sometime.

I almost forgot about our little jam session we had. How could I possibly forget something like that? What did it mean?

"Yeah. He's been here since the funeral, which I think is cool since he's Ben's brother. But isn't it sort of weird? Him still being here, I mean." Her eyes are wide as she takes a sip from her drink.

Yeah, it's strange. I've wondered the same thing, and when I asked him point-blank, he gave me an answer that sent me into a complete spiral. I still don't know what to make of it and haven't braved asking him about it further.

"Yeah, definitely," I say, not wanting to elaborate. As in, yeah,

I'm the reason he's still here. Whatever that means. We're just friends.

Friends.

"I've noticed you two hanging out more lately, which is nice. I think he needs a familiar face in a crazy place like this. I just didn't know if he said anything about his reasons for staying."

At this, I down the rest of my drink. I can feel my cheeks betraying me as they turn a soft shade of pink, matching the color of my favorite pair of Converse.

"Oh? You know something! Spill."

I shake my head. "Nothing. I don't know why he's still here. Maybe he just misses his mom," I offer with a shrug.

We both know that's a lie, but it's the best I could come up with on a moment's notice. Kelly sees straight through it. She has a way of doing that.

"Nope, that's not it. Come on, love. Tell me what's going on. Why is he here working at our tavern?"

I love that she said *our* tavern. Another gentle reminder that these people, *Ben's people*, still have my back. Even though he's gone, the people who care the most are still here, cheering me on. I take a deep breath and place my hands on my cheeks, resting my elbows on the table. A long sigh escapes me, and I stare down.

"He said he stuck around because of me," I say so softly that it almost comes out as a whisper. I'm not sure she heard me because she goes silent. The only sounds are the whir of a coffee machine in the background, moms chattering with their kids, and the soft clinking sound of utensils against plates.

When she finally breaks the silence, her voice has lowered an octave to avoid listening ears. "Because of you..." she repeats, astonished.

I nod. "Yeah."

"What does that mean? Jude... Does he have feelings for you?"

I was afraid she would ask me this. I'm not sure I want to

know the answer myself. Because I have no idea what the truth would do to me if I were ever brave enough to find out.

"I... I don't think so. We're just friends. I think he feels guilty for not being closer to Ben, and I think a part of him doesn't want to leave because of that guilt. You heard him at the funeral, right? That was the first time I ever heard him speak like that about his brother, and I could tell it had been eating at him for a while. I think he's just hurting, like we all are, and needed a change of scenery."

I don't know if that's the full truth, but it takes some of the focus off me... For now, anyway.

She nods in agreement. "Yeah, you're probably right. That makes sense."

She pauses.

There's more. I can always tell when she has something else to say, because she'll pause, chew her lip, and then release it right before she launches into whatever she was holding back.

"But if he's starting to develop feelings towards you, please be careful with your heart. I'm not saying he's a bad guy, I don't know him all that well. But I care for you like I would a sister, and I know how fragile your heart is. Bottom line, I don't want to see you get hurt," she says, reaching across the table and taking my hands in hers.

"We're friends, that's all," I repeat, more to myself than to her. If I say it enough times, maybe it'll stay true. We can't be more than friends. He has to know that, right? I'm sure I've made myself clear. And it was I who asked him to come over, and I asked him to hold me. He hasn't stepped out of line at all.

Asking him to hold me had been harmless. Nothing else happened. But it's a dangerous line to have crossed. One I never should've allowed to happen. If lines are getting blurred, it's my fault, not his.

"Okay, love. I believe you. But if it *does* become something more, keep your heart protected, okay?"

"It won't."

"Will you at least promise me?"

There's nothing to promise her, but I do it anyway.

"I don't like him like that. Ben will always be the love of my life," I say through clenched teeth. I'm not upset at her, I'm upset at the circumstances, and at Ben for putting me through this.

I know none of this is anyone's fault. Yet, somehow, it eases the pain a little if there's someone else to blame.

"I know that, dear. I know. I trust your judgement. Please just promise me for my peace of mind. And then I'll drop it. We don't have to talk about it anymore."

My hands still in hers, I quickly nod my head. Ready to put an end to this conversation. This is not the direction I pictured it going. I'm sure we have someone's attention in here by now, but I don't dare glance around.

"I promise," I say resolutely, letting our hands drop back down to the table.

She nods her head gently and offers me a soft smile. I fake a smile back and eat the rest of my sandwich.

I already know the promise is useless, because I'm not sure we were ever really friends to begin with.

CHAPTER 44
Jay

t's Friday, and Jude has barely spoken a word to me all week. I've still been eating lunch in the office every day, but she's obviously changed her schedule. I don't understand why—or what I did. Maybe it doesn't have anything to do with me at all, and she just needs space. I shouldn't be quick to make assumptions, that never does anyone any good.

I should talk to her. That's hard to do, though, when she hasn't been around. I saw her leave with Kelly a little while ago. I haven't seen Jude talk much with anyone else, but the two of them seem pretty close. And Jude needs every little piece of sunshine she can get right now.

As I'm finishing up my lunch, something colorful catches my eye from the shelf next to the bulletin board. I ignore it at first, but curiosity gets to me, and I go over to see what it is. When I get up close, I quickly see that it's a scrapbook. The front cover is covered in sparkling jewels, cutouts from a newspaper, and a collage of pictures.

It's not my place to look through it. Yet somehow, my fingers have a mind of their own. Before long, I've flipped through every single page. Inside the front of the album is a note in bubbly handwriting that reads:

Hey, love, Brian & I put this together for you as a keepsake. This may cause some tears, but with any luck, they'll be healing ones. I also hope it helps you reminisce about all our good times, because we've had plenty over the last decade. Love you like a sis!
Xo, Kelly & B.

Kelly and Brian seem like really good people. From what I've heard from others around here, they were the closest couple to Ben and Jude. Brian is also a firefighter and had been there with Ben the night he died. It tears me up inside anytime I think about it.

Most of the pictures are from the tavern over the years. The pictures are in chronological order from oldest to newest. The last picture in the album is an image of Jude on stage singing. She's playing guitar with her eyes closed, and Ben is sitting on a barstool near the stage watching her with love in his eyes.

Jude is still in love with Ben, and probably will be for a long time. When you lose someone the way she lost Ben, I'm not sure it's something you can ever move on from. Not completely. Their hearts were tethered to each other the day they said "I do." I know because I was there, and I remember.

I've never had the privilege of experiencing a love like they have. I've only experienced tiny glimpses of love. I'm not sure I'll ever experience an everlasting one. Some things just aren't written in the stars for everyone.

I keep reading over the final words Kelly wrote in the back of the scrapbook for Jude:

This is not the end of your story, this is just the next chapter.

I wonder what Jude thought about this when her friend gave it to her. A part of me is filled with regret for peeking, but a larger part of me is glad I stumbled across it.

This scrapbook is full of memories I could've been a part of, but I chose differently. If only I could take it back and tell him yes when he asked me. We could've been business partners. Jude wouldn't have to deal with all this on her own. She wouldn't be left scraping up the pieces, because I would've already been here. Yes, I'm here now, but does it matter? What if I'm too late to fix what's beyond repair?

Jude doesn't return when Kelly does. When I try to casually ask Kelly where Jude is, she says she has some errands to run and probably won't be back in until Monday. A sinking feeling settles in the pit of my stomach. Maybe she is avoiding me after all. There's only one way to find out.

Me: Hey

It's lame and way too casual for everything racing through my brain, but it's all I've got. Slow, baby steps. I'm worried I've already scared her off, and I don't want to make things worse than they already are.

She replies within a few seconds.

Jude: Hey, back. What's up? Everything okay at the tavern?

Me: Oh yes, it's fine. I'm just seeing if you're okay.

Jude: Yep, all good. Just have to run some errands this afternoon.

Me: I gotcha. Can I ask you something?

Jude: Okay

Me: Did I say or do something that upset *you?*

At this, she doesn't respond for a few minutes. The dots appear and then disappear. My stomach clenches in knots, waiting in anticipation.

Jude: No, it's nothing like that… I have too much in my head and need a little space. Sorry, I haven't been around as much. Busy figuring things out.

Me: I get that. There's always too much in my head. If you ever wanna talk about it, I'm a pretty good listener. Just wanted to check in.

Jude: Thanks, I appreciate it.

Jude: Actually, I might have a favor to ask if you're up for it.

Me: Okay, shoot me with it.

Jude: How would you feel about playing my guitar for me

tonight? I have a song picked out that I'd like to try. But, seriously, no pressure. It's last-minute.

Me: Of course, count me in! Will we have a little time to practice beforehand?

Jude: Yes, I can bring us a bite to eat, and we can practice for a bit.

Me: I still have my old guitar at my house, if you're okay meeting there?

I know it's a risk asking her to come to my house. But I recently tuned up my old guitar and have been playing quite a bit more lately. It's been a good distraction from smoking while I'm home. I can't whip out my guitar at the tavern and burst into song when I have a craving. Still, it's something. I wonder when Jude last set foot into Mom's house.

Jude may call the whole thing off. I don't know how often Mom invited her and Ben over, or what memories Jude has of our childhood home. The chance that Mom will be there is also pretty high.

Me: You know what...

I'm in the middle of typing out a text backtracking my invite, when she beats me to the punch.

Jude: Okay, we can do that. How's seven? I'll still bring us food.

Me: Yep, perfect. See you then.

Jude: What were you gonna say?

Me: I was making sure that you were okay with coming over. I understand if it's too triggering for you to be there.

Jude: That's okay. I can't avoid it forever. I'll be there.

Those same three words that I'd said to her not that long ago. I could only hope we were both willing to hold onto our promise to each other.

CHAPTER 45
Jude

Walking into Ben's childhood home immediately sends me into a time warp. It feels like ages have passed since I was here last. I wonder if this is similar to how it felt for Jay to step across the threshold for the first time in ten years. That had to have felt strange, to say the least.

Ben spent a lot more time here with his mom than I ever did. Not that I wasn't fond of Rita, because she truly is a great mother-in-law and grandmother to my kids. But she rarely invited all of us over. I saw her mostly when she'd pop into the tavern from time to time, which had been less and less over the years after Ben's dad passed.

She still manages all the finances, but generally from the comfort of her own home. Ben met with her a few times a week to check in and see how things were going. For the most part, they left me out of it. I have a feeling, someday soon, I'll need to start looking into the finances myself. Unless it's something she still wants to do. If that's the case, I'd never dream of taking that away from her. It's a conversation we still need to have. It feels a little strange being here now, like I'm a stranger walking into somebody else's space.

Luckily, when I arrive, I'm not greeted at the door by Rita, but by Jay. I picked up some Chinese takeout on the way, and he immediately leads me down the long, familiar hallway to his bedroom. The first room is an office, where Jay's dad, Scott, used to work, followed by Ben's and Jay's rooms, which sit across the hall from each other. The master bedroom is at the far end of the hallway. The doors to both the master and Ben's are shut, thankfully.

I hold my breath as we walk past Ben's old room. I'm not sure what that room is used for now, since it's been years since Ben last used it. But still, the memories are there, and the ghost of him lives in every room in this house.

I place my palm gently over the door of his room, as if I could sense that he still somehow belongs here. The wooden door doesn't feel any different beneath my hand. Still. I find myself longing for little pieces of him. As though holding my hand here can magically absorb everything that reminds me of my husband.

Jay halts when he notices I'm no longer right behind him. He tilts his head over his shoulder and studies me carefully, his gaze softening.

"You can go in if you'd like. I'm sure Mom won't mind. It probably looks the same as the day he moved out. Mom never did manage to redecorate after he left for college. I won't be surprised if it's still the same," he offers.

I appreciate the gesture, but I'm not sure I'm ready to face his childhood room yet. Not today. It's already a big step just agreeing to practice here.

I shake my head, slowly removing my hand and letting it fall to my side. "Thanks, but that's okay. Maybe some other time."

He smiles encouragingly and leads me into his bedroom, where I'm immediately taken back in time. Jay's room is like a snapshot in time. His walls are covered with black-and-white posters of popular bands from the '70s and '80s. But my eyes are drawn to the one in the corner, near his guitar stand. It's a large poster of The Beatles, and in bold printed letters are the words from the song Ben used to sing to me throughout our marriage: "Hey Jude."

I'm stunned, and without even realizing I've moved, my fingers are caressing the poster as if I can't decide if it's real or not. It is. I'm sure I look like I've lost it.

Maybe I have, just a little.

Without turning around, because there are now tears that have found their way into my eyes, I quietly ask him, "When did you get this?"

I can sense his presence close behind me. The scent of him is warm and woodsy, with that same subtle hint of smoke and leather again. It stirs a strange sense of pleasure that I don't fully understand.

"I can't remember exactly when I got it, but it was after Ben left for college. It was sometime when I was in middle school and started getting more into music."

He had this before he even met me? It's not that unusual, really, it's not. Who doesn't like The Beatles? But why this particular poster? With the very nickname that Ben branded *me* with.

I love finding out little things like this. These are the little treasures I keep tucked away for extra hard days. No day has been easy since Ben left this earth, but I don't think I've lived through the worst days yet. It's the little things, like seeing an old poster with my name on it, that brings me joy in this moment.

I reach down and pick up Jay's gorgeous onyx Ovation Balladeer guitar and hand it to him, giving him my best smile. Because at this moment, it's real. Even if whatever is—or isn't—going on between us is unclear right now, I'm sure of one thing.

"Let's make some music. I'm ready."

CHAPTER 46
Jay

Jude decides to open the night singing an acoustic cover of the song "Good Years" by Nina Nesbitt. She told me a few hours ago, when we were practicing in my room, that if she didn't start the show, there's no way she'd have the courage to get up there. I don't think it would have mattered when she sang; every single time she sings, I'm blown away by the gravity of her voice.

After we practiced together for a couple of hours, she left to go home and finish getting ready. Thirty minutes before we were due on stage, she texted me she was ready, and I came and picked her up.

I zone out as we perform the song. I've been told my voice isn't terrible, but it's more of a lack of confidence, especially if I don't have my guitar with me. It's been a while since I last played. I have a newer guitar in LA, but this one belonged to my dad, and he taught me everything I know.

By the time she sings her final note, there's not a dry eye in the room. There's even a touch of moisture collecting in the corners of my eyes. I've never heard the song before today, but I'm fairly decent at picking something up quickly, especially when the melody isn't too complex.

I'm slowly learning more about Jude's style of music. She enjoys songs that make you feel *something*. The lyrics are simple, yet deeper than they first appear. When you take the time to really listen, you understand more—and Jude's voice has a way of taking you there.

Whatever deeper emotion she's experiencing, you're bound to feel it too. I don't know how she does it, but it's a natural gift she has. She has a quiet confidence about her. She's not openly proud, but I think she knows she's good. I can tell by her expression when people are applauding her that there's a part of her that enjoys the recognition. I mean, who wouldn't? And it's well-deserved.

Yet, another part of her—the part only I see—is the side that wants to shy away from it all. She's sung her piece and accepted the praise, but now she wants to retreat into her quiet space. There's a soft flicker in her eyes that almost seems to whisper *I'm good to go now.*

We end up sticking around for a couple more songs before heading out. There's still a buzzing energy in the tavern: people talking, people laughing, and kids by the stage swaying and dancing along. There's something about all of it that makes you feel like you belong. Even though I know I'm still far from ever belonging here.

Once we're settled back in my car, I look over at her. I can't help it. Tonight, she's wearing a golden-colored dress that's light and summery, swaying gently back and forth as she walks. Her hair is half pinned up, with the rest flowing down her back.

Every time she has even a small fraction of her hair down, I'm tempted to reach out and run my fingers through it. It looks so unbelievably soft. I wonder if pieces of it would snag along the rough calluses I've earned from working with my hands over the past decade.

I'm quickly removed from my thoughts when Jude faces me, her golden eyes locking on mine.

"Thanks again for doing that with me. It was... it felt good being up there again. I mean, it was hard, emotionally, but I still did it, ya know?" She beams at me, her smile reaching her eyes.

Not that her smiles aren't often genuine, but since I came back, I've noticed she doesn't give them out freely. Not to just anyone.

She reserves them like a treasure, waiting for the right moment. I'm honored that she trusts me with them. I can't help being a little curious about what she's thinking. Why do I care so much? Why does it matter when it never mattered before?

Because I never let it matter. I pulled myself away from the things and people that were once important to me, starting with my own family.

"Yeah, you did. You should be proud. I loved seeing you up there," I say before I have the chance to think it through. My cheeks flush, and I pretend to focus on something in the darkness outside my window. I hope she gets what I'm trying to say, but all I heard come out of my mouth was the word *loved*.

A beat of silence passes between us before Jude dares to speak.

"You were great too, you know. You are far more talented than you give yourself credit for. Ben never mentioned that you could play like that."

Her voice is soft and light, but it trails off slightly at the mention of his name.

I chance a small glance over at her. She's looking straight ahead, toying with the ends of her hair. I let my eyes linger for a moment before pulling my gaze away. I have to, for my own good. Maybe for both of us.

That's because Ben didn't know. He wasn't around to know

anything of importance about me. I was six years old when he graduated from high school and left for college. We might've been brothers biologically, but our bond never had a chance to grow. We didn't have a fighting chance to be close, and the one chance he'd given me, I'd blown it.

"He didn't know. My dad taught me when I was in middle school, and I had a makeshift band with some buddies in high school. Nothing serious, mostly just messing around. I've always loved music," I admit quietly, reminiscing.

"I'm sorry you and Ben weren't close."

I can feel her eyes on me, and I glance over, forcing myself to make eye contact. I want to see her sincerity up close.

Her gaze is soft, and she's stopped playing with her hair, her hands gently resting in her lap. She surprises me by offering one of her hands. Trying not to question what it means, I take it in mine. Her hand is warm and soft against my rough, weathered skin. If she minds, she doesn't show it. Our fingers link together, and I lift my gaze to meet her eyes.

"Thank you for saying that. It's okay. I just wish I did things differently. I'm not sure why I pulled away like that, but it wasn't right. It wasn't fair to any of you."

And I mean it. It's one of my biggest regrets. One I may never be able to forgive myself for. I can only hope that someday she will.

Our hands still locked together, she nods her head. "Yeah, I get that. I have regrets, too."

This pins me to the spot. Jude has regrets? I know she's not perfect—we're human after all—but what regrets could she possibly have?

"Like what?"

"Oh, lots of things. The night I found out about Ben... I was so angry at him. Selfishly angry. The kids had been fighting all day, and I did my fair share of yelling and time-outs. Let's just say, I wasn't the best mom that day." A small sliver of a smile spreads across her face before it vanishes.

I memorize it in case it doesn't return for a while. She can be okay one moment, and then be overcome by a flood of sadness the next.

"He was supposed to be bringing us food on his way home. Because by that point, I was too exhausted to prepare anything. He was doing *me* a favor. And then he'd gotten a call and was out saving other people's lives, while I was here, worried about what we were going to eat. It was so petty of me to feel and think that way. But I did. I was angry at him while he was saving lives and sacrificing his own.

"That's how much pain I've been in. I'm still in pain, and sometimes I'm still so angry at him for leaving me like this. Everything is such a mess."

Her grip on my hand suddenly tightens, and on instinct, my other hand finds its way to our interlocked fingers. I gently stroke her knuckles in a soothing rhythm.

I wish I could do more for her, but I know it would be borderline inappropriate. We might be holding hands, but it doesn't mean anything. She probably holds hands with Kelly and who knows who else. This doesn't mean anything more than what it is. It can't.

"But tonight, I didn't feel angry up there. Even though I was singing about all the good years we had together—and that alone was so hard—it was okay somehow. I felt pain, and yet I was also okay. I know I'm not making sense, Jay, but I didn't feel alone, or angry, or broken. I felt like *me* again. Just a tiny glimpse. Just during that song. But for a moment, I was me." Tears brim in her eyes, making them appear watery, and a single tear trails down her cheek.

I reach out and swipe it away, tucking a stray curl behind her ears. She's frozen beneath my touch, unsure of my next move. The only sounds in the car are the soft purr of the engine and the rise and fall of our breaths, moving in sync.

My eyes fall to her lips. I want to kiss her so badly. I've been thinking about it a lot lately. Especially after that night at her house when the power was out. I almost did it then, but it wasn't the right time.

Here, in the parking lot of the restaurant, isn't exactly the most romantic place either. The right moment may never come. And if it feels right for me, will she be ready? I'm so scared of doing something to push her away from me for good.

"Jay..." she stops me in my tracks.

Can she tell what I'm thinking through the desire shining in my eyes? I want her, but I don't think she feels the same way about me.

"Yeah?" I breathe out shakily. I don't know what's happening between us, but it's definitely something. At least it is for me.

"What are you doing?" she asks me softly. It doesn't come out accusatory, just curious.

I'm asking myself the same question.

"I don't know," I answer honestly. "What do you want me to do?"

My question stuns her into silence. She draws back slightly, pulling her bottom lip between her teeth, removing her hand from my grasp.

That's it, I've done it. I've broken the spell; whatever was holding us together before is gone.

She shakes her head, looking away from me. Closing herself back off. Shutting me out.

"It's too soon for anything, Jay. I can't," she whispers.

"Right. I know," I say, more to myself than to her. I'm well aware she's not ready, but that doesn't stop my heart from betraying me and racing every time she draws near.

"I like being around you, but I meant it when I said we can only be friends. I can't move on. It doesn't feel right."

"I know, and I wouldn't ask that of you."

"Jay... Do you have feelings for me?" she asks me, cutting to the chase.

I know I need to answer her honestly. No point in dodging it.

"Yes." Wow, I really went for it. No turning back now.

"But you hardly know me..."

"Doesn't matter. I know enough to know that I like you."

"Even though I was married to your brother for ten years?"

"Yeah."

"Even though we have two kids together and I'm now a *widow*," she says the word widow like it's a dirty word.

I flash back to our first interaction, when I called her out on her lack of cursing. I can't believe I'd been so crass. So petty. Before I came back here, that's exactly the man I was. Maybe nobody else can tell, but I know I'm already not the same man I came here as. I'm far from perfect, but better.

Jude makes me want to be a better person. Not just for myself, but for her too. Losing my brother brought me back to a place I cut ties with. But if I missed out on saying goodbye to my brother, I've also missed out on the one person who might be the miracle that helps turn my life back around.

Because of Jude, I want to start living my life differently. I've made a lot of mistakes and have a countless number of regrets, but every time I'm with her, I no longer desire the things of my past. I want this new life, and I want it with her.

"Yeah. I still do."

"Why?" she asks me. Throwing me off guard. She's desperate to get down to the heart of the matter. My heart. My intentions.

"Because those are just pieces of you, but they don't make up all of you. Ben was a piece of you, and so are your kids. But you're also more than just the pieces of your past. You're bright, and smart, and care about the people you're with. You're a great listener... I can spew a lot of nonsense sometimes, and you aren't quick to brush me off like most people do.

"You didn't ask for any of this, and I'm not saying it's been easy because I know it hasn't. But even though life has given you the most horrific circumstances, you haven't given up. You're so strong, even in the midst of your pain, you still show up and work hard for the tavern and your employees. You're still fighting for what's important."

With a shaky breath, Jude finds my eyes again. "And what's that?"

"You."

"Me?"

"You said so yourself. Tonight, you were given a tiny glimpse of the person you used to be. You aren't lost, Jude, you just need to be reminded of who you are. And for what it's worth, I see you. I really do."

She doesn't say anything else as I drive her home. Before she gets out of the car, she gives my hand one final squeeze.

"Thanks, Jay, for everything you said tonight."

I'm not entirely sure how to interpret the meaning behind her words, but I nod in acknowledgment. I'll take whatever she gives me.

"Of course. I rarely say things I don't mean. I may blurt things out, but at least I'm honest." I shrug my shoulders, offering her a small smile.

"I like honesty. Keep being honest with me, okay?"

"I will. And Jude?"

"Yeah?"

"I know you aren't ready for anything right now, and that's okay. But if that ever changes... I'll be here."

She bites her lip again, her hand slipping away from mine. I let her. I'll always let her decide what she's ready for.

"Of course. I will. Goodnight, Jay."

"Goodnight, Jude."

I drive away, singing the song we sang earlier, with the scent of her lingering in the car long after she left.

CHAPTER 47
Jude

There are two weeks left in June. It's funny how time can go by in a blink, and also creep by slower than molasses. It's no secret that I'm flying back to Indiana at the end of June to be with my parents and children for the remainder of the summer. Now that it's right around the corner, it almost doesn't seem real.

Ever since our conversation last Friday night, neither of us has brought it up. Maybe it's for the best. Not that I'm purposely trying to sweep it under the rug, it's just that I don't know what to do about it. It's been nagging at me ever since, but I don't think it'll do either of us any good to hash it out. I don't understand how he could've developed feelings for me so quickly... We started as strangers.

Now? We're far from it. At least to me.

But that's where I have to stop my train of thought. Because who knows where they will go if I let them. I'm scared to find out. Besides, I can't do that to Ben. I know he's not here anymore, but he's still in everything I do. Everywhere I go, he's there in the back of my mind whispering to me to *slow down*. Or maybe that's just the wiser side of me, warning me not to jump into anything new. Especially with *him*. Because he isn't just anyone... he's Ben's *brother*.

That isn't lost on me. I'm not usually one to worry about what other people think, but I can't help it with this. What *would* people think about me if I went from one brother to the next? I'm sure the gossip page would have a field day with that one. Jay and I aren't that far apart in age. He's only five years younger than me, but I've never been with anyone younger. It shouldn't be a big deal, and I think it's more a matter of who than our age difference.

But it's not just that. Ben's only been gone for a month. I can't already have feelings for somebody else. Everything in me screams that it's just *wrong*. Isn't it? I don't know if there's a wrong or right. There isn't a guidebook to healing.

How soon is too soon to start dating again? Six months, a year, two years, three, four? Never?

The pain of losing the love of your life never goes away. What happens when you start to love somebody else? What happens to the love you had before? Is it possible to love somebody new in the same way you once did? Will your love grow stronger or weaker because that part of you is lost forever?

I don't have any answers. I try my best not to let my thoughts go there. But occasionally, they do. Rather than lying here hour after hour, tossing and turning, sometimes I reach over and pull out my phone, and I shoot a quick text to Jay to see if he's still awake.

Most nights he is. I shouldn't be so shocked that he's having trouble sleeping, too. We carry on a conversation via text message until one of us falls asleep.

I don't know if it's dumb to be messaging him like this, but I truly do believe he cares about me, feelings aside. He's becoming someone that I can trust—with the little things as well as the crazy things that keep me up at night—because something is keeping him awake as well.

Me: Hey, you up?

Jay: Yeah. Can't sleep?

Me: Unfortunately, no. I can only handle so many Gilmore Girls episodes back to back.

Jay: LOL! Mom and I used to watch Criminal Minds together.

Me: I'm trying to fall asleep here, not be scared out of my mind. Pass!

Jay: True! Have you tried listening to music?

Me: No, I didn't think of that. I usually just have the TV on in the background. Does music help you?

Jay: Yeah, it does. Can I send you something?

Me: Of course.

Jay: One moment...

Me: Standing by.

I close my eyes, resting my phone on my chest as I wait for him to respond. Only a couple of minutes later, I feel the vibrations coming from my phone. I pick it up, a smile instantly forming across my face.

When I open the text message conversation, I see that he's sent me a link. It's for a playlist that he's titled: Jude and Jay's Playlist.

My heart skips a beat without permission. He made me a playlist? *For us?*

My fingers tremble as I hover over the icon, then click play. I close my eyes as the first song begins. It's a cover of The Beatles' song "Hey Jude." I'm instantly brought back to the night at the tavern when everyone was there to honor Ben. In a crowd of many, our paths somehow crossed. Our eyes locked as my six-year-old courageously sang my song on stage. My song, my anthem.

As that song is finishing and before I can move on to the next one, another text comes through.

Jay: I hope it's okay that I made this... I know how much "Hey Jude" means to you, and I wanted it to be the first thing you hear when you listen to it. That song is meant for you. I know things are a bit confusing between us right now, but please know I would never take that song away from you. I also chose a few songs that remind me of you. I hope that's okay and that I'm not pushing you in any way. I know how much music means to you. I hope this helps, in whatever way you need it.

I'm too stunned to reply. I underestimated Jay's character entirely. I'd been so quick to write him off because he wrote us off five years ago. I also tried to reach out to him when Ben couldn't get through, and my texts had gone unanswered then. But I feel heard now. Something in him has changed. Changed for the better. Maybe nobody else can see it, but I do. I see him. Just like he sees *me.*

Sweet dreams, Jay. See you tomorrow.

I know I shouldn't leave him unanswered, but I do for now. I close my eyes and hit play again, tuning into the next song. I'm not sure when I'll finally drift off. But I know one thing's for sure:

I've been wrong about Jay...

And the time we have left together this summer is quickly running out.

CHAPTER 48
Jay

Tonight we are performing "Guidebook to Healing" by Jamie Miller. I found the song when I was putting together the playlist. It took me about three nights to complete the list. I kept going back and forth, memorizing lyrics, second-guessing how they might resonate with her. Hoping somehow to inspire her to keep singing, to keep making music.

It's hard to believe we only have one more week before she's gone, spending the rest of the summer in Indiana. I'm glad she's getting some time away. She needs her family as much as they need her. She's shown me pictures and videos of her kids, even introducing me to them once while on a video call. She cheerily exclaimed, "This is Jay, say hi!"

Nova and Riley greet me with as much warmth as they would anyone they were familiar with. They have a way of making me feel as though I belong. And for a while, I didn't belong anywhere. Jude has a way of making you feel like you are exactly where you are meant to be.

We haven't discussed what is going to happen when she

returns in early August. Even though Mom and I haven't discussed it in a while, I'm also painfully aware that my six weeks will be up soon as well. I'll have to make a decision. A big one at that.

I can give up the tavern to Jude and walk away for good. Or I can stay and help her in whatever capacity she wants me. If that means running the tavern as business partners or letting her take the reins fully, I'm happy to do whatever. I missed out on my chance to run this place with Ben, it wouldn't be fair of me to dictate this path for her. It has to be her decision, not mine. I hope she'll want me to stay, because I'm starting to believe that's what I want too.

A lot has changed for me in the short time I've been back in Bethel. I've not only cut back on smoking... I'm down to half a pack a week, which is saying a lot. I hope, little by little, I can continue cutting back. Not just for my health, but because I want to.

I feel different since I first set foot back in my hometown. If, by the end of all this, I don't stay... I won't be leaving as the same man who first arrived.

It's true that Jude helped kickstart most of these personal changes within me. She's made me strive to be better. Losing Ben has a lot to do with it, too. It puts things in perspective in ways I've never thought about before. Losing your brother does something to you. Because of it, I'm not the same. There's no going back to before.

I'm still not entirely sure I fit in here, but I know I don't belong in LA anymore. Nothing and no one is waiting for me there. Well, maybe my buddy Kyle. But he'll survive. He's got his girlfriend and his father, who's currently under investigation for fraud. I have no idea what Kyle will do with his life now that the business is shut down, but if I'm being completely honest, I'm not bothered by it. That's his life. I'm okay starting over here.

The tavern is slowly growing on me, and I can see myself accepting ownership and belonging here. Someday. The rest of the staff is slowly but surely warming up to me. I think Kelly's openness with me is rubbing off on everyone else. Small steps. I'm okay with that.

We are going on in about fifteen minutes. Our song is midway through the set list. Jude's worked up the courage to let someone else go first this time. I believe that woman can do anything she puts her mind to. Who am I to disagree?

"You ready?" Jude places a hand on my arm, her eyes bright and dancing with excitement. I love seeing these joyous glimpses of her. It's rare, and I soak it in every time.

At that moment, my phone lights up with a call. I glance down at the screen and curse under my breath when I see who it is.

Now is not the time. Whatever he has to say can wait. I let it go to voicemail. I can call him back later. Or not. I got away from all of that for a reason. I'm here now.

I'll be here.

I meet Jude's eyes and offer her a small smile. Her eyebrows quirk up with worry, and I do my best to wave it off. I don't want her to fret, it's nothing important. Whatever it is can wait.

Only it can't. My phone flashes again with Kyle's name. *Great.* As much as I want to, I can't leave him hanging. I motion with my hand towards my phone, already bringing it up to my ear.

"Sorry, I need to take this real quick. I'll be right back." Before I can reassure the worry in her gaze, I move quickly past her and make my way out front to where we first met. It feels like a lifetime ago now.

Only, at this moment, I'd give anything for it to be her out here with me.

CHAPTER 49
Jude

t's been twenty minutes since Jay walked out to take a call, and he still hasn't returned. We were supposed to go on five minutes ago, and he's nowhere in sight. I wonder what that was all about. He seemed flustered when he saw the name on the screen. His features went from soft and elated to dark and fearful. Who called him? What are they talking about? Should I be worried? Should I go out there and check on him?

Before I can make my way outside to see if Jay's okay, Kelly comes up to me, her blonde ponytail swishing back and forth.

"Hey, love, are you performing soon? I've already bumped the next artist up, but what's going on? Where did Jay go?" she asks me, concern etched across her face and her blue eyes flashing with worry.

"He had an important call he had to take, but I honestly thought he'd be back by now. I'm getting ready to go check on him," I say, folding my arms across my chest, peering over her shoulder to see if I can see him from here.

"No, that's not what I mean. He left. I saw him get in his car and leave. He's not here." She reaches out to touch me, and my eyes instantly well up with tears.

He *left*? He told me he'd be right back. He knows what performing this song means to me. After all, he was the one to find it for me. It was among the many great songs he added to my playlist.

Panic instantly takes over. Did something bad happen for him to just leave in a hurry like that? I'm torn between finding out where he went and giving him space in case he has to handle an emergency. My thoughts go directly to his mom. I'll shoot her a quick text, just to make sure she's okay.

But then I look up and see Rita coming over to me. She's wearing a similar expression as Kelly. What's going on?

"Did you see where Jay went?" I blurt out as she gets close enough.

She shakes her head, her eyes locking with mine and rooting me to the spot. Her posture slumps slightly, as if his absence weighs on her too. I've never seen her shoulders slumped in such a way before, probably because she never had any reason to until now.

In all the times I've been over at Jay's house to practice our songs, she's only popped into his room once. It'd been a quick greeting before she retreated to a different room, giving us back our private space.

"I'm sorry, but I didn't. I was just coming over to ask you the same. I knew you two would be on soon and didn't want to miss it. Did he tell you where he was going?"

I shake my head, fighting back tears.

She nods as if trying to put together all the pieces that I can't.

"Okay, dear. I'll go check on him. He wouldn't leave you hanging like this if it weren't for a good reason. Try not to worry too much, okay? I'm sure it's all fine. Now go, don't let this ruin your night. You were born to be up there."

Sometimes bad things happen. I'm sure nothing terrible has happened. It's a thread of hope I'm choosing to hold onto anyway.

A small tear escapes and makes its way down my cheek. I sniffle and wipe it away with the back of my hand. Rita and I haven't been close over the years, but I'd like to start trying to get to know her better. Something I should've done a long time ago.

Being around Jay has taught me that while some things can't be fixed or changed, the things you *can* change, you should while you still have the chance. If something needs mending, like a broken relationship, there's no better time than the present to start working on the repairs. He's right.

I don't understand why he left without saying goodbye. But I still need to do this. For me. When I close my eyes, I'm reminded of how the music makes me feel. How it makes me come alive.

I'm not going to let this setback ruin my night. I can still get up there and do the hard thing.

I ended up singing "Dancing With Your Ghost" by Sasha Alex Sloan, instead of the one we rehearsed. It didn't feel right performing that one without him. I fell in love with this one as well. A song I've had on repeat since Jay sent me his playlist. It screams every single thing I've been feeling since Ben left me behind.

Tonight, I believe everyone in the room feels it too. People are tapping their toes in a steady rhythm, some are humming along, even though it's clear they've never heard this one before. But they're here with me. Present in a way I've never experienced before. I sing with all that I have left in me. By the time the final note ends, my face is streaked with tears.

Ben, I miss you... I'd give anything for one more dance with you, my love.

It's not until midnight that I get a text from Jay. It's short and doesn't say much, but I suppose it's better than not saying anything at all.

Jay: I'm sorry I missed our song. I'll make it up to you, promise. Are you free tomorrow? If so, I'd like to take you somewhere. Let me know what time works best.

Me: Yes, I'm free. Six o'clock would be fine.

I go to bed with a heavy heart as I sink beneath my covers. It felt good to sing another song, yet I can't shake this nagging feeling about Jay. Something's wrong, something he's not telling me.

I thought we'd both been honest with one another. But he seems to be sorry for abandoning me tonight. Maybe he'll give me more details tomorrow. I can only hope for as much.

After all, he said he was sorry for missing *our* song. The lines between us aren't clear. If anything, they just keep getting blurrier by the minute.

CHAPTER 50
Jay

never meant to hurt Jude. I know I shouldn't have walked out on her like that, but I didn't feel like I had much of a choice when Kyle called. He needs my help with something.

He got himself tangled in a mess with his dad and their business. *Our* business. When I answered the call, he sounded completely distraught and beside himself. I finally got him calmed down a bit and hung up, but then the texts started coming through and didn't stop.

Kyle needs me to come back home. He said he needs me there to help him fix this. As much as I don't want to go back, he's my oldest friend. I can't just leave him hanging, no matter what we've been through together. Maybe it's because of that I feel like I have to. I need to.

Home. LA stopped being that the moment I left, barely over a month ago now. It feels like that was a lifetime ago.

I told him I have one more week here, and then I can fly back and settle some things with him. Jude's only here for one more week as well, and then we'll both be gone. And I need to make it up to her. I left her in a vulnerable place last night, and I've got to remedy that. I can't leave without telling her goodbye.

I just hope she can forgive me for dashing out like that. Kyle and I have been best friends since middle school. We go way back. I thought I left on a clean slate, but he called me in desperation. He doesn't have anyone else he can turn to, and we both know I wouldn't be able to say no. At least this one last time.

While I'm there, I can grab the things I left behind, especially if my trip to LA is only temporary and I'm coming back to Bethel. Back to Jude. I know what going back to LA now will look like. I know the repercussions of my actions.

But do I?

It's Saturday, and my shift ended at six. As soon as I clocked out, I headed straight home to shower and freshen up. Jude has the day off, as she does most weekends, and I can't help the nervous energy pouring out of me. I have been doing better at cutting back on my smoking, but I'm fidgety now as I wait for Jude to come out of her front door. I need something to do with my hands.

I barely have the thing lit before she exits her front door. I soak in her presence for a moment as she locks up her house before she turns around and faces me. I quickly extinguish the cigarette and stuff it into an empty container.

Today she's wearing a soft pink sleeveless top, the color of tulips—the same shade as her nails the day our paths first crossed again. Her hair is down, swept back in a matching pink headband, and she's wearing jean shorts that show off her sun-kissed skin. I can't help the smile that creases my face when I glance down at her feet. Pink Converse.

I laugh as she opens the passenger door and sits down beside me.

"What's so funny?" She smirks at me as she secures her seatbelt.

"Nothing," I say, shaking my head and putting the Prius into reverse so I can slowly back out of her drive.

"No, it's definitely something. Tell me."

"It's your shoes."

At this, she snorts.

Man, her laugh. It sounds like pure magic. An even rarer treasure than her smile, and I'm quick to memorize the way it sounds, soft and vibrant like a favorite song.

"What about them? Not a fan of Chuck Taylor, I take it?" Another softer laugh escapes her.

"No, I love them. Especially when you wear them." There's that sneaky word again that keeps finding its way into our conversations. I know I'm just talking about her shoes, but who am I kidding?

I love more than just her shoes.

At this, her olive skin flushes pink, perfectly matching her pink ensemble. I love how she can pull off any color. Blue or black, something vibrant like yellow or orange, and of course, pink—it doesn't matter. Everything looks good on her.

"Thank you. This pair is my favorite," she says, smiling down at her feet.

She plugs her phone into the charging cord attached to my car. At first, I think her phone has died. But again, this woman is filled with surprises.

Music starts pouring through my speakers as I drive to our destination. I recognize the first song immediately. She's pulled up the playlist I made for her. For *us*, really, but I didn't say that when I sent it to her.

She reaches over for my hand, and I enjoy the way her slender fingers tangle up with mine. I don't know what any of this means to her, but I know what it means to me. If I think about it too much, we'll both be in trouble.

She sings along with the track that's playing. This one's a bit sadder than the rest I put on the list. It's about all the negative thoughts that we experience as humans.

It reminds me of her story of the night Ben died. How she was struggling emotionally that day, and how Ben was the calm to her storm. How she's been so angry at him for dying and leaving her.

But then she said something that I haven't forgotten. She said that even though she's angry at him for leaving her and their kids behind, the one thing that lessens the pain, even a fraction, is music.

Singing, specifically.

When I'm singing, the anger lessens... and for a moment, I'm me again.

I've also dealt with anger issues. I wish I turned to music to lessen the pain, the guilt, and the regret. Instead, I turned to women I'd use as a distraction to make me numb, alcohol to make me forget, and cigarettes to take the edge off. I should've turned to music. I should've picked up my guitar sooner. Would it have eventually led me here? There's no way to know. But I have music back in my life again, because of Jude. There's a lot of good things in my life that are because of her.

I don't tell her where we're going, but it takes a little under an hour to get there. It's seven-thirty now, and we have at least half an hour before the sun sets. As we pull through the gates, she's already rolling her window down and sticking her arm outside, waving it in movements that mimic the ocean; testing the breeze.

We've come on the perfect night. It's warmer than I'd like, but it's not as hot as it has been the past couple of weeks. The sun is starting its descent, and the temperature has already dropped by a couple of degrees.

We pull into the state park, one I came to a bunch when I was younger. But this is the first time I've ever brought anyone else out here with me. I hope she isn't disappointed in my attempt to make this night special for her. A peace offering for standing her up last night.

I should've told her we'd be hiking a little ways, but I made sure she had on closed-toed shoes rather than flip-flops or sandals.

She squeezes my hand once before letting it go, unfastening herself from the seat. When we both get out, she smiles up at me.

"I haven't been here in forever," she breathes out, turning in a slow circle as if taking it all in for the first time.

I feel my stomach pinch with excitement.

"Yeah, me either. Mom and Dad used to bring me here when I was younger."

She folds her arms underneath her chest, and I do my best not to let my gaze linger there.

"Did Ben ever come out here?" she asks me carefully, biting her lip. As though she's trying to keep the sadness from spilling out.

"To the Gloss Mountains?"

She doesn't say anything, just nods.

"Yeah, probably. Mom and Dad really liked it out here. I mean it's nice because it's not far away, you can easily spend an afternoon hiking around here, and then be home before it gets too late."

It's not a big state park. There's no designated areas for camping or lodging; it's just meant for day trips, but it's a neat place to explore regardless.

"Yeah, it's gorgeous," she agrees, looking around at the cliffs that jut out in front of us.

I pop the trunk, pulling out two backpacks. I hand one to her, placing the other on my shoulders.

"Ready?" I ask before she can ask me anything else.

She nods, and we start hiking the Cathedral Mountain trail. In my opinion, it has some of the best views of the sunset. We should make it up there in plenty of time.

I just hope she enjoys it as much as I think she will.

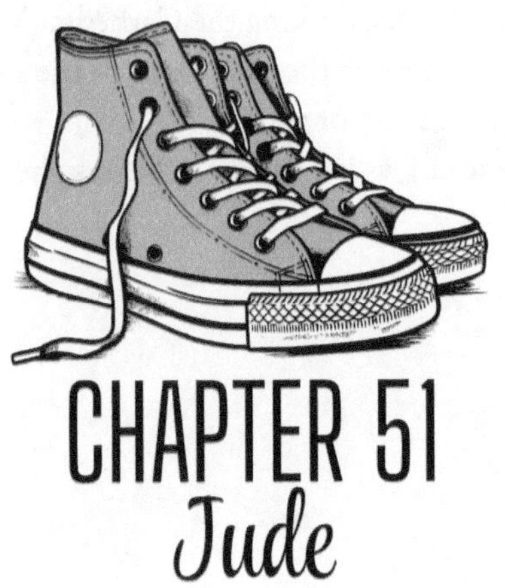

CHAPTER 51
Jude

He wasn't kidding. The view up here is breathtaking. I made it to the top without too much effort thanks to my Zumba and Pilates classes. But he's in better shape than I am.

He pulls out a folded blanket from his backpack and hands me some bug spray. He's thought of everything, and I'm touched by the small gestures. I hate the feeling of being sticky, but mosquitoes can get bad this time of year, and I don't want to chance it. It's thoughtful of him to do all of this in the first place. He's a hard person to stay mad at, I'm coming to find out.

I forgave him before he'd even apologized. My parents taught me to forgive easily, and it's stuck with me. And now I know first-hand that life is far too short to hold grudges. Time isn't promised, and I won't waste what little I might have.

In the bag, he's packed us a nice picnic— sandwiches, a salad, and a bag of Kinder mini chocolates for dessert. It's sweet and thoughtful, and I'm stunned he came up with all of this in such a short amount of time.

At the bottom of the bag, there's a Bluetooth speaker if we want to listen to music later. Of course I want to.

I'm leaving one week from today to go back to my hometown, to spend the rest of the summer with my family. It doesn't erase the small tug of longing I feel here, though. Here with *him.*

After we finish our food, he puts our trash away and scoots closer to me. So close that our legs are touching. He feels like a paperweight. His very presence is steadfast and unwavering. I'm not sure I've ever been this close to him before, except for the time I asked him to hold me when I needed to fall apart.

There's not many people I would let in like that. I'm not even sure why I broke down with him that night, but he didn't even hesitate. He didn't make me feel anything but safe and secure, two things I hadn't felt in a long while. Not since Ben... But if something like that ever happens again, I think I'll allow it to happen.

I'm slowly letting my walls down around him. He isn't perfect, I know that, but neither am I. It's not always the perfect person you need—just the right one at the perfect moment.

I can't help but think about how many times he's seen me cry. He's seen me at my lowest, and he's also seen me on a literal mountaintop. Small, Oklahoma-sized mountains that is, but still.

He's seen all of me, and he hasn't run from any of it. If anything, it's drawn him in closer somehow. It still blows me away when these thoughts creep in, as they often do lately.

We sit quietly and stare out over the tops of the hills and valleys at the fields below, watching the sunset paint the sky in a kaleido-scope of colors.

"Jude..."

Suddenly, I sit up taller and lean in close enough to grasp him by his shirt. I don't want to hear what he has to say right now. I need to do this or I may lose my nerve completely. I don't know what's come over me. It's like I lost control over my body.

His gaze turns to me, and he whispers my name against my

skin, sending shivers down my spine. I don't give myself time to think or question what I'm about to do, I just tug him closer.

I crash my lips to his in the fading light. His body stiffens, alert. I've caught him by surprise. Like a crack of thunder, my body pulls away, flooded with instant regret. I shouldn't have done that. I'm not sure what came over me, but my stomach churns. How could I have done such a thing?

I'm still in love with my husband. He may be gone physically, but he's still everywhere I go. He's in everything I see and say and do. I can't escape the memory of him. And now I can't escape the guilt I feel for putting my lips on somebody else's.

How could I?

Jay must sense my sudden agony. I feel him gently reach out and wipe the tears flowing down my cheeks. I'm shaking, but not from the cold. I'm shaking because of what I've done. The mistake I've made. I've just made everything ten times worse.

"Jude, hey... please don't cry. Hey, look at me," Jay says, his voice low and soft, as if he were speaking to a small child.

Right now I feel like one. I feel extremely small.

"Do you want to talk about it?" he asks.

I shake my head, wiping my eyes with my shirt. I look out over the horizon, taking my eyes off him. I can't look at him. I can't see the look of hurt written on his face.

He takes a minute before speaking again, allowing me a little time to gather myself. Put myself back together as best as I can. I appreciate his thoughtfulness, because I'm Humpty Dumpty, and I just had a terrible fall.

I can't fall for somebody else. Jay deserves someone who can give their whole selves to him, not only half. I'm not even sure I can offer half of myself. Maybe a third. Maybe none at all.

"Hey, um, I meant to say this before, but I'm sorry about last night. Some stuff I thought I'd taken care of before I came here isn't resolved. I'll need to take care of it after you leave."

I'm thankful for the topic change. The last thing I want to do is discuss the kiss. I wait for him to elaborate more. When he doesn't continue, I hesitate. I don't want it to sound like I'm trying to pry into his business, but I feel like he owes me a clearer explanation after abandoning me. It's not like him to dart out like that, especially when we were minutes away from performing together. I was counting on him.

"What kind of stuff? If it's okay to ask," I say, hesitating.

He shrugs his shoulders, leaning back on both of his hands.

"You can ask me anything, Jude. I mean that. And that kiss just now?" At this, he pauses, and I feel his heavy gaze lingering on me.

I look up at him, bite my lip, and shake my head. The kiss is the last thing I want to discuss right now.

"I just want you to know you don't need to feel bad about it, okay? I recognize that look in your eyes and it's regret, isn't it? Well, don't. We can talk about it some other time, but it doesn't have to be tonight," he sighs, his breath gently tickles my face as he breathes.

I just nod, unsure if any words would come if I tried. Something's happening to me, and I'm not exactly sure what it is.

"Anyway, my friend's name is Kyle... We go way back. We were buddies when we were in middle school. His dad offered him a job in Los Angeles after high school, and he asked me to tag along. Ben was moving back to Bethel when my parents asked him to run the tavern. I didn't have anything waiting for me here, so I told Kyle yes. It's a long story, but basically the last ten years have involved a series of failed attempts and poor life choices.

"I love my friend, but his dad's not a good business manager. He's run every single thing he's touched straight into the ground. I should have figured it out sooner, but I gave him the benefit of the doubt for Kyle. It just recently came to light that his dad was doing some shady stuff under the radar and got caught again. It's really bad this time, and Kyle needs me to go back home so I can help him figure out some things."

At this, I let out a small gasp. He's never mentioned any of this to me before. I had no idea. I wish he told me sooner. Not that I could have done anything or offered any advice, but he doesn't deserve this. Sure, it's not the same as losing your husband, I get that, but it's something real and painful that he experienced. I wonder if that's another reason he hasn't been in any hurry to go back.

"Wow, Jay. I'm so sorry. I had no idea. You should've told me."

This time, he puts an arm around me and tugs me close, pulling me into him.

He glances down at me and whispers against the top of my head, "Is this okay?"

"Yeah," I say softly in response. Somehow, it's okay. As long as I don't overthink it, it's okay. Moment by moment.

"To be honest, Kyle doesn't even know where his dad is, and he's a mess right now. I'm not sure how I can help him. He just said he's in trouble and needs me as soon as I can get there.

"I spent most of the night making phone calls. Employees we knew from previous jobs with his dad. Most didn't answer, and the ones who did had no idea where to find him. A few even said he doesn't want to be found and that we should just leave it alone.

"I even tried calling Kyle's dad, hoping he'd answer for me, but I think he has my number blocked because it didn't go through. It was a long night with little progress."

I don't know what to say. I don't want Jay to go back to LA, especially since he just told me his ex-boss is a criminal. I don't want him getting involved in that mess. He has a history with Kyle and his dad... What if he's already involved? How much do I trust him?

He must feel me tense beneath his touch, because he turns his head towards mine, "I had nothing to do with the business going down, Jude. You know that, right?"

I want to tell him that I do know. That I know the *real* him. The real Jay greets me every morning when I walk into the tavern. He sits with me in Ben's old office, where we spend our lunch hours talking about simple nothings. He brings me pizza in the pouring rain and holds me when I crack wide open from the weight of my grief. He sings with me. Makes playlists full of songs he picked out just because he wanted to. He plans romantic hikes up Gloss Mountain. And every time I've asked him anything—*anything*—he's always been honest with me.

Like now.

Yet, this one thing hangs over him like a dark, looming cloud. I want to believe that he's telling me the truth. I want to trust that if he says he needs to help out his best friend, then that's enough. I want to leave it at that and move on.

So, why can't I?

But the truth is, I don't know anything about the life he had before he came here. Before Ben's death brought him back, he removed himself from the family entirely. I'm just getting to know him for the first time. How can I be so sure that this is the real him? What if it's all been a show to get close to me?

What if I'd gotten it all wrong? Maybe he isn't here to heal with me after all. Maybe I'm not the reason he decided to stick around. Maybe it's all for the tavern since he lost his job in LA...

"I'm not sure..." I say, slowly backing away from him. Where it's safer, more secure.

He gently grabs my shoulders, turning me towards him so we can see eye-to-eye.

"Jude, I'm telling you the truth. Look, I care about you. A lot. I've never lied to you, and I'm not going to start doing that now. I may have made some dumb mistakes in my life, but it's because of *you* that I'm a better version of the man that you first met. I was broken, too, and lost. But Jude, I'm not lost anymore," he says, tears welling in his eyes.

I want to believe him so badly. Why is it so hard to trust someone again?

Be careful with your heart.

I promised Kelly. Not that I won't allow myself to start having feelings for anyone else, but that I would protect my heart. Have I been protecting it the way that I should? I'm not so sure anymore, the lines are all blurring together.

"W-what do you mean?" I stumble through my words.

"I'm not lost anymore because you found me. You make me feel at home. Like I belong here, owning and running the tavern with you."

The ground drops out beneath me. This. *This* is why he really came back? Wait, he owns Second Verse?

"What do you mean, owning it with me?" I ask.

He looks confused. "I'm fifty percent owner of the tavern with you. I'm here because my mom asked me to stick around for a bit to help you while I decide if I want to stay and run the business with you. But I'd never do anything you're not comfortable with. Did you really not know that I own it?"

I shake my head. I had no idea. His dad must've split ownership between the brothers when he passed. That's why Ben wanted Jay to come back and run the tavern with him.

Why wasn't I ever told? I should've known that's why he's here. It was never about me. It was about money. He lost his job in LA and this was a sure thing. And now that I know he might be into some shady dealings, I'm even more concerned. I will *not* let Ben's dream be ruined by anything illegal.

He must see the answer on my face because he seems desperate now. "You have to know that I would never hold information back from you. I thought you knew! Please, Jude. I'd never do anything to intentionally cause you harm. I... I think I'm falling in love with you."

At this, my jaw drops open. I blink back the tears that are forming as the sky blackens around us.

"No... You don't mean that. Take it back."

Tears begin to fall, ruining whatever could've potentially been between us. I know deep inside somewhere that I'm messing this all up. But it's a car crash I can't turn away from.

"No, I can't do that. I know you're not ready, but I love you, Jude." Pain is written across his features. His light, sand-colored hair moves in gentle patterns with the breeze.

I knew this would all come to an end eventually. Whatever this is, it's over. I'm not ready for it. We're both in over our heads. We got swept up together. But we are never meant to be *together*.

It isn't supposed to be this way. Not like this.

I close my eyes and, for a moment, all I see is Ben's face. I can't stop the flood of tears that come. I don't even try. How can I possibly love someone else? I can't let Ben go. I can't do it. I don't think I'll ever be ready.

I don't want to hurt Jay, I really don't. And I do think his feelings for me are real. I'd be lying if there wasn't something stirring in me, too. But I won't allow it. I can't. Especially not now, when I don't even know if I can trust him with Ben's tavern. My tavern... but I guess it's Jay's too.

It wouldn't be right. It wouldn't be fair.

I've only ever loved one man in my life, and he's gone. Gone for good. How am I supposed to have anything left to give when I already gave everything to the one person who was meant to be with me forever?

"I can't be with you, Jay. I don't understand what's going on between you and your friend... and you're just now telling me that the tavern has belonged to you all this time. You can't just drop a bomb like that and expect me to be okay with it. I need some time to clear my head. To try and understand what's really happening." I grit out, my entire body shaking.

I feel his warm, calloused hands gently grip the sides of my cheeks, his fingers swiping at my stream of tears.

"Jude, look at me."

I force my eyes open. I can hardly make out his features through my blur of tears.

"I have never once lied to you, and I never will. I'm sorry I didn't tell you. I honestly thought you knew. And I didn't think it was that big of a deal anyway. It doesn't change anything."

I scoff at this. That couldn't be further from the truth. Of course, it changes things. It changes everything. When I asked him why he was still here—why he hadn't left right after the funeral—he told me it was for me.

Now I know they were all lies. What else has he lied to me about? I'm not sure I should've ever trusted him.

"It changes everything, Jay. I think maybe it's best that we spend some time apart."

Hurt flashes in his eyes, and I quickly glance away before I change my mind. I should have known that being friends is more than either of us can handle. I'm not sure 'friends' is the right word for whatever's been going on between us, but whatever it is, it can't be more than that. I have to do a better job at protecting my heart.

"Is that what you want? Time apart."

No, it's not what I want. I want my husband to still be alive so I don't have to choose. So I don't have to make this hard choice. Because it needs to be Ben... or nobody at all.

"If you just want to be friends, I can respect that, Jude. If you want something more, but aren't ready yet, I'll wait for you. However long that takes, I'll wait. But you have to tell me what it is that you want."

My heart is pounding so loudly, I wonder if he can hear it. I'm sure he can feel it through his hands, still holding softly onto my face.

"I think you should go. Your friend needs you more than I do." It hurts me to say it, but it's the truth. While I didn't plan to run this business alone, I'm not so sure I want him in charge.

Both Jay and Rita kept me in the dark about him owning half the tavern. If they were on my side and truly interested in helping me run the tavern, they wouldn't have hid this from me. I have to believe that Ben didn't know, because I don't want to consider the possibility that he may have known too.

"I'm so sorry if I hurt you, Jude. That's the last thing I want to do. Just, please, be honest with me. Do you want me to stay? Stay and run Second Verse Tavern with you?"

I came here tonight with hope in my heart. Hope that maybe we can be more than friends someday. Maybe, just maybe, we can see where this thing goes. But now I know that it won't be going anywhere. This is where our song ends. And it wrecks me. *Wrecks me.*

I finally shake my head. "No," I whisper.

He's silent for a beat, and all I can hear are the sounds of crickets chirping and the buzzing of summer around us.

"You don't mean that, do you? Can we please talk about this some more? If this is about us, I can give you more time. All the time you need. I'm not in any rush."

I shake my head. "You can't stay here. I need you to go back home, where you belong."

His gray-green eyes lock with mine. For a moment, he holds me there, frozen in time. There's not a trace of anger in them, only sadness and pain. I can't say he doesn't see the same thing in mine. I hate that this is even happening, but I'm glad I found out the truth now. When was he going to tell me? Did it just slip out tonight by accident? It doesn't matter now.

This is goodbye.

"Okay, I will, if that's what you want," he says, shrugging his shoulders and fidgeting with one of his pockets.

I haven't seen him smoke recently, but that doesn't mean he's quit. I can tell this conversation is upsetting him, but I'm hurt by this, too.

He should've told me sooner.

"It is." That's all I can get out. If I open my mouth to say more, I'll take it all back.

But I know it's already too late. The damage is already done. On both sides.

CHAPTER 52
Jude

don't see much of Jay in our final week together. After I finished crying my eyes out in front of him—yet again—I pulled together what little composure I had left, and we drove home in silence. I might've even drifted off while little, dark thoughts played like shadows across my eyelids.

I didn't see or hear from him again until a few days later, when the week started. It's like the raw pain of a wound right after you decide to rip off the Band-Aid. In a sense, that's exactly what we both did that night.

He dropped a few bombshells on me. First, that he lost his job in LA because his boss is involved in something illegal. He hadn't gone into much detail about that. The second being that he's half owner of Second Verse. And third, he's falling in love with me. Also, I can't forget that I *kissed* him! The entire night had been filled with surprises.

He's in love with me, and I don't know how I'm supposed to respond. What am I supposed to do with that? Sending him home is the best thing to do.

Right?

I have no idea what I'm doing. I sludge through the days, making sure to FaceTime the kids at least every other day. Kelly tries a few times to invite me out to lunch with her, like we do from time to time, but I decline. I'm not in the mood to explain what happened and how I feel. I'm not even sure I know where to begin.

I'm not eating much, and I can hardly sleep. I either skip lunch altogether, or eat a quick bite at home. I feel numb. Maybe the real loss is starting to sink in, and I don't know what to do with it, how to handle this new heaviness that's weighing me down.

Also, there's a part of me that misses Jay's company. We got too close, too quickly, and I got burned. I wasn't ready. Despite Jay promising me that he'd wait for me, I can't ask that of him. I'm not sure I want him to in the first place. But this? Stay friends and risk it all, or play it safe and send him away. I wanted this, chose this, yet somehow I don't like it. Not at all. But I know it's the right thing to do.

I'm in a dark place, and I don't know how to pull myself out of this funk.

It's not until close to ten p.m. Thursday night that I get my first text from him all week.

Jay: Hey, just wanted to check in.

Me: Thanks. I'm good.

I'm not, but I don't know where to start. I can't explain all the terrible thoughts that have been running through my mind the past couple of days.

Jay: Jude, please don't shut me out. What's going on? I'm worried about you.

Me: Don't. You have bigger things to worry about.

Jay: Because you made them out to be. You're the one who told me I should go.

Me: That's exactly what should happen.

Jay: Should it though?

Me: I'm not even going to try and guess what that means. But yes. It's better this way.

Jay: For me or you?

Me: I don't know.

I let out a loud sigh and close my eyes, pulling the covers up over my head and trapping the heat underneath. My body feels like it weighs a thousand pounds. I don't think I can move if I wanted to.

Jay: Are you okay? Really?

Me: No...

Jay: Can I come over?

Me: No.

Jay: Jude... please let me help you.

Me: I don't think you can.

Jay: Maybe not, but I could try if you'd let me.

Me: How?

Jay: Any number of things. We can talk about it or sit together in silence. We can listen to music or count the stars out tonight. We could watch another one of your favorite movies. You can tell me more things about Ben or show me that scrapbook you had in your office.

Me: You know about that?

Jay: Yeah, sorry. I didn't mean to snoop. It's a beautiful album, though. Kelly did a great job.

Me: I haven't opened it yet.

Jay: Oh.

Me: Yeah, I wasn't ready. I couldn't do it.

Jay: Do you have it with you now?

Me: Yeah. It's in my closet.

Jay: We can look at it together?

I pull the covers off my head and sit up at this. Tears instantly prick the corners of my eyes, and I blink them back, trying to make out his words as I read them again.

Would he really do that with me? He would. The Jay I know absolutely would. But why? Why is he always so quick to say yes when it comes to me, no matter how hard or uncomfortable it might be for him?

Here's a guy who admitted he has feelings for me. I'm still in love with his dead brother, yet he would drive over here just to look at old pictures and reminisce with me. It hits me straight in my gut. I'm a terrible person for constantly pushing him away. I want to draw him closer to me, but everything in me screams I can't, and I freak out. I don't feel like I deserve to have somebody close to me again. I'm so conflicted and confused by all of this. I don't know how to handle any of it.

Me: You seriously mean that?

Jay: Yes, absolutely. I rarely say things I don't mean, Jude. And I mean this one hundred percent.

Me: Okay

Jay: Okay, as in you want me to come over?

Me: Yeah, before I change my mind. Which seems to be happening a lot lately. I'm sorry.

Jay: Don't be. I said I was okay with waiting.

Me: You did say that.

Jay: Okay, see you soon. I'll forgive you if you change your mind on my drive over.

Jay: But please don't. LOL!

Me: You're ridiculous. And I won't.

Jay: I know. Okay, see you.

I fall asleep before he pulls into my driveway.

CHAPTER 53
Jay

t's ten minutes shy of eleven o'clock when I arrive at Jude's house. I've always admired her house. It's a large, white, farmhouse-style home with white board-and-batten siding, trimmed in black. The front porch light is on as I make my way to her door. There's already a steady swarm of bugs near the lights, but I ignore them to get to Jude quicker.

She doesn't greet me at the door, so I hesitate for just a moment, wondering if she'd rather I text her first and let her know I'm here. Maybe she decided to take a quick shower. I know she's expecting me, but it feels weird to knock on somebody's door this time of night.

I send her a quick text to be safe.

Me: Hey, I'm here. Just letting you know.

I wait a couple of minutes before mustering up the courage to knock. I knock three times and wait.

Nothing.

I knock again, but still nothing. I hope she's okay in there.

It's probably nothing major. She doesn't seem like herself tonight, though. I know what depression looks like, and she seems rather low. She never mentioned struggling, but maybe she doesn't know how to? Or doesn't want to burden me with anything else. Although it wouldn't have been a burden. Far from it. My mind instantly goes to the worst-case scenario, and I reach for her door handle and give it a slow push.

It opens easily. She left her door unlocked for me. Of course, she did, because she trusts me. Or she wouldn't have wanted me to come in the first place. But then again, what if she's changed her mind and doesn't have the guts to tell me through text? What if this is it this time?

Goodbye.

I ease the door open slowly, taking in my surroundings. No candles are lit like the first time, but she does have a couple of lamps glowing softly, casting light into the kitchen and living room, which shares an open layout just inside the entrance.

"Jude?" I call out softly.

I don't want to startle her. I can't shake the sinking feeling in the pit of my stomach that something isn't right. Normally, she's quick to greet me.

It doesn't take me long to check the first floor and move closer to her room. I pass her tall bookshelf in the hall and come to the entrance of her bedroom.

Her door is wide open, and a soft light is beckoning to me from within. I have to know if she's okay. I can't wait a second longer. I take one long stride into the room and hold my breath for what awaits me.

A rush of air quickly escapes my lungs as I take in the sight before me. I've found Jude. She's sound asleep and softly snoring. A small laugh escapes me, and I freeze for a moment, hoping the sound doesn't wake her.

Her phone is still clutched in her hand, resting on her chest, which rises and falls with each breath she takes.

I have to decide what I should do. I often second-guess myself, but not this time. Without even thinking, I slip out of my sandals and make my way over to the other side of the bed. The side of the bed that remains cold and untouched, forgotten.

I don't know how she'll react when she wakes up and finds me lying next to her, but I try not to think about that. For now, this is all I want. If this is our last moment together, so be it. We both leave Oklahoma in two days. Her to Indiana and me to California. This might be the only chance I ever get to be this close to her. One last time.

I lay on top of the sheets, trying to still my movements. The last thing I want is to spook her and send her into another panic. I would never intentionally hurt this woman. I *love* her. It's crazy even thinking that, much less admitting it to her. But I couldn't help it. It was going to burst out of me sooner or later. It just happened a lot sooner than either of us was prepared for.

Whether or not she feels the same remains unclear. But it doesn't change the way I feel towards her. With her wild brown curls falling in waves around her pillow, I scoot in as close as I can. I reach out and touch her hair lightly. A feather touch. Nothing more than a whisper.

I tell myself I'll go before she has the chance to wake up. But for now, this is what we both need. I said I would be here for her, and I've kept that promise. Just like I intend to keep my other promise to her as well.

Because I will wait for her. As long as it takes. I'll return to Bethel once I get everything settled back in LA. I'm scared partly because I'm not entirely sure what she wants.

But she didn't sound okay. And it's hard to leave her like this, even though she made it clear she doesn't want me here anymore.

Had she meant it when she said that? Does she really want me gone?

I don't want to cause her any more pain. She's had enough pain in the last few months to last a lifetime. If she truly wants me to go, I will.

And this time, I'll go for good.

I never meant to keep anything from her. I care about her. But the more I'm around her, the harder I'm falling for her. I want to help her with the tavern. I want whatever she wants.

Even if that means this will be my last night with her. Because come morning, it just might be goodbye. For good.

CHAPTER 54
Jude

can't remember the last time I slept this well. I don't even recall falling asleep; it just sort of happened. Even with my eyes closed, I can feel the warmth from the late-June sun kissing my face. Along with something else.

I stretch my legs out and feel the familiar warmth of someone else. I turn on my side, snuggling deeper into the sheets, and pull the blankets around me. Then I feel something brushing along my hairline. More like a someone. I let out a contented sigh. *Ahh.*

Gentle fingers are stroking my temple in a soothing pattern. I dare to move closer to the center of the bed. The strokes along my temple turn into a head massage with strong, gentle fingers weaving their way in and out of my tangled mane. I let them. Ben. *Benny.*

I could stay like this forever. For a moment, I wonder if I'm still dreaming. I blindly reach out my arm, surprised to be met with someone else. I'm not alone.

Soft lips press against the skin of my forehead, and I can't help but wonder if this past month and a half has all been some terrible dream loop I've been stuck in, and I'm finally waking up after all this time.

My eyes fly open with a sharp gasp. It's not my husband beside me, but Jay lying face-to-face with me, his fingers tracing slow, lazy circles along my jawline.

No, no. How did I let this happen? How did I allow someone else to get this close to me?

It strikes me like a jolt to the chest, raw and undeniable, and I back away from the man beside me. As though I've burned him, he yanks his hand out of my hair, cursing under his breath. But there's something soft in his expression. He's not running away like I'm trying to. Trying to escape whatever this is. Whatever may or may not have happened between us.

Wait, nothing happened, right?

"Jay?" I whisper, my voice coming out scratchy and raw with morning sleep and confusion, like my body hasn't caught up to the shock of finding him there. I slowly sit up and reach for the tumbler of water I keep on my nightstand. I take a long drink through the straw before finding his eyes again.

I can see now that he's still fully dressed. He's wearing a fitted black T-shirt and jeans. The man slept in jeans. Maybe nothing happened after all. I'd remember, right? Then again, the last thing I remember was texting him to come over, and then everything faded to black after that. I'd fallen asleep. But why is he still here if I hadn't been awake to know that he came in the first place?

"What are you doing here?" I ask, even though I'm pretty sure I already know the answer.

He runs a hand over the stubble along his jaw and lets out a soft sigh. He props the pillows up behind him, shifting his body higher to meet mine.

"To make sure you didn't change your mind." He smiles at me with a sleepy grin.

I wish he weren't so handsome. Like obnoxiously cute. His sandy-blonde hair is disheveled and messy like I've never seen it before, and his eyes look sleepy. Like maybe he had a good night's sleep, too.

I shake my head slowly, rubbing a corner of the bedding between my fingers. Back and forth.

"I didn't, but I also didn't mean to fall asleep before you got here. It was... a rough night, and I'd been more tired than I realized," I say, offering him a small smile back. What I need right now is coffee. I don't even know what time it is, but we both have to be at the tavern later this morning.

"Yeah, you were out like Sleeping Beauty. But I didn't mind. I was hoping not to wake you," he says softly, his grayish-blue eyes dancing over mine.

"I'm sorry, I thought you were Ben," I say quietly, closing my eyes before the tears come. I wait for the first one to fall, but it doesn't come. My eyes are dry somehow.

At this, he reaches for the hand that's been toying with the edge of the blanket. His hand is warm and comforting in mine. Slowly, I open my eyes back up and look over at him.

"Don't be. You don't have anything to apologize for. You're allowed to feel things, Jude," he says honestly.

I know he's right. How is it that he can be so patient with me? How does he do that?

"You seriously stayed here the whole night?" I grin sheepishly.

He returns the smile and shrugs his shoulders playfully. "I couldn't walk away."

I don't know what to say to that. That's been happening more and more with him.

A beat of silence passes before I open my mouth again. We both end up trying to speak at the same time.

"Do you want me to make some coffee?"

"Are you up for some reminiscing?"

I quirk an eyebrow at him. "I'll make the coffee, and then we can sit on the deck and look through the pictures together if that's what you mean."

"Yeah, that's what I mean," he says with a soft smile. "Sounds great."

"This is not the end of your story, this is just the next chapter."

Kelly's handwritten words echo in my head all morning. Her scrapbook is beautiful and so well thought out. I can't believe she took the time to put that together for me.

She told me she originally planned to give it to me and Ben for our next anniversary, which would've been next month, but knew I needed it a little sooner. She's not wrong.

I wish it hadn't taken me so long to look through it. The tears had come, but somehow they didn't feel like sad, broken tears. It felt like healing. It was exactly the way Jay had described it earlier this morning, "reminiscing."

After several cups of coffee, flipping through each page, and sharing memories of Ben, we eventually parted ways. I needed to finish getting ready before heading over to the tavern, and he needed to do the same. I still haven't gotten around to packing my bags yet. I leave for Indiana first thing in the morning, and he'll be flying back to LA not too long after.

Before we parted ways, I asked if he'd be willing to sing one more song with me tonight before we both left. He smiled and said sure. It was hard to tell exactly what he was thinking. I knew I hurt him the other night when I told him that I wanted him to go back to LA, but now I'm not sure I meant that.

It isn't my place to take the tavern away from Jay if he really wants to run it. With me. Maybe I'd been quick to jump to conclusions. I'm not sure what I want, and I know that's not fair to him. Maybe he's right, and I do need some more time.

Yet, despite everything I put him through, he stayed with me all night. Nothing happened between us, but how would I feel if something had? I'm not so sure I would've stopped it had he made the first move. After all, I did kiss him first. Even though we haven't talked about it since that night, he didn't sound like he regretted it. He told me not to regret it if I did. *Do I regret it, the kiss?* No. Yes. I don't know.

My emotions might be all over the place, but I think I'm starting to fall for him. Piece by piece, I can feel him breaking through the walls I put up when I lost Ben. I just have to let him fill up those spaces rather than trying to force him out.

Jay chose the song this time, it's the song "Little Did I Know" by Julia Michaels. It's a song about how love can catch you off guard. How you think you have everything planned out, and then someone comes along and changes everything.

The moment Jay came back into my life, everything changed. I'd been quick to write him off, thinking he was this cold and callous person who only cared about himself. But I'd never been more wrong about someone.

He's proven himself time and time again that he's genuine. He does care, and he's sorry for how he handled things in the past between him and his brother. He came here filled with guilt and regret. He might still carry a few, but he's changed, too. For the better. He's not the same man who walked into this town, and he won't be leaving the same. I can only hope when he returns— when we both return, that neither of us will go back to who we were before.

CHAPTER 55
Jay

Mom doesn't understand why I'm leaving. I hate the thought of lying to her, but I know I can't tell her the real reason why I have to go back. Kyle's in trouble and needs my help, and she would just worry even more and beg me not to go. Not again.

Maybe, by not telling her the full truth, I'm causing more harm than I need to. My six weeks are up, and I'm on a plane back to LA. The place that was home for the last decade. I know exactly what this looks like on the outside. She asked what this means and if I'll be coming back. The truth? I don't know.

I didn't promise Jude anything; I know better than to do that. Promises could easily be broken. In case this turned into something more challenging than just helping my friend locate his dad, I couldn't leave Jude hanging like that.

I remember something she said to me at the beginning of June: *Well, I hope it wasn't for nothing. I hope when you decide to leave, it'll have been worth something.*

I care about her too much to promise my return. I won't give her false hope. I want her, it's more a matter of if she wants me back. It's too late to turn back now. I need to fix this first.

I can only hope she'll understand.

I told Mom that I need more time to process. That I need to go back to LA and make sure that's what I want. Whether that means starting again in Cali or staying with Jude and Mom in Bethel.

Jude told me that day, sitting on top of the cliff, that I belong in LA. I never really belonged in Bethel to begin with. Who am I kidding?

Sure, I spent the entire night in bed next to her. Close enough to breathe in her light jasmine scent, close enough to hear her soft breaths next to me. But she doesn't feel the same way that I do.

She thought I was Ben lying next to her in *their* bed. Because why wouldn't she? Why did I ever think I had a fair shot with her? I played it off like it didn't bother me, but it did. It stung worse than I let on. She's still grieving, I know she is, but when it comes to Jude, I'm ready to dive into just about anything with her.

I told her I'm willing to wait, and I meant it. But realistically, how can I hold onto something that's already slipping through my fingers? She doesn't want me in that way. Not the way that I want her.

For now, this is what needs to happen. Maybe this time apart, whether it's just for a little while or for forever, will give us both some answers. Because it's killing me not knowing.

As the Oklahoma fields roll by like a tumbleweed out the airplane's tiny window, I can't help but wonder if she's hoping for the same thing.

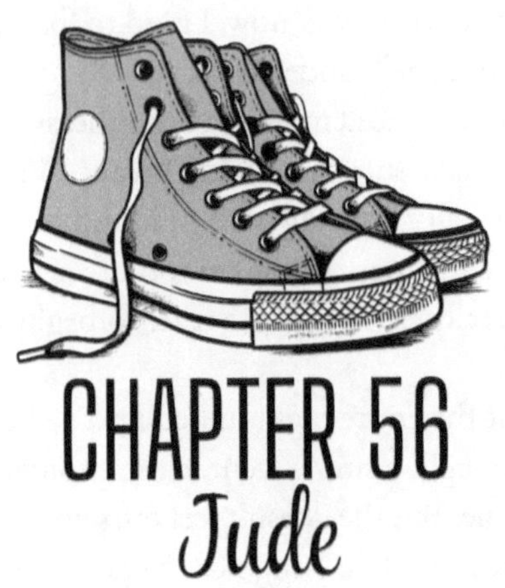

CHAPTER 56
Jude

can't believe I survived so long without seeing, holding, and hugging my babies. Seeing them now, it's like they've grown older before my eyes. How has it only been a month?

My parents and my kids picked me up from the airport, and we spent the past three hours traveling from the airport back to my parents' home. Both Nova and Riley talked a mile a minute. I had a hard time keeping up, and probably didn't get every single detail, but it was refreshing to hear their voices after so long apart. Face-Time has its perks, but it's not the same.

I'm grateful for the time I had without them, but I also didn't realize just how much I desperately need them. I don't want to go this long without them anytime soon. I hope I'll never have a reason to.

There are only two more days left in June before it is officially July. I'm spending a couple of weeks in Indiana before we all fly out to the beach. Mom and Dad surprised the kids with an all-inclusive, kid-friendly beach resort in Jamaica for the last two weeks in July. It's very generous of them. After everything they've already done for the kids this summer. I do my best to forget that this trip was supposed to be for our eleventh wedding anniversary. In hindsight, I'm grateful they didn't cancel the reservations. Any chance at escaping reality these days, I'm in.

The remainder of the summer flies by in a flash. The days turn into another week gone by, and before I know it, we're already packing up our bags to head back home. *Home.* Funny how home can mean different things in different phases of life. Sometimes, home means the literal place you go to at the end of a long day, or in this case, a long trip. But other times, home is simply where your heart is. And my heart? Well, it's in several places.

Part of my heart is here with my family, in Indiana. The other part is in Bethel, Oklahoma, where I spent the last decade building a family and life with my husband and our two wonderful kids. A large piece of my heart was buried with Ben.

But there is another fraction of my heart that rests in the hands of his brother. One of the last people I ever expected to fall for, Jay Whitley.

I can only hope he still feels the same way about me when I return. We haven't communicated much since we both got on separate flights and flew in opposite directions.

I've texted him a couple of times, and he always responds. But his texts are short and straightforward. No smiley face emojis or anything. Maybe he's just busy, helping out his friend. I don't fully understand it all, but I try not to let it bother me too much. I want to trust him. I want to believe the things he said to me.

I wish that I had been more present when it came to running the tavern while Ben was still alive. Sure, I made appearances, and I know the staff well, but I have always separated myself from work and my personal life. This had easily become a large part of Ben's life. The people there were his second family. I've never allowed myself to get close enough for that kind of bond to form.

Without him here, it all falls to me now. Every responsibility he took on effortlessly for the last ten years has fallen into my lap. I wasn't prepared for the weight of it all then, and I'm not sure that I am now.

I'm barely getting by, caring for myself and the kids. Every day is a new challenge. Some days I wake up and make it through the day okay, without any meltdowns or panic attacks. Other days, it's a miracle if I even make it out of bed before early afternoon. But I am doing the best I can. Step by step, moment by little moment.

And I've had some time to think. A lot of time, actually. I don't want to run this place by myself. I never should've left it all to Ben, but he honestly loved every second of it. I love it too, just not in the same way he did. It means something else to me. Every time I walk through the doors, I not only picture him here, but I can also hear all the songs we used to sing. He wasn't much of a singer, so he didn't perform with me on stage, but he was always there.

I shouldn't have been so hard on Jay. I was hurt when I found out he had just as much right to this place as I did. As Ben had. I got scared because I realized how unpredictable the future can be, and I didn't want to say yes to something when I had no idea how it would turn out.

The truth is, I may never know what's in store for this place. But I do know one thing: Ben tried to get his brother to partner with him in this business. He wanted to give Jay a chance—long before I knew it was a possibility.

What if he's telling the truth? About all of it.

I don't know him well, but I know enough about him to believe that he had nothing to do with all the illegal stuff that went down with his boss. That isn't his fault. He was just in the wrong place at the wrong time. Like so many of us have been.

I have to believe what he said is true. I want to be someone that he can trust. He wouldn't have given me all of that information if he didn't trust me with it in the first place. I believe him. I trust him. I can see that now. And now I have to have faith that he'll decide what's best for him and this restaurant. It's just as much his as mine. It should've been a part of his life all along.

I can't rob him of that now. That isn't fair of me to decide that for him. He should be allowed the choice. If he truly wants to be here running this place with me, he should be given that chance. It may still crash and burn, but neither of us will ever know if we don't try.

Time has a way of uncovering the truth, and soon I'll find out if he meant everything he said.

I'll be here. But will he?

I want him to be.

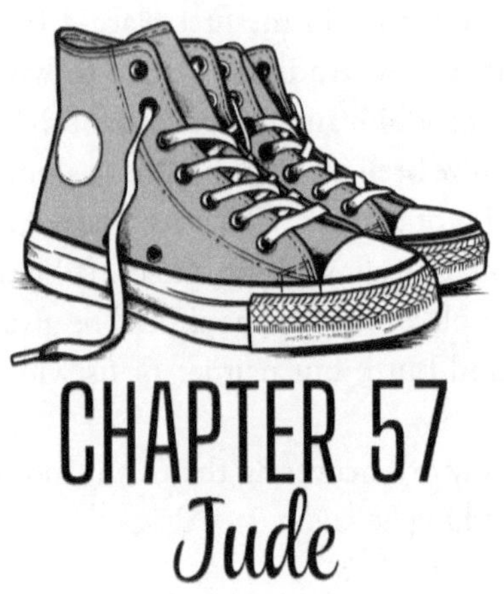

CHAPTER 57
Jude

t's August first, and also the first Friday since we returned a few days ago. The kids still have two full weeks before school starts back up again, and they're bouncing with restless energy. I haven't given much thought about what to do with them during the day while I'm at the tavern, but luckily, Kelly has the day off today and offered to watch them along with her four girls.

Kelly's girls are sweet and get along well with my kids, so I'm not worried about it. Once school starts back up, it won't be an issue.

Kelly shows up right at nine with her arms full of goodies. She has at least three grocery bags full of food and snacks for all the kids, and her oldest, Alona, is carrying two to-go cups of coffee. She's the best.

I haven't had a chance to catch up with her since all the whirlwind events with Jay, and then spending the rest of the summer in Indiana. I took the album Kelly made so I could show my family. We laughed and cried as we reminisced about Ben.

I miss him so much.

As soon as Kelly arrives with her kids, Nova and Riley run up to them, wild with excitement, already deciding who will play who in their favorite game called "family."

After they all retreat downstairs, I turn to my friend and she opens her arms for a big bear hug.

"I missed you, Kells," I say in a rush, her arms wrapping tightly around me. They're warm and comforting, like a campfire on a cold autumn night.

"You too, love. Seriously. Don't leave me like that ever again. Okay?" She moves me an arm's length away, holding firmly onto both of my shoulders, her ocean-blue eyes locking onto mine.

I nod my head and motion towards the coffee she brought. The to-go cups have cooled down, so I pop them both into the microwave for a quick reheat.

"Oh yes! I got you a coconut caramel latte, hope that's okay," she says, handing me the cup labeled Coco C once it's warmed up.

"It's perfect, thanks." I pull out a chair at the kitchen table and plop down. She grabs the remaining coffee and does the same.

We start with small talk, catching up on the little things. I tell her about the kids' summer and their time with my parents. I then pull out my phone and show her several pictures from our vacation on the sandy beaches of Jamaica. It'd been the perfect getaway. Something we'd been needing for a long time.

When it's about time to say goodbye to the kids and make my way over to the tavern, Kelly asks the question I'm sure she was building up to the whole conversation. "So... tell me what happened between you and Jay."

We've both finished our coffees, and I stand to leave, but at her question, I freeze.

My breath catches in my throat. *Jay.* Will I be seeing him today for the first time in a month? We went from seeing each other just about every day to almost radio silence over the past month. But that's all it'd been, right? A parting of ways? A "hey, see you later" kind of thing. Or had I mistaken it, and it was really a goodbye?

"What do you mean? Nothing happened." I say, folding my arms across my chest. For some reason, I suddenly feel defensive, even though I have no reason to be.

She raises one of her perfectly plucked blonde eyebrows at me, tilting her head to the side.

"Really, Jude? Try again. Something was definitely going on between you two." Yeah, something happened between us, but what exactly, I'm not sure. We had a connection, there was a flicker of a spark, but had I been too quick to snuff it out before it had the chance to ignite?

Somehow, I feel like this is partly my fault.

"Yes, fine. Okay. But I'm not sure how to explain it. I mean, we started to form this connection, you know? But I think I messed it all up. I haven't been able to let Ben go yet, and I just... I'm not sure I'll ever be ready to try again with somebody else, you know?"

"And by somebody else, you mean Jay, right?"

I mean, anyone. I'm not sure I can see myself living life with anyone else. But for my own sake, I hope that I'm wrong. Because I don't want to be alone forever. That's not how I want to spend the rest of my life, and I think Kelly knows that about me.

"Jay, the boy next door, anyone," I say, waving my hand in the air as if I can make the next man of my dreams appear out of thin air. He doesn't.

"You live out in the country, love. You don't have any boys next door." She laughs, soft lines creasing around her eyes in a grin.

I shake my head, rolling my eyes. "You know what I mean."

She nods at this. "Yeah, I do. Look, I meant what I said when I told you to protect your heart. But now it just seems sad all over again. And I want to know why. Why did he leave, Jude?"

Why did he leave? It wasn't that long since we last talked face-to-face, but it might as well have been ages ago. A decade ago. A lifetime.

"He had some things to take care of with a buddy back in LA," I say, robotically. I'm numb again. I didn't think it was possible to miss two people at the same time. A man that I could never be with again, and another man that I was hoping to see again, but maybe I'd gotten it all wrong. Tipped the scales too far.

She chews her lip, pondering this.

"Did he say when he's coming back?"

I sit back down, gravity pulling me into the chair. My legs are anchored to the ground. *What?* I thought... I thought he would've come back by now. It's been over four weeks since we last saw each other. I thought that'd be plenty of time to work through things with his old business partner and return home. *Home, back to me.* But I told him to leave... I practically shoved him out the door. I told him it was for the best, that he didn't belong here—that LA was where he belonged.

I've been so foolish.

What was I thinking? No wonder he hasn't returned. He thought this is what I wanted from him. Being friends had been too much, and also not enough. Said things I can't take back. And now I've pushed him away for good, making him think whatever sparks we had between us meant nothing.

But he isn't nothing. Not anymore. Not to me. What have I done?

I hear the loud scraping of a chair near me. Kelly is rising out of her seat and slowly making her way over to me.

"Jude, what's wrong? What is it, love?" she says, turning my face gently towards hers.

I glance up at her with blurry eyes. I shake my head. I can't get the words out. I've ruined any chance I had at a new start. A new beginning. A second chance.

"He's gone, Kelly. I pushed him away, and now he's not coming back. I'm too late." I choke out as the tears spill over. I'm a constant teeter-totter. I never know when the tears will come. But they always do.

"Oh, honey... don't say things like that. You can't be sure of that," she offers, trying to reassure me.

She tugs me closer, resting my head on her shoulder as I sob. She just holds me there.

"I am. It's too late."

She draws back slightly so our faces are only inches apart. Her blue eyes hold mine intently. She doesn't back down.

"You're right—some things do pass us by. But not everything. I don't think it's too late to remedy this if that's what you want. Jude, I have your back. You know that. I always will."

I want to believe her, but it's so hard. Jay is miles away, living his life, and he's probably already forgotten about me. After all, he left this place once. How hard would it be to turn away from it all again? He hasn't been as attentive in our text messages lately. Maybe he's already moved on. From this town, from the tavern, and from *me*.

"What do you want, Jude?"

"I don't see how it's possible..."

"Do you want him to give you another chance?" she asks me.

It's all I can do to nod my head. The words I need to say don't come.

"Okay, then I think I have an idea."

"Okay," I say, not feeling super confident in whatever idea she has up her sleeve, but I'm willing to at least give it a fair shot. I'm willing to try anything at this point.

I'm not certain about a lot of things lately. Tomorrow is not promised, but if given a chance to make things right with him, I'd like to try again. I'd like to try something new with Jay.

Maybe, just maybe, I'm starting to believe in life after love after all.

CHAPTER 58
Jay

can't believe it's been an entire month with barely a word from Jude. Yet, a small part of me expected this to happen. She'd realize that I'm not what she wants and just needed time away from me to realize that. Of course, I hadn't allowed her the space to see that with me always there.

I only wish there wasn't any space between us. I left with memories of her soft skin next to mine, her hair in between my fingers. And the final song we sang together. A song about learning to trust and confide in someone new. I thought that would be us, but I guess I had it all wrong. I should've known better, and I did. But it didn't stop my heart from going after hers anyway.

When I arrived back in Cali, Kyle had been a wreck. Distraught over losing another business with his dad, and then his dad hiding from authorities when they came with a warrant for his arrest.

Fortunately, we were able to track him down within a couple of days. It hadn't taken us long to figure out where he was hiding.

We were smart about the whole thing, of course. Kyle and I

have a mutual friend who's a cop, and once we were sure of his dad's whereabouts, he tagged along with us. We found his dad's truck and caught him pulling up to Kyle's mom's house. They'd been divorced for years, but after everything fell apart, it seems like they rekindled something.

In the weeks that followed, I finalized the paperwork and officially moved out of my apartment and into Kyle's place. I told him it was temporary, but he didn't seem to mind.

He has a spare room, and I don't have much. It's nice to have my Range Rover back again. But that's all I've missed from my life back here. To be honest, I'm missing Jude and the liveliness that the tavern brought to the small community. I can't find those things here.

I'm stuck in a hard place. A place I no longer want to be stuck in.

I've wanted to text Jude so many times. And there are a couple of times she texted me, something simple like: *The air feels different here,* or *I've had your playlist on repeat today, can't get these songs out of my head.* But I didn't know how to respond to any of them. I'm not sure what she meant. I can't see her face-to-face, and I'm trying to protect my own heart from completely shattering. She wanted me to come back here, and she wouldn't have said that if she hadn't meant it, right?

Kyle invited me out with him and his girlfriend tonight. They've got a favorite bar they hit most weekends. I politely declined, though. Before my path crossed with Jude's, I'd been reckless. I often partied and drank on the weekends, but not anymore. Somehow, it doesn't feel right going places without her. Eventually, that feeling will pass, but the wound is still fresh. It stings not having her around.

One of the times we sat in the office at the tavern having lunch together, she mentioned a new idea she had for the tavern. She wants to bring in a wider audience for their Friday Open Mics. She said she thought about starting up a Livestream on their website where anyone can tune in live and get to enjoy the performances from anywhere.

I thought it was a great idea and arranged everything before I left. I asked Mom for help—without telling her why—and she stepped up without hesitation.

I keep checking in with Mom to see when they'll be ready to start streaming live, and every time she tells me that I should come back home and see for myself. Relentless. She isn't wrong, though. I shouldn't be miles away in a different time zone. I'd still be there now, had Jude just given me—us—a chance. But she didn't want that. Whether she just needs space, or more time to process everything, the reasons why don't matter.

All I know is that she doesn't want me there. She made that clear. And even though I'm back here, back "home," it doesn't feel the same. At least I know that the tavern is in good hands. I know her well enough to trust that she'll love and cherish that place just as much, or more, than my brother did.

After Kyle and his girlfriend leave for the bar, I sit at my computer and half-heartedly search for some more jobs. Suddenly, I get a message request from someone on my Instagram page. I open it up to see a link. I've gotten enough links in my life to know what it is without even opening it up. Before I returned to Bethel, I probably would've been tempted to view it, but now I'm only filled with disgust. At myself. There's only one person I have on my mind, and she's miles away.

Before I can exit the webpage, another message pops up, but this time it isn't a link. I skim it quickly.

kel-star89: Hey Jay! I promise it's not spam! Which, I know, makes it sound even more like it is. Just trust me, you'll want to watch this. You can thank me later!

What. In. The. World. Who is this? And why should I trust them? Yet, something in my gut is telling me to open it. I have no idea what it could be and why they are sending this to me, but I have a feeling I should click it and find out.

I click on the hyperlink and close my eyes. I hold my breath and count to three. *One, two, three.*

I release a long breath and open my eyes. My jaw drops at what I'm seeing.

My laptop nearly falls off my lap as the screen now reads: The Second Verse Tavern Presents: Live Open Mic! CLICK HERE TO VIEW.

I'm in awe. I can't believe they finally have it up. She actually did it. Jude had a vision, and I got to be a part of helping it come to life. I move my mouse over the link. I have no idea what to expect, but before I can second-guess myself, I click the link and a video fills the screen. It's a crisp image of the stage I've grown familiar with over the summer, and on it is a woman I'd recognize anywhere.

It's Jude, opening the set for tonight.

Do you believe in life after love? I remember asking her that forever ago. It wasn't my smoothest line. I was such a different person when I first met her.

Jude laughed and asked me if I was seriously quoting Cher. I absolutely was. And now, Jude is belting out the lyrics to that very song on the livestream for the entire universe to see.

Only, this isn't a version I've ever heard before. No, nothing quite like this. Jude has her eyes closed for most of the song, and as she drags out the final note—chilling me to the bone—she finally opens them.

An incoming message pings on my laptop, and I glance at it before the notification disappears.

kel-star89: Are you watching?? Please tell me you are. Just a thumbs up will suffice.

I'm not entirely sure who this is, but I have a pretty good guess based on the screen name. Kelly. I'm thankful she reached out. I can't believe I've gone this long without seeing Jude.

kel-star89: This is Kelly, btw. Ya know, from the tavern. Keep watching!

I knew it. I don't know how they managed to pull this off, but I can find out the details later. Right now, I don't want to miss a thing.

I turn my attention back to the only person in the room I care about. Jude.

I know she can't see me, but when the song ends and the applause dies down, she looks directly into the camera. If I didn't know any better, it feels a lot like she's staring directly into my soul. Does she know I'm watching her?

Before I have time to ponder why she chose that song, she starts speaking to the camera.

I lean in closer and turn up the volume.

"I'm not sure if you're out there somewhere listening... I hope you are, because I have something to say." At this, I'm on full alert. I situate the laptop so I can see her perfectly. I miss those eyes, and her perfect smile, and the way her hair falls in waves around her.

She adjusts herself on the barstool, crossing her legs. She's wearing that same bright pink dress I first saw her in the night I found her outside, flushed and desperate for an escape. Her hair is pinned up with a few soft curls falling loose around her face. And of course, bright pink Converse to match. I wouldn't want her any other way.

"When you came back into my life, I didn't believe in life after love. Truly, I didn't. The love of my life had been ripped away, and I thought that was the end for me. I had no idea how I'd ever move on. I'm still not sure. But you once asked me if I believed in life after love, and, at the time, I thought it was a joke.

"I've had time to think—really think— about what that question means to me. And now, I do believe in life after love. I believe not all broken things are lost. Some things can be found. Some things can be mended. You and I were both lost and broken when our paths crossed. I hated you at first. But slowly, little by little, you chipped away at my armor until you broke through. You never gave up on me.

"In the end, I pushed you away. I thought that's what I wanted. I thought it was for the best. But I was wrong. It wasn't for the best. It tore me apart. I just wanted to tell you: I believe. *I believe.*"

Before I have time to think it through, I do what I should've done from the start.

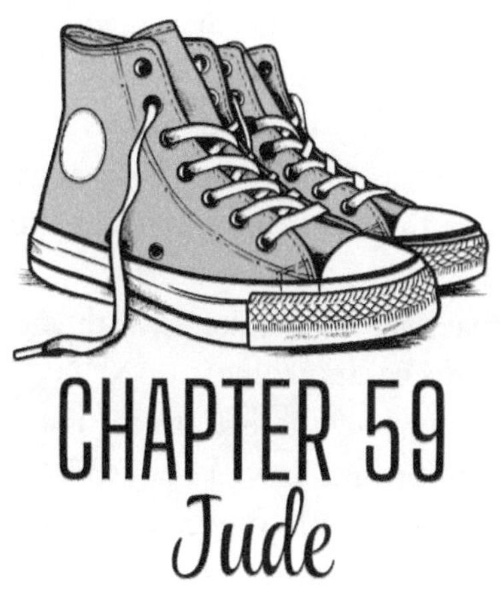

CHAPTER 59
Jude

'm shaking as I exit the stage. I can't believe I said all that. But I mean every single word. I hope it was the right thing to say. Kelly had the idea to send him the link directly, to be sure he would see the song. I hope it all worked out on his end. That he hadn't been busy with something else, or someone else. But it's done. I've never done anything like that before.

I'm generally a private person when it comes to personal matters, especially when it involves the inner workings of my heart. I may not be fully ready to dive into a new relationship yet, but I'm ready to start trying. I don't want to spend the rest of this crazy, unpredictable life alone. I had someone willing to stand by my side, and I did the worst thing possible. I pushed him away. Told him I wanted him gone, when that wasn't the truth. I realize that now.

I don't want to hide from my feelings anymore, even though they terrify me. Falling for somebody else is scary. It's messy, hard, and comes with challenges I've never had to face... like allowing myself to fall for someone, even though it's a constant, internal battle of right vs. wrong. Yes or no. Stay or go.

But he needs to know how I really feel. Jay will know I was talking to him, and I don't care if anyone else in Bethel figures it out. I'm tired of hiding. I feel as though this huge weight has lifted off me. I feel lighter. Brighter. More confident. No matter what the outcome is, at least I spoke from my heart.

Sometimes that's all you can do. Go with your gut. Trust your instincts. Pray for the best outcome.

I never even told him the live stream is up and running. I haven't reached out to him in weeks now. Now the whole world knows I'm falling in love with somebody else. I can only hope the one person who needs to hear it the most was tuning in. I found this particular acoustic cover version shortly after he asked me if I believed in life after love. I love that song, but the auto-tune pop version isn't exactly what I was looking for. I stumbled upon this one, sung ironically almost a decade ago by YouTuber Madilyn Bailey.

As soon as I set down my mic, I left. I know it was a risk to sing that song and say what I said live for the world to hear, and I can't stay here. Not without him. Not knowing if he'd ever see it, and wondering if I missed my chance. It was Kelly's idea—she doesn't know the history of that particular song, but her idea was to say something to him directly over the live stream, just in case he's listening.

There's a small chance that he could watch it now, even if he missed it. The video will be archived on the website for some time. But my phone is dead, and I need to charge it.

I need to get back to check on the kids. It's been a long day. Business seemed busier than usual, and there were a few technical issues with the streaming. Luckily, it all worked out just in time. But I need to be home.

I make it out to my car, dump my purse in the passenger seat, and start my car. Before I can plug my phone into the charging cord, there's a soft knocking sound on my window. I jump and turn to see who's tapping on my window.

Whew, it's Rita. I'm not sure who I was expecting it to be, but I'm thankful it's a familiar face.

I roll my window down and peer up at the tall woman. Ben was the spitting image of his mother, broad-shouldered and tall like a mountain. They both had hair the color of midnight and eyes that matched.

She bends over to get a better view. "I'm sorry for scaring you, Judith. Er, I mean... Jude. Sorry, um, do you have a minute?" She clears her throat and motions towards the seat where I previously dumped all my things.

I unlock the door and quickly shove everything into the backseat.

I don't know whether to be more shocked that she called me Jude for the first time or that she's sitting in my car. Did I trip and fall on my way out of the tavern? Am I dreaming?

I shake the crazy thoughts out of my head and glance over at her. She takes up most of the room in the seat, just like Jay. Funny.

She seems nervous and fidgety, and toys with the hem of her skirt. She looks over at me, offering me the smallest of smiles.

"Is everything okay?" I ask.

She quickly nods and turns her focus back to the hem on her clothing. "Yes, I'm sorry for barging in on you like this. I've been meaning to talk to you, and I saw you leaving in a rush. I figured it was now or never. I mean not *never*, never, but you know," she says with a chuckle.

I have no idea what she's going on about, but I offer her a small smile in return.

"I guess I'll start by saying that I'm sorry I never called you Jude. I know my Benjamin always called you that."

I nod my head even though she's not looking at me anymore. I stare in front of me at the entrance of the tavern, watching as people come and go.

"It's okay, really. My parents always called me Judy growing up. But I've always been Jude to him. It just stuck."

Her eyes flick up to mine when I say this. She nods with understanding, her eyes wet with moisture.

"I'm not sure why I never did, and I'm sorry about that. I can start calling you Jude from now on if you'd prefer. You'll have to be patient with me, though. I'm getting older every day and may not get it perfect every time." She laughs again softly, her skin crinkling near her eyes.

"That's okay. Thanks, I appreciate that."

"Anyway... Jude, what I want to talk to you about is Jay."

At the mention of his name, I force myself to look away. It's too painful to think about him right now. After I sang my heart out to what felt like an empty room. A room where I saw only him as I belted out every line.

"Oh," is all I manage to get out. This can't be good. I always get the impression that she doesn't like me much, that she'll never see me as someone good enough to have married her firstborn son.

"I'm not sure what you did to my boy, but I want to say thank you."

Wait, what? I turn my head back in her direction and shift my body towards her. She can't possibly be serious. Thank you? For what? If anything, she should be yelling at me because it's my fault I broke their family this time. He's all she has left, and I ruined that for both of them.

"Thank you?" I grit out, not understanding.

"Yes, dear. You saved that man. You changed him. Don't think I didn't notice, because I did."

I'm stunned. Shocked. I don't believe this.

"But he left because of me. I said some terrible things to him that I didn't mean, and now he's gone. It's all my fault. You should be blaming me."

She shakes her head softly, her fingers pausing for a moment in her lap.

"I don't blame you for anything, Jude. Maybe you just aren't ready yet. Maybe neither of you are. Whatever was said between you two can be worked out."

"Worked out how? He's thousands of miles away and doesn't want anything to do with me."

She shakes her head again and starts digging around in her purse for something. I'm growing impatient as exhaustion catches up with me. I haven't been sleeping well again, not since... Well, that ship has sailed. It was over before I let it begin.

She places a white, folded-up piece of paper on my dashboard. My eyes flicker over to the paper and back up to meet hers. What is this? What does this have to do with anything?

"I think this might help. Read this after I leave, somewhere in private, and I think you'll understand that he wants *everything* to do with you."

My hands shake as I reach for the folded piece of paper. I have no idea what this is or what to make of anything she's saying to me.

"What is this?" I ask, looking down at the note in my shaking hand.

"Open it and you'll see for yourself. Call me if you need anything, dear. It's all going to work out in the end. You'll see."

But how can she be so sure? I need to hurry home so I can see for myself what is in this mysterious letter that has all the answers.

I highly doubt it holds all the answers, but I can only *hope*. I haven't forgotten all of my faith just yet.

CHAPTER 60
Jay

As soon as her song ends, I pull up a new internet tab and start searching for available flights. I can't believe I've gone this long without giving up and going to see her. It's risky and crazy, I know, but I can't sit around here, in a room that isn't mine, when I know how she feels about me.

How could I have been so blind? Or maybe she hadn't known how she felt until now. She needed some time to process everything, and I don't blame her for that. Not one bit. She's not someone I can stay mad or frustrated at.

Since day one, I let her call the shots, and that hasn't changed. Neither has the way I feel about her. I'm crazy for this woman, and I need to hold her in my arms and remind her exactly what she means to me.

I shoot a quick message back to Kelly, thanking her for sending me the link. I'm so glad she did, and that I trusted her enough to click on it. I can't imagine not seeing Jude's performance. The earliest I can get to Bethel is a late flight on Saturday evening. Mom will most likely be willing to pick me up, but I hesitate briefly as my mouse hovers over the "buy now" option.

This is what Jude wants, right? She picked that song on purpose, knowing what it means to me, something just between us. And then she looked at the camera directly, as though she was somehow talking straight to me.

She sang that song in the hopes that I'd been listening. Right?

I hit submit before I can second-guess myself. I'm doing this, it's done. I'm packing up my things and I'm going home. Home to Jude. For good this time.

I can only hope and pray that this is what she really wants. Leaving Bethel all those years ago was the biggest mistake I ever made. Going back now—for her—might just be the second. I'll find out soon enough.

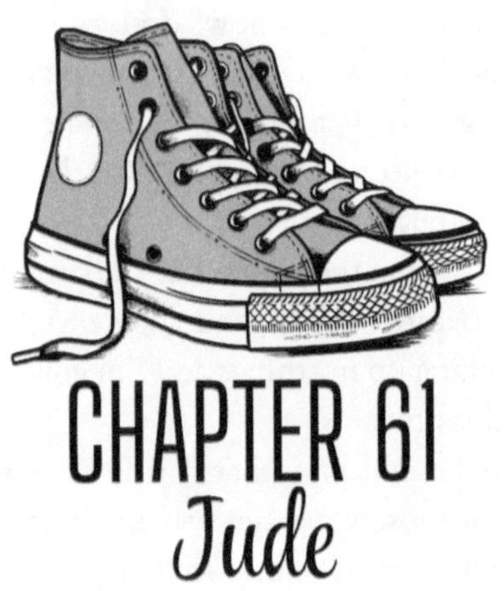

CHAPTER 61
Jude

t's almost ten by the time I pull into my driveway. I shut off the car and quickly make my way inside, the note burning a hole in my purse. The kids are fast asleep in their beds, and I say a quick thank you and goodbye to Kelly and her kids before they leave.

I pull on one of Ben's baggy old T-shirts. It's black and white with The Beatles walking across the iconic Abbey Road. I turn off all the lights except for a small lamp on my nightstand and climb into bed with the note.

I take a deep breath and slowly unfold it.

I gasp and cover my mouth with my hand. I recognize the writing right away. It's Ben's. He wrote this... whatever *this* is. I bite my lip to keep the tears at bay and scan my eyes over his comforting, yet awful handwriting.

I stifle a laugh because it's terrible and hard to read. He's always had the worst handwriting, but I love it anyway. I loved him in the small things and big things, and I want to soak in every little piece I have left of him. Like this old band tee and this messy letter. I settle in to read what Ben wanted to say.

I'LL BE HERE

I BELIEVE YOU ONLY FIND TRUE LOVE ONCE
IN A LIFETIME
AND I FOUND YOU
DARLING I FOUND YOU

CAUGHT ME IN A HAZE
I COULD LIVE FOREVER THIS WAY
GIRL, YOU'VE GOT ME SPELLBOUND
LOVESICK FOR YOU, ONLY YOU.

FOR ALL THE DAYS I'M GIVEN
I'LL BE HERE
FOR ALL THE MOMENTS TIME ALLOWS
I'LL BE HERE
COUNT ME IN, READY TO DIVE IN
DARLING THIS IS WHERE OUR STORY BEGINS.

Okay, I was kidding myself when I thought there wouldn't be tears. After I make it past the first line, I'm already a goner. The waterworks start whether I want them to or not. When did he write this? And why didn't he give it to me?

My eyes scan the page and see that there's more to the song. But the rest of the lyrics are written in a slanted, unfamiliar scrawl. When I see the name beside the rest of the lyrics, I have to choke back a sob. Because it says Jay. *Jay?* I wipe my eyes with my blanket and continue.

Jay:
Nothing is the way it seems

Tomorrow isn't promised
Yet, I found you
Darling, I found you.

Two healing hearts
Hoping to start again
Living through the pain
Of yesterday.

It only took a moment
When I laid my eyes on you
The spell had been broken
Darling, it was always you.

This promise I can keep
I'll be here
Even on the days you feel like giving up
I'll be here
Ready and willing, no matter the cost
This is where I'll be, darling.

When I finish, I read it again. And again. I cannot believe the two most important men in my life would write me a song. Ben started it, who knows how long ago, but he never finished it. Then Jay came along and wrote the rest. But there's a third, important part that's missing from this. I make myself a cup of coffee, sit down with my favorite ink pen, and get to work.

It's nearly midnight by the time I'm finally satisfied with my piece, but it's complete. The perfect love story. One that I thought was over the day I lost my husband, but had somehow only been the ending of that chapter in my life. Today, I'm turning over a new page so I can learn what it looks like to live again.

Jude:

Hope had been lost
The day my love died
I thought I had you for a lifetime
But time often lies.

A cruel and desperate cry
I didn't know how to begin again
Until I found you
Darling, I found you.

You picked me back up
Got me on my feet
You saw the real me
The girl I'd hidden underneath.

I'm not going anywhere
I'll be here
Please take your time with me
Treat my heart with care
Darling, you'll find me here.

Count me in, this is where our story begins.

I could only hope and pray it's not too late to try again.

CHAPTER 62
Rita

The moment I got the news that my baby boy was coming home, for good this time, I was nearly beside myself. The call arrived moments after Jude finished her song. It was the first song the tavern has ever aired live for an online audience.

He tuned into our live stream and saw the whole thing. I couldn't have been more grateful that he had. What a sight she was to watch on that stage! Benjamin was always too humble about her talent, but she's seriously the best I've seen come through our doors in a long, long while.

Benjamin changed this place from the ground up and made me a proud mama. I miss that boy more than anything else. At least I thought that until Jay walked out on everything he had here a second time.

The second he called, I picked up, worried something had happened to him in California, and I'd be the one flying out there to see him. To fix whatever damage he did. But I was wrong. He's coming home. For good. He's going to be *here*.

When I got off the phone, I rushed out to find Jude. I had

planned to tell her about Jay, but instead I ended up handing her the song lyrics I found. She needs to know how he feels about her before he comes home.

I found the lyrics in Jay's bedroom. I went in there to clean after he went back to LA. I ended up sitting on his bed, and wondering where on earth I'd gone wrong.

For years, I blamed myself for Jay leaving. I was too hard on him growing up, or maybe I wasn't hard enough. Maybe I pushed him out the door, or maybe it'd been a little of me and Benjamin both. I don't know.

But my eyes caught on something sticking out of his dad's old guitar. At first, I was surprised he hadn't taken the instrument with him. He left his guitar behind to collect dust the first time he went to California. Now... I heard them practicing songs together night after night.

I haven't heard him play like that in ages. I wasn't sure he still knew how. But he does. It's like playing has never left him, and he's never walked away.

Tucked in between the strings was a white, folded piece of paper. *How odd.* I hesitated a moment, knowing I shouldn't be nosy. But if it was something important he left behind, I'd need to make sure it got back to him, and I figured a little peek couldn't hurt. I sobbed when I saw Ben's chicken-scratch handwriting. I read through every single word in a puddle of tears.

When I came to Jay's addition further down the page, I worried my heart would stop beating. This was the most beautiful and heartbreaking thing I have ever read in my entire life. I know how much Benjamin had loved Jude. But I had no idea my baby boy had fallen for her as well. I had a feeling he might have a crush. Call it motherly intuition. But not to this extent. I had no idea how deeply he truly feels for her.

He wasn't clear why he was so quick to leave after the six-week time frame I gave him. But none of that matters anymore. I just need him back home. And I need Jude to see this, so she, too, could know and understand just how much Jay cares about her.

I gave it to her when I saw an opportunity, so she'd know the whole story before Jay gets home. I think I'll let his return be a surprise. When it comes to love, sometimes that can be the best kind.

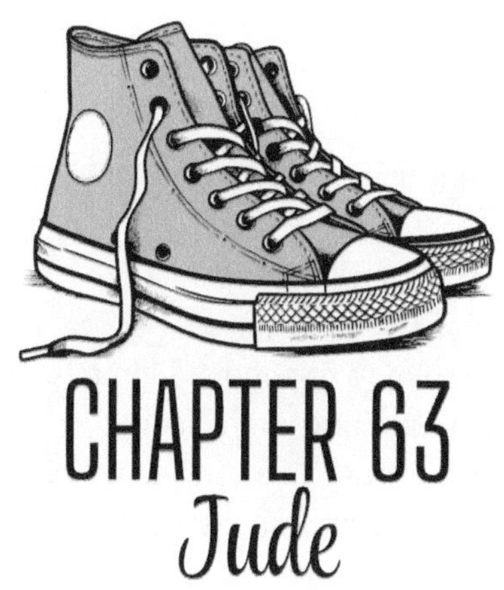

CHAPTER 63
Jude

'm wide awake when the text comes through. I had the day off today and spent most of it keeping the kids entertained and practicing the chords for the song I'll Be Here. I don't have a lot of time to get it right, but my goal is to perform it during next week's Open Mic.

At 11:05, my phone buzzes with a new message.

I've been practicing in the basement, hoping I don't wake the kids with the sound of my singing and guitar. I take a break and swipe to read the message. My heart instantly skips a beat. *Jay.*

Jay: Hey, Jude.

Me: That's ironic, because I'm currently taking a sad song and making it better.

Jay: Really? Is that what you're doing right now?

Me: Yeah, kind of LOL

Jay: What if I told you I'm here?

Me: Here?

Jay: Yeah, can I come in?

Me: OH! Hold on a sec, be right up.

I don't wait for him to respond as I jump to my feet, throw my phone on the couch, and race up the stairs.

I throw open the front door and don't give Jay any time to speak before I throw myself into his arms. I may not be sure of a lot of things, but I'm sure of this. I'm in love with this man. I really am.

I'll be here.

He kept his promise.

CHAPTER 64
Jay

The second she pulls away from me, I hold her face between my hands, tugging her back in close to me, our lips crashing together. The kiss is deep and urgent, yet gentle at the same time. Two people riding out the same waves together. We're in sync. In harmony. With our lips locked and our bodies pressed against each other, it feels more like a warm embrace. I can't get enough of it. Enough of her.

I've dreamed of this moment since the day we met outside Second Verse. With her bright pink dress, coordinating shoes, and matching soft pink lips.

Her lips. I came home for this. For *her*. And now, she's finally mine to love. I don't know what the future holds, and I know tomorrow isn't promised. But the love I have for her isn't going anywhere.

My hands move up into her soft curls, and I suddenly want my hands to be everywhere. But I'll move slowly, because now that she's finally in my arms again, I don't want to do anything that could risk her pushing me away. We need to take this slow and move at her pace, not mine. I meant what I said about waiting for her.

It wasn't that long ago that I craved one-night stands. But there's something different about Jude. She's worth waiting for. I want to take my time with her. I'll take whatever she wants to give me.

I pull back slightly, allowing us both a moment to process this. Take in what's happening between us. I want to see if it's doing to her, what it's doing to me, by the look reflected in her eyes. I don't want to push her too far or too fast. I want whatever she wants. I've never wanted that with anyone else before. Not until now.

Maybe it just takes the right person coming along at the perfect time. It's funny though. Because there never really is a "perfect" moment. We met under very imperfect circumstances. We met in possibly the darkest, most grueling places we would ever find ourselves. Yet she is the small beacon of light that will change my entire world. She became my future, and that altered *everything*.

I search the golden flecks mixed with browns and greens in her eyes. She quickly gives me the answer I'm hoping for.

"I want *you*, Jay," she whispers breathlessly, her eyes dancing with want.

I believe her, but I also love and respect her enough not to rush this. Desire or not. Of course, I want her in that way. I'd be lying if I said I don't think about her in the most intimate way. And maybe someday, she'll want that too. But for now, that's not what this moment is about.

"Slow down there, tiger. Come here."

She quirks one of her eyebrows up at me, but doesn't ask any questions as she closes the space between us. As soon as she's close enough, I slip my hands beneath her thighs and hoist her up against me, breathing in her sweet scent as I carry her over to one of the couches in the living room. She giggles against my neck and it tickles.

I love her laugh. I think I'm starting to love everything about this woman. She's incredible. It wasn't that long ago that we sat on this very couch, working through one of her many puzzles together.

I sit down first, and then guide her into my lap. Her legs are wrapped around my middle and, for a moment, we stay just like this. Her head rests on my chest, her breath slow and steady, like waves kissing the shore. She's the calm to the storm that's often wreaking havoc on my insides.

I hold her close with one hand and use the other to run my fingers gently through her curls. Up and down, back and forth. She murmurs quietly against me, the vibrations of her soft noises sounding through my body.

After some time, I break the silence. "It was hard being away from you... I missed this. Being with you," I say, continuing to stroke lazy lines through her hair.

For a moment, I wonder if she fell asleep, but then she stirs and gently lifts her head off my chest, tilting her head up towards mine.

"I missed you too..." she admits softly. "Why did you come back? I honestly didn't think I would see you again. I hurt you."

I gently tuck her head back against me, while moving my hand to her back, drawing little shapes.

"I was hurt, yeah. And I don't always forgive easily. You already know that about me."

"What was different this time?"

What was different this time? Everything... but mainly her. But it also has to do with me. I've wanted to change. I don't want to hold onto grudges anymore. I've been tied to my own regrets for way too long. It's time to let it all go.

"I meant what I said before I left. I just want you to be happy. If that means you running the tavern without me, I'm okay with that. If you want me here with you, then I'm here. Jude, I'll follow your lead. I've been living by my own rules for so long, and look where it's gotten me. Absolutely nowhere. I'm so tired of running. I'm done. I'm not going anywhere unless you say the word."

She stills for a moment after I finish. I can't tell if she's processing or if she's crying. I wrap both arms around her in a gentle hug.

"But what about what you want? What do you honestly want, Jay? If my opinion didn't matter to you, what would you choose?"

I don't hesitate. I turn her chin up towards mine so I can make sure she hears what I'm about to tell her.

"I would choose you. I never would've left in the first place. I can't change what I did in the past, but I'm done running and hiding. I'm here. For the long haul. I want to stay here with you and be with you. For as little or as much as you want me, I'll take it.

"I love you, and I mean it when I say I want the best for you. I know true happiness may seem like a far-off dream for you, and I get that. I'm more than okay waiting on your timeline. It doesn't need to be on my time. I'll be fine, okay? I just want you in my life. I'm tired of saying goodbye to the people I care about the most, and that includes you, Jude."

Tears roll down both of her cheeks, and I press my fingers to the wetness, wiping them away.

"I want that too. All of it. I want you. I want you to help me run this tavern. I can't do it alone, and I don't want to. Ben would want you to be here running it with me. I know he would. But more importantly, I want you here too. I don't have all the answers for what our future may look like, and that scares me a little. But I'm willing to give us a shot. I'm willing to give you a second chance. Please, don't go. Stay."

I nod my head, tears brimming my eyes, and I bring her lips back to mine. Warm and sweet and *mine*. As long as she will have me, just like this, I'm not going anywhere. She deserves the whole world and more. I'll spend the rest of my days trying to give all of that to her. This isn't our final song, it's just the beginning.

Because we have each other, and that's enough. It always has been, and always will be.

It's getting late and I should leave, but I don't want to. Not so soon after I got her back. With Jude still in my lap, I lift her up and carry her to her bedroom. When we make it to her bed, I lower her down gently onto the mattress. As I start to peel back the covers so I can tuck her in, she grabs the front of my shirt, tugging me closer.

Our faces are inches apart, and I can't help but smile down at her. She's perfect. Perfect for me.

"Can you stay with me tonight? I want you to," she says to me softly. I search her eyes for hunger and don't find any, only a tenderness that nobody has ever offered me before.

This woman has me wrapped around her finger. I'd do anything for her. And right now, I'd love to stay by her side. I want to let her know that she's safe with me. I want to earn her trust completely. Show her that she can trust me, and that I'm really not going anywhere.

"Of course I will. Do you need me to get you anything?"

Smiling sleepily, she shakes her head and rolls onto her side. I take the hint and ease into bed beside her. She's facing the night-stand, so I pull the covers around us and inch closer, wrapping an arm around her and drawing her in.

"Is this okay?" I whisper against her soft blanket of hair spilling over the pillow we're sharing.

"Yes," she whispers.

"Please don't ever be afraid to tell me if something I'm doing isn't okay. I want you to be comfortable with me," I tell her.

She reaches for the arm that's around her and finds my hand, interlocking our fingers together.

"I'm comfortable with you, Jay. But if something ever comes up, I'll tell you. I promise."

"Goodnight, Jude."

"I love you," she says so softly I almost miss it. In the next minute, she's already sound asleep.

CHAPTER 65
Jude

Time flies when you're in love. Jay and I have officially been dating for six months now. I know that isn't considered long in the dating world, but our world isn't like everybody else's. I never would've dreamed I'd become a widow at thirty-two, left to navigate the waters of single motherhood while running a full-time business.

Time doesn't slow down to make room for grieving. But Jay is one of the most patient people I know. He's already been there for many of my "firsts." He surprised me by coming back here in the first place, and then Ben's birthday rolled around. We spent the day going through old pictures and silly videos—laughing until we cried, then crying until we laughed again.

We celebrated with the kids and his mom. The kids helped make a cake for their daddy. And then, of course, the holidays that came quickly after: Halloween, Thanksgiving, Christmas, New Year's, and up next, Valentine's.

I survived each one with a river of tears, but never had to face any of them alone. He was there with me through them all. Sometimes he'd cry too, and other times he simply held onto me until I cried myself dry. He's so good to me. More than I could've ever imagined.

I was nervous the first time I officially introduced Jay to my kids, but had been pleasantly surprised when both Nova and Riley welcomed him with giggles and immediate tickle fights. That used to be Ben's wheelhouse, not mine. I love the little rascals with my whole heart, but wild games are not my thing.

He loves playing and spending time with them. When I'm busy or after a long day, he offers to watch the kids for me so I can have a few minutes of me time to shower. I think he genuinely wants to spend time with them. Whether that means playing Candy Land or Floor is Lava for the hundredth time, he doesn't seem to mind. They're a huge part of me and what makes me who I am, and he wants to be involved as much as possible.

He's invested in them as much as he is in me. If I had even the slightest idea Jay would eventually become a part of my world like this, I probably wouldn't have believed it. It took almost losing him before I was able to see the whole picture.

Jay and I sing together every Friday night. It's the one night we let the kids stay up late and join us at the restaurant. Second Verse Tavern.

I remember asking Ben when we first got together how his mom and stepdad came up with the name. He said it was because, for his mom, his stepdad Scott was her Second Verse. She'd gone through a tough divorce when Ben was about ten and never dreamed she'd find someone else. Believe it or not, she met Scott one night here at the tavern. The rest is history.

History that still lives on through the name of this sacred place. Now, the name shares a new story. A story of *my* second verse. The person I gave a second chance, because life had given one to me as well. Losing Ben has been the hardest thing I've ever had to endure. But finding love and hope again through Jay has been nothing short of amazing.

Jay and I sang the song we all wrote together a month later, in honor of Ben. *I'll Be Here.* Ben will always be my first love. But just because someone is your first, doesn't mean they'll also be your last.

Jay would become my new song. A song I never expected to write and live out. And while our story is far from perfect, it's still very much ours—a harmony I never saw coming, but somehow needed all along.

He saved Ben's last song for me, and now we can continue writing out the rest of our story. One note at a time, lyric by lyric. There's no such thing as the perfect song, but there are certain melodies that stick with you for a long time.

BONUS CHAPTER
Ben

ey Brian, can you bag me up some food for my wife and kids? I've gotta head out, the kids are losing it. Possibly my wife, too." I laugh, even though it's not funny. I could hear the stress in Jude's voice.

This kind of thing happens more often when I'm not there. When I get home, the kids seem to change their attitudes. They could be pulling each other's hair one moment, and running to wrestle with me as soon as I walk into the room. The little devils run full force at me, swinging their little arms, and do their very best to try and tackle me to the ground.

Jude usually stands there glowering at me with her pink lips in a pout and her arms folded across her chest. After ten years with that woman, I'm still just as in love with her as the day we met.

"Yeah, sure thing, boss!" Brian, our head chef at the tavern and my best friend, yells to me from the kitchen.

I shake my head, a grin tugging at my mouth.

"You don't need to keep calling me that, you know!"

Brian pops his head out of the small window and rubs a hand

through his beard. He's always had more facial hair than me. I could never pull it off, and Jude would probably have a cow, honestly, if I ever decide to grow it out.

"Yeah, you keep saying that. But technically, you are my boss!" he retorts.

I roll my eyes and motion with my hand for him to get back to grabbing me a to-go bag.

I feel a buzzing coming from my back pocket. I reach for my phone and answer it.

"Yes, dear," I answer, assuming it's Jude. It doesn't take me long to figure out that it's not Jude. It's my fire chief. There's a fire, and I'm needed on the call. We've been in such a dry spell this season, and there's been more and more fires popping up as a result.

I push open the kitchen doors to get Brian's attention.

"Hey man, we've gotta go. Just got a call. There's a really bad fire north of town."

Brian and I have known each other for years. He's the first person I hired full-time to run the kitchen. He's an excellent chef. I'm not just saying that because he's my friend. People come from all over to eat his food.

About five years ago, he asked me to join the fire department with him. Jude wasn't exactly thrilled about it, and probably still isn't, but she also didn't stop me from signing up. Honestly, I just love helping people. Even if it's just one life, that's still one life I've made a difference in, and that matters to me.

I think that's why Jude finally agreed to let me go. She loves what matters to me. I don't deserve that kind of love. Yet she gives it to me freely.

"Yeah, sure. But what do you want me to do with dinner for your family?"

My mind is already pumping full of adrenaline. I completely forgot about taking them food.

"Here, I'll take it. We shouldn't be gone too long. The crew is already on their way out there. We need to go!"

He passes me the large bag of food, shouting out quick orders to one of our other top chefs as we run out the doors together.

I'll be home soon, Jude. Don't worry about me.

The fire is way worse than we thought. This time of year, the grass is bone-dry and in need of a good rain. A rain that doesn't look likely anytime soon. The blaze started in a small farm field. Within minutes, it had spread to the house on the property. From what I'm told, an elderly couple lives there.

We have to stop this fire from spreading. And we need to get these people out. That's my number one priority right now. I send up a quick prayer, like I always do before charging into a fire this big. Then I run headfirst into the burning house.

I find the husband first. He'd been asleep and passed out from the smoke fumes choking the home. We get him out. Next, we find his wife. But the moment we pull her outside, she bursts into tears, quickly becoming hysterical.

"My baby! My baby! My grandson's still inside. Get him out, please. My baby, get him out!"

The word "baby" slams into me, and suddenly images of my own kids flash through my mind. Novelle on the day she was born, her golden skin and eyes like her Mama, soft brown curls framing her face... my Nova. And Riley, my sweet boy with dark eyes like mine. The one who gives the best hugs.

I have to save this woman's grandson. If it were my house on fire with my wife and kids trapped inside, I'd do everything in my power to get them out. I'd sent Jude a quick text on the drive over, while Brian drove. It wasn't much, but hopefully we can calm the flames and head back home soon.

I rush back into the engulfed house. Windows are breaking, boards are splitting, and the sounds are nothing short of a nightmare. It suddenly dawns on me that I forgot to ask her for the boy's name. Or maybe she told me, and I got distracted by thoughts of my own family and kids. His grandmother mentioned his room is upstairs, and that he's most likely still in there. That's when I hear it faintly, someone shouting his name over and over like a song on repeat.

Jay, Jay, Jay.

The same name as my brother. He's around the same age as when I left my Jay for the first time, at age six, when I graduated and went away for college. Then I returned years later, engaged, and I hadn't exactly welcomed him into my life with the warm embrace I should have. This little boy shares a name with the brother I often forget about. That's the funny thing about family though, you never forget completely.

I have to get this boy back to his family so they can be the ones to wrap him in a warm embrace. Safe and sound. Safe at last. *I'm coming, Jay.*

I shout his name now, hoping I can get to him in time.

Finally, after clearing the ground floor and making my way up to the second floor, I find the little boy crouched in the corner of a bedroom, sobbing into his hands. I quickly scoop him up, place an oxygen mask over his face, and carefully make my way back over to the stairs. But they're gone. Flames climb the walls and engulf the stairway, making it impossible to go back the same way I came.

Okay, this is looking pretty bad. But I'm not going to panic. I just have to find a different way out. I can typically think quickly on my feet.

"It'll be okay, Jay," I tell him as I look around for an escape.

He's still crying, but he's also holding onto me tightly as though his very life depends on it. I'm his *only* hope.

I duck into the first room I find and immediately go over to the window. I yank it open and shout down to my crew.

"I've got him. We're trapped. I need help now!" I yell, trying not to panic. I can't recall another time I've ever felt this scared. I have to put on a brave face for this little boy. Jay's counting on me. I have to stay focused and get him out of here as soon as possible.

Brian extends the long white ladder up to the second-floor window. He quickly climbs up and holds his arms out for the little boy. The moment he looks down and sees his grandparents waving wildly up at him, his entire face lights up with relief. He stretches his little arms out to Brian, latching them around his neck as they quickly make their descent down the ladder.

The flames are growing hotter by the second. I don't have long. This entire place will be nothing but smoke and flames within minutes. I wait until Brian safely gets the boy on the ground before I turn around to climb out of the window.

What are the odds that my brother and this boy share the same name? I don't think it's some crazy coincidence, it's something deeper than that. Because how else could you explain it? *Jay*. His name is Jay.

If I make it out of here alive, Jay will be the first person I'll call after my wife and kids. I tried to reconnect with him five years ago, but maybe I should've tried harder. Maybe I was the reason he ran off in the first place. Maybe it's not too late to fix what's been broken. Things between us have been broken for far too long.

That's when I hear it. Something worse than fire crackling in my ears, windows shattering, and sirens screaming in the distance. It's the sound of this entire house breaking. Crumbling like a house of cards, with me in it. The sound of the end.

Can be found on both Apple Music and Spotify

Hey Jude | Glee Cast Version
Good Years | Nina Nesbitt
Guidebook to Healing | Jamie Miller
Bad Thoughts | Rachel Platten
I Knew It, I Know You | Gracie Abrams
Little Did I Know | Julia Michaels
Dancing With Your Ghost | Sasha Alex Sloan
Believe | Madilyn Bailey
Rest | Dean Lewis & Sasha Alex Sloan
Where I Want to Be | Forest Blakk

"I'll Be Here"

Written by Ben, Jay, & Jude

BEN:

I BELIEVE YOU ONLY FIND TRUE LOVE ONCE
IN A LIFETIME
AND I FOUND YOU
DARLING, I FOUND YOU

CAUGHT ME IN A HAZE
I COULD LIVE FOREVER THIS WAY
GIRL, YOU'VE GOT ME SPELLBOUND
LOVESICK FOR YOU, ONLY YOU

FOR ALL THE DAYS I'M GIVEN
I'LL BE HERE
FOR ALL THE MOMENTS TIME ALLOWS
I'LL BE HERE
COUNT ME IN, READY TO DIVE IN
DARLING, THIS IS WHERE OUR STORY BEGINS.

Jay:

Nothing is the way it seems
Tomorrow isn't promised

Yet, I found you
Darling, I found you.

Two healing hearts
Hoping to start again
Live through the pain
Of yesterday.

It only took a moment
When I laid my eyes on you
The spell had been broken
Darling, it was always you.

This promise I can keep
I'll be here
Even on the days you feel like giving up
I'll be here
Ready and willing, no matter the cost
This is where I'll be, darling.

Jude:

Hope had been lost
The day my love died
I thought I had you for a lifetime
But time often lies.

A cruel and desperate cry
I didn't know how to begin again
Until I found you
Darling, I found you.

You picked me back up
Got me on my feet
You saw the real me
The girl I'd hidden underneath.

I'm not going anywhere
I'll be here
Please take your time with me
Treat my heart with care
Darling, you'll find me here.

Count me in, this is where our story begins.

AUTHOR'S NOTE

I'm not going to tell you what I was originally going to name this book. If you're anything like my seven-year-old daughter, you're reading this and scoffing at me, arms folded across your chest, the whole thing. I get it. It's not going away, it just wasn't right for *this* story. But that doesn't mean it won't be perfect for another story in the future. Don't worry, it won't stay a secret forever.

That being said, let me tell you a little bit about the inspiration behind Jude and Jay's love story. I hope you love it as much as I do. While this story is entirely fictional, there are always elements of reality in the stories that I write.

I have a friend who lost her husband in a tragic accident not too long ago. He left behind his wife, two kids, and his family. I learned firsthand from her just how painful that loss was for her and her family.

While this story is not a retelling of her story in any way, it inspired me to tell this one. It gave me a new perspective on life and what it could look like to have to walk daily through terrible grief. How does one go on living, when the one person in their life is not?

My husband is a mountain climber. Every year, he maps out hiking routes so he can cross another one off his list. It's both a beautiful and terrifying sport. Trust me, I know, because it scares me every single time he does it.

You won't ever see me summiting to the top. It won't happen.

I can write about it all day, but I just don't have the kind of drive or desire to ever try something like that.

A year ago, around the time the original title came to me (the one I didn't use), I had a terrible thought while he was gone on a hike.

Several actually.

What if he doesn't make it? What if he gets lost? What if he gets hurt and has to call for help? What if this morning was the last time I'll ever see him? People die climbing mountains, right?

Scary, horrible, terrifying thoughts that I couldn't control. Bad things can happen. They do. Life is unpredictable. Anything can happen at any given time.

Fortunately, for my husband and my brother, (his favorite hiking buddy) they were fine. Everything was okay, and they made it. Another one to check off their list.

That didn't stop the thoughts, though. *What if?*

And what do you do when you can't get a thought unstuck from your head? Well, if you're like me, you start writing about it. That's exactly what I did, and this story came out of it. This story was the mountain I chose to climb.

I can't fathom the thought of ever losing the love of my life. It hurts too much. It's impossible to go there. But for this story, I dove deeper than I ever have before, and I went all in.

I had to start and stop several times while writing this. It was getting too emotional and too personal. I had to take breaks. Many of them. Riley and Nova are spitting images of my own kids. Every thought I put into those two characters, I was thinking of my kids and what it would be like if suddenly I had to raise them on my own. It was a humbling experience.

Mina is based on my own mother, and in a lot of ways, Jude is me. She is and she isn't. I don't own a family business, and I definitely don't sing in taverns or on stage. I do, however, sing "Believe" by Cher at the top of my lungs in our kitchen at home with my family.

I also love pickles on pizza. Don't knock it until you've tried it, okay? And if it's still not your thing, hey, no worries. It wasn't Jay's either until that first bite, just saying.

This story, while emotionally heavy at times, is ultimately a story of love, hope, and redemption. I love the second-chance trope. I'm a believer in being slow to anger and quick to forgive. I simply took two imperfect people who, by the end, were perfect for each other.

I realize this isn't everybody's story. It's not mine either, but it might be somebody's. I realize loss and grief are not easy things to have to walk through. But I do know that you don't ever have to walk through the hard times alone.

The friend that I mentioned earlier is now remarried, and they have a sweet baby girl. That little girl was their second chance. Second chance at life and love. I like to think that life is like that too.

When given another chance at something, why not take it? Life is short, don't we know it. It's also too short to live full of regrets.

If you're still breathing, you're still living. This is your second chance to begin again. What are you waiting for? We're in this crazy life together. You and me. Let's do this.

About the Author

Delon Nicole Starkey is an author from Ohio. She lives there with her husband and two beautiful children. She's passionate about her faith, family, friendships, and writing. You'll catch her sneaking off to local coffee shops as often as she can.

Let's Connect!

Instagram: author.delonnicole
Facebook: Delon Nicole (author)
Goodreads: Delon Nicole
Website: www.delonnicole.com

Your Feedback Matters!
Please leave a review on Amazon or Goodreads!

AMAZON

GOODREADS

PROLOGUE - THE HOUSE ON MONARCH STREET

THE STRANGER BY THE POOL

The clock read a quarter to five. Thomas and his dad were expected home soon. I timed dinner to be done precisely at 5:30. It was nothing fancy, but they both seemed to favor my chicken parmesan, and it'd been a while since we'd eaten it.

To be honest, I barely remembered the last meal we all ate together. Mealtime was punctual, but, mostly, it was only my son and me at the table. My husband, Clair, usually took his plate into his office, but I'd hoped he'd make an exception for tonight. He wouldn't emerge until his work was done for the day and he'd downed at least a glass or two of wine. Maybe three or four, depending on the day he'd had.

The next day was Thomas' birthday. And not just any birthday; he would be turning thirteen. My blue-eyed boy was suddenly a teenager. They said time goes too fast, and they weren't kidding. A door slammed outside, startling me and pulling my attention away from the casserole in the oven.

Is that a car? It's not even five o'clock yet.

I paused, remembering my mother had mentioned earlier that

she'd be dropping off a cake. I clutched a hand over my fluttering heart, trying to slow it down, and laughed at myself for being so paranoid. Of course, it was just her dropping off the cake.

Who else would it have been?

The house was eerily quiet without Clair here. It was as if I'd become so accustomed to my husband's yelling that I didn't know what to do with the silence when he was gone. He didn't leave me alone often. He treated me like *I* was the one that couldn't be trusted.

Shaking my head, I opened the front door and rushed down the steps in case she needed help; I wouldn't have put it past her to bring a mountain of gifts. She spoils Thomas almost as much as I do.

Halfway down the steps, my feet skidded to a stop. The car in our driveway was unfamiliar. The tinted windows made it impossible to see who was inside.

With my heart pounding again, louder and faster than before, my feet acted before my brain had a chance to catch up. I scrambled back inside the safety of my home and slammed the door, chipping one of my nails in my rush to secure the deadbolt. People didn't show up at our doorstep. We ran a business, but nobody ever arrived without an appointment first. It was an unspoken rule that everybody just *knew*. I hadn't scheduled to meet with anyone today. Had Clair made an appointment and forgotten to mention anything to me about it? No, his business is like a child. Only he spends more time caring for it than he does his own son. He would never forget a meeting.

Peeking out the window from behind the curtain, I watched the car for any movement. Mom would have told me if she'd gotten a new vehicle. I knew it didn't belong to Mr. Foster, our groundskeeper, either. He lived close and rarely drove, opting to walk to and from our house. I glanced at the clock and realized he was probably getting off work soon and would be heading out for the evening. I should probably warn him about the strange car out front or, at the very least, ask if he might know who it belongs to.

Maybe he's waiting for a ride.

Worrying my lip between my teeth, my eyes landed on the clock again. 5:00. There had been no sign of movement from the car yet. I was getting more and more unnerved as the time lapsed. I hoped whoever it was left before the guys made it home. I didn't want to explain to Clair about the strange vehicle sitting in our driveway. Not that I could explain it. And it wouldn't have mattered anyway. I'd end up taking the blame regardless. I flinched at the thought.

Putting on a light cardigan from the hook by the side door, I exited from the back. I'd check the gardening shed first, where Mr. Foster spent a lot of his time. Once again, the thought of being alone in this monster of a house hit me. Leaves rustled from the nearby bushes, causing my heart to hammer in my chest. Suddenly, I desperately wished Thomas was with me.

Thomas had always been my biggest protector, more than a boy his age should ever need to be. With a small tug in my chest, I longed for the young boy he used to be. But I needed to remind myself he wasn't a child anymore. Thirteen made him a young man now.

Distracted by my wandering thoughts, I nearly ran right into the stranger in my yard. I skidded to a stop on the patio next to the pool, a few feet away from him. I slowly made eye contact with the man standing alone in my backyard, like he was waiting for me. I didn't recognize him. His dark eyes bore into me, daring me to step closer. I held my breath, my muscles frozen.

After what felt like hours, but was probably more like a few moments, he finally broke the silence. "Rachel, dear. Don't be afraid. I just want to talk to you." His voice was low and gravely, and he started edging towards me like a cat stalking its prey.

He knows my name!

My voice caught in my throat, too afraid to speak. What was happening?

My hands trembled like leaves on a windy day as he continued to creep closer. I took a small step backward, inching toward the house while being careful not to fall into the pool. The warm, chlorine-filled waters sloshed gently in the breeze behind me. If I took just two more steps, I'd fall in. Finally, I found a sliver of courage and held onto it. Barely.

"Don't come any closer. You need to leave. This is pr-private property."

He smiled at me in a predatory way, making me feel like prey rather than a human being. Goosebumps shot up my arms and along my spine.

Someone, please come. Someone. Anyone. Please.

He held out his hand with a disarming gesture, but something dark in his eyes told me he was anything but friendly. Everything in me was telling me to run. I wanted to...but I couldn't. My feet remained glued to the concrete.

"It's okay, doll. You don't need to be afraid of me. I want to talk to you about something. It's only business, Rachel."

There it was again—my name on that strange man's tongue. I needed to go. *Now!* His hand still extended, I shook my head at it, and my breath caught in my lungs. That was when my feet finally got the message to run.

I didn't make it far. He was faster. Stronger. Hands grabbed my waist and held me in place. It was all too familiar: the way his arms pinched my skin, the desperation. Even though he was a stranger, I knew that type of touch.

No... no! I have to get away. Why is no one coming to help me?

His words were muffled, drowned out by the sound of the blood rushing through my veins. Writhing in his arms, I fought and kicked to free myself. I might've been screaming, but it was all a blur. My nails dug into his arm. He roared in a mixture of pain and fury but didn't loosen his hold. The harder I fought to get free, the tighter he held onto me.

My son will be home soon. Tomorrow is his birthday. His father would be home as well, and—no, I wasn't fighting for him. I fought for my son. My sweet Thomas. I had to get away so that I could hold him in my arms once again.

A scream pierced the air. So shrill and urgent it broke through the silence of the warm summer day like a hot blade through butter. I couldn't tell if it was my own or from someone else.

Mom, is that you?

From the corner of my eye, I noticed someone coming towards me. I stretched out an arm in their direction, praying they would reach me in time.

The tight grip on my body finally loosened, and my body abandoned me as it went down, down. Fast and heavy gulps of air. It was like I'd forgotten how to breathe. My vision blurred, as something in my skull cracked, like the shell of an egg spilling open. Only *I* was the cracked egg, oozing away from myself. Water was suddenly everywhere. In my lungs, in my nose, in my throat, in the wound that felt like fire greeting the chlorine.

Only I can't breathe underwater. I don't think I can breathe at all.

Down...

Down...

Down.

My whole world shifted. And through it all, I heard voices shouting and screaming. Anger. *Could it be my own? Am I the one that's angry here? I suddenly can't remember.*

Stay awake!

Red water. No... Blood. I couldn't tell where it was coming from. I knew it had to be mine.

Down...

I couldn't keep myself afloat. Water filled my lungs like a

balloon. I wasn't going to make it. I wouldn't be eating cake with my son for his birthday.

No, no, no! I'm so, so sorry. I refuse to let this happen! I'm not done fighting for you, Thomas. I will make it out of here. And when I do, I will find you. Whatever it takes. I will find you and whoever did this to me. To us.

I will not leave you, Thomas.

I promise.